It was the laughter that woke her.

The giggles that came from grinning young mouths.

"No!" She struggled to sit up. A hand clamped onto her forehead, holding her down.

Another hand squeezed her cheeks, forcing her mouth open.

"No! No!"

She was fully awake. The smell of lighter fluid snaked into her nose.

"No!" She tried to sit up, to run.

Her attempt at movement sent pain roaring through her body.

She looked down.

Her legs and feet were on fire. The melting plastic garbage bags and the burning newspaper combined to produce an acrid, lung-piercing smoke. The Converse sneakers given her by the nuns melted and molded themselves to her cotton socks and, beneath that, her skin. The garbage bag around her legs was dissolving into the denim jeans. She felt heat gnawing through the fabric.

The old woman began screaming. . . .

By Judith Smith-Levin

DO NOT GO GENTLY
THE HOODOO MAN*
GREEN MONEY*

*Published by The Ballantine Publishing Group

GREEN MONEY

Judith Smith-Levin

FAWCETT • NEW YORK

A Fawcett Book
Published by The Ballantine Publishing Group
Copyright © 2000 by Judith Smith-Levin

All rights reserved under International and Pan-American Copyright Conventions. Published in the United States by The Ballantine Publishing Group, a division of Random House, Inc., New York, and simultaneously in Canada by Random House of Canada Limited, Toronto.

Fawcett is a registered trademark and the Fawcett colophon is a trademark of Random House, Inc.

www.randomhouse.com/BB/

Library of Congress Catalog Card Number: 00-190618

ISBN 0-345-42084-5

Manufactured in the United States of America

First Edition: August 2000

10 9 8 7 6 5 4 3 2 1

To the best gift that God ever gave me,
Jason William Levin
and to
The best gift that Jason ever gave me.
Jake
1982–1999

ACKNOWLEDGMENTS

My sincere thanks to:

Megan Farley
for her help in researching this
novel.

Marillyn Holmes
For the title idea.

Revé Mason
for sharing her potter's secrets.

Dr. Hal and Mrs. Joan Sandler R.N.
And Dee A. Odem R.N.
for the medical information.

and to:

Alice Volpe, my agent, and friend.
Whose support, laughter, and
good spirits keep me focused.

and to:
Beaumont, who was always happy to
see me. I miss your face.

TYGFMBTKNLAEIPA

PROLOGUE

The bench was a hard, yet comfortable old friend.

Molly Ludendorf favored this bench, and this corner of the park.

The old woman pushed her "house on wheels," a McKay's Market shopping cart, to the bench and sat down. She began ceremoniously preparing her sleeping quarters.

The night air felt crisp. She raised her head and sniffed.

"It will be coldt before mornink," she muttered in a thick, heavily German-accented voice.

Nearly twenty years of living on the street had given her skills meteorologists could only dream about.

She laid out a ragged pink wool blanket on the bench, patting it lovingly. It was a find, from a Hillman Avenue triple-decker just before it was knocked down.

Molly stuffed newspapers into a white plastic Stop N' Save bag, and put it at the head of the bench. A good pillow.

Dipping into her cart, she fished out a baby blue polyester sweater with a bleach stain on the front. She'd found it in the trash outside of the Laundromat on Second Street.

She had seen some men going through the trash can and had waited for them to leave. She'd had her share of trouble with homeless men in the years she'd been on the street. Thank heaven she was too old to be raped anymore, but then, you never know.

When the men left, she went through the can. She discovered the sweater at the bottom. She pulled it on, over her clothes. It was big, but that was good; she could wrap it around herself like a coat.

Again she reached into the jumble in the cart, taking out a

1

three-day-old copy of *The Wall Street Journal*. Carefully rationing out the pages, she wrapped them around her green Converse high-top sneakers, tucking the edges inside the shoes.

The nuns who ran the Saint Luke shelter had given them to her. She had dragged herself in on a cold, snowy night, her own shoes in tatters, barely clinging to her nearly frozen feet. The Converse sneaks were the only shoes they had that she could fit into. The nuns let her bathe, then gave her clean clothes, underwear, two pairs of pristine, thick white socks, and the shoes.

Once the shoes felt secure, she took out three dark green plastic garbage bags and smoothed them out on the bench. Selecting the one on top, she pulled it over her feet. The bottom had been cut away so that she could tug the plastic all the way up to her waist. She tucked it in to the band of her stained blue denim pants.

She took the second bag and pulled it up to her knees, then tucked it securely around her news-shrouded feet and legs.

Garbage bags were a miraculous invention, she thought. They held body heat like the finest goose-down quilts she'd owned in her other life, before the pain, before the alcohol, before the streets.

Holding onto the bag around her legs with her free hand, and pressing her ankles together to keep the paper in place, Molly lay down on the bench. She wrapped the third garbage bag around her body and pulled up the pink blanket, tucking it under her hips and thighs.

She felt warm and secure.

The breeze was beginning to turn cold. She pulled the dirty black hood of the nylon windbreaker she wore under the sweater over her head. She pulled the drawstrings tight. The hood formed an ear-warming shield around her wrinkled, dirty face. She pulled her crocheted brown woolen hat from inside her sweater and tugged it down over her forehead. The brim touched the bridge of her nose. On the chilly, light breeze, she smelled a sweet, pungent smoke, coming from the trees.

"Lowlife scum," she muttered to herself. Her heavy accent

gave the words a clipped and guttural sound. "All da drugs dey smoke and shoot, dey're killink da worlt."

She turned her back to the wind.

The bass-heavy beat of music rode on the air.

Molly pulled her hat down farther, trying unsuccessfully to block the sound. Dr. Dre and the prematurely departed Tupac Shakur, singing about partying in California, accompanied her into sleep.

The side of her head was cradled in the softness of her makeshift pillow, while her face pressed hard against the scratched, worn back of the bench, where it joined the seat.

She began to smile. She felt warm, full of the tasty spring lamb stew given to her at the back door of Jessie Mae's soul food restaurant. And now sleep, sweet and welcoming. Molly began to dream. She was home. In Munich, Germany, the city of her youth.

She saw herself. Young, tall, strong again, and happy. So very happy.

Her long, silken blonde hair floated back from her shoulders, as she stood on the balcony of her parents' home, smiling down at the young face looking up at her.

Dieter. The boy she'd loved before she sailed to America . . . before Oskar Ludendorf, his whining, sickly wife, and his sweaty hands, before everything.

Dieter was urging her to come down. His wide, plump face smiled up at her. She could see the freckles across his broad nose.

She reached out.

Suddenly she could barely see him.

The sun was in her eyes, a blazing, blinding light.

She started to sweat.

The heat from the sun gave way to the softness of rain pattering down on her outstretched arms and hands.

"Dieter," she murmured, as the rain softly touched her skin. She stretched out farther.

Immediately the heat was back.

Hot, burning. Painful, searing heat.

In her sleep, Molly Ludendorf shook her head.

"No . . . no," she said.

Dieter disappeared into the rays of that bright, agonizing sun.

"No."

It was the laughter that woke her.

The giggles that came from grinning young mouths.

"No!" She struggled to sit up. A hand clamped onto her forehead, holding her down.

Another hand squeezed her cheeks, forcing her mouth open.

"NO! NO!"

She was fully awake. The smell of lighter fluid snaked into her nose.

Above her she saw the faces.

They were young and white.

Through her watering eyes, she couldn't tell if they were male or female. All she knew was that they were laughing.

Some of them shook beer bottles over her, while another one sprayed a stinking liquid from a small red-and-blue can over her body.

"NO!" She tried to sit up, to run.

Her attempt at movement sent pain roaring through her body. She looked down.

Her legs and feet were on fire. The melting plastic garbage bags and the burning newspaper combined to produce an acrid, lung-piercing smoke. The Converse sneakers given her by the nuns melted, and molded themselves to her cotton socks, and beneath that, her skin. The garbage bag around her legs was dissolving into the denim jeans. She felt heat gnawing through the fabric.

The old woman began screaming.

A hand clapped over her nose. She opened her mouth wide, trying to breathe and to scream again.

Her remaining teeth erupted in pain, as something hard and bitter was shoved against them. Pain shot through her jaw as she bit down, trying to keep it out.

The hand pressed harder. Molly felt her bottom lip split, blood spilled down her chin. The pain was so great. She struggled, trying to keep her mouth closed, but it opened. Her brain controlled her body. She needed air.

An object was forced deep into her mouth, into the darkness behind her bleeding lips.

"No . . . mmmpph!" She struggled, fought, and tried to scream again.

With each agonizing inhalation, the object moved farther into her throat.

She gagged. A thin white liquid rose and surrounded the thickness of the thing in her mouth.

She could feel it moving.

Like a boat tumbling over a waterfall, it slid deeper and deeper into her throat, closing off the air, choking off the scream.

Her hands flew over her body, her eyes began to bulge, tears ran down her grimy, wrinkled cheeks.

The laughter.

She could still hear the laughter.

One of them was laughing so hard, it turned into choking. It sounded as if it were coming from the ground, behind her. As if the laugher had fallen, overcome.

GOD HELP ME! her mind screamed. *HELP ME.*

God didn't help.

The agony in her feet raced up her legs, and roared over her thighs.

Beneath her clothes, the flesh blistered and popped.

Heat filled her skin, then burst out.

Fire licked her garbage bags, her paper, her clothes.

It devoured the streams and puddles of the "cool rain" strewn over her.

She felt the last air in her throat, as it slid over and around the object that she couldn't cough up or swallow down.

Molly Ludendorf made a rattling, gurgling sound and felt her life whooshing out from her body. She willed her bulging, tear-filled eyes to see . . . to know who was doing this to her.

She turned her head.

The stinking rain now covered everything. Her hood, her hat. She felt the fire licking her face, like a demented dog.

The skin on her neck cracked and peeled.

The rough fibers of her crocheted wool hat adhered to her blistering skin.

As the fire claimed her eyes, one color devoured her final thought.

Red.

The reddest hair she'd ever seen.

Red, her blistering brain thought. Red, the color of flame.

CHAPTER ONE

At first it was the booming of the bass that assaulted his ears, and then the voices. High, male, yet eerily feminine.

Cody Stevens opened his eyes. That small movement seemed to let more and more of the sound into his throbbing head.

He turned over in bed.

The Bee Gees continued their assault, telling him he should be dancing.

Cody looked at his bedside clock. It was 6:45 A.M. The alarm was set for 7:00.

The Bee Gees vibrated in his brain now, stomping and singing. Their high voices sawing into his skull. He sat up.

Sometimes he hated his sister.

Cheyenne Stevens was fourteen years old, and she had discovered disco.

Their house rocked from morning till night with the throbbing beat of the seventies.

Cody rubbed his pale blue eyes. He was wide awake as the Bee Gees faded out to the absurdly light sound of KC and the Sunshine Band, singing "Boogie Shoes."

There was no going back to sleep.

Cody Stevens wanted to strangle the entire group that put together the *Saturday Night Fever* soundtrack.

He listened, until he heard Cheyenne's door close. The

sound was mercifully muted. He knew she was in her room, getting ready for the day.

Cody swung his long legs out and put his feet on the plush navy blue carpet. He sat like that for about five minutes, gazing at the red hair on his pale, freckled arms, and thinking about the night before.

He yawned. "Shit happens," he said out loud, and stood up. He scratched his testicles, and walked barefoot and naked to the bathroom.

Just as he started the shower, The Trammps urged him to "Burn, baby, burn."

David Riley and his twin brother Daniel kissed their mother good-bye and headed out the door.

Diane Riley stood at the window, waving at her two sons, watching them head down the early-morning, sunny street to the bus stop. Her "twin babies." They were seventeen years old, and sometimes she still had trouble telling one from the other.

When the boys were little, she dressed them differently, so that she could tell them apart. Still, they sometimes exchanged outfits and pretended to be one another.

Now at school they wore uniforms. The teachers made them wear different colored ties, so that they could distinguish Dan from Dave.

Sometimes the boys would slip back into the old joke, with Dan trading his red tie for Dave's blue one.

She used to laugh when they did it as children, but now she sometimes wondered if they even knew who was who.

The early years with her boys had been good times. Back when they were "the D Fours," Doug, Diane, Dan, and Dave. A real family, before her husband Douglas lost it.

"Middle-age Crazy." That's what her best friend Irene Kavaraceus used to call it. She knew that among her friends, their husbands' affairs with younger women were tolerated.

Diane wondered what those wives did, how they got through it. Where was it written that the wives from the beginning, the ones who went through the struggle to support him while he got *his* degree and began *his* business, had to be turned in, exchanged for a new model? One who would look good on his aging arm and make the other old men jealous.

On women, gray hair, wrinkles, and expanding waistlines were unforgivable. But on men the reality of aging was considered "distinguished."

Diane's mouth turned downward, frown lines etching themselves in at the corners. "Bullshit!" she said out loud. The words rang harsh and jarring in the sunny room.

Was there some great celestial rule book somewhere that said women were expendable, and that men could just go on, from woman to woman, no matter how gray, bald, fat, or stupid?

Well if there was, she was gonna bust the hell out of it. She was going to break every rule written.

She had given up her life in this union. She had stayed home, tending to the house and raising the boys. When they grew up, her time had gone to endless volunteer programs and projects. She had become a Stepford wife in every frightening sense of the word, right down to the plastic boobs.

On their eighteenth anniversary, after dinner and champagne, she'd gone to bed with her husband. He offhandedly mentioned that her breasts were beginning to "go south." Diane made an appointment for surgery the very next day. After they'd been "tightened and augmented," Doug refused to touch them because they didn't feel "real."

Diane sat down in a brightly upholstered chair, watching the empty, sun-filled street beyond the bay window. Doug had no idea of what she felt, how it had crushed her to hear his comments about her body. He acted as if she were the only one who had aged. For a time, she was despondent. She moped around the house in a state somewhere between tired and catatonic.

But things had changed. Love came when you least expected it, and from the most unlikely places. She was a witness to that. Love made you strong, able to do anything, like end a dead marriage.

"You've got a big surprise coming, Doug," she said softly. "Very soon, your 'perfect' marriage will be over. And when it's done, I'm not slinking out silent, ashamed of my years *or* myself." She wrapped her arms around herself. "And I'm not walking away broke."

She closed her eyes, and thought of their twenty-seven years together.

They had met at her sister Anne's eighteenth birthday party, in her own backyard. Doug was a friend of Anne's boyfriend Rick. He'd asked Doug to the party. The minute Diane saw him, she fell totally and completely in love.

When the handsome college man asked her, a high school junior, out on a date, she nearly died. They went to a movie, and left halfway through, both on fire. Doug drove to a secluded area, and they made love in his car. He took her virginity and her heart that first night.

Afterward, they stole moments to be alone. In the back of his car, in her house while the family was out, in dingy little roadside motels. Their passion, white-hot and blazing, consumed them both, leaving them sweaty, feverish, and filled with one another.

Unable to face a long future of medical school, internship, and residency without her, Doug asked Diane to marry him. Her parents had been against it, but in the end they gave their blessing, with one condition. That Diane get a college education, as she'd planned before Doug came into her life. She agreed. They married two months after her eighteenth birthday.

After graduation, Doug was accepted by the medical school of his choice, Stanford. They moved across the country, away from her family and everything she knew. It was there, in California, with Doug spending so much time on campus, that Diane realized what true emptiness and loneliness was.

He encouraged her to keep her promise to her parents, to go back to school. There was nothing she wanted to do. Doug talked her into studying nursing.

He painted a rosy picture of them working side by side, partners in marriage and career. She hadn't really wanted to be a nurse, but she did what he asked, and enrolled in classes.

Doug loved medical school, and fell deep into his studies. Diane pretended to be as consumed by nursing, but the truth was, she didn't care. All she wanted was to make him happy.

When Doug closed his books and climbed into their bed alongside her, nothing else mattered except their passion. Lying with her head on his chest, listening to him breathe, Diane told herself she didn't need anything or anyone else. He was her world.

"I was such a stupid little nitwit!" she said out loud. "I went through nursing school to help *him*!" A tear slid down her face. "Fat lot of good it did me. We never got to work together. I got pregnant and that was that." She smiled ruefully. "What a joke."

After they became the parents of twin boys, Diane's fantasy of love sustained by passion still burned. To her thankful surprise, Doug still wanted her, he still loved her body. But for a long time now, that had been over. That part of their lives had disappeared. She knew he was seeing other women, but she'd been able to accept that fact. She could refuse to see what was right in front of her, until Camille.

Camille Westfall was a young woman whom Diane had met through her bridge club. She had come into their lives and turned everything upside down.

"Cammie," as she was called, was Ellie Findlay's niece. She'd come to Brookport after a failed love affair in New York City. The girl loved Ellie more than her own mother, and when her love affair went south she asked if she could stay with Ellie and her husband Stan for a while. Ellie gladly opened her home.

At their weekly card game, Ellie stopped stuffing Diane's curried salmon puffs into her mouth long enough to say that her niece was nursing a broken heart and she needed to get out, to find work, and get her life started again.

"Right," Diane said softly. "She got life started again." Ellie had brought the plump, big-breasted, red-haired girl over to the Riley house. In spite of the fact that Diane felt she was "common," she had been charmed by her. She introduced Camille to Doug.

Less than a week later, Cammie was working as a clerk in Doug's office, and now . . . Diane sighed deeply.

Doug's longtime nurse Shannon Cooper was the first to tell her that her husband was having an affair. Diane knew that Shannon had phoned her out of loyalty, but the nurse wasn't telling her anything she didn't know. About three months after that phone call, Shannon, a devout, old-line Catholic, quit, saying she couldn't stand being in the office with "adulterers."

Though Diane never confronted her husband, Doug suspected she knew of his relationship with Cammie. He didn't really want to hurt his wife. He hadn't intended for this thing to get out of hand. He was bored, looking for something to make his juices flow again. He had thought the girl would be like the others. A few laughs for a while and then gone. After all, he still loved his wife.

Diane had matured from a pretty girl to a beautiful woman. He knew other men still looked at her. It made him proud at cocktail parties, and get-togethers, but for him, Diane held no surprises. They had lived through too much together.

Then Cammie came into his world, impressed by him, hanging on his every word, viewing him as some kind of superhero, one who cured patients, and saved lives. Just her eyes on him made him feel invincible.

When he'd first taken her to bed, she responded with an honest passion and fire that he'd long missed, and indeed, considered over in his life. The girl got under his skin. He was even thinking about leaving Diane.

The boys were nearly adults, and in time, they would understand. Cammie made him *feel* again. He was wise, sophisticated, and brilliant in her eyes. He needed that, as much as he needed food and water. Even so, he had to be careful. He had a longtime practice in this city.

Stubbornly clinging to the notion of general practitioner in a world of specialists, Douglas Riley was much loved by his patients. They saw him as a throwback to the days when doctors cared more about people than the bottom line.

They all believed in him as an upstanding family man. A pillar of the community. But he knew they'd drop him like a hot rock if they found out about his relationship with Camille, so he stayed with Diane, and she never said or did anything to make anyone think otherwise.

Diane got up from the chair, stretching her arms above her head. She noticed that whenever she sat for a period of time, her body ached. She was going to have herself tested for arthritis. Her mother had suffered from it.

She would have asked Doug to administer the blood test, but she didn't want him to see another sign of age creeping into her body.

As for now, she had her own way of easing the stiffness. She walked into the kitchen and pulled a bottle of Absolut vodka from the refrigerator. She opened the freezer and reached behind the ice cream and the twins' Milky Way and Snickers bars. Stretching into the space between the frozen lasagna and the frozen orange juice, her fingers touched the small, thick, hidden glass.

Taking the iced vodka cup and the bottle, she walked into the master bedroom. Facing the unmade bed, in which she had slept alone, Diane filled the frosted glass with the clear, cold liquid. She raised her arm, in a toast.

"Here's to you, Doug. You *bastard*!" She drained the glass and immediately poured another. "She who laughs last . . ." she said, and put the icy rim of the glass to her smiling lips.

CHAPTER TWO

Saint Francis Park was green, shady, and cold. Homicide Lieutenant Starletta Duvall pulled her lightweight dove-gray trench coat tighter around her. The breeze blew soft but chilly around her throat. It carried the pungent scent of burnt human flesh.

Star looked at the charred bundle at her feet.

"The first burned bum. A sure sign of spring."

"It's Molly Ludendorf," Homicide Sergeant Dominic Paresi said.

She looked at her partner.

"You sure?"

"Pretty much." He pointed to the burned rags clinging to the charred corpse. "Look at the clothes. They're the same ones she's been wearing since the Nixon administration. Besides, when the weather warms up, she likes to sleep in the park. The route guys say she likes this bench, near the statue."

He indicated the stone likeness of Saint Francis of Assisi directly behind them. "Besides, the bench is burnt too. She must have been sleeping when she was torched. . . ."

"And rolled onto the grass," Star said, pointing to the scorched blades of grass around the burned body. She stooped down and touched the lawn.

"It's damp now, dewy." She stood. "So she must have been lit up well before dawn, when the grass was still relatively dry."

Star looked at the ground. "It was cold last night. There's still patches of frost on the grass, but none anywhere around the body."

She looked again at the corpse. "That plus the degree of burns says she had to have been lit up for quite a while. Somebody had to have seen this. You'd think they would have at least called 911."

"In this pit?" Paresi said, derisively. "Believe me, while she was burning, I'm sure the fucks that hang out here probably beat feet to the Seven-Eleven for hot dogs and forties, and had a wienie roast!"

A sudden shaft of sunlight pierced through the trees. Paresi put on his sunglasses and squatted beside the body, a look of sadness mixed with disgust on his face. He clicked his tongue twice against the roof of his mouth.

Star recognized the sound. He made it when he was disturbed. She folded her arms and walked in a tight circle around her partner and the thing on the ground.

Paresi touched the brim of Molly's charred woolen hat, moving it back, exposing more of what was left of her face. A chunk of the burnt fabric broke off between his latex-gloved fingers. He dropped it beside the body, sighed deeply, and stood, looking down at her.

"She was a royal pain in the ass," he said. "Always fighting, yelling, and spitting at people . . ." He walked around the body. "But she didn't deserve this. It was a terrible way to die."

Star folded her arms across her chest and looked away.

"I guess she won't be calling anybody *nigger* anymore."

Paresi's azure eyes peered at her over his shades.

"So much compassion. What happened, you get up on the wrong side of the doctor this morning?"

She looked at him, her face stony. "I got up from my own bed this morning, thank you. Besides, Mitchell's out of town."

"That explains it," Paresi said. She was hanging tough, but he knew this scene was getting to her.

He walked around the bench, checking burn marks.

"So . . . whaddya think?" He stopped in front of her, again peering at her over his shades. "Cajun for lunch?"

Star thrust her hands deep into the pockets of her coat. She knew Paresi was seeing right through her. After nearly six years partnered up, they read each other like an old married couple.

Paresi knew this was a scene she'd carry in her mind for a long time, so he was using gallows humor to draw her out and away from the reality at her feet. It was something they both resorted to as a way of dealing with particularly revolting crime scenes.

"A little blackened chicken?" he asked, peeling off the gloves.

"Bite my butt!" she said, a little smile at the corner of her mouth.

Paresi laughed. "Drop your pants."

"Lieutenant."

Star turned toward the voice coming toward her. It was Detective Leo Darcy.

From underneath his khaki coat, a bright slash of neon green appeared. Leo was wearing his new spring jacket.

"Yeah, Leo?"

"I got this from under the bench." In his latex-gloved fingers, he held a scorched book of matches, with the name HAMPTON HOUSE HOTEL stenciled in gold on the partially burned shiny white cover.

Star looked at the pack. The Hampton House was one of the best hotels in the city.

"Think this was already here, or do you think it was used to set the fire?" Darcy asked.

"I don't know." She shrugged. "Even if it wasn't used to set the fire, it seems strange that it's here, in this park."

"Maybe we've got a high-class fire freak on our hands, or someone who was slumming, you know, looking for entertainment on or near this bench."

The chubby detective nodded in agreement, setting his clean-shaven jowls in motion.

"There's lots of activity around here after dark," he said. "You can get anything you want—boys, girls, blow, smack, crack, crank, ice, Special K. . . . You name it, the fine entrepreneurs down here can supply it."

Star looked around. "It's not the park it was when I was growing up, that's for sure."

"Yeah," Leo said. "It's a shame, ain't it, how the world is turning into a toilet."

"It's pretty sad, all right," she agreed. "Bag it up, Leo." She pointed at the matchbook. "We'll check it out."

"Right." The heavy man pulled a plastic evidence bag from his pocket and deposited the matchbook.

Across the lawn, Star saw the black, city-issued Medical Examiner's car pull up to the curb.

The door opened. She watched as the man got out and crossed the lawn. He was short and red-faced. His bowed legs propelled him heavily forward. The heels of his scuffed brown shoes gouged holes in the new grass.

"Lieutenant," he said, nodding at her.

"Dr. Spiegel."

Robert Spiegel was a deputy medical examiner, one of a crew that worked under Brookport's Chief Medical Examiner Dr. Mitchell Grant.

"This one doesn't take a Rhodes scholar," Dr. Spiegel said, pulling on his latex gloves.

"Yeah." Star stood over him, as he squatted near the charred remains. *They don't call you Speedo for nothing,* she thought to herself.

Paresi was right. Molly had died in agony. Her hands were charcoaled claws, and her mouth was stretched, gaping. She died screaming.

Spiegel gave a little grunt and waved his hand in a gesture of dismissal. He stood. "I've got another call. Tag her and bag her." He looked at Star. "It's pretty much open and shut." He peeled off his gloves and tossed them on the grass, near the corpse.

Star wanted to kick him. "When will she post?" she asked.

Spiegel shrugged. "Whenever . . . call the office." He turned and headed back to his car. Star watched him plowing his way across the grass.

"Thanks for all your help, Doc," she called out sarcastically. "Jerk!" She turned back to the body. Recollections of her run-ins with Molly Ludendorf unrolled in her head like a movie.

The old woman at her feet had tormented her for years, calling her names, spitting at her, even attempting to ambush her once, attacking her from behind. It was the only time Star had ever hit her.

While she was still in uniform, on patrol one night, Star and her then partner, an old-line vet named Tim Cochran, were the first to arrive at a fight outside of a run-down bar. As Star attempted to pull one drunk off of another, Molly jumped her from behind, trying to grab her weapon from its holster. Star quickly flipped the woman over her shoulder. Molly, on the pavement, grabbed again for the gun, and Star knocked her cold.

She looked again at the pitiful mass of burned flesh and rags at her feet.

"All those years of calling me nigger," Star said, softly. "Now look at you."

In her early days on the street, Star learned to ignore the

wackos and derelicts. If they got under your skin, they could make things twice as bad. If they knew you had a hot button, they didn't just press it, they *lay* on it.

The first time she'd been called nigger, she was a few days out of the academy, and she reacted. Tim Cochran pulled her off the man who'd said it, after Star had slammed him against a fence, her nightstick crushing his windpipe, in full view of a crowd.

Cochran turned the man around, cuffed him, and forced him to his knees to await the wagon. After he was taken away and they'd returned to their cruiser, Tim gave her some advice. He told her to never let anything get to her in public.

"If you react, that's all you'll hear for the rest of your time on the street. Don't let these stupid bastards rattle your cage!"

The people doing the name-calling were mostly mental patients tossed out when the Commonwealth could no longer pay for their care, or they were burnt-out druggies, winos, or just kids with big mouths. The insults mostly went in one ear and out the other, all of them except this one. Molly Ludendorf's hatred was real, not fueled by rage or liquor. It was cold, straight-up, heartfelt racist hatred, and it always hit Star where she lived.

Even filthy and living on the street, inside Goodwill drop-off boxes, Molly Ludendorf considered herself better than any black person, and that included Star. The woman's hatred was so vehement that she sometimes stood in the middle of the street screaming and spitting at black people.

She had been arrested more times than Star could count. She had even been hospitalized several times from beatings at the hands of those she tormented.

Star recalled pulling a derelict black man off the old crone. The man was choking Molly when Star, in uniform, arrived with the "just out of the academy" officer who was her trainee at the time.

The rookie, primed for action, jumped immediately out of the car, and headed for the angry man. Star grabbed him and held him back while she stood there, watching the man choke Molly.

The young officer couldn't believe what he was seeing.

Star just stood there. Her arms folded, her eyes dispassionate, watching the old woman's knees sag, as the black man throttled her. Horrified, the recruit stepped forward again. Star grabbed him, her grip hard on his forearm.

"Wait," she said. "Just wait."

Beside himself, the newcomer stood back. She was in charge, he had to respect that, but if she didn't do something, he was going to. No way he was going to watch this old woman be strangled right in front of them.

When the old woman's knees touched the ground, Star stepped forward and pried the black man's hands from around her throat. Molly dropped gasping to the sidewalk.

"I'ma kill her, I'ma waste that old bitch!" the man yelled. Star pushed him back against a building, holding him.

"Calm down," she said. "Calm down."

The man pushed away, but Star shoved him back, pinning him with her forearm against his throat.

"Calm down," she said, "don't make me hurt you."

The man breathed foul breath at her. Still she held on. "Calm down."

He sagged against the wall. "I'm okay, sis, I'm okay."

"Sure?"

The man nodded.

Star let him go, and looked at him. He was dirty, but he wasn't drunk, and he wasn't one of the regulars. He appeared to be just a guy down on his luck, who'd had the further misfortune of running into Molly Ludendorf. Star reached into her pocket and pulled out a ten-dollar bill. She handed it to the man.

"This is for food, hear me? Food."

"Yes ma'am," the man said. "I hear you. Thank you, sis."

"Food," Star said again. "I don't smell booze on you now, but don't play me. If you drink it up, I'll know, because this is my beat, and I'm gonna see you again." Her amber-colored eyes locked on the man's face. "And you'd better be sober. If not, I *will* lock you up, got it?"

The man nodded.

"When I cruise Beebo's Lunch in a little while, I want to see you through the window, at the counter . . . understood?"

She stepped closer to him, her voice low. "Because if I *don't* see you, I'm coming in, and if you're not there, I'm going to be totally pissed off the next time we meet, and I guarantee you, it'll be your ass. Got that?"

"Yes ma'am."

Star stood back.

"You ain't locking me up?"

She shook her head. "Not unless you drink my hard-earned money. Go on, I'll take care of this."

"Thank you, thank you, sis," the man said. "I didn't mean to hurt her, but that woman don't know when to quit, she just wouldn't stop."

"I know," Star said. "Go on."

"Yes ma'am." He waved the money at her. "Thank you kindly, and God bless you."

The man took one more look at Molly on the ground and spat in her direction.

"Now!" Star said.

"Gone." The man took off running, and disappeared around a corner.

Tran Nguyen was beside himself. "How could you do that?" he said. "How could you just stand there?"

"Get her up," Star said, walking toward the black and white.

Nguyen moved to help Molly stand. Partner or no, he was going to report this. He extended his hand to the dirty bag of rags on the sidewalk. Molly scuttled backward like a bug.

"Stay *away* from me!" she screamed.

Tran Nguyen turned toward Star. She leaned against the cruiser, watching, her arms folded. He reached out again for Molly.

The crone spat at him. "I sait, keep avay. Don' put your durty hantz on me, you goddamned yellow, slant-eye, dog-eatin' bastid!"

Nguyen turned to Star. She held out the radio.

He called for the wagon, and when it arrived, he gleefully tossed Molly inside. He even began referring to the old woman by the nickname Star had given her: Frau Hitler.

Tran Nguyen was a sergeant now, working out of Grand Theft, but whenever they met, they still laughed about his early days training with her, and his run-ins with German Molly.

"I'll have to call Tran and give him the news," she muttered.

"Hey."

She turned to see her partner holding out a tall, gray and red disposable cup. A creamy white froth peeked over the top.

"Ooh, latte grande," she said, surprised.

Paresi nodded. "I thought you could use a break." He handed her the cup. "Perfect foam, cinnamon, and lots of shaved chocolate."

"Outstanding." She smiled.

"That's better," he said, toasting her with his cup.

Star sipped her drink. It warmed her.

"This is great, where'd you get it?"

Dominic pointed across the park. Beneath a tree, near another bench, a young black man waved at her.

"His name's Norvel," Paresi said. "He says hi, and he wanted me to tell you that you are 'phat.'"

"What?"

"Phat."

"Oh . . . phat. P-H-A-T!" she said, grinning. "Plenty Hot And Tempting," they said together.

Star smiled at the man with the coffee cart, and waved at him. He waved enthusiastically back.

"When he told me to tell you that, I said, she's gonna slug me," Paresi said. "Then he told me what it meant."

"You should know that, Paresi, you spend a lot of time with Roland and Cole, they're always talking about some girl being phat," she said.

"Hey," her partner shrugged, "I just thought they liked big girls."

Star laughed and waved again at the young man across the lawn. "He's fine," she said. "Too bad he's twelve."

Paresi shrugged. "So he's young; you can train him. You know, bend him your way."

"You're . . ."

"A pig . . . I know. What's so wrong with training a young man? We all had to start somewhere. Older women know all the moves . . . capeesh?"

Star shook her head. "You know, Vee's my best friend, I know her like I know myself, and I just can't understand what she sees in you."

Paresi leered at her. "If you ask me nice, I'll show you." Their laughter was interrupted by a uniformed officer.

"Lieutenant Duvall, Sergeant Paresi, they're about to move the body now."

As they turned back toward the burnt corpse, Star caught sight of three young men, a few feet from the scene.

They were standing, watching the activity.

She knew there was a private, upper-class boy's school at the other end of the park.

Moneyed beyond political correctness, Bromleigh Academy had existed for over one hundred years in the rolling hills and mighty oaks of Saint Francis Park.

Though the neighborhood surrounding it had changed over the years, Bromleigh remained what it always had been. A haven of privileged education and good breeding. The school turned out a never-ending chain of spoiled, rich young men from Brookport's wealthiest families.

Though most of the money was generations old, lately new money had found its way to Bromleigh. Brookport's latest multimillionaires sprang from the computer industry. Spending their days and nights in front of computer screens and in the company of others like themselves, new money lacked the social graces of the old. Still, money is money, and the newcomers schemed, donated, and bribed their sons into Bromleigh.

However, not all of the students were wealthy. In the 1960s, when America found its conscience, the neighborhood surrounding Bromleigh grew darker.

The prestigious old school began offering scholarships to "worthy" neighborhood kids. The young men had to maintain a high grade point average for two years of junior high, and once accepted, they had to maintain an A average for their first semester at Bromleigh.

If they were able to do that, they finished out the remainder of their high school educations at the acclaimed institution. Ninety-nine percent of Bromleigh graduates went on to college, directly after graduation.

Over the years, the school's graduates of color had achieved great success. Several became high-powered attorneys, another won a seat in the U.S. Senate, and three became giants in medicine. Not a bad trade-off for the school to remain safe in the increasingly violent neighborhood.

Bromleigh sat on the hill, as it always had, above the squalor and poverty around it. Its students enjoyed a kind of privileged existence. They moved freely over the campus and into the park, without fear.

Indeed there had never been an incident involving a single Bromleigh Boy that Star could remember. It seemed that the ivy-covered, gray stone buildings inspired awe even in the area lowlifes.

She looked back at the boys intently watching the detectives go about their work, and then at her watch.

"It's just after ten o'clock," she said. "Why aren't those kids in class?"

Paresi looked at the young men.

"Tea break," he said, derisively. "They're Bromleigh boys."

"They don't look like troublemakers," Star said. "But they don't look like Bromleigh kids either."

"Trust me." Paresi stared at the boys. "I can spot little rich assholes anywhere."

"Now who got up on the wrong side?" she said.

"I just don't have a lot of respect for kids who have everything handed to them."

He shoved his hands into his pockets, his gaze never leaving the three boys, who stared back at him. "These muffs are groomed from jump to be assholes."

"Assholes that would torch an old woman?" she said.

The two detectives stared at the kids in front of them.

Two of the boys were mirror images of one another. One

wore a green wool baseball jacket with tan suede sleeves, over gray trousers. His twin wore a navy baseball jacket with gray leather sleeves.

The third boy was a tall redhead. He wore a long, black, capelike coat.

Star's instincts told her that he was the leader, the one who called the shots. They weren't causing any problems. Still, they made her uneasy.

The redhead nudged the twin nearest him with his shoulder. The three of them turned in unison and started across the park.

At the crest of a small hill, the twins continued over, disappearing on the other side. But the redhead stopped.

Star watched him.

As he turned, facing her, his coat blew back in the wind.

She caught a glimpse of a navy blazer with a red and gold crest on the breast pocket.

Even with the sun behind him, she could see he was smiling.

CHAPTER THREE

Back in the squad room, Star picked up the phone. She punched in the number of the Medical Examiner's office.

When the operator answered, she asked for Dr. Spiegel.

"Dr. Spiegel's office." His secretary sounded like a woman who drank.

"Hello, this is Lieutenant Duvall, the Seventeenth, Homicide," Star said. "I need to know when Dr. Spiegel is posting the female found burnt this morning in Saint Francis Park."

"Just a minute, Lieutenant." The woman put her on hold.

Star drummed her fingers while she listened to a dreadful Muzak version of "Tequila Sunrise."

"I hate this stuff they play while you're holding," she said.

Her partner nodded in agreement. "I know. 'Super Freak' with strings."

"If only," she muttered. "'Tequila Sunrise,' a great song, destroyed. I think the Eagles should regroup and sue." She made a face. "I'd rather listen to dead air than this."

Paresi looked up. "Maybe you should put a bug in Mitch's ear, suggest something new."

"Like?" she asked.

"How 'bout 'Another One Bites the Dust'?"

"Thanks."

"Or 'Shotgun.' That's good, and it's Motown!"

"Enough."

"Or some Grateful Dead . . ."

She tossed the enormous rubber-band ball on her desk at him. Paresi caught it in one hand and put it in the bottom drawer of his desk.

"Give it back," she said.

"Come get it," he laughed.

"Lieutenant Duvall?" The woman's voice was back.

"Yes?"

"Dr. Spiegel said he's not going to be able to work on that body until Friday, or maybe even Monday. Did you have any other questions for him?"

"Has it been identified?"

"No. Not positively."

"Okay. Are you sure he can't post it sooner?"

Star could hear the sound of papers rustling.

"I'm sure, Lieutenant. Since Dr. Grant is away, things are running a little slow."

"Yeah." Star sat up straight in her chair. "Thanks." She hung up.

"What?"

"Speigel's such a lox. He can't get to the body until Friday, or even next Monday." She looked at Paresi. "Which might be a blessing in disguise."

"Why? It's just Molly."

"I know, but the way those boys were standing around this morning makes me uneasy. I want Mitchell to do it."

"You can't let go of those kids, huh?"

"Guess not," she said. "It wouldn't surprise me to find out they torched her."

"Tell you the truth, I've got the same feeling," Paresi said.

Star rocked back in her chair and looked at him.

"In my heart, God forgive me, I think whoever did it deserves a parade, but still, it's a homicide. I can't just shine it on because it's Molly and I hated her guts. That's why I want Mitchell to do the post. Spiegel couldn't find his ass with both hands, but Mitchell won't miss a trick." She picked up the phone. "He's in New York, consulting on a case."

"What's he into?"

"He's supervising an exhumation."

"Yech!" Paresi shuddered.

"Amen." Star flipped a couple of pages on her desk calendar. "He's got a suite at the Plaza." She looked at her watch. "It's still early, he's probably not in, but I can leave a message."

"The Plaza? A suite?" Paresi mused. "Was the Four Seasons full?"

Star smiled. "He prefers the ambience of the Plaza." She punched in the numbers. "He says even Donald Trump couldn't ruin it."

Paresi smiled. "Ambience, huh?"

Star swiveled in her chair, listening to the phone ring in New York City. "That's right." She smiled at her partner. "Unlike you, Mitchell Grant is *not* a Motel Six kind of guy."

CHAPTER FOUR

Star opened her desk drawer and pulled out a fresh bag of Hershey's Kisses. The operator connected her to Mitch's suite. He answered on the fourth ring.

"Hello?"

"Hi."

"Hi yourself." His voice caressed her ear.

"I didn't expect you to be in," she said. "Am I interrupting something?"

"No, not at all, just drying off. Hang on a sec." Mitch ruffled a towel through his wet hair, and switched the phone to his other ear.

"Better?" he asked.

"Much."

"I spent most of the morning up to my elbows in graveyard mold and dust. I had to clean up, and the bath here is infinitely superior to the facilities at the morgue. I just got out of the shower."

She was silent.

"Star?" he said. "You there?"

"Just getting a mental picture."

"Hope it's of me, and not the mold and dust."

They laughed.

"Definitely you . . . and I like it."

"Yeah?"

She could see him as clearly as if she were in the room. His blond hair, damp and tousled. The sparkling drops of water shimmering on his broad shoulders and in the thick, golden hair on his chest. She closed her eyes and saw the smile that she heard in his voice. The single dimple on the left side of his mouth, and the way his beautiful full lips opened to display white, perfect teeth. She saw his green eyes filled with mischievous glee, as the tiny laugh lines at their corners deepened. Mitchell Grant smiling could take your breath away, but Mitchell Grant *wet* and smiling would make your socks roll up and down.

She sighed.

"Sounds like you miss me," he said, his voice a husky, soft whisper.

"Oh, I do," she said. "I really, really do."

"In a couple of days, Lieutenant, you can show me just how much."

She looked up. Paresi was watching her, an "I know what you're talking about" look on his face.

Blushing, she swiveled her chair around, her back to her partner.

"I need a favor," she said, all business.

"Anything."

Star turned back to face Paresi.

"We have a female, Caucasian, who was fired up sometime last night, or very early this morning. We believe it's Molly Ludendorf."

"German Molly?"

"We're pretty certain," Star said. "It looks like she was torched while she was still alive, possibly sleeping, in Saint Francis Park."

"Who would do that?" Mitch said. "She was a mean old biddy, but harmless."

"I know. Spiegel took the call, but he says he won't be able to autopsy her until later in the week, or even next Monday. You know how he is, so I was hoping you'd do it."

"Sure, I'll be back on Wednesday morning. I'll call in and set it up for midafternoon."

"Thanks. So how's your case going?" she asked.

"Exhumation is not a pleasant thing, Lieutenant," he said. "Especially after three years in the ground."

"Yikes." Star shuddered. "Poor you."

There was a muffled silence, as if he had put his hand over

the mouthpiece. Still, in the background, Star could hear a feminine voice.

"Mitchell?"

"Yes, sorry. Something I had to take care of."

"Do you have company?" Star managed to say around the lump growing in her throat.

From across his desk, Paresi's eyes questioned.

"My daughter," he said.

"Oh." Star's relief was palpable. Though this phase of their relationship was new and great, the doctor's reputation as a womanizer was never far from her mind.

"She and her mother are here in New York, doing some shopping. I was just directing her to a couple of charge cards that haven't yet reached meltdown."

"She sounds like a big girl," Star said, sounding inane to herself.

"She's a junior at Brown this year, so a new wardrobe is a must. Hang on."

She could hear them talking. Her name came up. She couldn't hear exactly what was being said, but the young woman sounded less than pleased.

Mitch picked up the phone.

"Done," he said. "She's off to put skid marks on my plastic."

"It's nice that you're being a daddy," Star said.

"That's your spin on it," Mitch sighed. "Personally, I think she looks at me and sees a walking charge card."

"Most girls that age see their dads like that. I used to drive my father crazy." She smiled. "He made me get a job to pay off my clothing bills."

Mitch laughed. "That's a plan, though in Robin's case, I can tell you, it ain't gonna fly."

Star laughed with him. "Is Carole Ann with her?"

"At the bar, no doubt knocking back champagne cocktails like iced tea. But that's all right. When we split, we agreed that our contact should be *never*," he said. "Enough about them, what about you? Outside of Molly, how are you?"

"Fine," she said. "It's spring, the weather's warming up, and Darcy's got a new jacket."

"Uh-oh," Mitch said.

"Right. Neon lime under glaring lights, green. If you look directly at it, your eyes burst and run down your cheeks."

Mitch laughed. "Ray-Bans all around."

"You got that right." Star smiled. "If I keep focused on not looking directly at him, I'll be able to see you when you get home."

"Then train those beautiful eyes on Dominic, because I've got something special for you."

"Is it bigger than a bread box?" she said, again turning her chair away from her partner.

"Depends on the size of the loaf."

"Sounds intriguing," she said.

"I think you'll like it, and if you don't . . ." Mitch hesitated, teasing her.

"Then what?"

"We'll figure something out."

Star laughed.

"I'll call you tonight," he said, "and tell you a bedtime story." His voice was soft, but with a husky sexiness that made her entire body warm.

"I can hardly wait." She turned back to face Paresi. "Bye, Mitchell." She hung up.

"Ain't love grand?" her partner said.

"As long as it doesn't involve you." She tossed a handful of the silver-wrapped chocolates on his desk.

"So when's he coming back?"

"Wednesday morning. He's going to post Molly in the afternoon."

"Good." Paresi went back to the report he was typing. "Sounded like you heard somebody in his room."

"He'd just gotten out of the shower. His daughter was there."

"That must have been traumatic." He looked at her. "You know, naked dad."

"I'm sure he was covered."

"Uh-huh."

"You know he has a nineteen-year-old."

"Yeah." Paresi nodded. "But I understand she's not too crazy about him, so what did she want?"

"His charge cards. It's new wardrobe time. She and her mother were going shopping."

"So where was moms?" Paresi said.

Star built a small mound of silver-wrapped kisses in the center of her desk. "Waiting . . . in the bar."

"Of the Plaza," Paresi said.

Not looking at him, she unwrapped two pieces of the chocolate candy, demolishing her carefully built hill. "Of the Plaza," she said, and popped them into her mouth.

CHAPTER FIVE

Mitch looked up at Star from the charred body on the steel table in front of him. Like the doctor and his assistant, the detectives were also masked and gowned. Though only her eyes were visible above the mask, he could see her distress, and turned toward his assistant.

"Crank the air please, Jason," he said.

"Yes, Doctor." The young man went to the wall and fiddled with the high-tech pad of numbers set into the thermostat.

There was an industrial hum from the fans and a rush of cooler, cleaner air flooded the blue-tiled room. It moved out the scent of charred flesh—a smell so strong that even the filtering masks they wore couldn't erase it.

With only three nearly intact fingers left on the corpse, which cracked and flaked with his every touch, Mitch resorted to another method of lifting a print. The way in which he did it made Paresi loosen the straps holding his mask and pop two sticks of Doublemint gum into his mouth. Star's stomach churned.

The doctor amputated just below the second joint of Molly's scorched right forefinger and removed the section of bone. He then slipped the dead flesh over his own gloved finger and held the flaking skin in place with the thumb and forefinger of his other hand. Slowly, and carefully, Mitch rolled the dead fingertip on a black-inked pad.

Star and Paresi looked at one another. He handed her a stick of gum.

"Thanks," she whispered, loosening her mask. "You wouldn't happen to have any Pepto-Bismol on you, would you?"

"There's a bucket under the table," Paresi said.

"Too intense, Lieutenant?" Mitch asked, not looking up from his grisly task.

She unwrapped the gum, quickly popped it into her mouth, and pulled her mask back into place. "I'm fine," she said, unconvincingly.

Mitch gently pressed the fingertip onto an ID card. The print was light, but readable. He handed it to Jason, who put it into a machine in the corner of the autopsy room. The machine whirred and clicked. Jason removed the paper it pushed out.

"Ama . . . Amaleah . . . Amaleah Ludendorf," he said, walking back to the table, reading. "Aka Molly. It's a match, Doc."

"What an unusual name," Mitch said, circling the body. He looked up. It sounds like Mozart, Amadeus . . . Amaleah. Is it Austrian?"

Star looked over Jason's shoulder. "You sure it doesn't say Eva Braun?"

The men in the room laughed.

Still chuckling behind his mask, Mitch leaned close to the charred mess on the table. Under the glaring, unforgiving lights of the autopsy room, it was an even more horrible sight.

The body, stiffened and blackened, lay on the steel table like some ghastly centerpiece.

Beneath the destroyed flesh, flashes of yellow, and in some places where the flesh was completely gone, white bone were visible.

Molly's face was the most horrible. One side of her head

was burned down to the skull; brittle strands of dirty white hair stood in sparse areas along her red, raw-looking scalp.

Her lips were blackened burnt strips, barely hanging on. Her remaining teeth, oddly white and spectral, shone through the shriveled skin left on her face.

"Looks like Molly had quite a good dentist at one time," Mitch said.

"She used to have money," Star muttered, wincing as the doctor opened the corpse's jaw farther. She closed her eyes as bits of flesh flaked and fell to the stainless steel table.

"Look at this." Mitch leaned down and ran a gloved finger inside Molly's dead mouth. "Porcelain crowns." He pointed out two teeth with visible slumped white globs in the back of her jaw.

"Here too," he said, turning the skull, causing more skin to float onto the table. "Gold. No melting at all."

Star looked away.

Mitch drew his scalpel carefully along the burnt flesh, making a cut into what was left of Molly's throat.

"Doctor, there's something in there," Jason said.

Slowly, Mitch pushed a gloved index finger inside the incision. Burned ligaments supporting the old woman's charred larynx broke away, and some adhered to his glove.

"How many cartilages make up the larynx, Jason?" Mitch asked.

"Nine," the young man answered without hesitation.

"Right." Mitch moved back. "Tell me what you see."

Jason leaned in. "The object is trapped between what's left of the thyroid and arytenoid cartilages."

"Excellent," Mitch said. "Do you think any part of it might be in the cricoid cartilage?"

"I don't think so," Jason said. "Whatever it is, it seems to be pretty solidly caught. I don't see any sign of it reaching down into the cricoid." He looked at Mitch. "Do you?"

"No." Mitch indicated the incision. "Do you want to go for it?" he said.

"Sure." Jason reached into the wound and gently moved the object back and forth. More blackened flesh fell to the steel table.

"I'll never eat barbecue again," Star whispered.

"Want to make another cut?" Mitch said, handing him the scalpel.

Jason took it and stood for a moment, looking at the body. "I don't think I can get through the tissue without really ripping the heck out of it."

"Sure you can," Mitch said, pointing to a place inside Molly's burned throat. "Start here."

Jason leaned over and slowly cut through the scorched, dense, tough tissue imprisoning the item in Molly's throat.

He reached into the incision. Star sucked in her breath. A sound whistled between her teeth. The item, visible now, was caught in a web of sooty membrane, still showing an opaque gray in some places.

"This thing doesn't want out," Jason said, pushing his fingers deeper into the wound. Star took another deep breath. The taste of her mask made her choke.

"Lieutenant?" Mitch said, his eyes on the body. "You want to take a break?"

"No." She cleared her throat. "I'm okay."

"I'm not," Paresi whispered.

Jason stepped back. "It's pretty tight in there, Doc."

"Let me try," Mitch said. He inserted his thumb and first two fingers in Molly's burned flesh, up to the knuckles. The still-glittering item moved slightly.

"Come on," the doctor said softly. "Come on out."

Jason stood on the other side of the body, leaning in. He and Mitch were almost head to head, peering inside the dead woman's throat.

"You want these?" Jason said, holding up a set of dissecting forceps.

"No thanks." Mitch shook his head. "It's coming." He caught the glistening, silvery object from the back. "Got it." He pulled it from Molly's throat.

Jason held out a kidney-shaped, stainless steel basin, and Mitch dropped the item into it. It hit with a sharp metallic ring that made Star's shoulders rise protectively.

The young man sent the piece once again scurrying around the metal basin, while he gazed intently at it.

"Do you know what it is, Jason?" Mitch asked.

"Nope." Jason shook his head, and made the basin rattle again. "But it seems kinda familiar."

Cody Stevens sat at his desk. His homework was done, and he'd answered all of his e-mail; now he was using his computer for other things. He smiled as the image on the screen took shape. The guys would love this one. He liked to draw, and electronic drawing was the best.

Like his friends, Cody had grown up around computers. When he was a little kid, his father had designed and produced games that made him a multimillionaire.

Sometimes when his dad was shitfaced, he liked to talk about the old days. How he started out with nothing. How he lived in a crappy one-room apartment and designed his first game on butcher paper that he stole from the place where he worked. "Real 'rags to riches' crap," Cody said out loud. "Probably a lie," he muttered.

Cody didn't remember ever being poor. Both he and his sister Cheyenne only recalled beautiful big houses in affluent neighborhoods, with this one being the best. His father had totally equipped this house with everything electronic. It was almost like living in a sci-fi movie. The only drawback was that neither his father nor his mother spent much time at home. In time, he'd gotten used to it. His sister too. She used to cry when she was little, but now she, like Cody, enjoyed the freedom.

That old cow that called herself the housekeeper dared not say anything to either him or Cheyenne. Besides, she didn't speak English too well anyway, so they pretty much did what they wanted, when they wanted. His parents had better things to do than sit around dealing with their two kids.

Jay Stevens was president of his own gaming company, though he no longer designed. Cody thought this was a good thing, since he felt his father was seriously out of touch.

His dad favored sci-fi and dark games, while the trend was moving more toward shoot-to-kill and war games. Still, there were the diehard mind-fuck fans, who loved his father's thinking games. Getting through spooky castles and dark forests filled with gnomes and evil fairies juiced them up. They had to think to survive. There were even fan clubs based on some of Jay Stevens's games, some as far away as England and Japan. Sometimes his father would bring home letters from some of these foreign geeks.

Still, once in a while Cody would try to talk to him, pitch him an idea or two, hip him to what was hot, but Jay waved him away, saying he was busy.

"Busy, right." Cody clicked the mouse faster. Most of the time the little roach just came home and got tanked. And as far as his mother was concerned, Cody barely remembered what she looked like. Brenda Stevens was a "socialite." Whatever that meant. "Who needs them, either of them?" Cody said. He had his friends, most of whom were in the same boat. That's why they'd come together and made the pact.

It was time for the second generation of game masters to make their mark. Someday, he and his friends were going to make more money than all of their fathers put together. They had big ideas, and they knew they had to refine, perfect, and test their theories. They wanted their creations to be so real, they'd have to be sold with vomit bags.

"Then we'll see who rules." Cody clicked the mouse, his pale eyes following the shape of the creature on the screen. It was looking good. It had the body of a bat and the leering, grinning face of a horned, scaly, horrendously fiendish-looking demon.

"Bitchin'," Cody said as he moved the figure around on the computer screen. "This guy is awesome! Much better than the other one. The guys are gonna go mad for this one."

He clicked his paintbrush icon onto the color palette, and selected a rusty brown shade, dragging it to the body of the monster bat. A click released it. Nodding his head in time to the latest Marilyn Manson CD, Cody refined and finished his painting.

He leaned back in his chair. "Way cool . . ." He grinned and then began laughing. "You look a lot like my dad," he said to the monstrous drawing. "All you need is a pair of stupid suspenders and an overpriced suit." That made him laugh hard.

His sister opened the door of his room.

Cody quickly double-clicked the window, causing the image to roll up, like a window shade, and dissappear from the screen.

"You know, when a door is closed, it usually means the person on the inside wants privacy," he said. "Next time, knock."

Cheyenne shrugged her bony shoulders and wrinkled her nose.

"Don't tell me what to do," she said. "You're not God."

"Don't be so sure," her brother said.

CHAPTER SIX

Star put two burgundy and white gold-rimmed dinner plates on the table, and tried not to think. Three weeks had gone by since Molly's murder, and they still had no leads. She didn't want to even consider that maybe because she loathed the victim, she wasn't trying hard enough.

Sharing this evening with Mitch was going a long way toward keeping her thoughts off the subject. As long as her hands were busy, her mind was occupied.

She laid a white linen napkin in the center of each plate, placed the silverware alongside, and went back into the kitchen for glasses.

Mitchell Grant stood barefoot in front of the open wall oven, his long form clothed in black jeans and a black breast-pocketed T-shirt. He was basting two perfectly roasted Cornish hens.

"Mmm, that smells so good," she said.

"Thanks." He put them back into the oven, and closed the door. "Another ten minutes and they'll be ready."

He moved to the cooktop and opened the lid on a pot of

wild rice. Steam curved gracefully downward into the stove's center vent, as he stirred the rice gently. "Almost," he said.

"How do you do that?"

"What?"

"Get things to come out together?"

He covered the rice and faced her.

They'd been "a couple" now for a few months, and the status of their relationship was a grapevine gossip staple in various city offices, including the police department and the medical examiner's office.

Star had known Mitchell Grant from her earliest days in the Police Academy, but had warily kept her distance. Still, even after years of being around him, one look from him could make her heart plunge to her knees. He was a singularly beautiful man. Exquisitely handsome, with a decidedly aristocratic cast to his features. If she had to describe him in one word, that word would be *elegant*. Even barefoot, in jeans and a T-shirt.

His tailored Italian wardrobe was as much a part of his legend in the department as his womanizing. Grant had a rep as a "hit-and-run" artist. Though she'd always been attracted to him, Star stayed away, even after his much publicized divorce. She had to be sure first of the depth and reality of the feelings . . . his as well as her own.

Spending personal time with him, and getting to know the man beneath the Armani- and Versace-dominated wardrobe, is what opened her heart. His warmth, his humor, and his support of her and the decisions she made allowed her to feel safe. She was beginning to trust him.

He took her in his arms. She rested her head on his chest. "You see, Lieutenant," he said, softly, "there's such a thing as timing, in cooking *and* in life. When things are perfect, and ready . . ." He squeezed her tightly. "They just fall into place."

She raised her head. He kissed her mouth.

She loved the taste of the man. His skin, his mouth. He had a natural sweetness that she found herself tasting even when they were separated. The kiss grew deeper. Star pressed herself against him.

"Play fair, Lieutenant," he whispered, kissing her ear.

She smiled at the feel of his body responding.

Mitch ran his hands over her back, and down, pulling her closer, pressing her body to his. He kissed her again. "Mmm . . . if we keep this up, dinner's going to be very cold and very late."

Star moved her hands over his chest, down his body, and underneath his T-shirt.

"I can wait."

They sat naked in his bed, dining from a tray on cold Cornish hen, microwave-reheated wild rice, perfectly steamed asparagus, and a mango chutney he'd made himself.

"You are such a good cook," she said.

"It's easy when you've got someone who appreciates it." He looked at her, his green eyes teasing. "And who loves eating it."

Star gazed at him. She loved looking in his eyes, flirting with him. The man released something in her, a daring, a feeling that never failed to surprise her. She looked at his shoulders, his chest, the golden hair growing there. He was like a drug. She knew it, and she'd stopped fighting it.

"Mmm. When everything tastes so good, a girl gets greedy."

"This whole night is worth that look on your face," he said.

She held out the last bit of Cornish hen. Mitch ate it from her fingers.

"Mmm." He licked her fingertips, then sucked her index finger into his mouth.

She put the tray of dishes on the table next to the bed, and poured the last of the wine into her glass. She sipped it, set the glass down, and leaned toward him. He kissed her, tasting Pouilly-Fuissé, the sweetness of mango chutney, and her own deliciousness. He felt her body against his, the softness of her lips, the heat from her skin. He gave himself up to the feeling rushing through him, devouring her mouth, her neck, her shoulders, her breasts.

"I love the way you taste," he whispered, kissing her again.

The phone rang.

"Oh no," she groaned.

Mitch lowered his head onto her shoulder and closed his eyes. He sighed, and leaned over her. "I'm sorry," he said, "but I have to answer."

"I know."

He kissed her on the lips and picked up the receiver.

"Hello." He looked at Star. "Hi, Dom. Yes, she's right here." He handed her the receiver.

Star looked sheepish. "I put my calls on forward," she said. "Sorry." She put the phone to her ear. *"What?"*

"I'm sorry to interrupt," Paresi said.

At the sound of his voice and the seriousness of it, Star sat up straight.

Mitch looked at her, his eyes questioning.

"What happened? Where are you?"

"In Saint Francis Park."

"You're off duty. What's going on?"

"Delaney called me. We've got another one here, and he thinks it's linked to Molly. He wanted one of us down here, so he called me."

"Another crispy critter?" she asked.

"Nope." Paresi sighed. "I would have preferred that to this."

"Okay, I'm on my way."

"Star . . . before you come down . . ."

"Yeah?"

"It's somebody you know."

Star looked at Mitch. "We're on our way."

The woman's body sat propped against a wall on the east side of the park. She looked like a discarded doll, her legs apart and her feet out in front of her.

Star saw the frizzy blonde hair glistening almost white in the darkness. A lump rose in her throat. Oblivious to the stares, she reached for Mitch's hand. No, she thought, no.

The portable battery-powered lights set up around the scene lit up that corner of the park. As she neared the body, Star's eyes smarted from the brightness of the lights. Still she could see the street people and druggies milling around the darkened edges, like shadowy extras in a horror film.

The cops and forensic crew parted, letting her and Mitch get close to the body. Mitch pulled a pair of latex gloves from his jacket pocket and snapped them on, as an assistant trained a bright light directly on the corpse.

"Dolores Causwell," Star said, her voice barely a whisper.

Paresi appeared at her shoulder. "I'm sorry," he said.

"Me too." Star moved closer to the body.

Dolores Causwell, Star's first bust, when she was just two weeks out of the Academy. The hooker and the cop crossed paths frequently in those early years, and had formed a strange yet solid friendship.

Dolores was a bottle blonde who favored heavy metal music, Cuervo Gold tequila straight from the bottle, and a Puerto Rican lap dancer named Téa Reyes. The two of them shared a very heavy heroin habit, and Dolores had come out of "retirement" to supplement their income.

"She's bled out," Mitch said, leaning over and touching the dead woman's ashen face. He squatted beside the corpse and gently turned the woman's head. "She's a little stiff, and she's cooling. She's been here for a while." He gazed intently at Dolores's neck.

Star walked a few feet away, looking at the ground.

Paresi stood behind Mitch. "Vampires?"

Mitch straightened up. His fawn-colored suede jacket caught the light. "Doesn't hurt to look," he said. "But my guess is she was involved in some kind of sex game that got out of hand."

Paresi nodded. "A definite hazard in her line of work."

Mitch looked around. "There's no blood."

"What?"

"Blood," Mitch repeated. "I don't see any, not even on her clothes."

"She wasn't killed here," Star said, walking back to the body. "There's no blood of any kind around her. She was dumped here. She died somewhere else."

"You're right," Mitch said.

Star moved to the left of the body. The woman's dead eyes

seemed to follow. Her hand was partially covered by the hem of her bright blue lightweight jacket.

Star crouched down. "Can I get a pair of gloves and some more light here, please?"

An assistant handed her the gloves and stooped beside her, aiming a high beam where Star pointed.

"What you got?" Paresi and Mitch moved closer.

Star pulled on her gloves and inched the fabric over with her fingertip. "Her fist is clenched, but I think she's got something in her hand, see it?"

"Yeah." Paresi leaned next to her. "Looks like something shiny."

Star straightened up and peeled off the gloves. "Let's get her hands bagged before anything else is done."

"Right." Paresi moved off toward the forensic team.

Mitch beckoned a member of his crew. He removed his gloves, took Star's, and handed both pairs to his aide. The woman put the gloves in a clear plastic bag.

"Thanks, Pat."

"You're welcome, Doctor," the woman said, snapping the bag shut.

Star took his arm and led him a few feet from the scene.

"Can we examine her tonight?" she asked.

"Yes." Mitch looked back and indicated the body. "Were you close?"

Star nodded. "In a weird sort of way." She pulled her coat tighter around herself. "Dolores was my first collar." She looked at the crumpled form. "You should have seen her then, Mitchell. About fifteen years and forty pounds ago, she looked like Kim Basinger. She was a fox and, in spite of what she did for a living, a really sweet girl."

Star sighed. "In the winter, when we worked her stroll, she'd bring coffee to us in the car." She smiled. "I was riding with Tim Cochran then, rest his soul. He loved piking the hookers. But with Dolores, he was always a gentleman. He was nuts about her, just like every other guy on the job.

"She and I were both new to the streets, so we had that in common. Where I had been trained as a cop, Dolores was just out there. She was a real innocent, unearthly. Not stupid or an airhead, just somebody totally without guile."

Star looked again at the body. "She'd go into Dunkin' Donuts to get warm, and whenever she spotted us, she'd always bring two coffees to the cruiser." She smiled at the recollection.

"One night I got the nerve to tell her I preferred tea, with the works. She laughed her head off. From then on, it was a large tea with lots of milk and sugar for me and coffee Boston for Cochran. She'd hand me the cup and say, 'We girls got to stick together, look out for each other.' In summer she'd bring us iced coffee and tea.

"When I was working graveyard, I used to spot her sometimes at two or three in the morning, still out there, no matter what the weather."

In the dim light, Star's eyes sparkled with unshed tears. "Sometimes, on really cold nights, if it was slow and I was riding solo, I'd let her warm up in the backseat. She'd get in the cruiser and we'd talk. She told me all about her daughter and how she got into prostitution. I mean, even when I locked Dolores up, there were never any hard feelings. She understood that I was just doing my job, like she was doing hers."

She looked back again at the crumpled form against the wall. Glistening tears inched down her face. Star wiped her eyes with the back of her hand, like a child.

"I used to tell her if she was going to sell it, she should hook up with a class house. Back then she had the face and body, stone call girl material. She could have made a fortune, but she preferred it on the stroll."

Technicians surrounding the body momentarily cut off Star's view. She turned away, wiping her eyes again and gazing off into the darkness of the park.

"Things went okay for her, until she got messed up with this crazy pimp, B. B. Penney."

"B. B.?" Mitch asked. "Like B. B. King?"

"Not hardly," Star said. "B. B. King stands for Blues Boy. B. B. Penney liked to call himself 'Big Black.' His real name was Ben. Benjamin Byron Penney. He was a real badass. He used to beat her senseless. I pulled him off her one night and slammed him a couple of good ones." She turned back to Mitch. "Know what he said to me?"

"What?"

Star's voice dropped to a masculine register. " 'When you leave, I'ma kill huh.' " Her eyes darkened. "Son of a bitch. He was a stupid, ignorant, dangerous bastard." She looked back toward the crowd around the body. "I asked her to go to a shelter, but she refused." Star felt the tears again sliding down her face. "She stayed because of her daughter; she didn't want to take Ronni out of the house."

"What did you do with him?"

"I locked him up for getting in my face, but he was on the street by morning."

She reached into her pocket and pulled out a small pack of tissues. She took two and wiped her eyes.

"One night, I got a call down to where she lived. When I got there, she'd taken a baseball bat to Ben. She ran him out to the street, chased him a couple of blocks, and beat his skull in."

She tried to speak, but her voice caught in her throat.

Mitch put his arm around her shoulder.

More tears ran down her face, and Star wiped them away.

"She caught him trying to have sex with her daughter."

Her body shuddered, and a deep sob tore from her.

"Ronni was just three years old."

Mitch pulled her into his arms.

Star clung to him, crying hard. "She should have killed the son of a bitch. Hell, *I* should've killed him. It was the sickest thing a man could do to a child."

She stepped back and wiped her eyes again. "He refused to press charges against her that night. It was the only decent thing that rat bastard ever did in his sorry life.

"After he recovered, he pronounced her a 'truly crazy white bitch' and let her go." Star blew her nose. "But there is a God. Ben hooked up with a little black girl named Valene Daniels in Philly. She did the world a favor and threw a few shots at him. She put three holes in that dented skull, and one in his neck. They told me that when the Philly PD got there, she was standing on the hole in his neck, and he was singing in the Hellfire Choir.

"I'm happy to say, his rep and Valene's story of abuse got her off on a justifiable. I think she should have gotten the keys to the city. She did everybody one hell of a favor.

"But it was too late for Dolores. He'd already destroyed her. After Ben, she went completely off men. She hooked up with a Puerto Rican lesbian, and they've been together ever since."

Star walked a few steps to a trash can, and discarded the tissues. She walked back to Mitch. "Somebody's got to let Téa know about this."

"What happened to her daughter?" Mitch asked.

Star looked down. "The last time I saw Ronni, she was going to juvie for nearly kicking an old man to death."

Mitch gently touched her face. "It's a rough world, baby. I'm sorry about your friend."

"Thanks." She put her hand on his chest. He covered it with his own. Star became aware of the eyes on them.

"People are watching us," she said.

"Let them." Mitch pulled her to him. "My only concern is you."

She closed her eyes, grateful for the comfort of his arms in the darkness of the park, away from the scene where her friend lay. "Thank you," she whispered, clinging to him.

She heard someone call his name. She reluctantly moved away. "Can we talk later?" she asked, wiping tears from her face.

"Whatever you need," Mitch said, walking her back to the scene.

"We need permission to move her, doctor." A jug-eared young man in a dark blue jacket, with CORONER written in white across the back, moved in step beside him.

"Pictures done?" Mitch asked.

"Everything's finished," the young man said. "Video too."

"Then let's get her covered and out," Mitch said.

Star stood alongside the doctor, the pain of seeing this particular corpse visible on her face.

"Hey." Paresi moved next to her.

"Yeah?" She turned to face him.

"One of the uniforms picked this up, a few feet from the body."

A clear plastic bag held a gold button. Star took it in her hand. "You got some light?"

"Right here." Paresi aimed a flashlight at the bag.

Star looked at him.

He nodded. "Uh-huh."

Mitch turned to look at what she held.

A distinct button. A golden wafer, with an emblem of a building, and a name stamped on it. BROMLEIGH ACADEMY 1895–1995.

CHAPTER SEVEN

The offices of the Medical Examiner's building were dark, yet on the floors below, the crypt, prep rooms, and autopsy suites were doing business as usual.

Twenty-four hours a day, seven days a week, on major and minor holidays, Brookport's dead were assured a place to rest on this their final journey from one world to the next.

Brought to the massive crypt by natural causes, accidents, fires, or as examples of acts of insane inhumanity, they found sanctuary.

Weighed, stripped, washed, cataloged, and shelved, they waited beneath white plastic sheets for the next leg of their trip. The introduction of sharp, invasive instruments soon revealed their reasons for being here, in this house of death.

They lay silent in the cold, with their belongings stuffed into paper bags and shoved between their toe-tagged feet.

Tonight, another client arrived, accompanied by a small entourage led by the chief medical examiner himself. The late-shift workers were unaccustomed to seeing their boss in the flesh, and most of them stared, especially the women.

Mitchell Grant walked down the corridor. Heads turned and jaws dropped as he passed, with Starletta Duvall and Dominic Paresi keeping pace alongside him. As they neared the weighing room, Jason Williams approached from the opposite end of the hall.

"Jason!" The doctor looked surprised. "What are you doing here? Are you working a double shift?"

"Yes sir," the young man said. "I switched with Kaminsky. He went out of town for a wedding."

"Well, glad to see you," Mitch said. "I can always use your help."

"What've you got?" Jason asked, as he followed the three of them into a chilly, green-tiled room.

A tall silver scale dominated most of the space. The brand name, Toledo, was written with a flourish across its black face in large old-fashioned white letters. The apparatus resembled the weighing machines you see on the highway.

Lying on a steel table, atop a metal plate, was the body of Dolores Causwell. Heavy chains, fastened to each corner of the metal plate, dangled to the floor beneath her.

A female technician appeared. In her gloved hands, she held a long, rounded pole. Height marks had been deeply etched into the wood. They watched as she laid the pole alongside the body, and carefully aligned it.

After getting the measurement, the woman put the pole aside and reached for a scuffed, ink-stained clipboard hanging near the scale. "Five feet ten and one half inches," she said as she filled in Dolores's height.

Mitchell Grant moved alongside her. The woman, whose photo ID badge read TRINA BOYCE, glanced at him. Her pale skin colored, then she dropped her pen.

Mitch picked it up and handed it to her. She smiled and dropped it again.

"Sorry, Doctor," she said.

"No problem." Mitch handed it to her again. "Are you done?" he asked.

"Oh." She looked flustered. "Yes . . . I mean no, the body has to be weighed."

"We'll take care of that." Mitch took the clipboard and handed it to Star. He pulled two pairs of latex gloves from the box on the shelf near the scale. "You can go now." He looked at the woman's name tag. "Trina."

Her face turned beet-red. "Yes, thank you, Dr. Grant." She bumped into Star. "Here's the pen," she said, handing it to her and turning again to Mitch. "If you need me, Doctor, just use the intercom."

Mitch smiled at her. "Thanks, I'll call if we need you."

The woman backed out of the room, her eyes on Mitch, her smile so wide Star thought her teeth might tumble out one at a time, like those of a cartoon character. She looked at Paresi and rolled her eyes. Her partner laughed.

Mitch tossed a pair of the surgical gloves to Jason.

"Thanks." The young man pulled them on.

"Let's get her up," Mitch said. He moved around the plate, collecting the hanging chains, bringing all four of them to the center, resting on Dolores's stomach. Jason tugged down the pulley apparatus and hooked it to the chains, locking the mechanism so that as the pulley rose, it created a pyramid of chains over the body.

There was a grinding of gears as the machine rumbled, lifting Dolores Causwell's remains up, allowing the needle to spin and settle.

"One hundred sixty-seven pounds," Mitch said. Star wrote the weight in the proper box on the form.

Jason pushed another button and the dull, scuffed steel plate slowly lowered, depositing Dolores back atop the table.

"What's with the hands?" Jason said, indicating the bags.

"She's got something in her right one," Star said. "From what we could see at the scene, it's shiny."

Mitch lifted the woman's wrist and removed the paper bag.

Jason leaned close and peered at the hand. It was tightly closed.

"I see what you mean," he said, touching the dead flesh. Dolores's fingers remained stiff and unyielding. Jason pressed firmly on the hand, using his thumb and forefinger to open her grip as much he could. Pressing down on her flesh, he felt the tip of the object with his thumb.

"It's hard . . ." He pressed again, this time moving enough flesh to get a small glimpse of the item she held. Straightening up, he faced the detectives. "It's metal, and shiny," Jason said. "Where was she found?"

"The park," Paresi replied.

"Near the school?" the young man asked.

"Right." Paresi nodded. "Against the wall, on the east side of the park."

"That's a rough area," Jason said, stepping back to look at the body. "She looks bad."

"She's lost a lot of blood," Mitch said.

"How much at the scene?" Jason asked.

"None." Star moved around Mitch and indicated the woman's wrists. "There's marks on her wrists, but they're not big enough to bleed her through." She looked up at the doctor. "You think this has anything to do with German Molly?"

"If it does, that means we've got a lunatic running around Saint Francis Park," Mitch said. He crossed the room and rolled a plastic-covered gurney alongside the table. "Let's get her down the hall and take a good look. Maybe once we get her hand open, it will tell us something."

The round, flat, black-numbered, white-faced Seth Thomas clock hanging over the door of Autopsy Chamber D, read 1:42 A.M.

The ceaseless whirling and hum of the fans bounced off the tiled walls.

Star watched the tall, brown young man standing across the table from Mitchell Grant. He had pulled back several braids from each side of his face and used them to tie back the rest of his hair. The overhead fluorescent lights shone down on him, highlighting the gold and copper colors in the long braids trailing down his back.

He leaned over Dolores, slowly moving a bright white lamp across the surface of her wrinkled, soiled clothes and pallid skin as Mitch, working with a powerful magnifier, painstakingly searched the body. When he'd collected what he could from the clothing and visible skin, he and Jason quickly undressed Dolores. They deposited her clothing, jewelry, underwear, and shoes into a large brown paper bag, while Star made notes of what had been removed from the body.

Beneath the harsh lights, the sins of Dolores Causwell's life stood out in darkened patches of collapsed veins and needle tracks on the insides of her arms and the pale, doughy flesh of her thighs.

Dr. Grant turned Dolores's body onto its side. Her flesh was chalk-white, except at the buttocks and the backs of her legs and thighs. What blood was left in her body had pooled there and turned those areas a nightmarish blackish purple.

"Oh . . ." Star's hand flew to her mouth.

Grant looked up.

Jason looked at her, seeing her eyes blink wet, and a tear rolling down her face.

"Sorry," she muttered.

Now Jason realized why Dr. Grant was taking such a detailed look at a body at this hour. He was doing it for her. For Lieutenant Duvall. He looked at Mitch. Even though he'd returned his attention to the body, Jason could see that the doctor's mind was on Star.

Grant got the dead woman's hand open. "Bingo," he said, and removed the small pewter piece from her palm.

Jason held out the metal tray. Mitch dropped it in.

As he'd done with the first piece, Jason rolled it around in the basin, again making Star shudder. He gazed at it and then rolled it again.

"You had the same reaction to the first piece we found in Molly," Dr. Grant said. "Have you seen these things before?"

Jason looked up. "I don't think so." He rolled the piece again. "Still, this one and the other one remind me of something."

"What?" the doctor and the detectives said in unison.

Jason shrugged. "I can't place it." He touched a gloved fingertip to the metal. "This is pretty thrashed." He looked at Mitch. "It looks like a chemical or something spilled on it. . . .

Still, it's kinda familiar." He looked at the three expectant faces watching him. "Let me think about it."

CHAPTER EIGHT

It was 8:20 A.M. and Jason Williams sat on the sofa in Mitchell Grant's office. After the doctor and the detectives left around three, he had returned to finish out his double shift in the morgue.

He was off at eight, but he remembered something about those objects they'd found with the bodies, and so he decided to stick around until Grant came in. He banked on the doc showing up at 8:30, as usual, even though he'd left so late.

When Dr. Grant arrived, Jason was waiting in his outer office. He told Mitch why he'd waited. The doctor patted him on the back, and called the Seventeenth, Homicide. They were waiting for Lieutenant Duvall and her partner to show.

Jason was tired, but pumped. Here was his chance to give something back to Dr. Grant.

He looked at the gold antique clock on Mitch's desk. The detectives should be showing up anytime now. He rolled his shoulders, trying to relax a kink between his shoulder blades.

"Your shoulders tight, Jason?" Mitch said, watching the boy flex and move his head from side to side.

"A little," Jason said.

"After we finish up here, have Lorraine call Dave Donato, my masseur. When he's finished, you'll feel like a new man. After that, go home and relax. Don't even think about coming back this afternoon."

"Wow!" Jason said. "Thanks, Doc."

"You're welcome," Mitch said.

Jason stretched his long legs out in front of him, and sipped from the cold, sweating bottle of IBC root beer he held in his hands.

"Root beer at this hour of the morning?" Star asked, entering the office and taking off her coat.

"A nineteen-year-old stomach." Mitch smiled.

Jason grinned.

"Hi, Jason." She tossed her coat on the sofa and sat down beside him.

Jason nodded. "Lieutenant."

"Looks good to me," Paresi said, walking in, his eyes red from too little sleep. He looked back over his shoulder. "Hey, Lorraine, got any more root beer?"

"Right away, Sergeant," Mitch's secretary answered.

Paresi dropped his coat on top of Star's and sat down in a chair next to the sofa.

Within seconds, Lorraine entered with a glass and a cold root beer. She handed them both to Paresi.

"I'll take your coats." She reached toward the two coats on the end of the sofa.

"You can leave mine," Star said.

"Mine too." Paresi set the glass on the coffee table and drank from the bottle.

"Very well," Lorraine said. She turned to Star, with a wide smile. "I've got some tea brewing for you, Lieutenant," she drawled.

"Thanks," Star said. *When pigs fly,* she thought. Star had no intention of drinking anything brought to her by Lorraine. It was no secret that the secretary, one of Mitch's previous conquests, hated her, and the feeling was mutual.

"Ah'm fixing it just the way you like it," Lorraine said. Her tight little smile didn't reach her cold blue eyes. "Plenty of milk and sugah!" She twinkled.

And lots of extra spit, Star thought to herself. "Thank you," she said. She knew Lorraine would rather be strolling through Hell in a gasoline bikini than making tea for her. No way she was drinking it.

Paresi held up his root beer, breaking the tension between the two women.

"Thanks for this, Lorraine. It's good."

"Glad you like it, Sergeant. Just let me know if you all need anything else." She smiled again at Star. "Hot tea coming right up."

Mitch leaned back in his chair, and rested his feet on top of his desk. He pointed to Jason.

"My assistant was waiting for me when I arrived this morning. Seems he remembers something about those two items we retrieved. Jason, the floor is yours."

The young man took a sip of the root beer. It was so cold he had a momentary "brain freeze." He liked that. Jason took another sip and a breath. He was center ring, and he loved it.

Mitchell Grant was his idol. Jason wanted to be just like him. Forensic pathology was an art, and Mitch was a Grand Master. The doc believed in him too—he had demonstrated that fact numerous times.

Now he had something that could maybe help him solve a case. Payback. He wouldn't let the doc down. Jason took another sip of the root beer, to clear his throat.

He put down the drink. His long, braided hair swung forward as he leaned toward the coffee table. He looked more like a rock star than a future forensic genius.

"My friends and I play a lot of computer and video games, you know, to relax." He looked at the trio in the room.

"I know lots of kids who are really into game-playing. Some of them even get into roles, you know, becoming the characters. It's cool, because in the game, you can be whoever or whatever you want to be. You can really get into it."

He picked up the root beer and sipped again.

"Some kids are militant, shoot-to-kill freaks, some are metalheads, into sci-fi and robotic stuff, and some are goths. They're the easiest to identify."

"Goths?" Star said.

"Yes ma'am." He nodded at her. "Gothics . . . they dress the part, you know, capes, lots of velvet and white makeup, like vampires, or noblemen from another age."

"Tom Cruise in *Interview with a Vampire*," Star said.

Jason nodded. "Exactly. There's lots of goths that are really into that whole vampire thing—they follow those books, and there are other groups that are into sci-fi, and they follow their thing, you know, space aliens, *X-Files*, *Star Trek*, *Star Wars*, all that."

"Are these usually college kids?" Paresi asked.

"Not always," Jason said. "I got into a game called Dragon World when I was in high school. In fact, when I went to Bromleigh, there was a whole bunch of guys who were into that sword and sorcerer stuff."

"You went to Bromleigh?" Star asked.

"Yes ma'am." Jason's cinnamon-colored skin glowed. "I was a scholarship student. You know, from the neighborhood."

"Jason's stats are impressive," Mitch said. "He graduated Bromleigh at the top of his class, and since he's been here, he's become my best worker."

Jason beamed.

"He's been working hard, soaking up the atmosphere and making a little money," Mitch said. "In September, he's headed for my old school, Harvard. Premed."

"Thanks to you," Jason said, nodding at Mitch. He looked at the detectives. "Doc got me a full scholarship, including books and room and board for my first two years."

"Way to go, Mitchell," Star said.

"He deserves it," Mitch said.

Paresi tipped his bottle of root beer toward Jason in a toast. "Impressive."

"It's the best," Jason beamed. "My mom was so happy when I got in, she cried for two days. Then she found out *everything* was paid for, and cried for two more!"

They laughed.

Jason looked at Mitch. "Doc says if I stay in the top ten percent of my class, the next two years are paid too."

"Outstanding." Star smiled at the young man.

"I know he'll do well," Mitch said.

"I want to be Dr. Grant when I grow up." Jason grinned.

"It's the Italian suits, right?" Paresi said.

"Definitely." Jason nodded. "*And* the ride," he said, a mischievous glint in his hazel eyes. "The Porsche is *slamming*!"

Paresi reached out and slapped him a high five.

Jason, comfortable now, leaned back on the sofa, lacing his long fingers together.

"After you guys left, I got to thinking about something that we used to do at Bromleigh. We read a lot of medieval literature, you know, lots of books with wizards and magic and stuff like that. There's a prof at Bromleigh who specializes in occult literature—it's a popular class. Anyway, he had us reading a book called *King Vikram and the Vampire*, by Sir Richard Burton."

Paresi looked at Star.

"Not that one," she said.

"No . . . not that one," Jason echoed. "Anyway, in this book, there was a thing called the Baital."

"Baital?" Star said.

"Yes ma'am," Jason continued. "In the book, the Baital is a bat with a human face. He's really smart and he can talk, you know, like directly to people. He spins stories and casts spells."

"A bat with a guy's face." Paresi shook his head. "I gotta get out more."

Everyone laughed.

Jason nodded. "It's pretty strange, all right. But later on, I started playing a computer game, called Vampire's Lair, and this thing was in it, only they jazzed it up, changed it some. In the game, they called it Batal. When you're playing, it can be male or female. It can take on any form. It comes out at night and it hangs upside down in the trees, you know, waiting for a victim."

"Wait a minute," Mitch said, swinging his feet off the desk. "I'm asleep at the wheel here." He turned in his chair and opened the small safe on the right side of his desk. He pulled out two metal pieces, each encased in a plastic bag. He put them on the desk.

"Take a good look at these, Jason," he said.

Jason stood and picked up the bagged pieces. He looked at one and then the other.

Indicating the one in his left hand, he laid it down on the coffee table. "Now that I remember," he said. "This one really sorta looks like the Batal. I mean it's burned and kinda melted, but you can still make out the shape of it."

"How does it kill?" Star asked.

"Like the vampire it is. It sucks all the blood out. But in the game, after it drains the victim, it spits fire and cremates what's left. It doesn't like competition, so it destroys its victims so they won't come back as vampires."

"Lovely," Star said.

"It's got real dead-looking skin, and it's always saying foul things."

"Not unlike the woman in which it was found," Star said.

"I knew that old lady." Jason reached for his root beer. "She used to hang around the school when I was there, always calling me and the other black guys niggers. She was pretty nasty."

"Yes she was," Star agreed.

"She probably pissed somebody off at Bromleigh and they got her."

The detectives and the doctor exchanged looks.

"Are you saying Bromleigh has the kind of kids that would do that?" Star asked.

"Well, ma'am," Jason said, "I know that lots of guys on the campus are into weird things. They play lots of games. Most of the senior and junior class is made up of computer geeks. Some of those guys have even built their own computers. They come from families that made big money in computers, and they are way into all that stuff.

"Role-playing games are very hot at Bromleigh. When I was there, everybody was into stuff like Vampire's Lair. In fact, that game was invented by the father of one of the kids who goes to school there. Everybody played it. It was so popular, there was even a club of guys who wore costumes and had meetings and stuff, all revolving around the game."

"Wow," Star said.

"A lot of those kids have money and not much else," Jason said. "They're always looking for a kick, you know, a bigger thrill than the one before."

"So they get into these games," she said.

"Big-time." Jason sipped his drink

"Do you know the current favorite?" Star asked. "Is it still the vampire game?"

Jason shrugged. "I've been out for a while, but my boys

still on campus say the big game now is Planet Fortress. It's a space alien war game."

Star picked up the second bag. "Any idea on this one?"

Jason peered at it. He shook his head. "I can't say. It looks almost like it's got wings, but it's so corroded, it's hard to tell."

"So a lot of these boys were really into the role-playing thing," Paresi said. "For some reason, that flips me out."

"It could get bizarre," Jason said. "Especially because it had to be done in secret."

"In secret?" Star echoed.

"Uh-huh." Jason took another sip of root beer. "There's rules on campus about what you can and can't do." He grinned. "Of course, rules are made to be broken."

"You ever break the rules, Jason?" Star smiled.

"No ma'am." Jason shook his head. "I couldn't afford to get kicked out. I mostly hung with the other brothers, we found other ways to have fun, ways that wouldn't get us expelled. Besides, we weren't really welcome to the game thing, but that was okay by us. We hung out and shot a lotta hoops."

Star kept looking at the two figures. She held up the first one and turned toward her partner.

"What?" Paresi said.

"This one drains the blood of its victim and then incinerates it." She held up the other one. "This one, we don't know what it is, but it was in Dolores's hand, and she was bled dry. Molly was burned, and Dolores was bled."

The three men looked at her.

"Not to mention the button at the scene," Paresi said.

Star nodded slowly.

"I think it's time to pay a visit to Jason's old school."

CHAPTER NINE

The greenery on the Bromleigh campus was in full bloom. Cherry blossoms crowded the branches of the trees lining the stone walkway leading to the administration building.

The school was over one hundred years old. Its buildings, masterpieces of Gothic architecture, graced the sprawling campus like so many jewels scattered across lush green velvet. Gray stone-fronted structures with wide marble steps and two-story stained glass windows stood before the verdant hills and endless lawns.

Star and Paresi crested a hill, their hair and coats tousled and blown by the chilly spring wind.

"Okay, so where's the building?" Paresi said, looking around.

"The sign said it's at the top of the hill." Star turned in a tight little circle. "This is the top, but I don't see any building."

"Maybe we're on the wrong hill," Paresi said. "There's another marker over there." He started walking. "I'll check it out."

Star turned again, spotting two students headed in their direction.

"I'll ask these kids." She stepped in front of them.

"Hi, excuse me," she said. "Can you tell me where we can find the administration building? We're looking for Dean Butterworth's office."

The two boys stared at her.

"The administration building?" Star repeated. "We're looking for Dean Butterworth."

The taller of the two stepped close to her, his wide mouth turned up in a grin.

"Hey, babe, no girls on campus, not unless you're here to party."

Star took her badge from her pocket, and held the gold shield close to his face. "Dean Butterworth's office . . . where is it?"

The two boys looked at each other.

"Whoa . . ." The tall young man backed up, his hands in the air. "A real live civil servant." He slapped palms with his friend. "Servant . . . that means you have to do anything I tell you, right? Give me anything I want?"

"Why don't you tell *me* what you want," Paresi said, stepping in front of Star. "The officer asked you politely." He got in the boy's smirking face. "I'm not so nice. . . . Where's Butterworth's office?"

The smirk faded. "Just around the curve, follow the stone path."

"See how easy that was?" Paresi said to the boy. He took Star's arm. "C'mon."

As they started toward the flat, curving stone walkway, the boy turned, cupping his hand to his mouth, yelling into the wind.

"Next time go easy on the garlic, Guido!" The two boys slapped palms, their laughter floating behind them.

Paresi turned, heading back toward them.

Star grabbed his arm. "Don't."

He stopped, the muscle in his jaw twitching.

"They're not worth the time or the paperwork," she said, pulling him gently. "C'mon, I see the building. Just let them go."

Paresi's eyes were invisible behind his shades, but she knew they were dark and furious.

She put her arm through his, drawing him close to her side. "Let's go."

On the roof of the administration building, at each corner, grinning stone gargoyles watched the officers approach. They stood as they had for over one hundred years, timeworn silent sentries, witnessing decades of change.

Griffins, with their lion's bodies and eagle's wings, formed granite guards on either side of the wide steps leading up to the leaded glass and mahogany double doors.

Star reached for the gleaming brass handle and pulled the door open for her partner.

"Thanks," Paresi said, walking in front of her. She fell in step beside him.

The two of them approached a sizable, intricately carved walnut wood desk. Star noted the chubby, dark-haired, round-cheeked boy seated there. He looked up. He had beautiful, thick lashes, and dark blue eyes. She saw the uneasiness in them. Beside her, Paresi made a slightly amused sound.

She smiled at the kid.

"May I help you?" His voice slid up and down, searching for a comfortable niche.

Star stepped in front of Paresi. "Hi, I'm Lieutenant Duvall, and this is Sergeant Paresi." She indicated her partner, who regarded the young man with undisguised amusement. "We have a two o'clock appointment with Dean Butterworth."

"Yes." The boy's voice caught in his throat and slid up an octave. "Two o'clock, police officers . . ." He pointed at the month-at-a-glance calendar centered on his desk. "It's right here, two o'clock."

Paresi moved alongside Star, his eyes hidden by his dark glasses. He looked down at the boy.

"So, junior, you wanna tell him we're here?"

"Yes sir," the boy said, and reached for the phone. "Have a seat." His voice slid again. "He'll be right out."

"Thank you," Star said. She pointed toward the burgundy leather sofa across from his desk. "We'll be over here."

They walked to the couch and sat down.

"You are such a menace," she said.

"What?" Paresi looked innocent. "What did I do?"

"First I have to keep you from breaking those two little snots outside in two, and now you come in here and play intimidation. You scared that poor boy stupid. These kids don't deal with cops every day, you know."

"No shit!" Paresi laughed.

"Why do you do that?" she asked, amused.

"Do what?"

"Paresi . . ."

Her partner shrugged. "I've been up all night, I need a little fun, that's all."

"Yeah," Star said.

Paresi took off his shades and dropped them into the upper pocket of his coat. "Okay, okay. I hear what you're saying." He indicated their surroundings. "I just have a hard time with this kinda place. It doesn't exactly scream 'come on in' to people like us."

"Speaking of us *ordinary* people," Star said, opening her purse. "I picked up our checks before we left."

She handed Paresi an envelope. He stared at it for a second, and shoved it into the inside breast pocket of his coat.

Star unzipped an interior pocket in her large, gray leather bag, and put her check inside.

"Remind me to hit the bank by four," she said, zipping the compartment. "If I don't, a couple of my checks are going to turn into prime, Grade A rubber."

"That's exactly what I'm talking about," Paresi said.

She looked at him.

"Think about it," he said. "We've been up all night, in our shoes over twenty-four hours, and yet here we are."

"So?" Star said. "It's our job."

"Right." Paresi's eyes darkened. "Don't you get it? It's *our* job. A job where we can get blown away by just walking in a door; and you're worried about covering a couple of checks.

"You think the people who send their kids here worry about whether or not the check for the light bill's gonna bounce?"

He pointed to her and then himself. "*We* do a job that could disappear us—" He snapped his fingers. "—in a hot second.

"*They* drive the best cars to their plush offices, where they plant their asses on the best leather and crack the whip on the rest of us. You could feed a family for a month on what they spend on lunch in a week. They don't do anything that could even make 'em sweat, let alone snuff 'em. We face death every single day, and you're worried about beating your checks to the bank. What's wrong with this picture?"

"Is this what sleep deprivation does to you?" Star teased. "Am I going to see you on the news, strapped to the max, wearing a bandanna around your forehead, taking hostages in the administration building?"

"I'm serious," Paresi said. "We stand hip-deep in crud day in and day out. In order to keep from going nuts, we tell ourselves we're doing a good thing, we're making a difference."

"Aren't we?" Star asked.

"You figure it out." Paresi leaned toward her. "We catch the bad guys, the courts turn 'em loose. Everybody's got their hands out, and everybody greases. The bad guys grease the lawyers, the lawyers show up in two-thousand-dollar suits, grease the judge, and the bastard's back on the street."

"What about juries?" Star asked, amused.

"Twelve nimrods in a box," Paresi said. "They don't listen to evidence, they don't follow what's happening, they're checking out which lawyer's got on the most expensive threads, and who puts on the best show. The only time anyone goes away is if they can't afford a high-priced suit. For those poor bastards, the Commonwealth steps in and sends 'em a kid. He's two hours outta law school, with his head up his ass, and the schlub ends up at the Graybar Hotel, and none of it matters."

"They go away," Star countered.

"So what?" Paresi fired back. "They don't count. They're just the workers, the mules, the pushers, the street scum. They don't rate, because they're replaceable. One goes down, send out another one. You don't make a dent till you trip the big fish, and they never get caught. They light up another Cuban, count their money, and keep on calling the shots. Meanwhile, the cop goes home and tries to figure out how to pay the mortgage and still get shoes for the kids."

"And that reflects on Bromleigh how?" Star said.

Paresi counted on his fingers. "The judge's kids could go here, the lawyer's kids could go here, hell, even the sleazo's kids could go here, if the pukes had enough brains to want something besides ugly gold jewelry and sharp rides.

"But a cop's kids?" He shook his head. "Not a chance. They couldn't get in here, at least not without swallowing a load of crap."

"You're right," Star agreed. "Bromleigh's expensive. But they give out scholarships to kids who don't have the money."

Paresi smirked. "And when did all that start? This pile of rocks has been here for over a hundred years. It wasn't until the neighborhood changed, and a couple of buildings ended up in ashes, that they figured they'd better do something."

"I'll agree on that." Star nodded. "The scholarship program began under duress."

"Damn straight," Paresi said. "They figured they had to pay protection, to keep this joint from being burnt to the ground. It never dawned on them that maybe some of those so-called 'low-class' neighborhood kids had the brainpower to be Bromleigh students, without all the bullshit they put them through."

He leaned toward her. "I hear they make 'em write essays about why they should be *allowed* to come here. Can you believe that?" His eyes held hers. "How many essays do you think the upper-class student body had to write? Most of 'em probably don't even know what an essay is. The only reason the little mooks are here is because their folks got serious bucks; not because they're smart or ambitious, but because they've got trust funds."

He leaned back, quiet. His eyes focused on a painting on the wall in front of them.

"Look at that picture," he said to Star. "Whaddya think it's worth?"

Star looked at the painting. "It's an Andrew Wyeth," she said. "And I don't think it's a print."

"It probably cost more than everything we own put together," Paresi muttered.

"Probably," Star said.

He stared at the painting. "You know, I've tagged along with Vee a couple times when she's gone over to the school where her boys are."

"She told me."

"It's a nice place," Paresi said, never taking his eyes off the painting. "But nothing like this. Roland and Cole are very smart kids. I'll betcha they're head and shoulders above most of the snotty little assholes riding through here on daddy's money, but Vee can't send them here."

He looked at her.

"And Jason, obviously that kid's got brains. But if you ask him, I bet he'd tell you he had to bust his ass to get in here. Look how hard he works for Mitch. I'm sure he worked like a slave in here too, just to get the education that these little skeezers take for granted. That kid works his ass off, and these mooks are in here, running around playing devil games!"

His gaze held her. "Want some more truth?"

"Hit me," she said, fascinated by this side of her partner. His relationship with Vee and her children was bringing out a maturity in him that she'd never seen.

"Mitch Grant is the only rich guy I've ever seen with any class. He's real. He doesn't have to do what he does. He's got enough cash to sit on his ass, sucking champagne for a couple of lifetimes. Still, he's out here every day. He doesn't break anybody's balls, he doesn't wave his cash in everybody's face, he just goes out and does it."

"That's true," Star said. "He lives well, and he doesn't hammer everybody with it. Don't you think there are others like that?"

"Hmph . . . a precious few," Paresi said. "Mitch came up with all the dough in the world, but he's not a stiff. He uses his money. He helps people. You *know* he's the 'scholarship' behind Jason's ticket to Harvard. Hell, he probably *owns* Harvard!"

Star looked surprised. "You think so?"

Paresi looked at her. "You don't? Where else is a kid from this neighborhood gonna get a full ride to Harvard? Mitch is the bank. He sees a kid with the stuff and he doesn't want it to go to waste for lack of dough, so he steps in, keeps his mouth shut, and helps the kid out. He's a stand-up guy. To tell you the truth, if it wasn't for the penthouse, the suits, and his wheels, I'd forget that he could buy and sell all of us."

"I never heard you talk like this," Star said, resting her hand on Paresi's knee. "I never thought you were this passionate about anything."

Paresi sighed. "I like having a good time as well as anybody, Star. But being around Vee and her kids . . . especially that little girl, Lena . . ."

A look of pure love crossed his face.

"Seeing what Vee goes through to keep them grounded, to raise them right . . . it makes you take a look at your life, especially when there's kids in it. You want them to have the best of everything, including education, because without it, they don't have a chance."

"Amen," Star said, softly, feeling the catch in her throat. She wanted to tell her partner he was sounding like a dad, but she didn't.

Paresi looked at his watch. "It's half past two, where is this jimoke? I wanna get outta here."

Star glanced toward the reception desk. "You're right. How much longer is he going to keep us waiting?" She sat farther back on the couch, and crossed her legs. "I'll bet Butterworth's some old guy with a bogus British accent, and one of those ratty tweed jackets with elbow patches."

The door to the office opened and a short stocky man appeared. Though his well-tailored black pinstriped suit made him appear slimmer than he actually was, Star could see the swell of his belly under the jacket.

"Detectives . . . please, come in," he said. His voice was strong, deep and heavily laced with Brooklyn. His thick, wavy, salt-and-pepper gray hair further surprised her. He looked as if he might have been a wild-eyed, frizzy-haired Deadhead in another life.

"Don't ever go for a job moonlighting on the psychic hotline," Paresi muttered. They rose and walked toward the office. The man stood beside the door.

"I'm Marshall Butterworth," he said, extending a large, fleshy hand.

Star shook it. Her hand disappeared, totally swallowed by his. "I'm Lieutenant Duvall, and this is Sergeant Paresi."

The man looked at Paresi. Star saw something in his eyes.

Her partner picked up on it too. For a second, she thought they knew one another, and disliked each other intensely.

Butterworth shook Paresi's hand, barely gripping it, and dropping it quickly. He turned to see Star looking at him. He attempted to recover.

"Please, go in, make yourselves comfortable. Would you like some coffee or tea?"

Paresi looked at Star. "No thanks," he said.

"Very well." He turned to the florid-faced young man at the desk.

"Alex, please hold my calls."

"Did he say calls, or balls?" Paresi whispered.

"Don't start," Star said.

When the door to the dean's office closed, Alexander Monroe looked around, making sure he was alone.

He pulled the phone toward him, taking another furtive glance around. He quickly dialed a number.

Cody Stevens answered on the first ring.

CHAPTER TEN

Marshall Butterworth sat with his hands folded on his perfectly ordered desk, looking at the two detectives seated in front of him as if they were errant students. The woman was all right, attractive in fact, but the Italian . . .

From the moment he saw him, Butterworth detested Dominic Paresi. To the short, round educator, Paresi represented everything he despised. The handsome face, the long, lean, muscular body, the cold, appraising blue eyes. All of it. He'd lived alongside Dominic Paresis all his life.

Pretty boys, getting through with a minimum of brains and

an abundance of balls. They'd been his enemy from the beginning, and now here was one in his office, flashing a badge and trying to make him believe *his* boys were reprehensible hoodlums.

"You're trying to tell me that you think Bromleigh students may have been involved in the death of that poor old woman found in the park a few weeks ago?" he said, his voice steady, attempting to hold Brooklyn at bay. "You think my boys would do something like that, burn a person, actually kill someone with fire?" Too late, he realized he'd pronounced it "fi-yuh."

"We didn't say that, Mr. Butterworth," Star said.

"Dean . . ." He raised a huge hand. "That's Dean."

"As in Martin?" Paresi said, straight-faced.

The man glared at him.

Paresi glared back.

Star put her head down. The tension between the two men was palpable. She just wanted to get the questions asked and answered and get out.

"Dean Butterworth, we are not accusing anyone of anything. We are simply trying to cover all the bases here. The death occurred within view of your campus, and three boys, wearing Bromleigh school uniforms, were on the scene while we secured the area and removed the body."

"They were curious," Dean Butterworth said. "Simply curious."

"Are you aware, *Mr.* Butterworth," Paresi said, "of any games of fantasy being played on this campus?"

The man's wiry hair actually stood on end. Star glanced at Paresi. He was loving it.

"Detective Paresi . . ."

"That's Sergeant," Paresi interrupted, "as in Pepper."

Star hid her giggle behind a cough. "Pardon me," she said, her eyes down.

"*Sergeant* Paresi, my boys are all well-brought-up young men. Bromleigh students are trained to be a cut above. We do not allow game-playing on this campus, other than chess, golf, tennis, archery, hockey in winter, and other endeavors of skill that mold young men to take their place in the world."

"Uh-huh," Paresi said.

Butterworth lowered his head. His round, blunt fingers twisted around themselves. What did this lowlife bastard think he was doing? There were no scandals and no problems under his command, and now these two, seated in front of him, had the nerve to try and tell him that maybe some of his kids were involved in torching an old woman. . . . No, not on his watch. Not now, not ever.

"Dean Butterworth," Star said. "The victim, a homeless woman named Molly Ludendorf, was known to some of the students here at Bromleigh. It's come to our attention that she'd harassed Bromleigh students in the past. . . ."

As if he hadn't heard her, Butterworth shoved his chair back and abruptly stood.

"Going somewhere?" Paresi said.

"Pardon me, Detectives," the dean said, Brooklyn bubbling beneath his words. "I can't help you today. You came on such short notice, and I have another appointment."

"Of course," Star said, gathering her coat. "We understand. You'll need time."

"Time for what?" Butterworth said, attempting to keep his voice level.

"To talk to us about those students we saw the other morning," Star said, slipping on her coat.

"It's impossible to locate three students without names or identification, Lieutenant," Butterworth said. "We have a very large student body."

"I'm sure you'll find a way to identify them," she said, beaming a smile at Butterworth's stricken face. "I can give you a pretty good description. One is a tall redhead and the other two are identical twins."

She pulled the strap of her purse over her shoulder. "That should narrow the field." She adjusted her bag. "Thank you for your time." She turned to her partner, who remained seated. "Let's go, Paresi."

"I have just one more question." Paresi said, not moving from the chair.

"Yes?" Butterworth stared down at him.

"How many computers on this campus?"

Butterworth took a deep breath. "Quite a few, Detective. We have them in our classrooms, our library, and most of the boarded students have them in their rooms."

"Are you aware of the fantasy games that some kids play on these things?" Paresi said, still seated.

Star saw the sweat that broke out on Butterworth's upper lip.

"Yes, Sergeant," he said. "I know there are such games, but as I said, they are strictly forbidden here at Bromleigh."

"And how do you enforce this ban?" Paresi asked.

Butterworth glanced at his watch and sighed.

"I have never imposed a ban, actually. When it came to my attention that these morbid games were popular pastimes for some teens, I called an assembly and forbade them on this campus. I then had the staff conduct a search of the computers that students had in their dorm rooms. They found no games of that nature."

"Uh-huh." Paresi finally stood.

Butterworth had to look up. It made him dislike the detective even more.

"So you just never checked again?"

"No need." The dean backed up two steps, so that he could look at Paresi without having to look up. "Bromleigh boys are honorable. They were instructed not to participate in the usage of such games, and they do *not* indulge."

"Yeah, thanks."

"You're welcome," the dean said coldly. He turned to Star. "I'm sorry to cut this short." He extended his hand. She shook it. He did not offer it to Paresi.

"Thank you for your time, Dean Butterworth," Star said, walking toward the door, with Paresi following. "We will be back, and soon. I'll make sure you get more notice next time."

"And I'll make myself available," he said, as they left the room.

Outside, Alex Monroe smiled and nodded as the two officers passed his desk. When they went out the double doors, he punched the lighted button on his phone.

"They just left," he said.

"Chill out, Al," Cody Stevens said. "No need to be uptight."

"I don't like seeing cops around; it makes me nervous."

Cody Stevens laughed. "They're cops . . . what do they know? They couldn't find Marilyn Manson at a PTA meeting. We got nothing to worry about."

"I don't know," Alex said. "Maybe nothing, maybe something."

Cody sucked his teeth. "I say it's nothing. You're the one who took the job in Butterworth's office to be our eyes and ears, just stay cool. If anything blows, you'll be the first to know."

"Yeah, I guess so," Alex said.

"Right." Alex could hear him drinking something, then he belched. "So, you comin' tonight?"

Alex looked around. "I'm not sure," he whispered. "After what happened, maybe we should just lay low."

"You lay low," Cody said. "I'm just gonna lay . . . get it?"

"Yeah," Alex said. The sound of Butterworth opening the door made him hit the hold button.

"Alex, please check on something for me." Butterworth laid his heavy hand on the boy's shoulder. "I believe there's a lecture on Myth and the Nature of Man being given at Randall Hall. I'm not certain if it's next week or the week after. Find out for me, and leave the information on my desk."

"Yes, Dean Butterworth." Alex made a note on the pad next to the phone.

"I'll be out for the rest of the day," the dean said.

"Yes sir."

Alex watched him leave the building, pausing on the marble steps outside the door to adjust his black overcoat against a sudden wind.

He picked up the phone and punched the lit button.

"Cody? You there?"

"Yeah man, I'm here. . . . What's it gonna be?"

Alex gripped the phone tightly and looked around again. "I'll be there . . . seven-thirty."

"Good man," Cody said.

* * *

"Did you enjoy yourself?" Star slid into the car.

Paresi settled behind the wheel, a smile on his lips.

"What?"

She buckled her seat belt. "You know what. You really got under his skin."

Paresi raised his hands, palms out.

"What did I do?" he said innocently. "I just asked him a couple of questions."

"Paresi."

"What?"

"The guy wanted to punch you out. Didn't you realize you were getting on his nerves big-time?"

Paresi shrugged. "That's his problem. He looked at her, an angelic smile on his face. "He didn't start sweating till *you* mentioned the three kids at the scene the other morning." He put the key into the ignition and buckled his seat belt. "As for me, I didn't intentionally try to bug him."

Star laughed. "Is that right, Sergeant Pepper?"

Paresi grinned. "I was listening to that album the other day with Lena." He faced her. "Did you know she's got quite a thing for Paul McCartney?"

"Yes," Star said. "She told me you gave her the CD. Vee said she's gonna show Lena a picture of the way Paul looks now, just so she doesn't have to hear the album again."

They laughed.

Paresi nodded. "She does listen to it a lot. I guess that was on my mind . . . you know, Sergeant . . . Pepper."

"Nice try," Star said. "But I think the next contact with Butterworth should be me, alone."

"Not a chance." Paresi started the car. "We're a team."

"Not when one of us runs the risk of the contact clamming up. Either he knows more about his boys than he wants us to find out, or he honestly has no idea. Either way, I intend to get to the truth."

"So we get there together," Paresi said. "That's what partners do."

"Not when one partner could get his lights punched out," Star said.

Paresi grinned at her. "He wouldn't hit you. . . . Besides, my money's on you. I know you could take him."

Star laughed. "It ain't me that's gonna get a face full of knuckles. I'm telling you Paresi, Butterworth's no wimp. Did you look at his hands?"

"His hands?" Paresi said.

"Yeah. His nails are manicured, but he's got working man's hands. He's done some kind of labor in his life."

"Maybe he likes to garden," Paresi said derisively.

"No . . . his knuckles and fingers look like tree trunks, and his palm is rough. Didn't you feel that when he shook your hand?"

Paresi stared at her. "Where are you going with this?"

"I'm just saying, don't underestimate him. That guy did some serious climbing to get to the position he's in now. That takes a lot of balls. If he knows anything, he's not going to let us take him *or* his boys down without a fight. We've got to be very careful how we come at him."

"You mean about the button? I notice you didn't mention it."

Star nodded. "I'm saving that for later. The first thing I want to do is run our description by Jason. Maybe he knows the kids we saw in the park. Before we talk to them, we should check those computers, and be really careful about it. This guy could make our lives hell if we don't do it right." She looked her partner in the eye. "I'm telling you, Paresi, Butterworth is not a guy to mess with. He's little, but he's tough."

"Yeah?" Paresi said, pulling away from the curb. "I'm tougher."

CHAPTER ELEVEN

Marshall Butterworth stood naked before his bathroom mirror.

Not a beautiful sight.

He was fat, he knew it, like most of the men on both sides of his family. His short legs and fireplug body were as much a part of the gene pool as his myopic dark brown eyes. Something you'd think his forebears would have considered when selecting potential mates. He'd long ago given up wishing and praying for a slim, muscular body. But now, in the glaring bathroom lights, he saw himself as she had.

She'd acted as if he were like everyone else. But she was a pro. Bought and paid for. No look of revulsion in her eyes, no gagging behind a lace handkerchief, as Anna Stein had done all those years ago, when he'd kissed her after their first and only date.

There had been other "ladies" bought and paid for, but this one, this one was different. She did what he asked, but even in that, there was a tender gentleness in her touch that set something loose in his heart and soul that he'd long thought dead and gone.

When they'd parted, he'd felt as if he were leaving a lover, instead of a paid assignation. He'd been a little rough with her, yet she forgave him. She told him everything was all right, that she was fine.

He'd stayed up all night, unable to sleep, unable to do anything but let his mind go back into the pleasure she'd given him, and the feelings she'd unleashed inside him. Before he knew what happened, it was time for work. He'd sleepwalked through the day, until the police officers arrived. After they'd gone, he'd had to find her. He'd left his office and gone searching. She was nowhere to be seen.

The thought that he might indeed have hurt her the night before, more than she said, came to his mind, but he fought it down. He went back to the park again, late in the evening, and she was still nowhere to be found.

Today, after classes, he would try again.

Marshall turned slowly under the unforgiving light and looked at his sagging flesh. Though she hadn't shown it, she had to have felt some degree of disgust for the hairy, ham-handed stranger touching her, and nearly weeping at the pleasure she gave him.

He stared at himself, his body reflected in the glass and staring back. A great, coarse mat of gray and black hair grew from his chest. It sloped thickly down over his drooping belly and disappeared beneath a roll of fat that nearly hid his genitals.

He turned, seeing himself in profile. The same thick hair covered his shoulders and upper back. It grew curly in the small of his back and over his large, lumpy behind. From the side, his penis stuck out slightly under the fat. He moved his thigh, making the wrinkled, sagging flesh of his scrotum visible.

A sudden vision of Dominic Paresi came into his mind.

"I'll bet that stupid dago bastard never had to pay a hooker in his life." Marshall snorted, remembering Paresi glaring at him, on his campus, in his office.

Did that guinea realize what he'd had to endure to have that office on that campus? Did he know that this career had been pounded out of sheer grit and balls?

Butterworth stood close to the mirror, his fingertips touching his image. He peered deeply into his own eyes, thinking back, remembering how he'd made up his mind when he was in the fifth grade, doing his homework in the back of the deli, that he was not going to be his father. He loved Isaac Butterworth, but he wanted his hands to be soft, and not smell of pickle brine and corned beef.

He looked down at his hands. They weren't his father's hands, but in spite of the manicured nails and the oceans of hand creams and lotions Butterworth used, you could still read his past in them.

From the day he read about the Bromleigh Academy at the local library, he'd been obsessed with going there.

He remembered the photographs accompanying the text. They showed the campus in fall. The leaves in Massachusetts were vivid and colorful, like some celestial brush had painted the trees. Brooklyn leaves didn't look like that. They were dry, colorless, and dead, even in summer. He badgered his widowed father into getting the information, finding out just what he had to do to get in to that school.

By the time he graduated junior high, Marshall had turned himself into Bromleigh material, and he was accepted. His father, Uncle Aaron, and Aunt Cele had sold, hocked, and mortgaged everything they had to send him to New England. They bought him "good" luggage (Uncle Aaron had a friend in the business), paid his tuition, and gave him "spending money," so he'd be "like the other boys."

"What a joke," Butterworth said to his image. "Like the other boys. I was about as much like the other boys as the Pope at a bar mitzvah."

He had no friends, so he kept his nose to his books. He graduated first in his class and nailed a four-year scholarship to Yale, where he again graduated with honors.

He could have written his ticket anywhere, but the deli owner's boy chose to return to Bromleigh, wearing the custom-made navy blue blazer of a teacher.

It galled some of the proud white, Anglo-Saxon faculty, many of whom had been his teachers, but there wasn't a god-damned thing they could do about it.

"I promised myself," he said to his image. "I promised that one day, I'd come back, show them what a Brooklyn Jewboy could do."

At times it had been twice as rough teaching as it had been in his student days. He was unwelcome in the teacher's lounge, and a lot of the snotty little bastards he taught re-ferred to him as "the Rabbi," but he hung in.

He worked himself nearly into a nervous breakdown, and now, it had all paid off. He called the shots. The Mayflower blue bloods had to do what he said, and now, here comes this nobody cop, walking into his office, dumping on his boys.

"He picked the wrong guy to fuck with," Butterworth whispered to his image. "The wrong guy."

He reached into the shower and turned on the water. He had to make himself move, get going. He was late. First-period classes would be over by the time he got to the campus.

A hot spray jetted out from six different nozzles, all aimed at giving him both a cleansing and sensual experience. He stepped into the shower. A delicious little sliver of pain touched the tender spot on his shoulder, and passed through him.

He rested his head against the tile, aching for the blonde. For her sad smile, and the harsh black makeup ringing her dark child's eyes. She looked like a ruined angel. That's why he'd picked her up. He could see, as he drove slowly by, that she was different.

She was sweet, too sweet to be doing what she did for a living. Dealing with men like him. Ugly, sad, hopelessly lonely men, who paid for entry into her mouth and her body. He could end all that for her. He could end all her pain. He'd almost said that to her when she was in his arms, just before the world exploded.

Marshall turned his face to the water. She's all right, he said to himself. She's not hurt. She's fine. She said she was fine.

He turned beneath the hot spray, wincing as a raw sting of pain rippled across his back where the water hit him. He cupped his hands, letting the hot water puddle and overflow his palms. Marshall Butterworth's eyes closed, a deep sigh escaped his open mouth. He kneeled on the sand-colored tiles, feeling it again. The blood, warm, wet, and flowing.

CHAPTER TWELVE

David Riley stood outside the door of his father's suite of offices, dreading going inside. He looked at his watch. If he put it off any more, he was going to be late for class. He shouldn't have let his mother talk him into this. He didn't want to have anything to do with his dad. Doug Riley was a hypocrite, as far as he and Dan were concerned.

Did he really think they didn't know about him and Camille? His mom was chugging about a fifth of vodka a day and walking around with a lost look in her eyes. Did their father think they wouldn't notice?

Both his parents were playing a game, and he and his brother were caught in the middle. They were supposed to run around with stupid smiles on their faces, pretending that they were some big, happy family. What a joke. The Happy Rileys. Yeah, right. Even the Simpsons had a better gig. At least Homer wasn't fucking around on Marge.

Dave stood outside the door, looking at the highly polished wood, wishing he had the courage to take out his pocket knife and carve the truth into the gleaming, glossy finish. Just so the fools that flocked through this door, with his father's name spelled out in golden letters, would know what he really was.

"They think he's God," Dave muttered, shaking his head disgustedly. "Stupid bastards. God doesn't fuck the help."

He swallowed the rage in his chest and opened the door. The office was empty. No one behind the desk.

Dave started to leave, but just then Julie Curran, his father's office manager, popped up from behind the desk. Dave jumped.

"Hi Dan . . . or are you Dave?"

"Dave."

The woman smiled. "I didn't mean to scare you," she said. I was digging a file out of the bottom cabinet." She ran a hand through her curly, dark hair. "I'm so short, and the counter is so high, that when I'm down there, I tend to disappear." She laughed, a deep, robust laughter, that rang oddly in his ears, coming from such a petite body.

"Yeah," he said.

The woman grinned at him. "Boy, you two are downright spooky, I'm never sure which one I'm talking to. How does your mom keep you straight?" She grinned, showing capped teeth.

"She's used to it," David said. "Is my dad here?"

"He's with a patient, and he'll be a while. Did you have an appointment?"

"No. He just asked me to drop by this morning." He breathed a sigh of relief. "Tell him I was here, okay?"

"All right, but I'm sure he'd want you to wait."

"Can't." Dave shrugged. "I'm gonna be late for class."

"Okay." Julie dimpled. "I'll tell him you stopped in." She began writing on a pad with big-eyed puppies scampering across the top.

David waved and turned to go.

"Dave, wait." His father's voice stopped him.

Shit! his mind screamed. He turned. "Hey, Dad. I thought you were with a patient."

"I am," his father said. "I just came out to check and see if you were here." Doug Riley looked at his watch. "You're late."

David shrugged. "Yeah . . . well, I'm here."

His father walked up to the reception desk. Dave made no effort to move from his spot in the center of the room. Under the fluorescent lights, Dave noticed that his father's skin was pale and sallow, like he wasn't getting enough sleep.

All that double-time fucking, he thought to himself. His father beckoned him to the desk. He walked over, his head down, not wanting to look at the man.

"Listen," Dr. Riley said to his son, "we need to talk—you, your brother, and me."

Dave smelled his father's sweet, cinnamon mouthwash. It turned his stomach. He backed up. "Yeah, Dad, why don't you try coming home when we're all up sometime?"

The venom in his son's voice made the doctor wince. "I know it's been rough for you guys and your mom, but things are going to change."

"Great, Dad, why don't you send us a postcard?"

Doug Riley turned around and glanced at Julie, sitting at the desk a few feet away. She appeared to be engrossed in the file on her monitor, her curly hair standing stiffly away from her neck. She ducked her head, seemingly peering at the paper to the right of her keyboard.

She wasn't fooling Dave. He noticed that none of the fields on her screen had been filled since he and his father began talking.

"I've got to go back inside," the doctor said. "But I'll be home this evening. Tell your mother."

"You tell her," his son said, angrily turning away.

"Dave?"

"What?" The young man kept his back to his father.

"I called you in today about school."

"I know."

"You're not doing well."

David spun again toward his father. His face burned, his eyes blazed, yet his voice, steady and cold, came eerily through his barely moving lips. "Being late for first period helps a lot, doesn't it, Dad?"

David saw his father flinch as if he had been struck.

He fought down the smile he felt inside.

"I just thought we'd have some time . . . but I've got to get back to my patient. We'll talk later, at dinner."

"Right." Dave headed for the door. He looked back, and caught Julie Curran looking at him, judging him. He could see she thought he was rude and disrespectful. What the fuck did she know?

"Doug?"

The doctor and his clerk looked up.

Camille Westfall stood in the doorway. Her pink uniform stretched around her plump body, her heavy breasts strained the buttons on her chest.

Julie caught the look of total disgust on Dave Riley's face. What would make him look at Camille like that? He didn't know her. Julie's eyes darted to Dr. Riley. He looked as if his son had shot him. She saw the pain in his eyes. What was going on? What didn't she know?

She looked back at Camille, leaning against the doorway. The woman locked eyes with the boy. A contest. Dave looked away, and Camille smiled. What's going on, Julie said to herself. What was *that* all about?

Camille beckoned with a frosted-pink-nailed finger at the doctor. "I need you in back." She cast an eye at Julie. "Mrs. Timmons is ready."

Doug Riley looked at Julie. She quickly looked down at her keyboard. The doctor's face reddened. "I'll be there in a second, Cammie," he said, turning back to the anger-hardened face of his son.

His heart pounded at the look on Dave's face. Both of his boys were in trouble, and no matter what his feelings were in his marriage, he wasn't going to let his sons drift away. They had always been good students, but now they were failing, Dave doing worse than Dan. That's why he wanted to talk to each boy separately. His kids were coming apart and so was his wife. She had always been so fastidious with herself and the boys. From the time they were little, Diane had kept them clean and properly dressed.

He'd watched her day after day, year after year. She would methodically go through her morning ritual before letting them out of the house. Diane would "inspect" their clothing, their shoes, making certain everything was clean, polished, pressed, and in perfect order. She had been doing it since they were kindergartners. Even now, the boys expected it of her, but to him, she seemed to have given up, stopped caring about their appearance. How else could she not have noticed that Dave was missing one of those expensive buttons from his school blazer?

CHAPTER THIRTEEN

Ryan Cassidy was hungover, but that hadn't kept him from his eight A.M. class in occult literature. He had to be there. He was the teacher.

The previous night, spent drinking much Irish ale and reading much poetry (his own) to the regulars at O'Rourke's Pub, hadn't been as much fun as in times past.

Maybe it was because he could no longer hide from the fact that he was a failed husband, a failed father, and an amazingly failed poet.

Failed whoremaster had been added to his list a couple of nights before, when he picked up a woman in Saint Francis Park. He'd tried mightily, but he couldn't get it up. Not even a little bit. They'd both finally grown tired of her attempts. He paid her and let her out of his car on the east side of the park. He thought he'd seen a couple of his students lurking about in the darkness, but he'd been too drunk to be certain, or to care.

After yet another hard-drinking, sleepless night, he'd showered, cut himself twice shaving, and managed to get to class about five minutes before his first students straggled in.

That's what he appreciated—the tradition here at Bromleigh Academy. In a world of hurry-up, throwaway, and electronic isolation, Bromleigh still held on to the old-fashioned, outdated idea that the young men in attendance at the tradition-steeped house of knowledge cared about all the bullshit that went along with being a "Bromleigh Boy."

They didn't.

The thought made Ryan grin. All those tight-assed little

cretins wearing school ties and blue blazers could really give a fuck.

He cast a bloodshot look around the room. Look at 'em. Pink-cheeked, well-scrubbed, looking like some old fuck's idea of perfect youth. Well they didn't fool him. He had been at Bromleigh long enough to know the truth. He knew that inside, some of them were just like their counterparts in the surrounding neighborhood. Gangsters. Junior hit men and criminals.

Not hit men in the sense that they'd actually take an Uzi or an AK and cruise the neighborhood. Well, maybe a couple of them. But more than likely, these were the hatchet men of the next generation. The corporate raiders taking no prisoners, blowing apart companies and lives.

Oh yes, these merry little shits would indeed take great pleasure in destroying what's left of the world in the name of greed. They couldn't help it. They came from a long line of pigs and capitalist bastards. Coldhearted assholes whose only concern was the bottom line.

Ryan ran a slightly trembling hand over his dry lips. Like those empty-hearted fucks in every major publishing house who kept rejecting his life's work—his poetry, his very soul, delivered to them by Federal Express.

The second bell rang, signaling the end of grace period and the beginning of class. Ryan looked out over the empty, insolent pale faces staring at him.

There were two empty seats. Cody Stevens and one of the twins. He wasn't sure which one, since Dave and Dan liked to fuck with his head, but he was pretty certain it was Dave. Dan Riley had a more reptilian look than his brother, and Ryan recognized his cold eyes staring back at him.

The door to the classroom opened, and Stevens and Dave Riley came in together, both of them red-faced and giggly.

"You're late, boys," Ryan said, his voice still carrying the rasp of too many dark ales.

Dave Riley nodded to him. "Sorry, Professor Cassidy. I had a family situation this morning."

His brother looked at him, as if to say, *liar*.

Dave took his seat, still smiling at the unimpressed Ryan.

"And you?" Ryan turned to Cody Stevens, who was sitting with his long legs stretched into the aisle.

"I overslept," the red-haired boy said, shrugging his shoulders. "Sorry."

The twins struggled to hold in their laughter.

Ryan opened his mouth to say something, but decided against it. What difference would it make? These kids were beyond caring about anything. Hopefully, by the time they took their places in society, he'd have made it as a poet, living a tax-free existence in the green hills of Ireland. Or he'd be dead. Either way, he wouldn't have to suffer.

He picked up the book on his desk and turned to the class.

"We're going to be taking a look at the occult offerings in Victorian literature."

He expected the faces and the groans.

"Cheer up, boys." Ryan sat on the corner of his desk. "I think you'll like this assignment," he said. "We're going to be looking at the vampire in literature. Our next book is Bram Stoker's *Dracula*."

CHAPTER FOURTEEN

Jorge Velez decided to make one more run before taking his morning break. He hadn't even had coffee yet, and he'd been at it since six A.M.

He swung the green-and-white recycling truck easily around the corner of Preston Avenue and Fourth Street. He liked this neighborhood. Mansions, nice people, and all the recycling was clean.

He knew most of it had been put out by the maids and cleaning people. Working folks, just like him. They knew he appreciated clean bottles and cans to pick up. Still, every now and then he'd find a few funk-encrusted cans and nasty glass containers, but mostly things in the bins were clean. Even the newspapers were neatly stacked and not just tossed in.

He bobbed his head along with the music racing into his ears from his Discman. Wearing "personal" music devices was against company rules, but hey, who was there to see him? He started his pickups at six and was usually done by ten in the morning.

Besides, he liked Queen Latifah. Yeah, she was a little on the hefty side, but he liked women with tits and ass. These little boy-shaped broads did nothing for him. When he pounded it home, the only bone he wanted to feel was his own. He liked plenty of cushion.

"Yeah," he said, his head bobbing with the beat. "Give it to me, Queen."

He eased the truck near the curb at 1587 Preston. Two gallon-sized plastic jugs sat at the edge of the street. They appeared to have something inside of them. Jorge could see a darkness through the thick, white plastic. A black Labrador retriever paced in a tight circle, sniffing first one bottle and then the other.

"That's weird." Jorge took off his headset, put on his gloves, and got out of the truck.

"Hey, dog, get outta there," he yelled, approaching the driveway.

The dog ignored him and continued to trot between the two containers, sniffing furiously.

"Go on, mutt." Jorge waved his gloved hand at the dog.

The animal looked at him, whined, and continued sniffing.

"Dumbshit dog." Jorge moved closer. He didn't think the thing would bite him. It looked dumber than his Uncle Tico, who had the IQ of dirt.

"Get outta there." The animal stopped and stared at Jorge. It whined once and backed up.

"What is this stuff?" Jorge picked up one of the plastic jugs. He opened the top. The scent set the dog barking and howling.

"Madre de Jesus," Jorge said. He capped the bottle and **raced back to his truck.**

*   *   *

The police cruiser was parked across the driveway when Star and Paresi arrived.

Two uniformed officers approached the unmarked car as the detectives parked.

"Lieutenant Duvall?" one of the men said to Paresi.

"She's Duvall," Paresi said, getting out of the driver's seat.

"Sorry ma'am," the young officer said.

"It's okay." Star got out of the car. "What's the story?"

"I'm Officer Deitz," the ruddy-faced man said. "Mike Deitz." He indicated his partner as they approached the cruiser. "This is Dexter Sykes. Dex, this is Lieutenant Duvall and . . ."

"Paresi," Dominic said. "Sergeant Paresi."

Sykes, a man with skin the dark color of bittersweet chocolate and the eyes of a ten-year-old, smiled at Star. He had a pencil-thin mustache, an overbite, and large, soft-looking lips. He nodded. "Hi, Lieutenant. Sarge."

"What's happening here?" Paresi asked.

"Well, this is Jorge Velez." Deitz indicated the driver, who nodded at them. "He was making his rounds this morning and he came up on this."

"Yeah," Jorge said, his dark eyes checking out Star, wondering what he would have to do to get her to slap the cuffs on him. He'd enjoy that shit like a big dog.

"I was doing my job, you know." He gazed at her. "I'm a man who likes to do things right." His eyes roamed up and down her body. "No matter how long it takes."

"Are you speaking to me?" Star said.

Jorge sent his gaze for another spin. "Yeah. Just wanna get it through to you, I'm a *hard* worker."

"I'm up here," Star said. "If you're talking to me, please address me and not my legs."

Jorge grinned. "Yes ma'am." He let his gaze travel her body. "But you gotta know, that's a long way up."

"Make the effort," Star said. She turned and walked to the curb, where the two jugs sat. Paresi followed. He took out a pair of surgical gloves from his jacket pocket and pulled them on. He picked up a jug and popped the top.

"Whew . . ." The smell settled on his tongue. He spat in the grass and looked at Star.

"Blood?" she asked.

Her partner nodded.

"Swell."

She turned to Jorge. "Do you have a listing of who lives in this house?"

"Naw, but I gotta phone in my truck. I can call the office. One of the girls can give you any information you need."

"Can you bring the phone out here?" Star said.

Jorge's eyes took another spin.

"Uh-uh. It's not portable." He licked his lips. "You gotta go to the truck."

Star turned to Paresi. "You go. I don't trust myself."

He laughed. "Lead the way, amigo."

Jorge looked at Star. "Ain't the lady coming?"

Paresi clapped him on the shoulder, simultaneously turning and propelling him toward the truck. "George, my man, she's not even breathing hard."

CHAPTER FIFTEEN

Mitch leaned over the long teakwood table in the conference room of the Medical Examiner's office. The detectives stood on either side of him.

"The blood found on the curb this morning definitely belongs to Dolores Causwell. It's a perfect match with what was left in the body," he said.

"So somebody actually drained her blood into two milk jugs," Star said.

"Exactly." Mitch, still in green scrubs, reached across the

photos that were spread out on the desktop. He selected a close-up of Dolores Causwell's inner thigh.

Star and Paresi leaned in.

"See the bruise and the cut." Mitch traced a blue-tinged, bruised-looking area with his index finger. "Right here."

Star and Paresi leaned even closer.

"I see the bruise," Paresi said. "But what am I looking at?"

"It's her inner thigh." Mitch pulled another photo next to the one they were examining. "Here," he said. "This one might be easier."

"Oh yeah," Paresi said.

"Take a good look at that bruise," Mitch said, pointing to the photo. "There's a needle stick in there. She either shot herself up, or somebody else launched her before she died."

"How long would you say between the injection and her death?" Star asked.

Mitch turned to her. "The stick didn't have time to close. In living tissue, needle sticks begin to heal within minutes. I'd say she died within two to five minutes of the injection."

"Then they drained her from her thigh?" Star asked.

"No." Mitch straightened up and selected another photo. "Here's the cut."

He pointed to a small slit outlined on the photo in red grease pencil. The wound was partially buried in Dolores Causwell's pubic hair. Mitch pulled over another photo. "This one is better." The photo showed the same area, only in this one, the pubic hair was shaved, and the cut highly visible.

"The killer made the cut into the common femoral artery," Mitch said. "It's kind of like the trunk of a tree. It's about two inches long, and sturdy. That gave the killer a solid place to anchor the rubber tubing. After that, a syringe with an out jet to the tube was attached. . . ."

"And pumped her blood into the milk jug," Star said.

"That's what it looks like," Mitch said. "She was still alive when the draining started. Her heart was pumping. She became her own engine, pumping until her heart gave out. She expired while being bled."

"How'd they get the blood out if her heart wasn't beating?" Star said.

"The tests showed a large amount of Coumadin."

"What's that?"

"A blood thinner, used to prevent clotting in postsurgical patients," Mitch said. "The killer dosed her with a lot of it. Her blood was basically like water. After she died, it looks like some manual compression was used. There were bruises on her chest. Worst case, the killer sucked on the tubing, to keep it flowing."

"You mean like siphoning gas?"

Mitch nodded.

"Yech!" She shuddered.

"Seems to me we should be looking for somebody with a medical background, some kind of training, a doctor, a paramedic. . . ." Paresi said.

"Yes." Mitch nodded. "I agree. Whoever did this knew how to cut her, where to cut, what to use to thin the blood, and how to keep it moving, so that it could be directed into the jugs."

Star shivered again. "Jesus."

Mitch turned to her. "If it's any consolation, she was so high, she didn't feel anything. I found the hematoma and needle stick on her right inner thigh. I excised a portion of skin and the first layer of flesh from that." He picked up his notebook. "The lab confirms the Coumadin and traces of heroin in both the skin and underlying layer of flesh.

"Because she was high, she might have been a willing participant, not knowing or caring what was being injected. Maybe she thought it would enhance the high."

"So she was partying?" Star said.

"Big-time." Paresi muttered.

Mitch nodded. "Right, and she'd had a good hit before she was given the Coumadin. There was also chemical residue on the inside of one of the plastic milk containers—Triazate."

Star folded her arms, as if holding herself together.

"What's that?"

"Something you'd find in a high school chem lab," Mitch said. "It's a liquid that can be used to dazzle young kids. When you put a flame to it, you get sparkles like the Fourth of July. Pretty hot stuff when I was in high school, but nowadays I'm sure nobody even pays attention."

"Is it dangerous?" Star asked.

"Not really," Mitch said. "It's corrosive, like Drano on metals, but it won't eat through certain types of plastic, glass, or wood. If you touch it, you won't get a burn, unless your hands are wet."

"And it's used in high school chemistry classes," Star said.

Mitch nodded. "Yes. A lab is where you'd usually find Triazate, but nowadays anybody can get their hands on anything. Chemicals can be ordered over the Internet. It could have come from anywhere."

"I think it ties to Bromleigh," Paresi said.

Star faced him. "You just want to rattle Butterworth's cage."

Paresi laughed.

"We'll get back to Bromleigh," she said, "but there's something else to look at first."

"What?" Paresi sat on the edge of the conference table.

"The medical angle," Star said. "Whoever did this knew something about first aid and anatomy, right?"

Mitch nodded. "Yes, but I can tell you that Bromleigh has one of the best physical anthropology and anatomy courses in the Commonwealth, and it's *not* an elective. It's a prerequisite for graduation. Bromleigh turns out a lot of future doctors, but the board feels that a knowledge of the body and how it runs is a must for any well-rounded graduate, no matter which direction they choose to go in life."

"Sounds like grounds for seeing Butterworth to me." Paresi smiled.

"He's not going to like it," Star said.

Paresi laughed. "No shit, but hey, we're investigating a homicide, and traces of a standard high school chem lab ingredient, combined with where the body was found, and that button, gives us plenty of reason for another friendly visit, don't you think?"

"Yeah. I do," Star said. "But before that, Mitchell, I need your help."

"Anything."

"Vee is planning dinner tomorrow night for us—you, me, and Paresi. I want you to ask Jason to come."

Mitch looked surprised. "Sure, but why?"

"Well, first of all, he's a nice kid, and secondly, he's just a little older than Roland. . . ."

"And?" Mitch said.

"Well, I've been thinking about this game he talked about. I called Vee, and the boys actually have Vampire's Lair. I want to have Jason come over and play it with them."

"And the reason behind this is . . . ?" Paresi asked.

"I want to see them playing the game. I want them to explain it to me. Jason said that the first piece we found resembles the bat in the game, the one who sucks blood then cremates the victims, right?"

The two men nodded in agreement.

"Well, I was thinking, Molly was cremated, and Dolores was drained of blood, but she had another piece in her hand."

"Something that Jason couldn't identify," Paresi said.

"Because the metal was corroded," Star said. "Maybe from this Tri . . . tri . . ."

"Triazate," Mitch said.

"Yeah, the stuff that was in the bottles."

"I see where you're going," Paresi said. "You think if we see the game, observe them playing it, maybe it will kick off something."

Paresi and Mitch looked at one another.

"Humor me," Star said. "Ask him."

CHAPTER SIXTEEN

Star, Mitch, Jason, and Paresi sat at the dinner table with Vee and her kids. Laughter rang through the room.

"It's true," Vee said, "honest." She looked at Star. "Tell them what you did."

"Yo, auntie, come on, we want to hear," Cole, Vee's sixteen-year-old son said, a huge grin on his dark chocolate face.

Star looked at her best friend's youngest son.

"I don't know if I want this story to get out." Smiling, she turned to Jason. "Can I swear you to secrecy?"

Jason laughingly raised his hand. He was having a good time. He'd been hesitant to accept the invitation at first, even after the doc told him what the lieutenant wanted, but now he was glad he'd come.

"I swear, I'll never tell a living soul."

"Okay," Star said, to the smiles around the table. "I did it!"

"Oh, wack!" Vee's oldest, Roland, said, laughing. I wish I coulda seen that." He and Cole slapped hands. Lena, Vee's eight-year-old, grinned at Jason, and covered her mouth with her hand.

"I woulda been too scared to even look," she said, between giggles.

"Dead people can't hurt you, baby," Vee said. "It's the living you got to watch."

"Ain't that the truth," Paresi said, pouring more wine into his glass.

"Still, auntie, didn't you and mama know?" Roland asked.

Star looked at her "nephews." Where did her boys go? In their places, there were two young men watching her.

"The papers said Victoria Bailey died. Your mama and I went to school with her, so of course we had to go to the funeral," Star said.

"The funeral home was way out, about an hour from town, which should have tipped us off," Vee said. "We hadn't seen Vicki since high school, but people move, so we didn't really think anything of the distance. Your auntie drove all the way out there."

"It was early when we arrived." Star picked up the story. "There was nobody there except the funeral director."

"We told him we came for the Bailey funeral," Vee said. "He looked at us kinda funny, but he took us to the chapel, then he left."

"Fast!" Star laughed. "He was gone so quick, I thought he

was on wheels." She and her friend cracked up at the memory.

"Anyway, this was the biggest funeral chapel I'd ever seen," Vee said. "The middle aisle was about a mile long."

"It was dark, too," Star said. "The lights were amber, and low. So when we started up the aisle, we couldn't even see Vicki in the casket."

"I closed my eyes," Vee said.

Everyone laughed.

"As we were moving up the aisle, trying not to bump into anything, or trip, your mama asked me how Vicki died. I said the papers reported that she'd been in a fire."

"Then I said, how come the casket's open?" Vee's tone started the laughs rolling again.

"Right," Star said, grinning. "Your mother had a point. As we walked up the aisle, we got even more nervous. I mean why *was* the casket open?"

"Smoke inhalation?" Jason said.

"Right." Star looked at him. "That's what I thought, smoke inhalation. Sometimes there are no burns. Conceivably you could have an open casket."

"I didn't know anything about that," Vee said. "So I kept my eyes closed."

"And I had to maneuver both of us up this long, dark, spooky aisle," Star continued. "So we get to the casket, and Vee's eyes are shut so tight they've disappeared. She leans over and whispers to me, 'What does she look like?' "

Vee took over.

"Star didn't say a word. So I asked again. 'What does she *look* like?' "

Star shook her head at the memory. "I said, '*White*. She looks *White* . . . and she's got a Confederate flag in her hand.'" She pointed at Vee. "Her eyes opened . . . *wide*!"

The boys laughed, slapping palms. Lena giggled. Her sepia-colored shoulders, in a bright blue Tweety Bird T-shirt rose up near her ears.

"What did you do?" Mitch asked, grinning at Star.

"We decided to get the hell out of there. Obviously this was not *our* Victoria Bailey," she said.

"I guess the Confederate flag was the second giveaway," Paresi said.

"For real." Vee shook her head.

"I can still see her," Star said. "She had blue-black hair, that the cosmetologist had curled up like Harpo Marx, and she had about two inches of blue eye shadow on each eye and a whole tube of red lipstick on her mouth."

"How old was she?" Jason asked.

Star shrugged. "Who could tell? She was real thin, and I remember the ice-blue dress she was wearing; it was too big."

"She had little tiny hands, too," Vee added. "But they were big enough to hold on to that racist flag. She looked almost like a child . . . but her face was too old to be a kid."

"Yeah, and those pinched-up red lips looked like they might've been real comfortable sucking on a corncob pipe," Star said.

The table erupted in laughter again.

"I don't know why, but we looked at each other and got so tickled we almost lost it," Vee said. "We had the kind of giggles that you get when you know you're not supposed to laugh, and you just can't help it."

"Those are the best kind," Mitch said. "But your surroundings were definitely not the place to break out."

"Right." Star smiled at him. "So we turned around and started up the aisle as fast as we could, but it was too late."

"Mm-hmm." Vee nodded. "I looked up to see this *huge* man standing in the doorway of the chapel. He was so big and tall, he nearly filled up the whole area."

"But what scared me was all the people coming up behind him," Star said. "It looked like a reunion of the hillbillies in *Deliverance*. We were in big trouble."

Both women laughed at the memory.

"Lord, we had to think fast," Vee said. "That aisle seemed awful short on the way back up, and we were tickled enough to burst. Star looked at the 'Grand Dragon' and just about fell out."

"I couldn't help it. I was trying so hard to keep it in."

Vee laughed. "She started moaning and keening, she was

so tickled," Vee said. "I was trying to maneuver Star out the door, but Man Mountain was in the way."

"He looked at me," Star said. "And I'm choking by this time. Then he looked at Vee, and said—" She dropped her voice to a deep register. "—'What chu gals doin' in heah?'"

They laughed hard at the memory, with everyone at the table joining in.

"I knew that was the day we were going to die, so I started shaking and trembling." Vee pointed at Star. "Which made her worse."

"Now I'm choking *and* biting my lips. I'm turning blue, I'm holding it in so hard," Star said.

"I knew she was just going to let go and holler," Vee said, "so I looked at this big ole man and I said, 'Oh suh, you has to 'scuse my frien' here, she jes overcome, seein' Miz Bailey laid out like dat!'"

"When she started that stuff, I had to hide my face in her coat," Star said.

"Yes, you did, and I'm still waiting for you to pay the cleaning bill." Vee looked at Mitch. "You should have seen her, nose running, sobbing, gasping, choking. She was a mess, trying to hold in that laugh."

"The guy looked at me," Star said, "and asked where we 'gals' knew Miz Bailey from."

"I told him we was her cleanin' gals," Vee said.

"He bought that," Star said. "He stepped aside and we waded through the Ozark Mountain Daredevils. Up until that day, I'd only seen beards like that on Yosemite Sam and ZZ Top."

The table rocked with laughter.

"We got outside," Vee said, "and you would have thought we were FloJo, God rest her soul, and Jackie Joyner-Kersee. We hit that parking lot *moving*!"

"When we got in the car, I totally lost it," Star said.

"She laughed so hard, she couldn't drive until she looked up and saw Big Poppa standing on the porch of the funeral home." Vee laughed at the memory.

"I floored it!" Star grinned.

"We made it home in about five minutes." Vee giggled, and pointed at Star. "The girl was wheeling!"

"Mama, that's deep," Roland said.

Vee stood up. "Deep enough never to swim in that pond again. Everybody go on into the living room, I'll serve dessert in there."

Mitch, Paresi, and the boys got up from the table.

"Let me help you, Mama," Lena said. "She made a pie," the little girl said to Star. "Lemon meringue, my favorite."

"That sounds good, baby," Star said, caressing Lena's face. "You go in the kitchen with Mama. I'll be there in a second. I want to talk to the boys."

"Okay." Lena picked up two plates and followed Vee into the kitchen.

"Guys," Star said to the boys. "Your mom said you have the computer game Vampire's Lair."

"Yeah, we don't play it much anymore, but we got it," Roland said.

"Well, I want you guys to play it with Jason."

They all looked at one another.

"He's good at it, and he's helping us on a case. So I need to see the game in action."

Cole and Roland looked at Jason. "Cool," Roland said. "My brother here is the King Vampire, at least he was the last time we played. I wanna see you take his crown!"

He and Jason high-fived.

"Hey, I know I haven't played in a while, but ain't nobody getting my hat!" Cole said, grinning.

"We'll see about that," Jason said.

"The computer's in here." Cole led them to the small bedroom that Vee used as a home office.

"Get it set up, and I'll be in," Star said.

Mitch and Paresi took chairs into the room, to watch the boys start the game.

Star entered the kitchen.

"You need my help in here?"

"You, help in the kitchen? Girl, please." Vee set two beautiful lemon meringue pies on the table, and started measuring coffee into the coffeemaker.

"Lena, get the cream out of the refrigerator for Mama."

"Okay." The little girl went to the refrigerator.

"We'll be in your office," Star said. "The boys are going to show me how this game works."

"What is it you're not telling me?" Vee said.

"It's just a hunch," Star said. "If it pans out, I'll fill you in."

Two hours, two pots of coffee, and a lemon pie and a half later, the game was hot. Star was moving quickly through the dark woods, on her way to the vampire's castle. With each nocturnal creature eliminated, her score, at the lower right side of the screen, increased.

"I can see why kids get into this," she said, outmaneuvering a winged serpent, swooping down at her from a dead tree.

"Look out, Auntie!" Cole said.

"What? No! Oh no!" Star rolled the mouse across the pad, trying to get out of the way of the blue mist forming on the screen.

"Too late," Jason said. "That's Mordrake, the wizard. You're gone."

"No! No!" Star watched Dorla, the female figure representing her on the screen, explode into a bright, dripping ball of blood, which spattered against the screen.

"Yech!" she said.

"My turn." Jason took over. His hand on the mouse was fluid. Star watched his character, Zen, glide swiftly past the blue mist wizard and on into the forest.

"He's gonna make it, slick," Roland said to his brother. "You're gonna have to give up that crown, man."

"Don't think so," Cole said, as Jason's character was suddenly caught in a screen-sized spiderweb, which appeared from nowhere. In the web, Zen struggled, trying to use his sword. It fell from his grip. Jason clicked the mouse, trying to save it. No use. The sword fell into a dark, bubbling pool.

On the screen, from the bottom left side, an enormous orange-and-black spider appeared. Zen's mouth formed a silent scream as the spider crawled toward him. It opened enormous, drooling, dripping jaws and bit down, separating

Zen's head from his body. Blood spurted from his neck like a fountain.

"Spider snack," Jason said, laughing.

On the screen, Zen was dissolving into a putrid green slime.

"And I thought my death was bad," Star said.

Jason grinned. "I used to be able to outrun Organe," he said. "But it's been a while since I played this."

"My turn." Cole took his place. As the King Vampire, he could roam the woods, safe except for huge bog worms that came up through the forest floor and the sunlight which penetrated the darkness randomly.

Star beckoned Jason out into the hallway.

"I see why kids get hooked on this stuff."

"It's fun," Jason said. "But this one is pretty tame, compared to some of what's out there."

"You mean there are worse violent and bloody deaths?" She shook her head. "This thing is so bloody you can wring it out."

"Yeah, but it's not as gruesome as Death Dive or Dementia."

Star's hand flew to her chest. "They're worse?"

Jason nodded. "Oh yeah."

Star looked back. Paresi and Mitch were as engrossed in the game as Cole, who was dodging sun rays and still holding on to his title as King Vampire.

"Well, I noticed that one of the guards for the castle is the evil fairy."

"Maylink," Jason said. "The seductress."

"She had wings."

"Yeah."

"That piece we found on Dolores, it had something on either side, remember?"

Jason nodded.

"Wings?" Star asked.

Jason shrugged. "Maybe, but the piece was corroded. I couldn't really say just what it was."

"I'm going with Maylink," Star said. "She was the seducer . . . and Dolores was a hooker. . . ."

Jason nodded. "I see the connection."

"I also noticed that troll thing," Star said. "The one that kept popping up when you didn't expect him."

"That's Grendar. He's the cannibal gnome; he cuts up his victims and leaves them all over the forest. He especially likes to bury the pieces under the dark trees near the castle."

"Those big scary-looking ones," Star said.

"Yeah. When he buries a victim, the trees become blood trees. They turn red with the blood of the dead buried beneath them, and then the trees sprout bloodfruit, which the gnome thinks is pretty tasty."

"Oh, gross!" Star said, making a face.

Jason laughed. "You gotta be tough for this game, Lieutenant."

"I see," she said. "So what happens if you're alone and you want to play, do you take all the parts and play against yourself?"

"Nope . . . You can play by yourself, but the computer will become your opponent, taking as many characters as you program into the game. That's a good way to get good at it, because if you can beat the computer, you're kicking butt." He smiled. "Still, it's much more fun in a group, because you can take on the roles, do voices, sounds, that kind of stuff."

"Thank you, Jason, you've been a lot of help."

"Glad to do it, Lieutenant." He looked back into the office, where Cole was now safe inside the castle.

"I like your family," he said.

Star took his arm, and headed back toward the room.

"Me too." She smiled at him. "And tonight we added one more."

CHAPTER SEVENTEEN

Marshall Butterworth saw the two detectives approaching the building from one of his office windows. He knew they'd be back. The Italian wouldn't be the type to give up or give him any peace. Now he could finally stop waiting for the other shoe to drop.

Instinct had kicked in when he got up this morning. He'd almost expected to see them today, and though they'd made no call for an appointment, there they were.

He was glad he'd laced his morning coffee with a pick-me-up. He was up and out of his seat before they reached the front desk.

"Good morning, Detectives," he said, nodding, crushing a spearmint-flavored Certs between his back teeth. "You don't have an appointment, but I'm assuming you're here to see me. What can I do for you?"

He watched Paresi reach into his breast pocket and withdraw a folded packet of papers. Marshall's mint-scented breath caught in his throat. Search Warrant! his mind screamed. Hold on, don't panic!

"Morning," Paresi said, not looking at him. "We'd like a few minutes of your time." He indicated the papers and put them back in his pocket. "We didn't have time for an appointment, and we won't be long, we just have a couple of things we'd like to clear up."

"Certainly." Butterworth stepped back, gesturing toward the open door to his office. "Come in," he said, with confidence he didn't feel. The detectives crossed in front of him, entering his office. "Would either of you like coffee . . . tea?"

"No thanks," they said in unison.

"No calls, Alex," the dean said to the boy at the reception desk. He closed the door and went back to his desk. He stood, his hands on the back of his chair.

"Dean Butterworth," Star said. "When we were here before, we didn't mention that there was a second killing in Saint Francis Park. At the time, it didn't seem connected to the burning of the homeless woman. The victim was a woman named Dolores Causwell."

Butterworth's eyes rolled. His breath caught. Dolores. That's what she'd said her name was, the bruised angel he'd searched for . . . Dolores. "I'm sorry. Was she someone from the neighborhood?" He struggled to keep his voice steady.

"No," Star said. "She was a prostitute. She mostly worked the stroll near the main entrance to Saint Francis Park."

"How sad," Butterworth said. He licked his lips and closed his eyes, trying to clear his thoughts. He willed his body to stand still.

"Yes," Star said. "It is sad. It has now come to our attention that both Ms. Causwell and Molly Ludendorf, the homeless woman who was set on fire, appear to have been killed in a manner depicted in a popular computer game."

"I've told you we don't allow that type of activity on this campus," Butterworth said. His upper lip began to sweat, and a damp spot appeared on the leather where his hands gripped the chair.

"Yes sir, I know what you told me, but you also have to know that nobody can keep an eye on an entire student population, twenty-four–seven. We've heard that some of your students used to organize tournaments around this particular game. Face it, Dean Butterworth, you have no idea what these kids do in their off hours."

Butterworth felt such a pounding in his temples that he feared for a moment he'd drop dead from a stroke. Pain gonged around in his brainpan, rattling like old bones. "What do you want from me, Lieutenant?" The anger in his voice surprised both his visitors and himself.

"Are you all right, Dean Butterworth?" Star said.

He took a deep breath. "I'm sorry. This is difficult. You've come here before, with your questions and accusations, and now you're back, telling me that another unfortunate has died yards from my campus, and that you think my boys are involved."

"We never said where she died," Paresi said. His blue eyes looked cold.

Butterworth tried to keep his hands still. He dug his fingertips into the chair back. "I assumed," he said.

"I said she worked the stroll near the park," Star said. "But you're right. She was found in the park, near the east gate."

Paresi shot her a look. Star ignored him and continued.

"Dean Butterworth, we're not saying that anyone here is involved. It's just that there seems to be some kind of connection with the burning of the homeless woman and this second victim. The thread is the game that your kids have played. Granted, without your permission, but they've still played it in the confines of this school. We would like your help."

Butterworth took a deep, labored breath, and stared at Star. He felt the tremors in his hands crawling up his arms to his shoulders. "What can I do, Lieutenant?" he said softly.

"We need a listing of those students with computers in their rooms, and we need access to those computers."

Butterworth felt the sweat beneath his fingers pool, and begin to trickle down the hunter green chair.

"No. Absolutely not."

"We respect your position, Dean Butterworth, that's why we came here to ask. But we won't hesitate to use warrants and confiscate every computer on this campus."

"You can't do that." Butterworth's voice rose. "This school is private property. You cannot act on my campus without express permission from the owners, and that will never happen."

"Maybe not," Paresi said. "But a murder investigation supersedes your private property bull. . . . We can take this place down brick by brick if we choose."

Butterworth sat down heavily on the chair, thrusting his hands under the desk. He folded them between his knees, trying to halt the shaking. "My boys always follow the rules. No one plays those types of games on this campus," he said, squeezing his wet palms so tightly together he thought they might bleed.

"Then let us check the computers," Star said.

"No." Butterworth shook his massive head. "I don't care what you say, it's a violation of their right to privacy. I can't . . . I *won't* subject my boys to that."

"Very well." Star stood. "Thank you for your time."

The combination of Remy Martin and strong black coffee bubbled in his gut. He swallowed, tasting mint and fear. "Are you going for warrants?"

Paresi again pulled the papers from his breast pocket and waved them in the dean's direction.

"No need," he said. "We'll be in touch. Thank you for your time."

Butterworth watched them leave. When the door closed, he got up and locked it. He went back to his desk and buzzed the intercom.

"Alex, no calls."

"Yes sir." The boy's voice filtered through the black box.

Butterworth unlocked his bottom drawer, put the key back into his pocket, and pulled a nearly full bottle of Rémy Martin from the drawer.

He went into his private bathroom, locked the door, and opened the bottle. Still shaking, he swallowed the liquor straight from the bottle and closed his eyes.

"Dolores," he whispered. "Dolores."

CHAPTER EIGHTEEN

"Good move there, Star," Paresi said, walking alongside her toward their car, "telling him where the body was found."

"Oh come on, you know he's not a suspect."

"Maybe he should be." He looked at her. "And if you're gambling . . ."

"If he's got nothing to hide," Star said, interrupting him, "he'll stop us before we leave."

The car was in sight.

"Then maybe we'd better start crawling."

Star shot him a look and continued toward the car. She had opened the passenger door when Butterworth came hurrying down the flagstone walkway, calling after them.

"You win," Paresi said. "Check this out." With a malicious grin, he reached into the open car window and picked up the radio microphone from the dash. With his eyes on Butterworth, Paresi leaned against the car door and raised the microphone to his mouth. "This ought to send him to the ER."

"Stop that," Star said. "I don't want to kill him!" She put on her game face and turned to watch the red-faced, out-of-breath man thundering toward them.

"Is there something we can do for you, Dean Butterworth?"

"Yes," he panted, "yes." He stopped, and tried to catch his breath.

Star smelled alcohol.

"I understand you two are just doing your jobs, and I'll co-operate, give you any help you need."

"That means coming clean with us, Mr. B.," Paresi said. "We ask the questions, you answer 'em. We need to see the computers, and we're bringing in an expert to check and make sure that nothing gets hidden away, understand?"

Butterworth nodded. "It'll take a couple of days, Detective."

Paresi stared at him.

Butterworth sighed. "Would this afternoon be soon enough? I'm going to have to juggle a class or two, to get the boys all in residence . . . have them show you their machines and the contents."

"This afternoon will be fine," Star said, looking at her watch. "It's a little after ten now, would three o'clock give you time to do what you have to do?"

"Three will be fine." Butterworth looked relieved. "I'll see you in my office at three."

"Thank you. We'll be there." Star got into the car.

Paresi watched Butterworth walk slowly back toward the administration building. He waited until the dean disappeared inside. Then he got into the car.

"I think we'd better ask Mitch if we can borrow Jason. He's the one who'd know how to find anything those little pukes would try and hide."

"Yeah." Star looked out of the window. "He's nervous about something. Did you smell the booze on him?"

"No," Paresi said. "You sure?"

Star nodded. "Definitely booze, and it wasn't on him when we went in."

"Well, if he's sippin' in the office, we struck a nerve," Paresi said. "He's hiding something."

Star nodded. "I think so. We'd better talk to the captain about a search warrant."

Paresi smiled. "No need. He gave us permission, and if he starts having second thoughts—" He patted his breast pocket. "—I'll just wave these at him again."

Star smiled. "Just what *are* those?"

Paresi pulled the papers from his coat. "Copies of Zukowski's report on that double homicide over on Trenton Avenue."

Star shook her head.

"What? They were in the box. I grabbed 'em just before we headed over to Mitch's office, just in case. They look official, right?"

Star laughed.

"Besides, I'm gonna turn 'em in . . . it's the least I can do."

"Paresi, one day you're going to bust Hell wide open."

"You won't let that happen. You'll lobby for me."

"Yeah, right." She laughed again.

"C'mon, you know we're in this together for life and beyond. Partners stay partners. Besides, you'd be too lonely up there without me. Who's gonna make you laugh?"

"Redd Foxx," she said, smiling. "Now drive. We've got to talk Mitchell into letting us have Jason for a while."

*   *   *

Jason Williams stopped outside the door of the administration building. A sudden wind whipped his long braided hair around his face.

"You guys got permission for all this, right?"

"We wouldn't let you do anything that would get you in any trouble, Jason," Star said.

"I know." Still, he looked nervous. "It's just that I don't want anything to get in the way of my scholarship."

"Not to worry," Star said. "Dr. Grant okayed your being here, and he wouldn't let you get into any trouble."

"Okay."

"Ready?"

"Let's do it." He opened the door and allowed both Star and Paresi to walk in in front of him.

A dark-skinned young man with beginning dreadlocks sat at the desk. He looked up and smiled.

"Yo, Jason, whut up dog, whatchu doin' here? You grad-u-*a*-ted!"

"Hey DeVon." Jason extended his hand. The boy grinned, showing deep dimples in both cheeks. He shook Jason's hand, taking it through a series of slaps and squeezes—a "soul" shake.

Jason pointed to the officers. "We're here on business, to see Dean Butterworth."

"Oh . . ." DeVon Holloway nodded. "Okay, let me tell him you're here."

"Sergeant Paresi and Lieutenant Duvall," Star said, showing him her badge.

The boy grinned. "Right." He punched the intercom button, and became all business. "Dean Butterworth, sir, there's a Lieutenant Duvall and a Sergeant Paresi from the police department here. . . ."

Before he could finish the announcement, Butterworth rushed through the door.

"Jason," he said, surprised. "Jason Williams." He extended his hand. "Good to see you again, son, but I'm afraid right now is not a good time for a visit." He indicated Star and Paresi. "I've got some business with these folks."

"Good to see you too, Dean Butterworth," Jason said, shaking his hand. "But I'm not here for a visit. I'm with them."

Marshall Butterworth's eyes widened.

"Oh? Did you join the police force, Jason? I thought you were looking for a career in pathology."

"He's with the Medical Examiner's office," Star said. "But he's agreed to help us check your computers. Jason is very proficient with computers."

Jason's eyes linked with DeVon Holloway's. They exchanged smiles that threatened to turn into laughter. DeVon put his hand to his mouth, covering his grin. Jason looked away and coughed softly into his hand, regaining his composure.

"Jason is a former student, Dean Butterworth," Star said. "He's familiar with the programs used at Bromleigh, and I'm sure he knows all the tricks that students play. If something has been hidden, he will find it."

Butterworth cast a look at the young man as if he were extremely disappointed.

"I see," Butterworth said. "And this is perfectly legal, even though he's not a police officer?"

Paresi patted his breast pocket. "He's *our* expert," he said.

"Very well." Butterworth sighed. "I guess we'll start in the Delamore Building. That's our largest residence. The boys are waiting."

Behind the officers and Dean Butterworth, Jason extended his fist. DeVon smiled and tapped it with his own.

CHAPTER NINETEEN

Cody Stevens handed Dave Riley a beer—one of the expensive, imported German brews his father hoarded in the downstairs bar.

"So, did the cops turn up anything?"

Dave shook his head. "Nah. They brought that black kid, you know, the one with the hair, the guy who was the major campus brain when we came in."

"Jason Williams," Dan said.

Dave nodded. "Yeah. Remember how he shook up the professors when he started wearing his hair like that?"

They all laughed.

"Yeah, him and the other niggers, yelling all that shit about their racial heritage," Cody snorted. "Like those apes got a heritage."

Neither of the twins said anything, but Cody's racist rants bothered them. They didn't share his views, but he was the King Vampire, so they kept quiet.

"So, they went through and looked at everybody's setup, right?" Stevens asked.

"Yeah."

"Was Butterball there?"

"Yeah. He came through with the two cops and Jason."

"Did you recognize the cops?" Cody took a deep swig from the bottle and belched.

"Uh-huh, from the park the other day. The woman, you know, she's a babe."

"For a monkey," Cody said.

Dave and Dan looked at one another.

"Anyway, it was her and that guy that was with her, you know, the tall, dark one."

"The greaseball," Cody said. "Looks like he should be making pizzas."

"They went from room to room," Dave continued. "Jason searched all the disks, and I gotta say, he knew all the tricks. He knew exactly what to look for."

For the first time, Cody looked concerned. "He didn't find anything, did he?"

"Nothing," Dave said, tipping the neck of the beer bottle toward the floor, watching the liquid inside creep up toward the open end. He didn't like beer, but he couldn't tell Cody that.

"So even Alex got his disk clean in time?" Cody asked.

"We checked his disk before they got to his room," Dave said. "He was nervous, but I think they probably chalked it up to cops fucking around in his room."

"Excellent," Cody said. He spun in his chair and reactivated his sleeping computer.

"Let the games begin."

Star sat with Mitch, cuddled in the oversized, cream colored chair in her den, watching Christopher Reeve and Jane Seymour fall in love in one of her favorite films, *Somewhere in Time*.

Near the end of the movie, Christopher Reeve lay dying in his room at the Grand Hotel, on Michigan's Mackinac Island. As the hotel staff broke into the room, Star sighed deeply, and dried the tears running down her face.

Mitch kissed her wet cheek and pulled her closer.

"Thank you for sitting through this with me," she said, resting her head on his shoulder.

"Actually, I like this movie," he said. "I think it's one of Reeve's best films."

Star looked at him. "I didn't know you were a fan."

"I am," Mitch said. "I think he's an extraordinary human being, and if anyone can come back from what he's endured, he's going to do it. The man has a will that's unshakable."

Star stared at him. "You're full of surprises."

Mitch smiled. "I admire Christopher Reeve, that's all. I think *Street Smart* is one the best movies ever made. You ever see it?"

Star nodded. "Mm-hmm. It was the first time I ever saw Morgan Freeman play a badass."

"He carried it off, don't you think?" Mitch said.

Star lay back in his arms. "Yep . . . he was great." They watched the screen, as Reeve was once again with Jane Seymour in a heavenly reunion.

"I love this film," she said.

"That's because the story's all about the power of love, Lieutenant." Mitch pulled her onto his lap.

Just hearing the word from his lips made her nervous. They'd never exchanged I love yous, and she wasn't sure she was ready to. Though she knew he had been faithful since their coming together as a couple, she still couldn't quite give up her fears that he would resort to the ways that made him legendary.

"I guess," she said softly.

She felt his arms tighten around her.

"You know another film I like that he's in?" she said.

"Which?"

"Remains of the Day." She tried not to think about how good and right his arms felt holding her.

"We have similar tastes, Lieutenant," Mitch said. "That's also one of my favorites. It's another lesson film."

"Lesson?"

"Yes," he said, as the credits rolled. "The lesson that love is the most important thing in life." He kissed her shoulder. "In the end, nothing else matters, does it?"

A sense of panic raced through her. She wasn't ready—she wasn't ready.

"Thank you for letting Jason help us out today," she said.

With his mouth against her shoulder, she felt his smile.

"Are you changing the subject, Lieutenant?"

"No. I just thought about Jason."

Mitch took her hand and raised it to his lips. He gently kissed her fingers. "Okay, I'm scaring you, so let's talk about Jason." He leaned back against the chair. His hands rested on the arms. "He got such a kick out of today, I'm afraid he's going to start thinking about police work instead of pathology."

Missing his touch, and immediately sorry for her reaction, Star leaned against him. Even though he knew what she'd done, he hadn't beat her over the head for it. He was patient with her. He always seemed to be giving her space. Maybe, just maybe, if she tried, she could relax and let this thing happen.

"Not a chance. He loves what he does, and he idolizes you."

"He's a good kid." Mitch gently moved his hand lightly over her shoulder, and down her arm. She loved his touch on her skin. She let herself relax, giving over to the feeling.

"Yes, he is," she said, and turned in his lap, gently running her fingers over his chest. "He was a little concerned at first, though, that he could mess up his chances for that Harvard scholarship."

"Never," Mitch said.

Star swung one blue-jeaned leg across his hips, and straddled him. "That's what I told him," she said, looking directly into his eyes. "Especially since it's coming from you."

"What?"

She wrapped both arms around his neck. "I didn't tell Jason, but I know you're the one paying his way."

"Busted, huh?" He smiled.

"Yes." She kissed him. "I think it's wonderful."

"Thanks."

She kissed him again. He ran his hands down her back.

"Mmm." He rested his forehead against hers, a low, throaty moan rising from deep inside him. He kissed her neck. His hands moved up her body. He stroked her skin, and held her face in his hands.

"You really make it tough to come clean," he said, looking directly into her eyes. "But before you get too thrilled with me, I have to tell you that there really *is* a foundation."

"Oh?"

"Yes. The Olivia Katherine Grant Foundation."

"Is that your mother?"

"No. My sister."

"I didn't know you had a sister," Star said.

"She died a long time ago."

"I'm sorry."

"Me too," he said, a note of sadness in his voice. "She was the best part of my family."

Star climbed off of his lap, and settled next to him in the chair. "What happened?"

Mitch was silent.

"It's okay if you don't want to talk about it," she said.

"No, I want you to know." He took her hand. "But it's still rough for me, even after all this time."

"If it's too much, I understand," she said.

Mitch kissed her hand. "I was going to tell you anyway." He looked at her. "I don't want any secrets between us."

She covered his hand with hers. "Whenever you're ready."

Mitch's eyes took on a faraway look, and a little smile crossed his face.

"Livvy was six years older than me, but my earliest happy memories are of her. She was more of a mother to me than our mother ever was." He looked at Star and grinned shyly. "She even used to wash my hands. She said I never got them clean enough." He raised his free hand, turning it, looking at it. "I would purposely leave dirt under my nails and between my fingers, just so she'd haul me to the bath, and wash my hands for me."

He looked at her. "Sometimes, I still feel the softness of her hands, soapy and slippery, on mine." Tears appeared in his eyes. "Stupid, huh? . . . What we hang on to?"

Star hugged him. He held her close, cradling her against his body.

"Livvy's was always the hand I held on to. Our mother was too busy being a social maven to care about us. She'd hand us over to Maude Logan, the nanny, and off she'd go."

"That must have been terrible for you both."

He nodded. "I used to wonder how Livvy survived before I came along. She was all alone with two empty, cold people. Our parents were the kind who should never have had children."

He leaned on her, his head resting on her breast.

"Livvy was my world. Then, one day, she was gone."

Star held him, gently stroking his hair. "What happened?"

Mitch closed his eyes. "The summer that she turned seventeen, we had a change in our usual routine. The family didn't go to our summer house at Lambert's Cove, on Martha's Vineyard. We stayed in Boston. My father had some kind of lecture series going at Mass General, and Mother decided we should all stay home. Livvy and some friends decided to spend a day in Rockport, and then go on to the Cape for a week. I begged her to let me go, but her friends didn't want some bratty eleven-year-old hanging around."

Star rocked him gently.

"My sister knew I was going to be alone with the vultures, so she told me that she wanted me to take the time that she'd be gone, and think about someplace I wanted to go. Just the two of us. She promised when she came back, that she'd take me anywhere I wanted. She said we'd spend all of our time together, just the two of us, doing whatever I liked. She kissed me good-bye, and promised to call me every day." He sighed. "That's the last time I saw her alive."

"Mitchell." Star hugged him.

His grip on her body tightened. "After she left, I spent most of my time pouring over every map, globe, and geography book I could find. I went to the library and took out a book on China!" Laughing, he shrugged his shoulders. "I was eleven."

Star smiled with him. He looked at her. "My sister. She was something. She kept her word, she called *every* day. And not just the hello, how are you calls—we talked, sometimes for over an hour. She wanted to know what I was doing, if I was eating, if I was reading. She used to choose books for me—Mark Twain and Robert Louis Stevenson were her favorites."

His eyes shone with unshed tears. "Imagine being seventeen, hanging out with your friends, and taking the time to call your little brother every day." He ran his hand along her denim-covered thigh. "I lived for those phone calls."

"What about your mother?"

"Constance held daily luncheons and 'tea' parties. The gettogethers were her excuse to booze. Somehow she felt if she served twenty-one-year-old Scotch out of her best crystal, it wasn't drinking. It was 'being social with the girls.' "

"Your mother's name is Constance?"

"Was," Mitch said. "Constance Mayhew Grant. Her ancestors came over on the Mayflower, which is really nothing to brag about, considering who those early settlers were, but she never let anyone forget it. And woe be to the fool who called her Connie.

"She was a blue-blooded harpy from the word go, and she never gave a damn about me or Livvy. I think we were both accidents, especially me.

"Once we were born, she gave us to the nanny and spent all of her time either shopping for junk to impress the rich, tired old bitches that came around to swill her liquor, or brow-beating the cook and the rest of the help into submission."

"You had a cook?"

"How do you think I learned?"

Star smiled. "I can see you in the kitchen, being a pest."

Mitch shook his head. "Willie Lee always made time for me, and teaching me to cook gave us a lot of hours together."

"Willie Lee?" Star said, guardedly.

"Willie Lee Thornton," Mitch said, warming to the memory. "She was a beautiful, brown-skinned, Mississippi-born angel who came into our lives when Livvy was twelve and I was six. We both loved her to death. We owe any kindness in us to Willie Lee."

"Part of the family, huh?" Star said, instantly ashamed of the bitterness in her voice.

Mitch looked at her. "I was a child, and I loved her. When I became a man, I loved her. I still do."

Star saw the truth in his eyes.

"I know this is probably hard for you to hear, Star, but our ties to Willie Lee weren't just rich white kids hanging out with the help. She was a good woman. She had a lot of love, and she gave it to her family, and to my sister and me.

"Our nanny, Maude Logan, was a nice woman, but she be-lieved in rigid standards for handling children. It was Willie Lee who provided the hugs and kisses, and the affection that anything living needs and deserves. She had a husband, Cordell, and two sons, Freeman and Emery. In the summer, her sons would come by late in the afternoons, before she got off. They were always welcome."

"In the kitchen?" Star said, before she caught herself.

"In our home," Mitch said. "Our front door didn't have a sign saying WHITES ONLY."

"I'm sorry," Star said.

"It's okay. For all their faults, neither of my parents were bigots. They were just people who thought of no one but themselves.

"When the boys would come by, if my mother was around, she was happy to see them, at least as happy as she could be to see anyone who wasn't there to fawn on and idolize her.

"Willie Lee and Livvy would make sandwiches and lemonade, and we'd sit around the table and talk. She treated us just like she treated her sons. Equal hugs and kisses. Freeman, her oldest, is still a good friend of mine. Emery moved to Detroit some years back, but we keep in touch. The last time we were all together was at Willie Lee and Cordell's forty-fifth anniversary, about six years ago. Cordell died a month or two after that, and Willie Lee died a year later."

"It must have been hard for you," she said.

"Devastating," he said, looking her in the eye. "I want you to understand, my family had money and prestige, but nothing else. Believe me, if Livvy and I could have changed places with Freeman and Emery, we would have done it in a heartbeat. They had joy. To tell you the truth, I was always a little jealous that they had her, and we didn't. Willie Lee loved me out of my despair when my sister died."

"I'm sorry," Star said, truthfully. "It's just something about hearing that 'she was one of the family' stuff, you know?"

Mitch nodded. "I understand, I really do, but I want you to realize that our relationship wasn't like that. When she died, I cried for weeks. I loved her. She and Livvy gave me the only mothering I ever had."

"Tell me more about your mother."

He sighed deeply. "Constance used to throw a few dimes at panhandlers and give our old clothes to 'the less fortunate,' " he said sarcastically. "She liked to think of herself as some kind of Lady Bountiful, the Brooke Astor of Boston. But the truth is, she was too goddamned selfish to give money or anything else to any cause but her own."

He took a deep breath. "My mother was a real work of art. Anyway, the final day of my sister's trip, Livvy called from Nantucket to say they were driving back that night. She told me to wait up, because she had a surprise for me."

He closed his eyes.

"You don't have to go on," Star said.

He looked at her. "I want you to know." He rested his head against her breast again. "She said they'd probably be in by ten at the latest. When eleven came and went, I knew something was wrong. I went to bed, and tried to sleep, but I couldn't. I kept seeing her, but when I tried to touch her, she'd disappear.

"The next morning, I came downstairs to find Willie Lee and the nanny in tears, while my mother and father sat dry-eyed like statues in front of a priest and two uniformed state police officers.

"Some drunken teenager from New Braintree crossed the line and hit Livvy's car head-on. Her friend Kara Billings was the driver, and the sole survivor. Marcia Harriman, Doris Kelly, and my sister died."

Star felt his arms tighten around her.

"Livvy was thrown from the car. Her neck was broken. She died instantly. It turns out being thrown free was merciful. Marcia, Doris, and Kara were trapped in the wreckage when it caught fire. Kara was able to get out, but she suffered lifelong disfiguring injuries. When she passed away, about ten years ago, she was still seeing those headlights coming at them, and hearing her friends screaming. They also found a dead black and white cocker spaniel puppy in the wreckage—Livvy's surprise for me."

"Oh, honey." Star hugged him.

He clung to her, his eyes closed.

"What about the teenager?" she asked.

"Died at the scene. No winners here."

Star held him tightly. "I'm so sorry, baby."

He kissed her chest, just above her heart. "When I turned thirty, I got both my share and Livvy's of the trust our father had set up for us. I took that and started the foundation. Livvy genuinely cared about people, and I couldn't think of a better way to honor her. She would have loved it."

"So Jason benefits."

"Yes," he said, regaining himself, his voice stronger. "He's smart, he works his ass off, and the only thing standing between him and his dream is money. So why shouldn't he get some help? His grade point average all through junior high and Bromleigh was outstanding. You've seen him work. He's got the touch, and he *earned* the grades to get him into Harvard. Nobody rigged anything for him, or dumbed down anything. He's a brilliant kid, so why shouldn't he have a chance?"

She touched his face. "Paresi said you were the scholarship fund."

"Really?" Mitch said. "How'd he know?"

"I guess he just felt that about you. He said you're the only rich guy he's ever seen with class."

Mitch laughed softly. "Dominic's a character."

"Yes he is."

Mitch looked deeply into her eyes.

"Thanks for letting me tell you all this. If Livvy and Willie Lee were around they would adore you."

"Think so?"

"No doubt," he said, pulling her to him. "No doubt at all."

CHAPTER TWENTY

Captain Arthur Lewis sat at his desk. He had been having a fairly decent day. In fact, it had been going so well that he was thinking of stopping at the market and bringing home a couple of porterhouse steaks and a good bottle of red wine. He was about to pick up the phone and call his wife, to tell her to just whip up a salad because he was bringing dinner home, when the phone call came.

Dean Marshall Butterworth of the Bromleigh Academy had managed to sound both angry and suitably chagrined as he related the activities of the day before. He described it from the moment Starletta Duvall and Dominic Paresi stepped into his office.

Now the two detectives sat silent and meek in front of him, neither one of them looking into his cold blue eyes. In fact, they looked more like chastened schoolchildren awaiting mom or dad to rescue them from the principal's office.

What was he thinking? Nowadays, kids *gunned down* the principal. Maybe his detectives had the right idea, even if they'd gone about executing it in a terribly stupid way. Luckily for them, he'd managed to convince Butterworth that what they did was entirely within the boundaries of their investigation.

"So." Lewis finally spoke. Star and Paresi sat at attention, their eyes on the captain.

"Let me get this straight. You two took it upon yourselves to search every computer in every dorm room and common area at Bromleigh Academy."

"Yessir," Star said.

"Uh-huh." Lewis's eyes locked on her. "And, in place of a computer expert, you took a kid that works at the morgue to verify the results, correct?"

"Yes, Captain." Star nodded. "That's absolutely correct."

Lewis had to fight to control his laughter. She was definitely Lenny Duvall's kid. He remembered some of the scams he and Star's father had concocted during their years as partners. When she tilted her head in that manner, he could see his old friend in her face, and Lenny was smiling.

"I see," he said, leaning back in his chair. "And at no time was any warrant produced to search the premises, correct?"

Star nodded. "Correct."

"Still, due to some papers flashed by Sergeant Paresi, Dr. Butterworth, the dean of the school, felt he had no recourse other than to allow this search?"

"I didn't flash anything, Cap'n," Paresi said. "I happened to *glance* at some papers that I had on my person, and Dean Butterworth *assumed* that I had a warrant. It's not our fault he jumped to conclusions."

"And just what were those papers, Sergeant?" Lewis asked.

He saw Star aim her "don't antagonize him" look at her partner, but Paresi was too busy enjoying himself to notice.

"Detective Zukowski's report on that double homicide over on Trenton," Paresi said, grinning.

Lewis closed his eyes, and shook his head.

Paresi winked at Star.

"You two lucked out this time," Lewis said. "When Butterworth called to complain, I asked if he'd given you permission to enter the rooms and look at the machines. He said that he had. I told him he didn't have a complaint. But—" He leveled a laserlike gaze at the two detectives. "—If it happens again, the two of you will be pumping gas down in the motor pool, got it?"

"Yes, Captain, we understand," Star said, ignoring Paresi's smile.

"Now, after all this drama—" Lewis indicated their report. "—you came up with bupkis?"

Star nodded. "There was nothing on any of the computers we checked, but that doesn't mean they aren't playing. The programs can be dumped and then reinstalled. Jason said he could use a data-retrieving program to salvage what was dumped, but we didn't want to push the envelope."

"Good thinking," Lewis said. "So, what's happening on the Causwell case?"

"The blood that the recycling guy found at the curb was hers," Paresi said. "We had the neighborhood canvassed, but of course nothing turned up."

"That's right." Star nodded. "The occupants of the house where the blood was found are in Europe, on an extended holiday. We traced their domestic help to a service in town called Maid For You. They told us that the house has been empty since March. They have someone go in and do the dusting, but nobody's living there just now."

"What about the maid that does the tidying?" Lewis asked.

Star looked at the notebook on her lap. "Her name's Estelle Packard, and the last time she was at the house was two weeks before the blood was left at the curb. We're meeting with her this afternoon, to take a look inside the place. The agency has permission to act in an emergency, and they felt this qualified."

Lewis nodded. "Good. What about the recycling bin the bottles were in? Did it belong to that house?"

"The bottles were actually left on the curb. That's another reason they seemed unusual to the pickup guy," Paresi said.

"But there are bins," Star added. "They're kept outside, next to the garage. This house has an open driveway, no gate. Anybody could have had access to them, but they didn't appear to have been touched."

She again looked at her notebook. "As for the dog at the scene, he belonged to a family a few streets over. They had no information."

"Great," Lewis said. "What's next?"

"We're gonna check out the milk jugs," Paresi said. "They had traces of a chemical that's mostly used in school labs."

"Right," Star said. "Loman's on that. He's checking the supply houses in the area that sell to the public schools and to Bromleigh."

"But the bottom line is that Bromleigh is the common denominator," Lewis said.

"Exactly," Star agreed. "It always comes back to that school." She closed her notebook. "We're not trying to harass Dean Butterworth," she said. "But the facts all point to something happening on that campus."

"Then get to the bottom of it," Lewis said, waving his hand in dismissal.

"We're on it." The detectives stood up.

"Paresi?"

"Yeah, Cap'n?"

"Make sure you leave Zukowski's report in the basket. He caught hell from me for not turning it in on time. And *apologize*!"

Paresi nodded. "I'll do that, Cap'n."

Paresi and Star drove slowly down Preston Avenue to the intersection of Fourth Street. The house where Dolores Causwell's blood had been found was the second from the corner.

The detectives drove up the long driveway and parked behind a black-and-silver-paneled Toyota pickup truck, with the letters *ota* painted out, so that it read *Toy.*

As Star approached the truck, a petite, timeworn, flame-

haired woman jumped out of the cab. Star noted that she had
the leathery skin of a veteran sun-worshiper. She wore tight-
fitting jeans on a short but still trim body, a gaudy western
shirt, and red leather cowboy boots.

"Hi, you folks from the police?" Star thought she sounded
like Dolly Parton, if Dolly had smoked three packs of cigarettes a day for thirty years. Her smile made the detective
think of a grinning death skull.

"Yes, I'm Lieutenant Duvall, and this is Sergeant Paresi."
The woman shook their hands.

"I'm Estelle Packard, I'm the one what cleans up around
here."

"Sorry if we're cutting in on your off time, Ms. Packard.
We appreciate your meeting us here," Star said.

The woman waved an aged hand which sported shiny, fake
hot pink nails.

"Call me Stelle, and don't even think about it. I think this is
downright excitin'! I'm gonna have lots to talk about when I
get to my line-dance club this afternoon."

"We'd appreciate your not saying too much," Star said.

The woman's heavily lined and mascaraed watery blue
eyes lit up. "Oh, I get it. Just in case somebody's up to somethin', you don't want everythin' out in the open . . . wanna trap
'em, huh?"

Star nodded. "Something like that."

"Well, y'all can count on me. I won't say a word, but when
it's all over, honey, I'm gonna spill like a leaky bucket." She
laughed at her own words, exploding in a deep phlegmy
sound that made Star want to wrap her whole body in plastic.

"Come on." The woman waved her hand. "We can go in
through the back." She led the detectives under a brick
archway and around to the rear of the two-story, Tudor-style
house.

A large redbrick patio held three round tables with four
chairs at each. The furniture was covered with white plastic
tarps. A variety of colors blossomed from long white flower
boxes and red clay pots that bordered the edges of the patio.
The raised area looked out onto a vast yard and gardens.
Across the lawn, within view of the back windows, stood

a white gazebo with Victorian gingerbread borders and a peaked roof.

A few feet past that was a long, glass-enclosed area, through which Star could see an Olympic-sized swimming pool. Opposite the pool was a small redwood building, with a hot tub steps away. She guessed it housed a sauna. She looked at Paresi.

His eyes were on Estelle Packard as she upended a small, bronze, long-eared hare, crouching at the top of three red-brick steps. It seemed to be peering into the lotus etched-glass French doors. Estelle punched a number into the nine-digit keypad embedded in the underside of the hare's belly. A little door sprang open, and she plucked out a set of keys.

Paresi looked at Star, an "are you kidding" look on his face.

Estelle opened the doors, which led to the dining room. It was a magnificent space. Endless pale peach-colored walls, bordered with spotless white baseboards, stretched to the second floor.

Star looked up and realized the house was built around itself. From the second story, you could walk around and look down on the dining room, kitchen, and what she suspected was a living room on the other side. Through the open area, leading to a hallway to the other side of the house, she saw a painting that appeared to reach from the first floor to the second. She recognized the frenzied, spattered colors. It was a Jackson Pollock, and it was an original.

"Wow," she muttered.

"The kitchen's right through here," Estelle said, leading them through another open area to their left, and into a huge, sumptuously outfitted, white and cobalt blue, French-styled, top-of-the-line, state-of-the-art kitchen.

"You could bowl in here," Paresi said.

Star nodded. "Not to mention roller-skate."

Estelle, not hearing them, walked to a cabinet. "The agency told me you were interested in the recycling," she said, opening the glossy, spotless white cabinet doors. "Something about milk jugs left at the curb."

She stepped back. "Here's where we put the things to be left outside."

She indicated a built-in set of tilt-out bins, beneath varnished pinewood shelves. The shelves were well stocked with paper towels, dishwasher detergent, linen counter towels, and assorted kitchen cleaning supplies.

"You can look in here," Estelle said, "but we never put out milk bottles. Both Mr. and Miz Fletcher don't drink nothin' but single-malt Scotch, the older the better."

She laughed again, and Star felt her flesh crawl.

" 'Tween you, me, and the fencepost, I have myself a little sip of it now and then, when they ain't home."

Paresi opened each of the three plastic-bag-lined but empty recycling bins. He ran his hands over the tops and down the insides.

He looked at Star. "Spotless," he said. "We got nothing."

Star made a clicking sound with her tongue. "Swell."

Paresi closed the bins and the cabinet doors. The three of them went back outside. At the truck, Star turned to the woman, who was walking alongside Paresi. She reached into her pocket and handed Estelle a card.

"Thank you for your time."

"Oh shoot, sugar, I'm enjoying this. No need to thank me."

Star smiled. "That's kind of you, Stelle." She pointed to the card. "If you remember anything, or if something comes up, please give us a call."

The woman looked up at Paresi. "Oh, I'd love to call," she said, grinning, exposing nicotine-stained teeth.

Paresi handed her one of his cards. "Make sure you ask for me," he said flirtatiously.

"I'll do just that," Estelle said.

Star watched her flutter her jet-black Maybelline-caked lashes at Paresi.

Oh brother! she thought to herself.

Paresi helped the woman into her truck, and the detectives headed back to their car.

"You have no shame." Star laughed.

"Can't hurt to let her think she's still got it. You never know what she might remember," Paresi said, and slid in behind the wheel. "Besides, she reminds me of my Aunt Sofia."

"Who's Aunt Sofia?" Star got into the car.

Paresi started the engine and backed up into a wide turn-around area off the driveway. Estelle backed her Toyota alongside their unmarked car.

"Y'all have a good day," she hollered over a Garth Brooks song blasting from her deck.

Paresi waved at her. She grinned, and pulled off, barreling down the long driveway.

"So tell me about Aunt Sofia," Star said as Paresi pulled out, following the truck.

"She was my mother's oldest sister. I never once saw her without a cigarette. She had that same kind of brassy dyed-red hair." He laughed. "Aunt Sofia was strictly an in-your-face, stand-up, take no prisoners broad. She smoked long pastel-colored sticks in a mother-of-pearl holder. She ordered her cigarettes from France. My sisters used to fight over the cartons they came in. They were pastel too, with some kind of foo-foo artwork all over them."

"I can guess what happened," Star said.

Paresi nodded. "Right, lung cancer. It caught up with her when I was twenty-two." He smiled at his recollections. "She was a pistol," he said. "She was raising hell and flirting right up until they threw the dirt in her face."

"I hope I go out like that," Star said. They remained behind Estelle's truck. She could still hear Garth.

"Hope the old girl doesn't think we're following her," she said.

"She'd dig it," Paresi said.

"You're probably right," Star said, as Estelle's truck ran the stop sign and disappeared around a corner.

"Maybe not," Star said.

Paresi came to a full stop at the octagonal red sign.

"Want me to go after her?" he asked.

"No, it's okay. She's rushing to spill her guts to her *line-dance class*," Star said in a perfect imitation of Estelle's smoky, country twang. "Let's just cruise the neighborhood."

"There's not much to see," Paresi said. "Most of these places got high fences around 'em or twenty-mile driveways."

"I know," Star said. "I just want to look around, that's all."

Paresi shrugged and turned left. They crisscrossed up and down the wide, placid streets.

"Ever notice how wide the streets are in rich neighborhoods?" Paresi said. "You could double-park on this street and still have a couple of open driving lanes."

Star nodded. "I know. . . . I guess they need the space for all those big cars."

Paresi nodded, but didn't say anything. They rode in silence for a while.

"Doesn't this strike you as a *Stepford* kind of neighborhood?" Star said.

"What do you mean?"

"Look around. We've been up and down these streets at least a dozen times, and we haven't seen a living soul. Doesn't that strike you as weird?"

"Now that you mention it, yeah." Paresi drove slowly. "Maybe they're all swimming in their backyard glass-enclosed pools."

"Yeah." Star grinned. "How 'bout that? Wouldn't you love to swim in that thing?"

"I'm sure it's cleaner than the Y or the gym," Paresi said.

"Amen," Star agreed. "I'm so paranoid about germs now, I won't swim in a public pool anymore."

Paresi glanced at her. "Take it up with Mitch, I'm sure he'd put one in your backyard. Just tell him you want to swim naked, and he can join you."

"You're a pig, Paresi."

They both laughed.

As they drove, a large cast-iron gate, facing them at the end of the street, swung open. A Silver Mercedes station wagon pulled out, and passed on Paresi's side.

"Son of a bitch!" he said.

"What?"

"That kid in the car, didn't you see him?"

"No, I was looking at the woman driving."

Paresi looked at his partner.

"It was the kid from Bromleigh . . . the fat one, the one who works for Butterworth."

CHAPTER TWENTY-ONE

Star watched Phil Bamberger walk into the lunchroom at the Seventeenth Precinct and barely recognized him. He and his identical twin brother Richard worked Vice, and for the entire time she'd known them both, they'd been involved in one undercover operation after another. She'd never seen them clean-shaven, or even clean for that matter.

Phil, the older of the twins by three minutes, kept his blue-black hair cut in a stiff military brush, while Richard wore his long and usually greasy.

She contemplated the man headed for their table. He wore his hair cut in a full, precise, every-hair-in-place manner. His black suit draped his body with an easy elegance worthy of Mitchell Grant. Like Dr. Grant, he walked as if the world belonged to him. As he moved closer to their table, Star blinked and gave a low, appreciative wolf whistle.

"Philly . . ." she said. "Look at you. Wow!"

Phil Bamberger smiled. It was the first time Star noticed that he had dimples.

"Like it?" he said, turning around, modeling the suit.

"Very hot," she said. "You look good."

"Nice threads, Philly." Paresi pointed toward the counter. "Want something to drink? Coffee, a soda?"

"No . . . no thanks."

Paresi indicated the empty chair next to him. Phil sat down. "Thanks for your help on this one," Paresi said.

"No problem, Goombah. Can't let the Lieutenant walk into something she can't handle." He winked at Star.

Star gave him a "yeah, right" look and poured milk into her tea. "What are you working on?"

Phil folded his large hands on the table.

Star noticed his nails were professionally manicured.

"Drug deal," he said. "I'm a high-rolling, high-living kingpin."

She whistled again. "I'll say."

Phil Bamberger smiled at her. "So you really like this look?"

"Very sharp," she said.

"Hugo Boss." He indicated the suit.

"I thought so," Star said. "Mitchell likes his line too."

"I thought about Mitch Grant when I put this character together," Bamberger said.

"Why? You think he looks like a drug dealer?" Star asked, grinning.

Phil laughed, and shook his head. "Not hardly, but he is a very sharp dresser. I figured I should go class instead of flash."

Star took another sip of her tea. "Good thinking," she said.

Bamberger sat back in the chair. "What can I do for you guys?"

Paresi pointed at Star. "We've been working on a couple of murders in Saint Francis Park, near the school."

"Bromleigh."

"Right," Paresi said. "There's lots of activity around that place."

Bamberger nodded. "No shit. That park really heats up at night, and lately some parts of it rock even in broad daylight."

"We've noticed," Star said. "That's why we want to do a little undercover. Two bodies in the park within weeks *ain't* good."

Paresi leaned on the table. "We figure if we hang down there and maybe scope out some of the nightlife, we'll pick up something on these killings."

"Right," Star said. "We need to talk to the regulars, the ones who hang twenty-four–seven. Somebody had to have seen something."

"Good luck," Bamberger said. "Even the scuzzos down there have a code. They don't rat, no matter what."

"I know you're undercover, Philly," Paresi said, "but how much do you know about the murders in the park?"

Bamberger shrugged. "Not much. Only that that old douchebag German Molly got roasted, and I heard some hooker turned up the other night."

"Dolores Causwell," Star said.

"No shit." Phil turned toward her. "I didn't know who it was, I've kinda got my hands full doing my thing, but I'm sorry about Dolores. She was an okay broad."

"Yeah," Star agreed. "She was good people, and I don't want whoever killed her to get away with it."

"I hear you." Phil leaned back in his chair and unbuttoned his jacket, exposing more of his finely tailored gray silk shirt. "My brother Rich is out there. Have you talked to him?"

Paresi nodded. "I talked to him this morning. The only thing he had to offer was that the newest thing with Bromleigh boys is hanging out in Saint Francis after dark and getting laid."

"Our future leaders," Star said.

Bamberger looked at her. "I'm not around the park. I've been working out of a penthouse on Exeter Drive."

"Money row," Paresi said.

"Right . . . Gotta live the life, you know." Phil smiled. "Hey Star, wanna be my lady for a while?"

"As tempting as that is, I'll pass," she said. "I've had my experience with living in luxury, and it ain't all it's cracked up to be."

"What we wanna do, Philly, is hang out in the park and scope out the activity," Paresi said.

"You clear this with Lewis?" Bamberger asked.

Star and Paresi looked at each other.

"I hear you." Bamberger pulled his chair closer to Star and lowered his voice. They leaned in to hear him.

"I'm currently supplying a lot of the crack, coke, and heroin floating around down there, at least Luca DiBartola is."

"Luca DiBartola?" Star said.

Phil pointed to himself. "Me . . . I'm Luca. I'm a major

player from Chicago, relocated here to beef up my operation. My roots are in street gangs, and I've done very well for myself."

"So, Luca," Paresi said, "how come you gotta be a guinea? Why can't you be . . . Ramon Rodriguez?"

They laughed.

"Look at me, ya chooch!" Phil said, spreading his hands, palms up.

"You could be Sheldon Bernbaum," Paresi said.

"Yeah?" Bamberger said. "When's the last time you heard of a Jewish gangster?"

"Meyer Lansky, Bugsy Siegel," Star said. "It's been a while."

Bamberger pointed to Star. "What she said."

"You got a point." Paresi grinned. "Just don't embarrass the family, capeesh?"

"Capeesh," Bamberger said.

"You got a runner for the mooks that hang in the park?" Paresi asked.

Phil smiled. "Yeah, Mr. Eugene 'Two Toes' Chandler."

"Two Toes?" Star said.

"Yeah. He's only got two toes on his left foot. Seems he got his foot caught in an escalator. He was trying to boost some leather jackets from Mayfield's downtown. When he got made, he tried to make a break on the escalator."

They cracked up.

"Oh, this guy is brilliant." Paresi grinned.

Phil nodded. "Right, he got his fake Air Jordans caught and dragged into the mechanism. The stairs ate up most of his foot."

They laughed some more.

"So, Eugene, now known as 'Two Toes,' being very *sharp* on the uptake, decided he needed a more lucrative form of work, without all the wear and tear on the bod."

"So he's hustling drugs in the park," Star said.

"Bingo. He gets a nice piece of change, and he don't have to do too much. He's been working with a couple of pimps, Stanley Johnson and Dushon Davis."

"Silk and Baby D," Star said.

"It always cracked me up that Davis calls himself 'Baby,'" Paresi said. "That bastard's big enough to swallow Godzilla *and* an order of fries."

"But he's cute," Star said. "Besides, the girls named him Baby, because his skin is soft as a baby's behind."

They looked at her.

"Hey, I'm not speaking from personal experience here," she said. "The girls like to talk to me."

"Well, between you, me, and Spaghetti Boy," Bamberger said, "Baby's gonna find himself real popular in prison. Him and Silk both. They work with Two Toes. They get a good cut of what he sells in the park. That's his tax for them letting him work that area. And it's a very lucrative gig. These guys are handling some major dough. Two Toes also spies on the girls and reports back. He tells Silk and Baby which ones are keeping back money and which ones spend more time flyin' than blowin' and humpin'. Sometimes, he even tunes 'em up when the pimps don't want to get blood on their fancy shoes."

"Amazing," Star said.

"Ain't it?" Phil smiled. "Believe me, we're close, and when these assholes go down, it's gonna be be-yoot-ti-ful!"

"I'm sure," she said, "but I was talking about the amount of effort they put into this stuff. I hate the violence, and the killings. I hate seeing young men dead and dying on the streets, but when you think about what they do with the drug business . . ."

The two men stared at her.

"It's amazing," she said. "With no education, no training, they bring in major money. They recruit sellers, they supply, designate, and protect. Imagine what they could do with someone teaching them, training them. These guys could run IBM or something."

"Don't tell me you're going soft, Starletta," Phil said.

"Not hardly," she said. "But I can't help but think about the wasted lives."

"Granted, some of these humps ain't bad guys," Bamberger said, "they just want what they think everybody else has . . . a good life. But they're killing people to get it. I wouldn't have a problem with that if they only killed each other. It could save the city a lot of money, you know. Tag 'em, bag 'em, burn 'em, and forget 'em; but that's not what happens. These pukes kill innocent folks, old people, kids. They gotta go down."

"So, is Richie working the park?" Paresi asked.

"Sometimes . . . You wanna hook up with him?"

Star leaned toward Phil Bamberger. "Since Paresi and I are going be out there with our asses hanging out, we'd like to know that backup is close by, if we need it."

"You expecting trouble?"

"Not really," Star said. "But we know that Bromleigh is in the center of this mess. Those kids are playing some kind of game. The murders are mimicking a computer game called Vampire's Lair."

"You think they're playing the game for real?"

"I don't know. But we want to prevent another murder."

"So far, the victims have been throwaway people," Paresi said. "Molly and Dolores, a bag lady and a hooker. We just wanna check around down there, you know, observe, get a bead on what's happening."

Phil nodded. "Done. I'll get Richie to call you this afternoon, he'll make sure you got cover."

"Thanks," Star said.

"So . . . Star?"

"Yes, Philly?"

"You gonna dress the part tonight?"

"Pardon?" Star said.

Bamberger spread his large hands in a "helpful" gesture. "You know, something really short and tight, something hot?"

Star smiled sweetly at him. "I will if you will."

Paresi cracked up.

"You know, I had to think about that." Bamberger grinned. "At least let me cruise you in my new ride, pick you up, make it look legit."

"Thanks," Star said, "but I'm not planning on getting into any cars."

"But you wanna make it real, darlin'," Phil said, smiling.

She smiled back. "Not *that* real."

CHAPTER TWENTY-TWO

The east end of Saint Francis Park was the darkest area of the sprawling greenbelt. A small, poorly lit street ran between the east and west entrances and spilled onto Harrison Boulevard just beyond the gate.

This was the most populated area for commerce.

Star walked slowly along the rim of the park, wearing black jeans and black crepe-soled walking shoes, and clutching her short, bright red woolen jacket against the chilly night air.

Across the street, Paresi sat on a bench near the corner, his eyes on her. He was dressed totally in black. Jeans, leather jacket, high-top sneakers, and a baseball cap, turned backward. He looked like any other thug come to the park to do his nightly commerce. Under his jacket, tucked into an inside pocket, a Walkman gave his jacket a slight bulge.

Far from playing music, the machine picked up every sound as Star walked "the stroll" across from him. A tiny microphone was planted in a gaudy pin that she wore on her jacket, its tough, yet microscopically thin, practically invisible, wire threaded through a buttonhole and down her body to the inside waistband of her jeans. There it plugged into a tiny, battery-powered generator nestled inside a special clip-on pouch, which rested flat, under the fabric, against her skin. Her black turtleneck sweater concealed the apparatus.

The bright red beret she wore slanted and low over her right ear hid a tiny listening device. This setup was new. She'd been miked before, but this latest gadget allowed her to hear Paresi, as well as be heard by him. She knew he always had her back, but still, it made her feel safer.

As she turned to begin her walk back toward the park, a

slick black Lexus slowed in front of her. The driver honked the horn. Star walked toward the automobile. The man pulled to the curb and stopped.

Star leaned down, looking in the window.

"Hey, darlin'," the man in the car said, smiling at her.

"Philly." Star leaned against the open passenger window. "What are you doing?"

Officer Bamberger grinned. "Making you look good, sweetness. Why don't you hop in?"

"I told you, I don't need any help. Paresi is across the street, and your brother's around somewhere."

Bamberger nodded. "I know. But my old pal Two Toes just hipped me that Willie Chester is on the way down here."

"Who's Willie Chester?"

"A righteous asshole pimp outta Dorchester that ain't plugged into the party line. He's a traveler, likes to take his women to the money. We got a big convention in town. Funeral directors!" Phil laughed. "Willie's here till it's over. A lot of the gentlemen have rooms in the Morton Hotel, just across the north end of the park. That area's considered 'safe,' so they like walking around, taking the night air, dig?"

Star nodded.

"Willie rides his women hard. He likes to tune up his girls, and anybody else who gets in the way. If he sees you, he's gonna hassle you, so get in the car and we'll take a little spin."

Star looked across the street. Paresi nodded at her.

"Swell." She got into the car. Phil Bamberger pulled away from the curb.

"Now what?" she said.

"I gotta keep you clear for at least twenty minutes, a half hour. We don't want the upright citizens to get suspicious."

"Okay."

"Willie will make his sweep, pick up his dough, and you won't have to worry about him for a couple of hours."

"Fine." She fiddled with the pin on her coat. "Paresi, you there?"

"Right where you left me," Paresi answered. "Tell Philly I said to keep his hands off of you."

"Don't worry," Star said. "I can handle this."

"Bet he's telling you to be careful with me." Phil Bamberger laughed.

Star smiled. "So now you're psychic." She spoke to Paresi. "We're going to get lost for about a half hour. I suggest you do the same, I'll call you when I'm headed back."

"Got it," Paresi said. "I think I'll take a walk."

"Not without me," she said.

"I'm a big boy, Star," Paresi answered. "I'm just gonna peep the action on the north end. Philly's got me curious."

"Okay. But be careful."

"Right," Paresi said. The connection went silent.

"Don't worry about him; Paresi can take care of himself." Phil Bamberger piloted the Lexus around the corner at Harrison and Third.

"I know," Star said. "It's just that Lewis doesn't know we're out here and if something happens, he's going to have a fit."

"He has a fit on a daily basis," Bamberger said. "That's what keeps his heart beating. Nothing's going to happen. I got an eye on you, and Richie and a couple of the guys outta the squad got you as well."

Star looked at Bamberger. "Thanks, Phil, we owe you."

"Nah," Bamberger said. "No debt at all. I know it gets rough sometimes, seems like we spend our lives sweeping back the garbage and we never quite get a handle on it."

"Amen to that," she said.

"So sometimes we gotta go a little out of our way. I know Dolores Causwell was special to you. She liked you a lot too. Whenever we picked her up, she always asked us if you were working. She used to say you were a stand-up broad."

"Really?" Star said.

Bamberger nodded. "Yeah. She said when you locked up a girl, you took the john too. The guys always let the john go, but you would lock 'em up, no matter how sorry they said they were, or how much they pleaded. She appreciated you for that."

Star laughed. "Well, the way I see it is that there are two people involved in the crime. I never could figure out why the guys would just let the johns take a hike. They're buying, they're just as guilty as the girls."

"Yeah, but guys understand other guys buying it."

"And women don't?"

"Nah . . . I mean, women don't really understand what's be-hind it."

Star half turned in her seat. "C'mon, Philly, don't give me that 'no strings' bull."

"That's what it is, Star. We got needs. Sometimes you just wanna get off. You don't need to feel nothing beyond that. You take a woman out a couple of times, she wants a commit-ment, and sometimes all we want is the drawers."

"Tell me something I *don't* know," she said. "A lot of guys think with their shorts."

"Not me." Bamberger wheeled the black car down Arlington Street, past the shops and hotels near the north end of the park. Star looked for Paresi. She didn't see him.

"I'm a stand-up guy," Phil said. "I mean sometimes I get needy, yeah, but when I'm in a relationship, I like it to be one woman. I'm not a player."

"Then you're a real diamond, Philly," she said. "You're going to be very good for some lucky woman."

Bamberger glanced at her. "Thanks," he said. "That means a lot, hearing you say that."

She looked at him. "It's the truth."

They rode in silence for a few minutes, then Bamberger pulled up to the curb where he'd picked her up.

Star opened the car door and turned toward him. "Thanks, Philly."

"Anytime, baby."

She got out and closed the door.

"I got my eye on you," Bamberger said.

Star waved and walked back toward the bench where Paresi sat.

Bamberger watched her in the rearview mirror for a few minutes before he pulled away from the curb.

"Gotta love that Philly." Paresi's voice filtered through her earpiece. "Always pitching."

"You heard us? I thought you shut the box off," Star said.

"Why would I do that?"

"You're dangerous with that thing."

Paresi nodded at her from across the street. "That's why you love me. Welcome back."

CHAPTER TWENTY-THREE

Star had been on the stroll for over three hours, and she was freezing. She clutched her red woolen jacket tightly around her body, wishing she'd worn a heavier coat.

"If we do this again," she muttered into her microphone, "I'm wearing long johns."

Across the street, her partner laughed.

"How are you keeping warm?" she whispered.

"You really want to know?" he said.

"You're a pig, Paresi."

He snorted into the mike. She laughed, and jammed her hands into her pockets. I gotta find those old fur-lined mittens of mine, she thought. Fancy gloves ain't gonna cut it out here.

She looked at the women passing her. They seemed oblivious to the cold. Some wore high heels and practically nothing else. Bare legs, micro-mini spandex skirts that barely covered their butts, and halter tops seemed to be the preferred uniform.

"Damn," Star muttered at the apparition stalking toward her. The woman wore a silver one-piece halter-topped bathing suit and a see-through, wraparound silvery cloth tied around her waist, stopping midthigh. Her pale skin had a blue tinge as she stepped high in her silver stiletto heels. She wore her white-blonde hair pulled tightly back from her face. Big silver bracelets clamped on each of her wrists. Her fists were clenched. She looked like some comic book villainess.

As they neared one another, the blonde looked at Star. Her glitter-shadowed eyes seemed vacant. Star nodded. The woman ignored her.

Star turned, watching the apparition pass. The woman's hair dangled down her bare back in a long silver-threaded braid. Her bathing suit turned out to be a thong. Her pale behind shone through the glittering, nearly transparent wrap.

"Yikes!" Star said.

"That's an outfit I'd pay to see you in," Paresi said from across the street.

"You first," Star said, turning to take another look. "I hope whatever she's on is keeping her warm."

"She's feeling nothing," Paresi said. "Guaranteed."

"Here comes Philly again," she said.

Phil Bamberger cruised by, and pointed with a thumb over his shoulder. Star looked in that direction.

"Hey," she said, "Richie's over there."

"Where?" Paresi said.

"Near the entrance. See him?"

"Oh . . . yeah," Paresi said. "I see him. . . . Jeez, he really blends in, don't he?"

"I'm going by," she said, walking toward the entry gate.

Richard Bamberger stood with a scuzzy-looking group near a bench. They were smoking weed and drinking out of brown paper bags. A ghetto blaster, near one of the men, hurled the sounds of Busta Rhymes across the park.

She strode up the dirty sidewalk toward the group. "You're right," she muttered into the mike. "He does this real good. I think he likes it."

Richie Bamberger, in filthy jeans, motorcycle boots, a dark watch cap, and a tattered army fatigue jacket grinned wolfishly as she approached.

"Hey, mama!" he shouted. "How much to get me someuh that?" The men he was with locked on to her, shouting, whistling, calling out to her.

Star kept walking.

"C'mon, sugarhips," Richie called out. "Talk to me."

She looked over at him and smiled.

The men hooted and howled as if she'd taken off her clothes.

Richie licked his lips and took a few steps toward her.

"C'mon, girl . . . whatchu say?"

Star smiled at him again and flipped him the bird.

The men fell all over themselves laughing at Richie for being shot down.

He responded by grabbing his crotch and wiggling his tongue at her. She turned her head to hide her laughter.

She went through the gates and turned left, heading toward another entry. She could see Paresi on the bench. She walked his way. As she passed, Paresi saw the man trailing a few feet behind her.

"Heads up," he muttered.

"Got him," she said. "Right behind me?"

"Right."

"I caught him earlier, when I was up the street. He was watching for a while."

"Not a problem?" Paresi asked.

"I don't think so," she said. "He's just cruising. I'm not worried."

"He might be nuts."

Star laughed. "Then he fits right in."

"He's moving up," Paresi said.

Star fought the urge to turn and face the man. She let him come to her.

"Hey, baby," she heard him say.

Star could smell the booze on him. She didn't say anything, and kept walking.

"Hey, mama!" the man yelled. "I'm talkin' to you, baybee!" He started to laugh. "C'mon, Boo, don' be like dat."

He ran his words together and attempted to keep step alongside her.

Paresi shifted on the bench, watching them.

She felt the man grab her arm.

She turned, pushing him off. He grabbed her again, holding her arm tightly.

"Get off me, man!" she said, with genuine anger. "Back up!"

"C'mon, Boo." The man grinned stupidly, his hands up. "I just wanna talk a li'l bizness witchu, dat's all, jes a li'l biz."

"Take a walk," she said, moving again toward Paresi.

"C'mon na, baby." The man walked behind her. "Don' treat a brother lak dat! Look." He rammed his hands into his pockets and pulled out a handful of bills. "I got money, Boo. I can take care bizness, hear dat?" He laughed wildly.

"I don't want to hurt this guy," she muttered into her mike. "Do something."

Paresi laughed.

"Thanks," she whispered through clenched teeth.

"C'mon sugah!" The man reached for her again.

She spun, facing him. "Back up off me! Don't follow me. You can't afford it, okay?"

The man raised his hands again and staggered backward, grinning foolishly.

"Hey, babe . . . I jes' wanna mak' us bof happy. . . . You know, I got money, I can do the do, all I need is you wit' yo fine self."

Star turned and walked away.

He followed. "Oooh-wee, girl, you sho' gotta lotta junk in yo' trunk, gon' make me do somethin' wild here." He grabbed her butt.

Star spun around and slapped him. *"Get off me!"*

Paresi grabbed the man from behind.

"Take a hike, man."

"Hey!" The man lurched backward. "Who you?"

"The lady is mine, and she don't wanna play, got it?"

"Hey, baby . . ." The drunk looked at Star. "You got a white *pimp*? Whut up wit' dat?"

"He ain't white," Star said. "He's Italian . . . Sicilian, you know, the crazy ones that'll cut your throat soon as look at you." She drew her finger across her neck, then pointed it at Paresi. "He's crazy, man. He'll cut you!"

"Naw, shit!" The man turned a drunken gaze on Paresi and said something fast and low.

"What did he say?" Paresi turned to Star.

"He said, he ain't out for no trouble," Star said. "He just wants to play, that's all."

Paresi grinned at her. "You understand him?"

"Sure."

They both laughed. The man stood weaving, grinning drunkenly.

"Tell him, Boo, tell him I be living large tonight, jes' wanna have some fun."

"What did he say?"

"I do believe the gentleman is speaking Ebonics," Star said. "Complicated by the fact that he's speaking it in the dialect of Drunk!"

Paresi laughed. "Hey, I've been known to speak a little Drunk myself," he said. "But that's Sicilian Drunk, I guess it's different."

"For sure," Star said.

The man leaned forward, and his breath nearly knocked her flat.

"C'mon, Boo, I'ma fool for a woman wit' junk in the trunk. . . ."

"Junk in the trunk?" Paresi said.

"He likes my butt," Star said.

"Hey, man." Paresi shook the drunk gently. "That's my girl, okay, and she costs more than you make, so move on. Okay, pal?"

"I dunno," the man said. "Y'all don't know what I got. Name yo' price."

"Two hundred thousand dollars," Star said, with a straight face.

"Two hunnert dollas?" The man looked surprised. He reached into his pocket and produced a thick lump of bills. "Hey, I got dat!"

The detectives looked at one another.

"I'll finish this," Star said. She took a deep breath, held it, and stepped toe-to-toe with the man.

"Two hundred *thousand* dollars," she said slowly, "then you got to *suck my dick!*"

Paresi burst out laughing.

"What?" The drunk looked surprised.

Star turned her head, took another breath, and got back in his face.

"You got to suck my dick." She leaned so close, she could see his pores. "I'm a *guy*, asshole!"

"Aw naw!" The man backed up. "Aw naw!"

Star reached for her fly. "Wanna see?"

The man weaved drunkenly, stumbling backward. "Naw, shit! I ain't into no freaky-deaky. Naw . . . nooooo baby, you got the wrong man. . . . I'm all man, don' be doin' no fag shit."

"Then get to steppin'," Star said, her voice two octaves deeper than usual.

"Ain't gotta tell me twice." The man stepped back. He looked at Paresi. "Shouldda figured dat shit out for my *damn* self. . . . Yo' pimp near bout pretty as you is."

"Thanks," Paresi said. "But between us . . ." He pointed to Star. "He's got the big ones. Solid brass." He grinned at Star. "C'mon, baby, jump up and down. Let the man hear 'em."

Star cracked up.

The drunk shook his head and staggered away across the grass.

"Poor bastard," Paresi grinned. "We really screwed up his evening."

"Let's make it up to him by saving his life," Star said. "He's got a lot of money on him."

"I'll holler out for the squad to pick him up," Paresi said.

Star watched the man staggering through the trees. "Good. Somebody's bound to beat him senseless and take his money. And I think he's had enough for one night." She looked at Paresi. "What time is it?"

He looked at his watch. "A little after two."

"We haven't seen any Bromleigh kids, and the girls have been getting into cars with *men*, no fresh faces. I'd say this night has been a wash," she said.

"I agree." Paresi took her arm and began walking her deeper into the park, toward their car, parked on the other side, near the decimated bandstand. They stopped in the darkness, where they could still see the man. Paresi pulled out his cell phone and punched in 911.

"Police Emergency."

"This is Sergeant Paresi, Seventeenth, Homicide."

"Go, Sarge," the dispatcher answered.

"Get the route guys over on the east side of Saint Francis Park, we got a D.K., African American male, wearing a gray jacket and dark pants. He's carrying a wad of cash."

"He's down," Star said.

"He just took a flop, face plant on the green, near the gate by the fountain. Forget the squad, send the wagon."

"On the way, Sarge."

Paresi looked at Star. "I say we hang for a minute, until they pick him up."

She pulled the collar of her jacket up. "Okay."

"Cold?" her partner asked.

Star hunched her shoulders. "Freezing," she said.

"Hey, you coulda had two hundred dollars, bought you a warmer coat," Paresi teased.

"Lucky me," Star said, shivering. She looked at him. "Are you going to give me your jacket?"

"What? You think *I'm* a gentleman?" Paresi laughed. "Come here." He pulled her into his arms. "Isn't this better? Now we *both* stay warm."

They stood, arms around each other, watching the fallen form of the man near the trees.

"So do we do this again tomorrow?" Paresi said.

"I'm game," Star nodded. "Maybe we'll have better luck. Tomorrow's Friday, kids are out of school for the weekend. Should be more action." She looked at him. "And I'm wearing long johns!"

Paresi laughed. "As long as Lewis doesn't hear about what we're doing, I guess we can make another run." He hugged her tighter. "You know, if he finds out we're out here without his permission, we'll be working the park for real."

"I heard that," Star said.

The sound of the sirens made them turn toward the gate. The white police wagon, blue lights flashing, roared past them, around the bend, heading for the fountain.

"They got him," Star said.

"Right, let's book." Paresi put his arm around her shoulder, and they continued their walk toward the car.

"You know, you're crazy," Star said, putting her arm around his waist.

"What did I do?"

"Jump up and down, let me hear 'em!" She laughed.

Paresi grinned. "Hey, just going with the flow, my man. Just going with the flow."

CHAPTER TWENTY-FOUR

The second night in the park was colder than the first. Star pulled her faux leopard coat tighter around her body, and congratulated herself on her decision to augment her outfit with knit tights and a leotard. The extra layer worn beneath her black pants and tan crewneck sweater provided all the warmth she needed. A black beret, again worn low over her right ear, hid her listening device.

She'd bought the hip-length swingline wrap coat a few years back. Whenever she wore it, Vee referred to her as "Sheena, Queen of the Jungle." Still, she liked the coat, especially the way it swung out from her body. It reminded her of the coats Lucille Ball wore on the old *I Love Lucy* series. Besides, the fullness of it hid the bulge of the 9mm Baretta nestled in her shoulder holster.

Across the street, Paresi was on a bench, earphones on, his Walkman tuned in to pick up her every breath.

"Maybe we should head back over to the other side of the park," she muttered. "There's absolutely nothing happening over here."

Across the street, Paresi nodded nearly imperceptibly.

"Gurl, you betta git yo' ass off my turf."

Star turned.

A small, butterscotch-colored woman, wearing a too-big, Tina Turner–style wig, thigh-high white lace stockings, tight black leather hotpants, and a white rabbit fur jacket, stood, arms folded, tapping her five-inch, open-toed, black ankle strap shoes.

"Jasmine?" Star said.

"Lieutenan' Duvall, dat 'chu?" The woman moved closer,

141

peering into Star's face. "Gurl, what 'chu doin' out heah? I know cops don' make no money, but chile, things ain't dat bad, is dey?"

Star laughed. "I'm not working, Jas. I'm looking for something."

The woman moved closer. Star smelled a mixture of malt liquor and mint on her breath.

"You lookin' fo' da som'bitch been killin' peoples out heah in da park, righ'?"

Star nodded. "Got anything you can tell me?"

Jasmine shook her head, making the champagne-colored, spiky wig bounce. "Ain' nobody see nothin'."

"So what else is new?" Star said. "Let me ask you something, Jas."

"Whatchu need, honey?"

"Do you know anything about some of the girls getting picked up by boys from Bromleigh?"

The woman shrugged her shoulders. "Naw, I mean I hurd some o'dem otha hoes, ain't workin' wif my man, I hurd dey do boys sometime. Silk wouldn' put up wif dat kina shit, un-nerstan? Don' like nobody messin' wif kids."

"Any of the boys ever approach you?"

Jasmine's wig seesawed with the shaking of her head. "A couple, but I jes' tol you, I don' do no chillren!"

Star nodded. "I understand that, Jas, I'm just trying to follow up on some information. Is there anything you can tell me?"

Jasmine stepped closer to Star, lowering her voice to nearly a whisper. "Na, dis ain't me, but I kno' sometime, dem boys be takin' gurls off da stroll fo' som freaky pardy shit."

"Do you know where they go?"

Jasmine shrugged. "Don' axe me, I don' be in dat shit." She sniffled, and wiped her leaky nose with the back of her hand. " 'Sides, I don' do chillren, Lieutenan', I got kids mysef." She pulled her rabbit fur tight. " 'Sides, I heah dem boys likes to draw blood, and I ain't inta dat."

"Thanks, Jas. I didn't mean to insult you."

"You didn', I knows you jes' has to axe some 'barrassing stuff sometime, don' botha me. Shit, if I can help git dis mothafucka off da street, gurl, I ansa you buck nekkid an tap dancin', ain' nobody be insult."

"Thanks. Now move on and keep your big mouth shut."

"Oh, gurl . . . honey . . ." The woman grinned, showing large white false teeth. "Chile, I ain't gonna mess up nuttin'. I jes' tol you I wantchu' to git the bastid, but I gotta tell you somethin', sweetie."

"What's that?" Star said.

Jasmine backed up, waving her hands toward Star. "You got on too much . . . can't nobody see nuttin'. Dem pants gots to go. You gotta show som' meat." Her dark eyes traveled down to Star's comfortable, flat-heeled, black loafers. "An' honey, I know you tall, but 'chu need 'chu som' heels on." She reached out and touched Star's fake leopard coat. "But I gots to say, I likes dis. . . . Whar you git it?"

"Nolan's," Star said.

"Izzit real?"

"If it were, I'd have to arrest myself. . . . Now move, Jas."

The woman nodded, and the wig slid toward her left eye.

"I'm gon', jus' tell me sumpin'."

"What?"

"Where is Officer Cutie?"

"Who?"

"Yo' pardna', dat fine man you work wif . . . Paresi."

Across the street, on the park bench, Paresi waved.

"Ooooh, I din't even see him over dere. . . . Gurl, he look lak a stone O.G." She licked her shiny orange-lipsticked mouth. "But he sho' is pretty!"

"I'm sure he's pleased," Star said. "It's always been his ambition to be taken for a gangbanger."

"Mm-hmm . . ." Jasmine pulled her jacket tighter, looking at Paresi. "Gurl, he can bang me anytime, all night lon' to the breaka dawn, and fo' free!"

On the bench, Paresi pretended to mull it over. Star laughed.

Jasmine waved at him, grinning from ear to ear, showing those huge false teeth.

Star remembered a time when Jasmine had all her own

teeth, but heroin takes a lot from you, including your beauty and your teeth.

"Move on, Jas, and don't say anything about me being out here."

The woman turned back to Star and nodded, knowingly.

"Silk knowed it wuz you when he see'd you. He tol' me it was you, but I din't see yo' face, so I say uh-uh. But he say sho' t'was you."

Star looked at her. "Will he give me up?"

"Naw gurl, he wonts the bastid bust up too. Silk say he cuttin' inna bizness." She tugged again on her rabbit fur. "You know how rough it is out heah. A gurl always got to be watchin' herssef, but wif' dat crazy old woman and den Dolores turnin' up dead, honey . . . nobody wont to be peddlin' no pussy, we wonts to be home, safe wit our chillren."

"I'm working on it," Star said.

"You go, Lieutenan'." She patted Star's shoulder. "Dis my spot, but I'ma let 'chu have it tonight."

"Thanks."

Jasmine started to walk away, but turned on her high heels and teetered back.

"You do better if you sho mo' stuff," she whispered.

"One more time—" Star smiled. "—I'm not working, Jas."

"Still, you tryin' ta catch a freak, baby. You needs to bait yo' trap. Dog'll go for raw meat, not nuthin' all covered up."

"It's cold," Star said.

Jasmine pressed her large orange lips together. "Now you know, you ain't never lied. My ass so cold, my pussy done friz up. I can't work nothin' but my mouf."

Across the street, Paresi laughed.

"Do he hear me?"

"Everything you say."

The woman covered her face with her hands.

"Whydnt you tell me, Lieutenan'? *Now* I embarrass."

Two hours later, the action in the park slowed down. A few cars cruised the streets, but most of the women had disappeared, either going home or settling into someplace warm

for coffee and maybe a hit in a bathroom. Across from the
stroll, Paresi sat on the bench, his arms folded.

"You look cold," Star said.

"If I stay out here much longer, I'll be like Jas," he said, "all
friz up . . . the end of the Paresi line."

Star chuckled. "I hear you. It's dead, let's call it a night."

"Done." He stood and stretched, his body stiff with cold.

A scream rang out, followed by a gunshot.

"Gun!" The detectives yelled simultaneously. Star spun
in the direction of the sound, whipping her 9mm Baretta
from its shoulder holster. She dropped, crouching close to the
sidewalk.

Paresi sprinted across the street, Glock in hand. He
dropped alongside her.

"From the bushes," he whispered, pointing into the darkness to her left. "Over there."

Another scream pierced the night. They ran low, guns
drawn, in the direction of the yelling.

Crouched in the bushes, the detectives could see the woman
on her knees. She was a small Hispanic woman, wearing a
short red jacket and skirt. Her legs sported thigh-high, candy-
striped red and white tights. Over the tights she wore white
anklets with lacy trim. On her feet were a pair of red spiked
high heels. Star could see the toes of her shoes digging into
the dirt.

Her hair was long and dark, parted down the middle. One
of her red-ribbon-wrapped ponytails was being wrenched
tightly in the hand of the man holding the gun.

He pointed the weapon at her temple. "My next one gon'
be in yo' fuckin' head, bitch! I want my money!" He yanked
roughly on her long hair.

The woman screamed. "Willie . . . I din't make nothin', I
swear!"

"Gimme my money!" The short, slightly overweight, light-
skinned man ripped at her hair again.

Star motioned for Paresi to go to the other side of the
thicket. Staying low, he moved through the bushes.

Willie Chester's head shot up, like a gazelle grazing near a pride of lions. He listened. His long, Al Sharpton–styled, processed hair stood out from his neck.

Though he was moving as quietly as possible, Star could hear Paresi. She bit her bottom lip and took aim, just in case.

"Who in there?" the man yelled, craning his neck, looking behind him, still twisting the woman's hair.

Paresi stepped from the bushes, zipping his fly.

"Hey, man, just taking a leak, that's all." He raised his hands in the air. "You ain't gonna kill me for having to piss, are you?"

Star couldn't see Willie Chester's face, only his hair and the gleam of moonlight shining off the muzzle of the gun in his hand.

A twenty-two, she said to herself. You got to get right up on the target to do any damage. Paresi, her mind screamed, don't get any closer!

As if he heard her thoughts, her partner took a small step back.

At that moment, the woman in Chester's grip screamed in agony and raked her nails into the hand holding her hair. Willie Chester shouted and raised his arm to strike her with the gun.

Paresi's Glock was in his hand so fast, it seemed like an illusion. "Drop the gun," Paresi said, moving to Chester's left, making the man turn to see him.

Willie Chester looked confused. "What? What is this?"

Star rounded the bushes and stepped into the clearing.

"He said, drop the gun."

Willie Chester looked around, directly into the barrel of Star's Baretta.

The woman on the ground looked at her through pain-filled eyes. She gulped back sobs but didn't scream.

"Look, I don't wanna kill nobody," Willie Chester said, holding the gun pointed up. " 'Cept this bitch here." He yanked on the woman's hair. A low moan came from her. "I ain't out for no trouble. Y'all look like you doin' jes what I'm doin'." He turned toward Paresi, at the same time trying to twist in such a way that he could keep an eye on Star. She stepped back, toward his right, disappearing from his peripheral vision. "She yo' girl, right?" he said to Paresi.

Paresi didn't answer, he just moved again, to the left. Willie turned farther toward him. Star moved in closer.

"Tell yo' bitch to back off, man. Tell her this my bizness," he yelled. "It ain't got nothin' to do wit her, okay, man? We down, we unnerstan' one another, right? We bof bizness mens, ain't we? No need for nobody to be gettin' hurt, right?"

"Put the gun down," Star said.

Willie Chester turned to look at her.

"Bitch . . . you better git yo' ass gone fo' you get . . ."

Paresi tackled him from the side. Willie's grip on the woman's hair opened. Like a puppet on broken strings, she slumped down face first, wailing and crying out in Spanish.

The pistol flew from Willie's hand and landed on the grass a few feet away as they went down. Dominic wrestled the man over on his stomach and handcuffed him.

Star moved in, her weapon aimed at Willie's head. She took the badge from her pocket, and flipped the black leather fold-over cover with one hand. She waved the shining gold emblem in Willie's face. "That's Lieutenant Bitch to you," she said.

"What the fuck?" Willie Chester muttered through the dirt, pebbles, and grass in his mouth. He spat. "What the fuck is this?" he yelled. "You two fuckers tryin'na kill me? I wanna lawyer, hear me? I wanna lawyer right now!"

"Shut up." Paresi hauled the man to his feet. "You have the right to remain silent. So use it before you piss me off!" He shoved Willie toward the sidewalk.

Star holstered her weapon, slipped a tissue from her pocket, and carefully picked up Willie's gun. She checked the safety and put it in her pocket, then went to the woman. "You all right?" she said.

The woman reached out, trying to grab her, pull her close.

Star backed up, as the woman screamed in Spanish.

"I'm sorry," she said. "I don't understand you . . . no comprende . . . no comprende." She helped the woman stand. "Come with me."

"He . . . he kill me." The woman sobbed, clinging to Star.

"Damn right I'ma kill you, bitch!" Willie Chester yelled over his shoulder. "Yo frijole, taco-eating, worm-drinkin' ass is dead!"

"Shut up!" Paresi said, shoving Willie against a lamppost. "I can't hear myself think." He pulled out his cell phone and called for the wagon.

Willie kept muttering. "Gon' get a lawyer, punk. Gon' sue yo' ass good! You an' that bitch."

Paresi shoved the phone back into his jacket.

"One more sound, Willie, and I'm gonna knock out all those pretty gold teeth."

"He threatened me!" Willie yelled toward the small crowd gathered near the curb. *"He threatened me!"*

Paresi looked at the park regulars.

"Like they give a fuck, Willie. Notice how quick they called for help when you were scalpin' your girlfriend back there."

He turned to Star. "I'd say this undercover gig is over."

CHAPTER TWENTY-FIVE

Paresi was about finished with his second Floogie's Famous Burger when Frank McCoy pulled up a chair and sat down with the two detectives.

McCoy, having heard about the fiasco in the park the night before, called Paresi that morning, claiming he had information that might help them. Dominic hadn't wanted to deal with him, but he knew they needed to hear whatever the man had to say. McCoy's information was usually dead on. He had a network of snitches that most cops wouldn't spit on. The worst of the street scum all called Frank McCoy "friend."

Paresi looked at him. He had some stones for walking into

a cop bar, with his rep. But then, this guy was the kind of sick puppy that got off on being hated. He was a bad cop, and a coward.

As he approached, Paresi thought back to his third year on the job. It was about that time that McCoy had turned his back and let his partner go down in a failed undercover sting. He lied his way out of it, but everybody knew he'd hauled ass when the shots rang out. He left Roscoe Ballard to die, choking on his own blood on the floor of a filthy shooting gallery.

The only reason he hadn't caught a bullet from his own was the unspoken rule of cops protecting cops. Still, he was outcast, frozen out of the department and treated like a pariah.

Paresi watched him. McCoy walked with his head up, actually waving and nodding at a few of the guys. None acknowledged him, though they all stared.

Still, Paresi knew that just about every "blue" in the house had gotten solid information from McCoy. After IA cleared him in Roscoe's death, no one would go near him. In an effort to redeem himself, he became adept at aligning with some of the worst scum in the city. Through this unholy network of snitches, he amassed a great deal of information that went into solving some of the city's biggest cases.

Still, the departments, citywide, regarded McCoy as an insect. Most of his fellow officers wouldn't piss on him if he were on fire. But he'd served nearly twenty years and he deserved his pension. They just wanted him gone.

McCoy saw Paresi at a table near the back of the darkened room. He knew all eyes were on him, so he waved and nodded. No one blinked. It was okay. McCoy knew he was hated, but there was nothing anybody could do about it.

They liked to squeeze his shoes, give him the evil eye, spit when he walked past, but in the end, there was nothing any of them could do to hurt him. It became a game for him. He loved flaunting himself in places where cops hung out. That's why he chose to meet Paresi at Floogie's. Besides, he knew Paresi's partner would come with him, and there she sat. As he neared, Star turned in her chair, facing away from him.

Across the bar, Star locked eyes with Annie Wilson, an undercover Bunco officer from the Two-Five. Like practically every other female on the force, she'd had her run-ins with Frank McCoy. Detective Wilson grimaced as he passed her seat. Star nodded almost imperceptibly, agreeing with the disgust in Annie's dark eyes.

McCoy caught the eye action from the both of them. It didn't matter. Political correctness be damned, he still thought the only position for a woman on or off the job was on her back or her knees.

Star despised him, but the case came first, and she wasn't about to let Paresi walk into that bastard's web alone. She sat nursing a Pepsi loaded with ice and lemon. She hadn't trusted herself to eat, the sight of McCoy just might make her bring it up again. As she watched him approach, she realized that the decision had been a good one. She turned in her seat, away from him, now fastening her gaze on the sign hanging over the bar. The bright yellow neon had been shaped into a police badge. Under which, in bright blue letters was the word PIG. Beneath that, also in blue, were the words, PRIDE-INTEGRITY-GUTS.

McCoy pulled out the chair next to Paresi and sat down.

"McCoy." Paresi pushed aside the remains of his Floogie Burger with cheddar cheese, mushrooms, and grilled onions.

"Dom." Frank McCoy nodded at Paresi and turned his attention to Star. "How are you, *Ms.* Duvall?" He smiled.

Star stared straight ahead.

McCoy laughed. "Well, whaddya know, she won't even say hello to me. I must be *annoying* her."

Star turned in her chair. Her pale, amber-colored eyes regarded him as if he were an insect on a windshield.

His smile widened. Star thought of hyenas on the Serengeti. She said nothing.

"Tell your partner she's looking very lovely today," McCoy said to Paresi.

Paresi took a sip of his 7UP. "Get to the point. We don't have the time or the stomach to stay around you."

McCoy raised his hands in front of him. "Just making conversation, that's all."

Paresi glared at him.

"I hear you're sniffing around, looking for info on the ass-holes that mighta been in on the hag-burning and that hooker that got dead up there the other night."

"Your message said you had information. Spill it and get gone," Paresi said.

"In time, in time." McCoy leered at Star. "Tell your partner if she's nice to me, I could turn this whole case around for the both of you."

Paresi wiped his mouth with his napkin and shook his head. "Frankie, Frankie, Frankie." He leaned back, smiling at the man. "When are you gonna learn? The *Lieutenant* is here for the same reason as me, trying to solve a case, so why do you think you have to insult her? She hasn't spit in your face, and the way I see it, that's pretty gracious of her.

"Don't you know she's got the power to have your sorry ass working out your last days, cleaning puke and shit outta the wagons? What makes you think you have the right to roll in here and say something like that?"

McCoy shrugged. "What can I say?" His gaze fastened on Star, a reptilian smile crossing his thin face. "She brings out the beast in me."

Star stood up. "I'll be at the bar," she said to Paresi, and walked away.

Frank watched her cross the crowded room.

"I got such a hard-on right now. How do you stand it, Dom? I'd give my left nut to see her naked." He turned. "Tell the truth, you ever put it to her?"

"Stugotz," Paresi muttered.

McCoy grinned at him.

Paresi could see how much McCoy was enjoying this. He laced his hands together and cracked his knuckles, calming his urge to punch the guy. "Frankie, I try to respect you 'cause you're a cop, same as us. We all know you done some shitty things, and I'm trying not to think about how much I hate you. But I gotta tell you, one more remark about my partner and I'm gonna reach down your throat and drag your asshole out through your nose, got it?"

McCoy smirked at Paresi. "C'mon, man, you can't tell me you never thought about doin' her." He snorted. "Word is you have! Lots of times. Now I hear she's givin' it up for that rich bastard in the ME's office. How do you feel about that? She ever do both you guys together?"

On his feet, Paresi grabbed McCoy by the neck and yanked him out of the chair.

"C'mon, Frank, we're going outside. I don't wanna get your stinking blood on Danny's floor." He started dragging the man toward the door.

"*Hey!* Ease up, Dominic!" McCoy tried to pry Paresi's hands from around his neck. "Ease up! I'm sorry," he croaked. "I'm sorry."

Paresi threw him back in the chair. From the bar, Star watched.

"That's it, that fuck's outta here!" Dan Leahy, the retired Vice Sergeant who owned Floogie's, reached beneath the bar and came up with a gleamingly polished, mint condition, Louisville Slugger baseball bat. His first week on the job he'd taken it off of a drunken factory worker, intent on using it to crease his crew cut. Dan had kept it ever since, and now the bat resided at Floogie's.

"No, Dan." Star grabbed his arm. "Let Paresi handle it. He's not going to let it go on much longer."

Leahy laid the heavy piece of polished wood on the bar. "Okay, but if that fucker jumps one more time—" He indicated the bat. "—he's gonna be kissing baby."

Back at the table, aware of the eyes on him, Frank righted himself in the chair, trying to straighten his collar and retrieve what paltry dignity he had.

Paresi sat down, stone-faced. "You got something useful to say . . . say it, or get to steppin' before I rack your balls on the pool table."

The man breathed hard, and beads of sweat appeared on his face.

"Okay . . . okay." He took Star's half-empty glass of Pepsi and drank from it. He looked at Paresi. Dominic's eyes were a cold, dark blue.

"Years ago, I used to patrol over there."

"Yeah . . ." Paresi said. "So?"

"So there's an empty building just off campus, near the end of the park. It used to be part of the school, a lab of some kind. About ten, twelve years ago, the school sold off some of that property and closed the lab."

"And the importance of this is?"

McCoy cleared his throat, coughed, and took another sip of Star's soda.

"Once it was sold and shut down, the powers-that-be over at the school sort of forgot about the place, but sometimes the kids use it for a place to make out. Lately, I got word from some of the girls that Bromleigh boys are hiring hookers and takin' 'em over there for parties."

"Parties? What kinda parties?"

"A few of the girls claim that some of those little shits are into devil worship or something. They said some of the whores have been having weird blood rituals over there."

"Is the building visible from the campus?"

McCoy shook his head. "No . . . It's over behind the spot where the old rose gardens used to be. It's all covered with ivy and the area's overgrown. Go down to the back side of Felton Street, the park kinda doglegs there. Take a left, for about a block. Then you gotta walk a couple of yards, and you'll see the path. Like I said, it's overgrown, but if you know where to look, you'll find it."

"Okay." Paresi nodded at the man. "That it?"

Frank stood. "Yeah."

"Thanks."

McCoy picked up Star's glass and looked across the room, where she sat, watching him. He gazed at her and drained the soda, slowly snaking his tongue down inside the glass, licking it.

Paresi jumped to his feet. "You son of a bitch!"

Leahy grabbed his bat and leapt over the bar.

Paresi spun McCoy around, throwing him facedown onto the table. Plates and glasses shattered on the floor.

Paresi shoved Frank's face into the wood and yanked the man's arm up sharply behind him. "You just can't help it, can you, asshole?" Still holding McCoy's wrist, Paresi grabbed the man's thumb and bent it backward, applying a pressure that made McCoy scream.

Paresi pulled him up and hustled him toward the front door. "Still hungry, Frank?" He bent the man's thumb again. McCoy yelped, and rose up on his toes. "Wanna eat something? I'm gonna help you. I'm gonna rip your goddamn arm off and feed it to you, you miserable fuck!"

Leahy came up with the bat, his face reddened and contorted in his rage. "Get outta my bar, asshole!" he shouted. "Don't never come in here again, hear me?" He opened the door and Paresi shoved the officer out to the street.

Frank McCoy stumbled and fell against a parked car. Paresi was on him, pinning him against the dark sedan, his forearm across the man's throat, his knee against the man's groin.

"You listen to me, cocksucker. Cop or no cop, you even so much as *look* at my partner again, I'll shoot your fuckin' eyes out . . . got that?"

The man nodded.

Paresi smiled. "That's some boner you got there Frank. A guy your age should be proud." He put his weight on the knee that rested against McCoy's crotch. The man howled in pain.

"Oops . . . looks like you lost it!" Paresi shoved him to the ground and walked back into the bar.

Leahy waved the baseball bat. "You're banned, you fuck! Hear me? Banned! Don't never put your foot near my place again, *never*!"

Paresi walked back to the table. Around the room, cops applauded and whistled.

"Knock it off, you guys." Paresi's face looked dark. "I was just puttin' out the garbage."

Star approached him. "Thank you," she said, taking his hand. "I appreciate what you did."

He nodded at her, the anger in his face draining away with her touch. "It's okay . . . it's okay."

Leahy came back inside. "You all right, Dom?"

"Fine," Paresi said.

"The way you went over that bar!" Star patted him on the shoulder. "Wow! You still got it, Danny."

The man smiled.

"Yeah," Paresi said. "Thanks for the backup."

"Anytime." Dan Leahy nodded. "Nobody's gonna come in my place and insult another cop, especially Lenny Duvall's kid."

He turned to Star. "Your father was one of the best guys to ever wear the blue, and you been nothing but his kid, all the way down the line. Nobody's gonna mess with you in here."

"Thanks, Dan," Star said.

The older man put an arm around her. "It's okay. If things was different and I wasn't around, I know Lenny would be watching out for my girls. I'm just doing what he would have done for me."

"Thank you."

Paresi reached for his wallet. "Guess I'm buying you some new dishes, Danny."

Dan raised his hand.

"Forget about that. Your money's no good in here."

"Thanks." Paresi put his wallet back in his pocket. "If McCoy comes back, let me know."

Leahy looked at the door.

"He ain't comin' back. Believe me, he ain't never comin' back."

CHAPTER TWENTY-SIX

Star lay sleeping in Mitch's arms. When she had arrived at the penthouse that evening, he could see she was the walking wounded. So instead of going out, he decided they would stay in.

He made one of her favorite dinners—lime-grilled chicken and linguine with roasted eggplant and fresh tomato sauce.

After they ate, she told him what had happened that afternoon between Paresi and Frank McCoy.

Mitch had a very short list of people he honestly disliked, and Frank McCoy was at the top. He was looking forward to the day McCoy would show up on one of his steel tables. After what Star told him, he wanted it to be sooner rather than later.

After McCoy left his partner Roscoe Ballard to die during the shoot-out that followed their sting gone wrong, Mitch had performed Ballard's autopsy.

The man was the father to three children, with one on the way, when Frank bailed on him. It was one of the most painful cases Grant had to work as medical examiner. Cops on his table always broke his heart, but for Frank McCoy, he'd order up cake and champagne.

After they talked, he took her upstairs. The massage he'd given her had quickly escalated into fiercely passionate love-making that had left them both exhausted and beyond satisfaction. Now he was awake and she lay sleeping in his arms. They lay on their sides, her back against his chest, his body wrapped spoonlike around hers.

Moonlight shone through the floor-to-ceiling windows. Mitch loved looking out at the night sky and waking to sun-filled mornings. His windows were high enough that privacy was not a concern, and so he kept the drapes open. Light from the moon flooded the bedroom, casting a silvery glow on their naked bodies, making them gleam in the darkness.

Mitch rested his head against her shoulder, listening to her breathe, matching his breath with hers. He ran his hand lightly down her bare arm. Star sighed in her sleep and snuggled closer to him.

Mitch looked at his pale hand against her dark, lustrous skin and marveled at the difference in their colors.

His long fingers fanned out toward her shoulder. The moon tracked the movement, making her skin glow beneath his touch. He moved his hand slowly over her back, savoring the softness of her skin. He kissed her shoulder, her neck, in-haling deeply of her scent. A warm sweetness, blended with Shalimar perfume and womanly satisfaction.

His mind went to Frank McCoy and what he'd done. "Poor bastard," Mitch muttered against her shoulder. "This woman is so out of your league." He kissed her again.

Star moaned slightly. Mitch raised up on his elbow, and looked down at her face. She was still sleeping. He kissed her cheek and lay back, holding her. He closed his eyes and let his hand continue its slow exploration. Gently, tenderly, his fingers found her breasts. He cupped them, first one and then the other, softly squeezing, loving the feel of the weight in his palm. She sighed in her sleep and moved against him.

A ripple of electricity went through him, making his body tremble against hers. He squeezed one of her breasts again, marveling at its supple, comforting softness. He moved his thumb over her nipple, until it stood, warm and pliant under his gentle stroke. Mitch sucked in his breath, holding it, trying to control himself. Slowly, he breathed out, trying to quiet the pounding desire racing though his body.

The feel of her back against his chest was warm and gratifying. She fit him. Sudden thoughts of other women, with whom he'd lain in this room, in this bed, filled his mind. He banished them all from his memories. This was the woman he wanted in his bed for the rest of his life.

He raised up again and looked down at her. He kissed her again and lay back, burying his face in the skin at the nape of her neck, again inhaling her, filling himself with her.

He closed his eyes and thought of the way she'd listened to him when he told her about Livvy and his mother. He had been amazed to hear those words coming from his mouth. He told her things he had never shared with anyone, not even his ex-wife, Carole Ann. It was as if her caring, her warmth, all of it opened him. When she sat, quietly hugging him, listening to him, he felt something he'd always thought a myth, nonexistent, at least in his life.

There had been so many women, so much mad lust, so much expendable passion, but no love. And now, with this woman, this unpredictable, funny, tough, sweet woman whom he'd known and wanted for years, this woman who could see his soul, close up, and not run screaming, this woman had opened him, totally.

All of the love and need he'd buried for so many years hit him hard. So hard he nearly cried. He had to be with her, to be as close to her as possible. To be inside of her, be a part of her body. Reason was gone, control was gone.

Mitch moved Star's leg with his own, and used his body to find her center.

Sighing deeply, with his eyes closed, he slipped inside of her. The feel of her opening, even in sleep, to accept him overcame him with so much emotion, tears rushed to his eyes. Part of him felt guilt for this extraordinary pleasure he was taking, but he couldn't have stopped if his life depended on it.

Mitch held her against him, his heart pounding. His eyes closed. Just when he thought he was going to come apart, and be forever absorbed inside her, she laughed.

"You're awake," he said softly, against her shoulder.

"And you're sneaky," she said, moving back against him. "Just how much fun can this be, without me?"

She felt his smile on her flesh.

"You'd be surprised," he said.

"Oh yeah? Well, consider yourself busted." She moved away and rolled over, settling herself astride him. "You have to be punished, you know that?"

She forced his arms over his head, pinning him, holding him down by his wrists.

Mitch smiled as she leaned close to him. Her breasts, reflecting the moonlight, grazed his chest. The strength with which she held him both surprised and aroused him.

She kissed him, and murmured in his ear. "You got to pay, baby."

Beneath her, Mitch whispered. "Punish me," he said. "Show no mercy."

CHAPTER TWENTY-SEVEN

Paresi set a white paper bag on his desk and opened it. He put a tall, red-and-gray disposable cup, topped with a high white plastic lid on Star's desk and removed an identical cup for himself.

Next to Star's cup, he placed a chocolate croissant, wrapped in thin white paper. He put the other white-wrapped pastry on his desk and sat down.

He looked at the clock. It was fifteen minutes past eight A.M. Star was late. Paresi unwrapped his pastry, an almond-covered concoction filled with apples. He'd just taken a bite of it, and the first sip of his cappuccino, when he noticed the small white envelope propped against his desk lamp. He opened it. Inside, on thick white card stock, was a typewritten note.

> Your "theater" in the park the other night was riveting. The climax was most exciting. In appreciation for such fine entertainment, a gift for you and your partner has been left in the parking garage, near the elevator on the second level. My thanks for such an exciting show. Enjoy it.

"What?" he muttered.

"Sorry I'm late," Star said, tucking her purse into the bottom drawer of her desk. "I slept like a rock." She looked at the coffee and pastry. "For me?" She removed the top of the disposable cup. "Ooh, latte." She unwrapped the pastry. "A chocolate croissant. Paresi, if it weren't for Mitchell and Vee, I'd marry you." She pointed to the note in his hand. "Fan mail?"

Her partner hadn't even noticed that she was standing in front of him.

"Hey." She waved her hand at him.

He looked up. "Hi . . ."

"Thanks for breakfast." She inhaled the rich fragrance of the coffee. "Perfect start to a rainy day. Mmm, I do believe I'm becoming a latte junkie." She stirred the frothy crown and sipped her drink. "What is that?" Again, she indicated the note in his hand.

"A present," he said, handing it to her.

Star read it. "I just came from the garage."

"Did you by any chance go up to level two?" Paresi asked.

"Nope," she said, and wiped her hands on a paper napkin. "Let's go check it out."

The two detectives headed for the double doors.

Inside the parking garage, they ran up the stairs leading to the second level. Near the door to the elevator everything seemed normal.

"I don't see anything," Star said. "Do you?"

"Uh-uh." Paresi looked behind a pillar near the elevator door.

"Think we've just got some kinda screwball on us?"

Paresi shrugged. "I don't know. But I do know that whoever wrote that note caught our action in the park the other night."

"And it looks like they brought the note right into the station," Star said.

"Right," Paresi agreed. "There was no sign of it having been mailed. It was on my desk when I got in this morning."

"Well, obviously it got us to the garage, but why?"

Paresi walked to the other side of the elevator door. "I don't know. There's nothing here that I can see."

"Where's your car?" she asked.

"In my spot. Where's yours?"

"I didn't drive in today, Mitchell gave me a ride. I had him drop me in the garage to avoid getting soaked, *and* the gossip patrol."

"So your space is empty?"

She looked at him. "Uh-huh."

They headed for the stairwell. On the first level they hurried to the space with LT. S. DUVALL lettered on the gray concrete floor.

In the center of Star's parking space sat a large, robin's egg blue camper-sized cooler. A white ribbon, topped with a big white bow, was wrapped around it.

"I don't like this," she said.

Paresi reached into his pocket and pulled out his cell phone. He dialed a number.

"This is Sergeant Paresi, ring Special Weapons."

"You think this is a bomb?"

"I'm not taking any chances. I'm not opening it, and neither are you. This is what they do, so let them handle it."

Star watched her partner. She saw the muscle twitch in his jaw as he waited for someone to answer. Paresi was rattled, and it was contagious. She felt her flesh creep.

He spoke into the phone. "Yeah, hi, Sergeant Thomas, this is Dominic Paresi. Star Duvall and I are down here in the parking garage. There's something here in her space. It's a package and it looks suspicious. Could we get somebody to come down here and open it?"

Star watched him pace as he talked. "I don't know, it just looks strange. . . . Yeah, thanks." Paresi clicked off and put the phone back in his pocket. "They're on the way."

Arriving quickly, the special weapons team cordoned off the area around Star's parking space and carefully moved in on the package. When the cooler top was removed, a thin white vapor curled out of the opening. Paresi put his arm around Star and pulled her against him.

Charlie Cosgrove removed his protective head gear and mask. He stood up. "Lieutenant."

"Yeah, Charlie?"

He took off his thick gloves and beckoned to her. "I think you oughta see this."

Star could tell by the look on Charlie's face it was nasty. She and Paresi moved toward the cooler.

"Jesus." Paresi wiped his mouth and stepped back. "Jesus H. Christ."

Star closed her eyes, then opened them again. It was still there.

The head had been neatly severed and packed in ice, face up. A woman's dead eyes looked out at the officers. Her arms and hands lay across one another, as if folded on an invisible bosom. One dead hand held a plastic bag.

Star swallowed her disgust and leaned down. "I need gloves," she muttered. Charlie Cosgrove handed her a pair from his pack.

Swallowing again, and forcing herself not to look at the dead eyes, she tugged the black bag from the hand. It felt heavy. She opened it. Inside the bag, a shiny silvery piece winked up at her.

"What is it?" Paresi asked.

Star turned the bag upside down, dropping the piece into her latex-covered palm. She turned the dwarflike figure over. It was the very detailed, misshapen figure of a man. Over his humped shoulder, he carried a bulging bag. His metal face was twisted in a frightening leer. She held it out toward Paresi.

"Another move in the game," she said.

"Somebody's playing a *game* with you guys?" Charlie Cosgrove asked.

Star looked at Paresi. "Looks like it," she said.

"I think I'll stick to poker." Cosgrove went back to the ice chest. "Poor broad."

"Cover it up, Charlie," Star said, "and let's get Forensics down here."

"Done, Lieutenant."

Mitch sat at his desk. He looked tired but attentive as he watched Jason turn the plastic bag holding the metallic gnome over and over in his fingers.

"It's Grendar," Jason said. "He's the cannibal gnome, remember, Lieutenant?"

Star nodded. "He got Roland."

"Yeah. He's the toughest guard in the game," Jason said. "His only function is to keep the player from reaching the next level."

"By killing and dismembering the player," Star said. She looked at Mitch. "The player explodes in a burst of blood and kinda oozes down the screen."

"Nice," Mitch deadpanned.

Paresi laughed.

"I hate to admit it," Star said. "But it is fun."

"You really got into it the other night," Jason said. "I'll bet if you practiced, you could rack up some heavy scores. . . . You'd be the King Vampire."

"Queen Vampire," Star said.

"I don't think the game has a queen," Jason said. "Girls don't usually like this stuff."

"Violent and sexist . . . I wonder why not?" Star said. "But there are female characters—Dorla, and the evil fairy."

"Maylink, the seductress," Jason said.

"Right." Star nodded. "Actually, she and Dorla look a lot alike." She looked at Jason. "Isn't there something about the trees, and the blood? I can't remember what you said—you know, about the red trees."

"Oh yeah," Jason said. "The bloodfruit."

"Bloodfruit?" Mitch said. "I missed that."

"You were in the kitchen with Vee," Star said.

"Oh, right, she was giving me her lemon meringue pie recipe. What's the bloodfruit, Jason?"

Jason put the figure down on Mitch's desk. "Grendar only eats what he kills. So he butchers the bodies and buries them in various parts of the forest."

"Meal planning?" Mitch said, making them laugh.

"Kinda." Jason nodded. "He cuts them into seven pieces and then buries the pieces all around. His favorite place is the dark trees near the castle. They become blood trees, because the blood turns the trees red, and then the trees produce a bloodfruit that looks kinda like big cherries. It's the gnome's favorite treat."

Star shook her head. "That really puts cherry pie in a whole new light. Who thinks up this stuff?"

"Actually, Vampire's Lair was invented by the company that Cody Stevens' dad owns," Jason said.

"Who's Cody Stevens?" Star asked.

"He's part of that geek group at Bromleigh, the ones who are way into gaming. Remember, I told you that one of the kids' fathers invented Vampire's Lair?"

"Right," Star said.

"Well, Cody's dad owns Dartech, and Cody swears he invented Vampire's Lair, and a bunch of other really dark games. I think he's on the level, because he used to bring samples to school, and guys would learn to play stuff before it came out."

"Were you involved in any of that, Jason?" Paresi asked.

Jason shook his head. "Nope. Cody isn't too cool about brothers. He never offered, we never asked. But he bragged a lot about his old man and the free games and stuff. He said he was inventing a game of his own, something better than anything his father ever made."

"What does this kid look like?" Star asked. "Was he anywhere around when we did the sweep?"

Jason shook his head. "No, ma'am. At least I didn't see him. He doesn't live on campus. But once you see him, you can kinda peg him for a geek. He's tall, about six-two, skinny, and he's got red hair. He wears the school uniform, but he also sports a big black coat that looks like a cape. He likes to hang with a couple of other guys who are identical twins."

Paresi looked at Star. "Back to Bromleigh?"

She shook her head. "Not yet . . . not yet."

CHAPTER TWENTY-EIGHT

"Any idea on our bucket o' babe yet?" Paresi said, sitting down at his desk, facing his partner.

Star looked up from the photos of the grisly find of three days before in her parking space. "Nope."

"She was pretty fresh," Paresi said. "And the hands were intact. No fingerprints?"

"They have the prints," Star said. "It's just that there's been no report on them."

Paresi picked up a handful of the pictures. "Any cause of death yet? I mean besides having her head whacked off?"

"Mitchell said he's going to call with the findings." The phone rang. She picked it up. "Homicide, Lieutenant Duvall." Paresi could tell by her smile who was on the phone.

"Yeah, he's here," she said. "Pick up, Paresi. He wants to talk to both of us at the same time."

"Hey, Mitch."

"Hi, Dominic," Mitch said. "Star?"

"I'm here, go ahead."

They could hear the rustle of papers.

"Okay. Our Jane Doe was strangled."

"How could you tell?" Paresi asked.

"There was ocular petechiae."

"In English, Doc."

Mitch chuckled. "Sorry, Dom. Bleeding. Blood spots, small hemorrhages in the whites of the eyes. There was also bleeding in the mucosa of the lips inside the mouth. The hyoid bone at the base of her tongue was broken as well. There was enough flesh of the neck remaining to examine," Mitch said. "There were no marks on the outside, but there were deep bruises under the skin and impressions on the inside skin of the neck."

More paper rustled. "The under-the-skin impressions say the killer wore gloves."

"That makes sense," Paresi said. "No fingerprints."

"Right," Mitch agreed, "but the murderer didn't take into consideration the fact that force yields marks and bruises under the skin. If the strangulation is manual, without gloves, fingerprints can actually be lifted from the skin."

"But this killer wore gloves," Star said.

"Right," Mitch said. "But gloves impart their own information."

"Such as?" Star asked.

"The marks say that whoever did this didn't have the

strength to really choke this woman. Manual strangulation is very difficult. The victim is usually fighting. By covering the hands, the killer would add more weight, more strength to hold on."

"I can't see that a pair of regular everyday gloves would add too much of anything, other than the hiding of finger-prints," Star said.

"You're right, Lieutenant," Mitch said. "But there are *other* types of gloves. The bruising had to have come from a heavy kind of glove. A construction or a workman's glove, some-thing worn to handle heavy or dangerous equipment."

"I guess we start looking at construction sites," Star said, "but we don't have a clue where to begin. We don't know where she was killed. . . . The best we can do is hope the rest of her turns up."

"Having the rest of the body would make my job easier," Mitch said. "My take is purely speculation, based on what we have. Her nails were clean, no skin underneath. If I had the rest of the body I could find out whether or not she was raped, or if there was more trauma involved in this. It's frustrating."

"She'll turn up, sooner or later," Paresi said.

"What makes you think so?" Star asked.

Paresi looked at her across their desks. "Because whoever did this delivered the first pieces to you. They're not going to stop. They're enjoying this. They'll play it out."

"I think you've got something there, Dominic," Mitch said. "We'll just have to wait it out."

"Yeah, thanks, Doc. Later." Paresi hung up the phone.

Star spoke with Mitch for a few more minutes before hanging up. She picked up the pictures. "This is so sick."

"Yep," Paresi agreed. "And it's gonna get sicker."

She leaned back in her chair. "Where have you been for most of the morning?"

"City Hall. I was checking out McCoy's story, following up on who bought that patch of Bromleigh land."

"And?"

He sat down facing her. "I know who owns it."

"Who?"

Paresi gave her a cat-eating-the-canary grin. "The city."

"The city?" Star sat forward. "The city owns that part of the campus?"

Paresi nodded. "Yep. They bought it a while back, for development. I guess with the changes in city government, it just slipped through the cracks."

"So in essence it's public property?"

"If you stretch it," Paresi said. "The city owns it, but they've done nothing with it. So let's say we *could* find proof of illegal activity anywhere on that little piece of land—the owner of the property where the transgression occurred would be liable."

"You are going somewhere with this, right?" Star asked.

Paresi folded his arms and leaned forward on his desk.

"The city owns the land, *not* the buildings on the site. Any building still technically belongs to Bromleigh. So anything of a suspicious or extreme nature found in said building puts the school back in the spotlight and opens the way for a"—He crooked his fingers in the air, forming quotation marks—" 'real warrant.' "

Star smiled. "Oh, Paresi, your mind in the morning."

He nodded. "The way I see it, we should haul ass over to that deserted lab McCoy talked about."

"You're right," Star said. "If we'd talked to him first, we wouldn't have lost two nights hanging in the park."

"The park was cool," Paresi said. "We got to snatch up the illustrious Willie Chester, who I'm sure *never* wants to work his girls in this city again."

Star laughed. "He had some outstanding warrants in Boston and Springfield—they're fighting over him."

"See?" Paresi said. "If we hadn't been in the park, he'd still be scalping his girls and making life a pain in the ass for everybody else. And don't forget Jas—she told you that Bromleigh boys were taking girls to some secret place. So that just verifies what McCoy said. It's got to be the lab, it's close by."

"Yeah, she said she'd heard they did freaky stuff. She said she heard blood had been shed."

"Well, if that's true, and kids are doing that, then they're not going to be savvy enough to clean up after themselves,"

Paresi said. "There's got to be some kind of evidence left behind."

Star reached for her coat. "Let's roll."

"Let's roll?" He grinned at her.

She shrugged her shoulders. "I always wanted to say that."

The ivy, weeds, and brush nearly covered the small gray stone building behind the ruined rose garden.

"McCoy was right. If we didn't know where this place was, we never would have found it," Star said, picking her way carefully along the overgrown path to the front door.

"I'll say." Paresi plucked a thorny branch from his black overcoat. "This is way off the path."

Star tried the door. It wouldn't budge.

They pushed together. Nothing.

Paresi jiggled the rusted lock. "It's either locked or stuck like hell." He backed up. "There's got to be another way to get in here."

The two of them carefully worked their way around the structure, looking through the dirty windows as they searched.

"It's a mess in there," Star said, peering through a grimy pane.

"Yeah, well, housekeeping ain't what we're here for." Paresi continued toward the back of the building. Star followed.

"Let's try this door." He shook the door. It too wouldn't budge.

"Locked?" Star asked.

"Kids get in here, we're gettin' in," Paresi said. He moved a few feet back and rushed the door, throwing his weight on it. The door popped open.

"Wow, Paresi, brute force. I like that."

"Yeah?" He grinned at her and massaged his shoulder. "Good. Glad you're impressed. Now call an ambulance, I think I broke something."

She laughed.

He smiled at her. "Look at you, I'm telling you I could be hurt and you crack up."

"You're okay, aren't you?"

"Yeah, I'm fine," he said. "Just wanted to see that smile."

"C'mon." Star pushed open the door and went inside.

The room looked as if it had been bombed. Dirt and grime, combined with the overgrowth, kept most of the sunlight out. The space was dark and foul smelling.

Ruined counters, a filthy sink, and a surprisingly usable-looking chalkboard took up one side of the old lab. Broken glass covered the floor.

"Mmph, it stinks in here." Star put her hand over her nose and mouth.

"Here." Paresi handed her his Vicks inhaler. She took two quick blasts up her nose and gave it back. He inhaled after her.

"God, even the Vicks doesn't help," she said.

"Don't think about it." Paresi moved to the other side of the room.

"Where do they take the women they bring in here?" Star said. "It's a pit—there's nowhere to do anything."

Paresi kicked at an empty wine bottle. It rolled against a stained, filthy twin-size mattress. "There's a place to drink, and get laid," he said. "What more do you need?" He took a small black metal flashlight out of his pocket. "Hey Star, look at this."

She crossed the floor, broken glass crunching beneath her shoes. Paresi trained the light and pointed.

A length of thin, red rubber tubing lay on the littered floor. It was surrounded by a dark brown, smudged, sticky-looking stain.

"That looks like blood," she said.

"Uh-huh," Paresi said. "Lots of it, too."

Star pulled a pair of latex gloves out of her purse, along with a plastic evidence bag, which she handed to Paresi.

She stooped, running her latex-covered fingertip along the stain.

"Dry," she said, reaching for the tube in the center. It came up from the floor with a small tearing sound. Dark brown flecks clung to it. She stood, holding the tube carefully between her thumb and forefinger.

Paresi held open the bag, and she dropped the rubber piece into it. "Mitchell said Dolores was tubed," she said.

"Right." Paresi sealed the bag. "If we can prove that the blood on this piece of rubber and on the floor is hers, we can bust the fuck out of that school."

"Let's get out of here," Star said. "I can't take the smell anymore."

Outside, at the rear of the building, she inhaled the fresh air deeply.

"You okay?"

"I'm not going to throw up," she said.

"Good. Hope you don't mind if I do," Paresi said. "The smell in there is more than just filth."

"That's exactly what I'm thinking." She walked a few feet from the building and turned back, looking at it.

"Paresi." She beckoned her partner.

He moved alongside her. "What you got?"

"Look at this place."

Paresi stared at the structure.

"What does it remind you of?"

He shook his head. "Something that should be bulldozed to the ground."

"No, look at it . . . doesn't it make you think of those Castle Rock Burger places?"

Paresi stared at the squat gray structure. "You know you got something there. It's those crazy corners, like little towers."

"Turrets," Star said.

"Yeah." Paresi tilted his head, looking at the building from an angle. "They make it look like a castle."

"The trees of blood," she muttered.

"What?"

"In the game . . . the trees of blood."

"Yeah, so?"

"What Jason said. The gnome buries the pieces of his victims in the forest under the trees *near the castle* . . . the blood turns to fruit . . . and the fruit is the gnome's favorite thing."

"Yeah?"

She pointed to the trees. "The blood makes fruit that looks

like big cherries." She waved her hand toward the trees surrounding the old building. Pink and white blossoms swayed
in the soft breeze. "Paresi, these are cherry trees!" She
reached into his coat pocket. "Give me your phone."

CHAPTER TWENTY-NINE

Mitchell Grant walked out into the decimated yard, behind
the deserted chem lab.

"The rest of the puzzle," he said to Star.

"The other pieces?"

He nodded. "The torso, separated at the waist, the hips, and
limbs. I'd say with the degree of decomposition, they've been
in there about three to four days."

"Seven pieces," Star said.

Mitch nodded. "With the head and hands, exactly seven."

Paresi crossed the yard, cell phone in hand. "Hey, Star."

She turned toward her partner.

"We got an ID." He put the phone in his pocket. "Her
name's Camille Westfall. She worked for a Dr. Douglas Riley,
in the medical complex on Ravenswood Drive. She hasn't
been in to work for a couple of days, and nobody's seen her
around her apartment. The doctor put out a missing. The description matches the head."

"Well, I guess we're off to see Dr. Riley," Star said.

Paresi flipped the pages of his notebook. "Let's go."

"Hang on a minute." She turned to Mitch. "How long before she posts?"

He looked at his watch. "Since it's so late in the afternoon,
why don't I schedule her for first thing tomorrow morning,
around eight?"

"That'll work," Star said.

Mitch took her hand. "See you later?"

"Count on it."

"We're here to see Dr. Riley," Star said to the woman behind the desk, flipping open her ID. The gold badge shone beneath the bright office lights. "I'm Lieutenant Duvall, and this is Sergeant Paresi."

Julie Curran looked nervous. "Is this about Cammie?"

"Cammie?" Star said. "You mean Camille Westfall?"

Julie nodded. "Yes, ma'am. We called her Cammie around here."

"I'm sorry for your loss, Ms. . . . ?"

"Curran, Julie Curran. Both Cammie and me work for Dr. Riley. I mean Cammie used to . . ." Her voice trailed off.

"I gathered that," Star said. "May we see Dr. Riley?"

"He's not here."

"Beg pardon?"

The woman looked close to tears. She swallowed loudly and placed a thin hand against her breast.

"When the doctor heard about Cammie, he became very upset. He went home."

"May we have his address?" Paresi said softly.

A big tear slid down Julie Curran's face. "I don't think I can tell you that."

"Honey," Star said, "we're the police. You *have* to tell us."

She looked up. "He's gonna be mad at me."

Paresi nudged Star aside and took one of Julie's pale hands in his.

"Julie," he spoke softly, "we're not the bad guys. We need to get some information on Cammie, try to find out who killed her. You want us to catch the killer, right?"

The woman looked deeply into Paresi's eyes. Her chin trembled like a child's. Another tear slid down her face. She nodded. The tear dropped onto Paresi's hand. He never looked away from her eyes.

"Good. We want to do everything we can for Cammie. That means we have to talk to the doctor." Paresi's voice lowered, became softer. He was almost whispering. "That means we need your help."

He gently stroked her hand. "If you choose not to give it, that's fine. But you're impeding our investigation. I'm sure the doctor wouldn't like that." He leveled his azure gaze at her. "We're going to talk to him, with or without your help, Julie. So why not make it easy on us? The doctor won't be angry."

Julie's hand trembled in Paresi's. "He was so upset when he left."

Paresi's fingers moved softly over her skin. His eyes never left hers.

"I understand," he said. "Dr. Riley's lost someone that he knew, and if it turns out that he takes some of that out on you for helping us, then you just call me, and I'll take care of everything, okay?"

Talk about your snake charmers, Star thought.

The woman gazed at Paresi, mesmerized. Her chin trembled again, but her hand in his tightened its grip. "I'll write it down," she said. "He's very upset, though. He and Cammie were . . ."

"Were what?" Star blurted out, and instantly wished she'd kept her mouth shut. The woman looked like a frightened mouse.

"I can't say any more. . . ." She pulled her hand away from Paresi and tore a sheet of paper off of her memo pad. Beneath the scampering puppies, she wrote down Douglas Riley's address.

The woman who answered the door was totally snockered, but she put on a good face.

"Mrs. Riley?" Star said.

"Yes," she answered. Star watched her eyes struggling to focus.

"I'm Lieutenant Duvall, and this is my partner, Sergeant Paresi, we're . . ."

"You must be here about that poor unfortunate girl who worked for my husband."

Star looked at her partner. The look in Paresi's eyes confirmed what she was thinking. The woman was plastered.

"Come in." She beckoned them into a large, brightly furnished living room. "Have a seat, detectives. May I get you something to drink? Coffee, iced tea, a soft drink?"

"No thank you, ma'am," Star said.

"All right. I'll get Doug."

"Thank you."

Mrs. Riley turned unsteadily and headed toward the rear of the large house.

"She's shitfaced," Paresi said.

"You got that right." Star nodded. "I can't smell it, but I can see it."

"Vodka," Paresi said. "And plenty of it." He walked toward the sliding doors that led out to a deck and garden. "Must be all the pressure of keeping up this big-assed house."

"Mm-hmm." Star wandered over to the fireplace. She looked at the family photos displayed on the mantel.

"Paresi."

"What?"

"Come over here. Look at these photos."

He moved to her side. "Their kids, so?"

"Remember the day we found Molly?"

"Uh-huh."

"Remember those boys that were standing around, watching?"

"Vaguely."

"Well, I think these could be the guys Jason was talking about. Remember? The tall, skinny kid with the red hair—Cody—and the twins that he runs with." She pointed at the pictures of the two young boys, dressed in matching sailor suits on the mantel. "I'll betcha these are the twins."

"Star, there's lots of twins in the world. Besides, these are young kids."

"No. The picture's old. Look at what they're wearing."

"Sailor suits."

"Not them, the two women in the background."

Paresi chuckled. "What are you, the fashion police?"

"It's the shoulder pads. That big shoulder thing . . . women wore those in the eighties." She faced her grinning partner. "I'll bet this picture is about ten or eleven years old."

"You're right, Detective." Diane Riley stepped back into

the room. "Those are our sons, Daniel and David. They were nearly seven years old when that was taken, in 1988. We were going to Doug's new office. The one he's in now. It was quite a celebration."

She picked up the photograph and pointed at the two shadowy women in the background. "That's me and my friend Irene." She smiled at Star. "Irene Kavaraceus. Doug and I used to call her 'The Wild Greek,' Brookport's very own Melina Mercouri." She looked at Star. "You're so young, you probably don't know who that is."

"*Never on Sunday* is a classic," Star said. "One of my favorite films."

Diane smiled and turned back to the picture, remembering happy times. "Then you understand. That was Irene." Her eyes clouded for a moment. "My goodness she was fun, always kept me laughing."

With affection, she stroked the shadowy figure frozen in time and framed behind glass. "She's gone now, poor darling. A massive stroke, about five years ago."

"I'm sorry," Star said.

"Me too." She put the picture back on the mantel. "I miss her so much. Sometimes I fantasize that she and Melina met up in heaven, and they're having good times, two 'Wild Greeks' together." She turned to Star. "I don't want her to be lonely. She was my bestest girlfriend. That's what we used to call each other—'Bestest girlfriend.' I like to think she's got a 'bestest girlfriend' in heaven too."

"Girlfriends are important," Star said.

"Oh my yes." Diane ran her hands over her slim hips, as if shedding memories. "My husband is very upset about all this. He's freshening up. He'll be in shortly."

"Thank you, Mrs. Riley."

"Call me Diane, and please, do let me get you something to drink."

"Water with ice will be fine for me," Star said.

"All right. And you, Detective?" She looked at Paresi.

"Water's okay for me too."

Diane Riley seemed grateful for something to do. "I'll be right back." She headed again into the depths of the house.

Star and Paresi sat down on the overstuffed chintz sofa facing the fireplace. "Talk about one sandwich short of a picnic," she said.

"Maybe she's responding to the murder. You know, people handle death in different ways," Paresi said.

"Maybe." Star's gaze went back to the picture on the mantel. "I'll bet those kids are the ones we saw in the park. They don't really look that different."

"You can remember their faces?" Paresi asked.

Star shrugged. "I mostly remember that they were twins."

Mrs. Riley came back carrying a silver tray, holding two cut crystal glasses filled with crushed ice, a set of small silver tongs, and two cobalt-blue bottles of imported mineral water. She'd put a small crystal dish of lemon slices on the tray, along with a matching plate of sugar cookies. She set the tray down on the coffee table in front of them.

"I know you only wanted water, but I made these." She pointed to the cookies. "When I heard about Cammie, I had to do something, so . . . My boys can't get enough of them, and I made quite a few. Please, help yourselves."

"Thank you." Star picked up a cookie and bit into it. It was still warm, and it tasted heavenly.

Diane Riley used the tongs to pick up a slice of lemon. "Lemon?" she asked.

"Oh, please," Star said. "Thank you."

She turned to Paresi.

"Sure," he said.

"Lemon makes everything taste wonderful," Diane said. "At least that's what I think."

"I agree," Star said.

Diane Riley dropped lemon slices in both glasses and opened the two bottles of water. She filled Star's glass and handed it to her.

"These cookies are fabulous," Star said. "Do you mind?"

Diane handed Paresi his glass of water. "Oh no, please, help yourself."

Diane beamed, as Star reached for another cookie. "I'm not bragging, but they are scrumptious. My boys love them. In fact, they have me make them all the time for their friends up at Bromleigh." She passed the cookie plate to Paresi. "Here you go, Detective."

"Thanks."

"Your kids go to Bromleigh?" Star asked, looking at Paresi.

Diane Riley sat down in a pale green Queen Anne chair, facing the cops. "That they do. Both Dan and Dave. They're about to graduate. They're wonderful boys."

"I'm sure they are," Star said, finishing her cookie. "These are very good."

"My wife's quite a baker," Douglas Riley said.

The detectives looked up. He was standing near the entrance to the room. Though he'd tried to spruce himself up before coming in, both Star and Paresi could see this was a man on the edge.

He moved slowly toward them, his hand out.

"I'm Doug Riley. Cammie worked for me."

His wife stood up. "I'm going to let you all talk. If you need anything, I'll be in the study." She patted her husband's shoulder and left the room.

"We're sorry to bother you, Dr. Riley," Star said, "but we need to ask a few questions about Camille."

The man nodded. "She was my . . ." His voice broke into deep, racking sobs.

Star and Paresi looked at one another.

CHAPTER THIRTY

Star looked at the body on the autopsy table. It reminded her of some kind of horrendous jigsaw puzzle. Camille Westfall's head, which had been previously autopsied, was the first piece.

Below that, pieces two and three: her arms and hands, severed neatly at the shoulders. The upper body and lower torso formed pieces four and five. She had been severed neatly at the hip joints, like chicken parts.

Star looked at the woman's legs and feet, pieces six and seven. The sight of Camille Westfall's pedicured, baby pink–frosted painted toenails on her blue, bloated, decomposing feet gave Star a raging case of the internal willies.

"I have never seen anything like this," she muttered.

Though the body had been bisected and the internal organs basically cut in half, decomposition and escaping gases had caused the skin to rupture on the lower swollen torso and legs.

Mitch walked around the table, viewing the pieces from various angles, all the while speaking into the small microphone attached to his scrubs, giving the particulars on the appearance of the body.

"Usually the head is last," he said to the detectives. "But since we got it first, it's been done. So we'll begin with the torso." He picked up a scalpel and looked across the table at Star and Paresi. Neither of them looked too steady.

"This is going to be rough," Mitch said. "You two sure you want to stay?" he asked.

Star and Paresi nodded.

"Okay." Mitch pulled his eyeshield into place and looked at Jason. "Let's do it."

The young man positioned his own eyeshield, and edged the rolling utility tray nearer the table. He placed the long-handled branch cutter closer to the end of the tray, making it easy for the doctor to reach. The fact that Mitch used an ordinary garden tool to cut through the ribs and cartilage to expose the heart and lungs never failed to rattle Star. For infants and young children, he favored a linoleum knife. Either way, the sound of crunching bones during the process never failed to set her teeth on edge.

"Beginning the Y," Mitch said into the microphone. He made the first cut into the blue-tinged, swollen torso. The sharp blade of the scalpel sliced through the decaying layers of flesh from shoulder to shoulder, and then down.

Star concentrated on the small holes drilled into the steel

table, which allowed fluids and water to drain into the tank below.

"Son of a bitch!" Mitch said.

"What?" He surprised Star. Mitchell Grant was a man who rarely swore. "What is it?"

He backed away from the table. Something thick, viscous, stringy, and totally unpleasant clung to his hand. It dripped onto the floor and the disposable blue covers that protected his shoes and the legs of his scrubs. Mitch peeled off the soiled glove.

"Jeez." Paresi stepped back.

"What is that?" Star said.

"Silicone," Mitch said, tossing the glove into the trash. "She's got implants. They've ruptured." He took off the other glove, tossed it, and went to the sink in the corner. He washed his hands, dried them with paper towels, and went back to the table.

Jason handed him another pair of gloves. He pulled them on.

"This is going to get worse," he said. "I'm going to have to remove the implants. You two sure you really want to be here?"

"Yeah," Paresi said. "We're tough, right?" He nudged Star with his shoulder. The look she gave him made the three men laugh.

Dean Butterworth sat silent at his desk, listening to the two detectives detail their findings in the deserted chem lab.

"I sympathize with the death of another person," he said. "But Bromleigh has nothing to do with any of it."

Paresi looked at Star. "You want to tell him?"

Star shook her head. "No, you tell him."

"Tell me what?" Butterworth started to sweat.

"Even though the property is no longer owned by the school, the old lab is," Paresi said.

"What?"

He leaned toward Butterworth. "In short, Dino, a crime has been committed on Bromleigh property. That opens this whole baby yuppie factory up for full search and seizure."

"What?" The man's face reddened. "What do you mean, search and seizure?"

"Dean Butterworth." Star put her hand on Paresi's arm. "What my partner is saying is that Camille Westfall died in accordance with the game Vampire's Lair. Sections of her body have been found on Bromleigh property. Her employer is the father of two of your students. . . ."

"Dave and Dan Riley," Butterworth said, interrupting her. "I read in the papers that she worked for Dr. Douglas Riley."

"Yes," Star continued, "and the father of yet another student is the creator, manufacturer, and distributor of that game." She leaned forward in her chair. "Those boys were seen in the park at the site of the homeless woman's burning death a few weeks ago. I recognized the twins. They were with a tall, red-haired boy."

"Cody Stevens."

"Yes. It's his father who created Vampire's Lair and who owns the Dartech Corporation. They create, manufacture, and distribute these very dark games.

"We've also been talking to people who frequent Saint Francis Park after dark. Some of them have corroborated the fact that Bromleigh students are often in the area, attempting to and in some cases actually purchasing the services of prostitutes."

Butterworth was on his feet. "I won't hear any more! My boys would *never*!"

"Your boys would, and did, Dean Butterworth," Star said. "We've got witnesses to their soliciting women for sex. I want to talk to some of your older students, upperclassmen, beginning with those three that I've personally seen hanging around the park. If you won't remove them from their classes, I will."

Butterworth dropped back into his chair. His face turned pale, and beads of sweat dotted his forehead.

"I don't believe what you're telling me," he said. "My boys are well-behaved, well-raised young men. They do not frequent *prostitutes*!"

Paresi leaned forward, his eyes nailing Butterworth.

"Your *boys* are snotty, horny little twerps, and they like to play games," he said. "The kind of games that young girls don't play. Your little angels participate in blood rituals, *Dean.* A piece of tubing proven to have been used in the murder of Dolores Causwell was found on the floor of the old lab, in a pool of her dried blood."

Butterworth closed his eyes, struggling to block out the image of Dolores. Her sad, bruised smile, her heartbroken eyes. He wasn't fast enough. Star saw the profound mask of grief that momentarily appeared on his craggy face, then just as quickly disappeared.

"Tubing?" he said softly.

"Dolores Causwell was bled, Dean Butterworth," Star said. "The murderer shot her up with Coumadin, a blood thinner. Then her femoral artery was cut, and a length of rubber tubing was shoved into the wound."

"They literally pumped the blood out of her body," Paresi said.

"That's right," Star said, watching Butterworth's eyes. "Her life was drained into two plastic gallon-sized milk jugs."

She paused, letting him absorb that horror. "The jugs were found on a curbside, literally put out with the garbage."

Butterworth closed his eyes; his skin now gray and pallid. He ran a massive hand over his face.

Knowing she was on to something, and feeling no pity for the man, Star leaned forward and deliberately hammered him.

"Did you know there's about eighteen pints of blood in the human body, Dean Butterworth? When Dolores was found, she had less than four pints . . . in her *entire* body."

Butterworth's eyes watered. "Did she suffer?"

"What do you think?" Star said, her eyes on him.

Butterworth lowered his head, unable to look at her.

"The medical examiner *thinks* she was unconscious when she was tubed," Star said, "but there's really no way to tell." She gave him another straight-in-the-eye look. "All we can honestly say is that the shock from the cutting and the drug didn't finish her. Ms. Causwell's heart continued beating. . . . She was *alive*, Dean Butterworth, alive, while she was being bled dry."

She watched the man struggle to control his emotions, but she didn't stop. Her golden eyes bored into his. "Camille Westfall, victim number three, was dismembered. An ice chest containing her head, hands, and arms was delivered to the police station and left in my parking space a few days ago. The remainder of her body was found hidden beneath some floorboards in the old chem lab."

Butterworth slumped in his chair as if Star had physically beaten him.

She went on, her voice steady, emotionless. "The common denominator in all of this, Dean Butterworth, from the beginning, has been Bromleigh. Now we find that Camille Westfall worked for Dr. Riley. The twins are friends with Cody Stevens—I've seen them together myself. And Cody's father created Vampire's Lair and owns the company that manufactures it. Some of your boys have been involved in soliciting prostitutes in Saint Francis Park, and I don't think it's out of bounds to start our investigation with this tight little threesome."

She sat back in the chair. "With or without your permission, Dean Butterworth, my partner and I are going to talk to them."

Butterworth stood slowly. He seemed to have aged fifty years in the time they'd been in his office.

"I'll have them brought here," he said.

"Thank you," Star said.

Dean Butterworth walked slowly toward his office door, praying his legs would support him. He stopped, his hand on the ornate brass doorknob.

Star and Paresi watched him take two deep breaths before he stepped through, closing the massive door behind him.

"He's involved," Star said.

"Yeah, that's the read I get," Paresi said. He turned to face her. "You do good badass stuff. It's been a while since I've seen that in you."

Star shook her head. "I don't like doing it, but he's hiding something."

"Don't you worry," Paresi said. "He's sweating, and he's gonna crack. He won't be able to hold on to what he knows."

"Dolores is what got him. He must have been a customer," Star said.

"Whatever the connection," Paresi said, "we'll get to it."

He held up his hand. Star slapped his palm with her own.

In Butterworth's office, David and Daniel Riley refused to look at the two detectives. Cody Stevens slouched in a chair across from Star, glaring at her while she ignored him. He stretched his long, sticklike legs out and bumped her foot with his.

Butterworth looked at the three young men seated before him. "Boys, I'm sure you had nothing to do with any of the mischief that's been happening lately in Saint Francis Park. Still, these officers need to ask you a few questions."

"Mischief?" Paresi said. "Mischief?"

"Look," Cody Stevens said. "We know what's been happening over there. It's all over TV. They've even started talking about it being like a game my father sells, but we don't have anything to do with any of it."

The detectives stared at him in stony silence.

"Okay," Cody said. "I admit that my friends and I sometimes do dumb things—we're kids! But we'd never hurt anybody, and we'd never go against a rule that could get us kicked out of school."

Star watched him, her face and eyes expressionless.

Cody's skinny face reddened, his voice grew louder. "This isn't fair, you know, not fair at all. You can't come down on us because my dad makes a stupid game!"

Paresi's eyes narrowed. Dan and Dave looked at the floor, their eyes fastened to the golden fleur-de-lis pattern on the burgundy carpet.

Cody sat back with a slight grin on his face. "We really don't have anything to tell you."

"Your friends mute, Stevens?" Paresi said.

"What, sir?"

"Mutes." Paresi pointed at the twins. "You know, dummies. No talking."

"Detective, there's no need for rudeness," Butterworth said.

Paresi shot him a glance that made him shrink in his chair.

"What are you guys looking at?" Paresi said, getting up. "What's so great about this rug? You've never seen it before? Is it new?"

He walked over and stood so close to Dave that the boy's trousers brushed against his. "So, fellas, tell me, what am I missing? What's in the rug? Answers to our questions?"

"No sir," the boys said in unison.

"Then look at me." Paresi leaned close. "Look in *my* eyes." The twins looked at one another. Paresi took Dave by the chin and forcibly turned his face. "I'm over here."

Butterworth jumped to his feet. "I really *cannot* have you strong-arming my boys!"

Paresi turned toward the dean. "*Siddown!* I've had about enough of you *and* your boys." He turned back to the twins. "You guys tough?"

The twins looked at one another and then back at the floor.

Paresi reached into his breast pocket and pulled out an autopsy photo of the grotesque puzzle that had been Camille Westfall. He shoved it directly under David Riley's nose. The boy recoiled as if he'd been slapped.

"C'mon, fellas, you like blood-and-guts stuff, right? Well here, take a look. This is what it looks like . . . *for real.*"

"Sir . . ." David Riley leaned forward and clapped a hand over his mouth. "Please."

Paresi shoved him back in the chair. "No pukin' on the expensive carpet, junior." He thrust the photo at Daniel. "How 'bout you, slim? You a wuss like your brother? Is chickenshit a twin thing?"

Daniel closed his eyes and turned his head.

"I'm no pussy." Cody Stevens reached out a bony hand. "Let me see that."

Paresi handed him the photo.

Cody Stevens's thin lips tilted up in a smile.

Paresi looked at Star.

She nodded at him. "Dean Butterworth, we need to see Mr. Stevens alone."

CHAPTER THIRTY-ONE

Cody Stevens sat sullen in the chair, staring at the two detectives.

"I don't know what you want me to say." He smirked at Star and Paresi. "I'm a student, a juvenile—there's nothing you can do to me."

"We can haul you down to the station and kick your ass till you're bowlegged," Paresi said.

"Then we can call your mom and dad and tell them to come on down and be sure and bring the family attorney," Star said cheerfully. "I'm sure you have one."

Cody stared at her, his face blank.

"The lady is talking to you," Paresi said.

"She's threatening me," Cody said, his eyes locked with Star's. "Both of you are. Why? I haven't done anything."

Paresi turned to Star, a stern look on his face. "Lieutenant Duvall, are you threatening this fine upstanding young man?"

Star rolled her eyes and assumed a comical "thinking" pose. "Uh . . ." She stood up, her brow still furrowed, and went to Butterworth's desk. She picked up the phone and turned to Cody. "Nope!" she said, and punched the intercom button.

Alex Monroe answered.

"Could you please have Dean Butterworth come back into his office?"

"Right away, ma'am."

"Very funny," Cody muttered.

"You ain't seen nothing yet," Paresi smiled. "You're gonna be downright hysterical before we're finished with you."

Butterworth came back into the office. "What is it?" He

tried to sound gruff, but Paresi's look made him back down. "How can I help you?" he said to Star.

"We'll need Mr. Stevens's home phone and address."

Butterworth looked at Cody. The boy shook his head disgustedly.

"Why?"

"Two reasons," Star said. "First of all, we're sending a car over to get his parents and we need the correct address."

"And the other reason?" Butterworth queried.

"Oh!" Star snapped her fingers. "Excuse me, I seem to be having a senior moment. The warrant. We'll need the correct address for the search warrant."

Cody snapped to attention.

"What are you talking about? Why are you searchin' my house?"

"Not your house, junior." Paresi smiled. "Your computer."

A look of pure panic crossed the boy's face.

"Dean Butterworth, they can't do that, can they?"

"Yes." Star smiled. "We can."

Jay Scott Stevens was not amused when his secretary, Jenny Halliwell, stuck her head into his office and beckoned him. He ignored her.

The woman, red-faced, her back against the wall, tiptoed sideways until she was next to him. Blushing furiously, she leaned down and dramatically whispered that his son had been arrested.

"Can't his mother handle this?" Jay growled through clenched teeth.

"Mrs. Stevens can't be located," the secretary said out loud, and immediately clapped her hand over her mouth. She looked as if she were going to cry. "I'm sorry, Mr. Stevens, but the police said it's urgent."

Jay Stevens turned to Larry Michaels and Kevin Griffin, the two white-faced, nervous-looking men sitting at his round glass conference table. They looked as if they had just gotten a call from the governor as they were being strapped down to the gurney.

"I've got to go," he said, his eyes searching their faces for any reaction to his son's predicament.

There was none.

"I'll reschedule for as soon as possible," the secretary said.

Jay waved his small, perfectly manicured hand. His diamond pinkie ring glittered as he shooed her out of the office.

Both Larry and Kevin stood, faces visibly relieved, packing away the papers that had been strewn across the glass table.

Jay tossed his notes into the black alligator-skin Mark Cross case on the table, next to his laptop computer. He tried to rein in his anger.

Just when these two bastards were caving big time. Their game was going to be a blockbuster, but he'd be damned if he'd give them a break. The rights—lock, stock, and barrel—for a good sum. That's all he promised, and that's all he'd give. He could see inside their heads. They were hungry, and he was the king of the mountain. The best company for what they had to offer. He was offering a good deal. Not an extraordinary one, but they'd each take in a lot of bucks—though of course not as much as he would.

He snapped the locks of his case closed and caught the look that passed between the two men. A little smile crawled across Jay's thin mouth. They knew Dartech had a hard-on for their game, but they also knew Jay Stevens wasn't going to be the one getting fucked.

They were going to take what he offered and like it. He'd known it from the second they walked into his office with their off-the-rack warehouse suits and cheap shoes. The joust, the parry, the thrust, the win. No surprises—but still, he enjoyed the game. His whole life revolved around them. His imagination and fascination for games and computers had made him a very rich man. No more "dweeb-boy" getting shoved around campus. Hell, his old school even had a building named for him now.

He got a kick out of knowing that all those jocks who'd made his life hell were now fat, soft, outta-shape bastards, wondering where their pissant lives went.

None of them had acquired his riches, or his power. He was

the real King Vampire. And now he had to walk away from one of his biggest acquisitions ever, because of a kid. His own incompetent screwup son, Cody.

Jay's face hardened into an angry mask.

"I'll be in at eight tomorrow morning," he said to the two men. "Make sure you're both here."

He cast his cold blue gaze on them. "Any problem?"

The two young men shook their heads. "No, Jay," Kevin said. "Eight sharp, we'll be here."

Jay Stevens turned and, without a further glance, headed for the door.

Kevin and Larry waited until the massive black wooden door closed behind him before turning to one another.

"Can you believe that midget asshole is so damned hot? Can you believe he's the *top* of the shitpile? If we had money, we could put out our own goddamned game," Larry said.

"Yeah, but we don't, and this is the best place to be." Kevin started piling papers into his briefcase. "Even though he's fuckin' us around."

"Yeah, I dropped my pants and bent over at the door," Larry said. "But I still think nothing is worth his fucking ego and the shit he's forcing us to eat." He looked at the door. "I hope his son-of-a-bitch kid gets the chair."

The two men laughed.

"I'm sure his kid's a lot like him. All mouth and no dick," Kevin said. "Most likely, the cops are just trying to teach the little snot a lesson. You don't get the chair for that."

Larry slammed his tan imitation leather briefcase closed. "Too bad."

Jay Scott Stevens was over the rational limit. He drove dangerously close to the red Jeep in front of him. When it stopped suddenly, he came within inches of ramming it.

"Son of a bitch!" he shouted, pounding the horn. "What the fuck's wrong with you!" The woman driving looked into her rearview mirror and gave him the finger. Jay swallowed the bile in his throat.

"Bitch," he muttered, and honked again. What the fuck else is going to go wrong today?

The phone in his hunter green Jaguar rang.

"I had to ask," he said out loud, and picked up the phone. *"What?"* he thundered.

"Señor Stebens," his maid Lupe said, in halting English. "I sorry to call you, but I very scared. Just now some poleeces come to casa . . . say come to take Mr. Cody's compperter."

"Let them!" he yelled. "I'm on my way to the police station right now. I'll take care of it." He slammed the phone down.

By the time he reached the Seventeenth Precinct he thought his eyes were going to pop out and his head was going to explode, like one of his characters in Dementia.

After putting up with an irritating sergeant at the desk downstairs and being told nothing, he was directed to the Homicide unit.

He stood in the middle of the tacky room, gritting his teeth to the point of damage, and trying to control the rage racing through his short but carefully sculpted and toned four-times-a-week-at-the-Brookport-Athletic-Club body.

To further piss him off, a colored woman, who towered over him, was telling him that she had taken his son into custody.

"Are you trying to pin a murder on my boy?" His voice sounded stern, no-nonsense. He controlled his urge to scream at her. That's what lawyers and deep pockets were for.

"No, Mr. Stevens," Star said. "We're not trying to pin anything on your son." She indicated a bench against the wall. "Please sit down."

"No." Jay fiddled with the Windsor knot in his Talbott paisley-printed silk tie. "I'm calling my attorney."

"I don't think that's going to be necessary. Cody isn't under arrest." Star again indicated the bench against the wall. "Please, have a seat."

"What part of *no* don't you understand, Officer? I said I don't *want* to sit down."

"It's *Lieutenant*, Mr. Stevens. Lieutenant Duvall," Star said, making a point of looking down to meet his gaze.

"It doesn't matter." Stevens fixed her with cold eyes. "He's here. You people dragged him in here, and I'm not going to allow you to railroad my boy. I'll have your badge!"

Star folded her arms and smiled down at him. "You wouldn't like it," she said. "It would clash with your pinkie ring!" She turned. "The public phone is in the hall."

"I have my own," Jay Stevens answered coldly.

Good, shove it up your ass! Star thought to herself, walking away.

Glaring at her back, Jay pulled a trim black cell phone from his inside breast pocket.

Paresi appeared, a folder in his hand.

"Come with me." He led her around the corner, near the interrogation rooms. "You know how you have a day that's great, and it just keeps getting better?"

"Vaguely." Star pointed over her shoulder. "Take a look around the corner."

Paresi went to the end of the small passageway and glanced around the pillar at the man standing in the center of the squad room.

"Who's the dink?"

"Cody Stevens's father, Napoleon," Star said. "And if you think junior is a pain in the ass, wait till you meet the original. I came really close to punching him." She scowled. "He talked to me like he *owns* me!"

Paresi sized up the man speaking animatedly into the cell phone. A wicked grin spread across his face. "He's mine."

"No." Star pulled him back around the corner. "Let's do this by the book. I've got a feeling about it. Munchkin Man is already angry. He arrived ticked. So he's liable to say something that will make you kick his tiny ass, and then we'll all end up rolling around the floor."

She sat on a bench near Interrogation Room Two, and indicated her plum-colored short-skirted suit. "This is a new outfit, and I'm not about to ruin it because of that little jerk!"

Paresi sat down next to her. "And you look good in it," he said. "So you win."

"You're giving up that easily?" Star smiled. "I *must* look good."

"You do, and I just happen to be in a great mood. Camille Westfall's clothes have been found."

"Where?"

"In a Dumpster behind the kitchen at—" He paused for effect. "—Bromleigh Academy."

"Paresi . . ." Her grin widened.

"I know," he said. "It gets even better."

"Tell me."

"There was dried semen on her clothes."

"Oh . . ." Star's eyes closed. "Oh, this is so good."

"Now for the best part."

"More?"

"Would I lie?" Paresi said.

"What else?"

"Mick Slater just called from the lab."

"And?"

Paresi leaned close. "As expected, Shithead Junior's hard disk contained Vampire's Lair. But it's not exactly what the boys showed you a few days ago."

"What?"

"Let me finish," Paresi said. "It gets better."

Star faced him on the bench. "Okay, go on."

"In addition to Vampire's Lair, Junior also had different versions of another hot game, called The Seven Rings. It's another dark, blood-soaked game that his father is going to manufacture."

Star raised her eyebrows. "Going to manufacture? . . . What are you saying?"

Paresi's smile widened. "I'm saying that junior was planning a very big rip-off of dad. Seems little Cody was developing his own version of Vampire's Lair, and he's copped quite a bit out of The Seven Rings. It hasn't even hit stores yet, and he's copied and changed it, to . . ."

"Sell to another gamemaker," Star said.

"From the plans on his computer, he and his little chums have been working on their own game, but to pirate from his dad and sell to dad's competitors before dad can get his product off the drawing board . . . well."

"He's smarter than he looks," Star said. "And Napoleon doesn't have a clue that his son is stealing his empire."

"That's my girl," Paresi said. "Want some more?"

"Be still my heart."

"We've also got his e-mail and diaries, both of which are filled with references to the ritual ceremonies and parties in the lab. He's also pretty talkative about—and I'm quoting here—the 'pussy on the hoof' he picked up in the park."

Star leaned back against the bench, shaking her head. "This is too good."

Paresi winked. "I got more."

"Oh, Dominic."

He waggled a finger in front of her face. "You're gonna wanna kiss me."

"Tell me."

"Most of the mail is between Reptile Boy, the twins, and Alex Monroe, that fat fuck who sits outside Butterworth's office."

Paresi looked at his watch. "And, as we speak, all of the little shits are being rounded up and brought in here, to join old Cody and tell us exactly what they know."

Star leaned over and kissed Paresi noisily on the cheek.

CHAPTER THIRTY-TWO

Captain Lewis stood in the anteroom with Paresi. They watched through the one-way glass as Star spoke to the people assembled around the table in the interrogation room: the Riley twins, their parents, Alex Monroe, Dean Butterworth, Cody Stevens, his father, and their attorney, Lawrence Stockard.

"From the outset, I want to let all of you know that no one is under arrest." Star addressed this last to Alex Monroe who, without parent or representation at the table, looked as if he was about to burst into tears.

"Then why are we here?" Jay Stevens shot an icy look at Star.

"We have some questions regarding our ongoing investigation into the murders in Saint Francis Park," she said, not looking at him. "The clothing and personal effects of the latest victim have been located in a Dumpster in back of the kitchens at Bromleigh Academy."

Dean Butterworth hung his head and stared at the hairy backs of his huge hands.

Star turned toward Diane and Doug Riley. "The victim, Camille Westfall, worked for Dr. Riley."

At the mention of the woman's name, Riley's face paled, a thin sheen of sweat appearing on his skin. His wife looked concerned and slipped her hand over his. He never looked at her. He focused his eyes somewhere beyond the wall of Wanted posters he faced. Diane Riley curled her hand around her husband's. Dr. Riley's fingers remained still on the green metal table, nearly lifeless.

"May I have some water for my husband?" Diane Riley asked.

"Sure." Star headed for the door. "Would anyone else care for anything?"

Most of the occupants shook their heads, and one or two nos floated in the air. Star exited, closing the door behind her.

In the anteroom, she joined Paresi and Lewis.

"Are we on thin ice here, Captain?" she asked.

"You're doing fine, Lieutenant." Lewis leaned on the wall, his eyes focused on the group in the room. They all sat quietly for a moment, and then Alex Monroe began to talk.

"I'm sorry, Cody," he whispered.

"Shut up, shithead!"

"Cody Stevens, you are not to use that language or talk to a fellow Bromleigh student in that tone of voice!" Butterworth's eyes blazed. "I don't believe . . ."

Cody's father interrupted him. "Quiet, both of you! Don't you know they're watching us?"

Alex looked toward the mirror.

"You mean they're on the other side of that glass?"

"What do you think?" Jay Stevens said, looking at the boy as if he had the IQ of a mushroom.

"I thought that was only in the movies," Alex whispered.

"Shut up!" Cody snapped.

"I guess I'd better get some water for Riley," Star said. "He's not looking too good."

"Let me take it in." Paresi headed for the small refrigerator near the rear of the squad room. He plucked out a bottle of water and pulled a paper cup off the stack on the table in the corner.

Star and Lewis watched him enter the interrogation room.

"Who's for water?" Paresi said.

Diane Riley raised her hand. "It's for my husband."

"Good move, Paresi," Star muttered.

Paresi handed her the bottle and the cup. He looked at Riley. "How you doin' there, Doc?"

"Fine," Doug Riley said. "I'm fine."

His wife filled the cup with water and handed it to him. Paresi noted the shakiness of the man's hands.

"This has got to be rough for you," he said. "Camille West-fall worked for you, right?"

Doug Riley swallowed the water. He looked pained. "Yes." He took another sip. "She was part of my office staff."

In the anteroom, Star watched the twins. As their father spoke, they cast glances at one another. The distaste on their faces was also identical.

"Something's going on with the twins," she said.

"I caught that," Lewis said. "Get in there and see if you can't shake it out of 'em."

Star walked into the interrogation room.

"How much longer are we going to have to sit here?" Jay Stevens said. He leaned forward in his chair. His visible anger made his face as red as the suspenders showing beneath his charcoal gray suit jacket.

"Just a few more questions," Star said.

"We didn't bring an attorney. Should we have a lawyer for our boys?" Diane Riley asked.

"Actually, Mrs. Riley, no one needs an attorney," Star said, pointedly looking at the well-dressed, overweight man seated next to Jay Stevens. "No one is under arrest, this is just a talk."

Lawrence Stockard cleared his throat.

"I disagree, Lieutenant." He made a sweeping gesture around the table. "These young men are being railroaded. They all need representation, and since I'm the only attorney present, I advise you that I'm acting for every one of them."

"Well, aren't you a swell guy!" Paresi said. He pointed at the twins. "Does your fee double for them?"

"Keep it up," Stockard said, ominously.

"Let's just finish, okay?" Star said, trying not to show how much she was enjoying Lawrence Stockard's annoyed look. She and Paresi had dealt with him before. Both of them considered him something lower than snail slime. Lawrence Stockard was exactly the kind of attorney who gave credence to all of the lawyer jokes.

"The reason all of you are here is because of something we discovered on Cody Stevens' computer."

"What?" Jay Stevens said.

"The game Vampire's Lair."

"That's one of my company's games," Jay Stevens said. "Of course my son would have it!"

"Does your company manufacture diaries, Mr. Stevens?" Star said.

Jay looked at his son. "What is she talking about?"

Cody shrugged. "I've just been messing around, that's all."

"Messing around how? What did you write?" Jay Stevens said.

Cody hung his head. "Just some of the stuff that me and the guys talk about . . ." He looked at Star. "I made up a lot too."

Stevens turned to Star. "You read my son's personal diaries? We're here because of an adolescent's fantasies?" His little body trembled with rage. "You had my son's computer confiscated for this?"

"Is that true, Lieutenant?" Stockard began scribbling on his legal pad.

"Uh-oh, he's writing. . . . That triples the fee, doesn't it?" Paresi stage-whispered to Jay Stevens. Even the boys **couldn't keep straight faces.**

"The computer was confiscated under Probable Cause, Mr. Stockard," Star said to the attorney. "There have been three murders in and around Saint Francis Park. The killings mirror the deaths of characters in the game you manufacture and your son and his friends were playing. Your son's diaries clearly indicate that he and his friends hired prostitutes to participate in rituals connected to this game."

"Why didn't I know about this?" Jay Stevens demanded of his son.

"It wasn't any big deal," Cody mumbled. "Besides, you don't care what I do."

"What did you say?" Jay Stevens's face darkened with blood, his eyes bulged.

Cody looked directly at his father. "I said you don't give a damn what I do. You never have!"

Stevens rose out of his chair, with his fist clenched, as if to strike his son.

Lawrence Stockard grabbed his arm. "No, Jay!" He pulled the man down. "Sit, just take your seat. Get hold of yourself. We don't want any more trouble."

Jay Stevens sat back in his chair, breathing audibly. His small, sharp-featured face was mottled with rage.

His son looked down at the table, his thin hands shaking.

Lawrence Stockard turned to Star. "Unless you have something that ties my client, or any of these boys, into those killings, Lieutenant, you're looking at a very big wrongful arrest case."

"Nobody's under arrest," Star said, her eyes locked on Stockard. "Read my lips: Nobody is under arrest—" She looked around the table. "—yet."

"Don't try to intimidate these kids, Star," the attorney said.

Star shook her head, and smiled. "It's *Lieutenant* Duvall, Mr. Stockard, and I'm in charge here. That means you're playing on my field. So play nicely or I'll have to detain you."

"Is that a threat?"

"It's a fact." She stood at the head of the table, looking the attorney in the eyes. "Your client and his friends have bragged about picking up prostitutes in Saint Francis Park. One of the murder victims was a known prostitute named

Dolores Causwell. Ms. Causwell was a tall, statuesque blonde woman. There is a reference to a, quote, 'big blonde bitch' in young Mr. Stevens's e-mail."

At the mention of Dolores Causwell, Marshall Butterworth's hands went slick with sweat. The room was closing in on him. He felt as if he were going to start screaming and never stop. He squeezed his hands together, entwining his fingers so tightly that his hands turned white from the cessation of blood flow. He leaned forward in the chair and began to silently pray, his lips unconsciously moving, until he realized Dominic Paresi was staring at him.

"Dad . . ." Cody's eyes looked startled.

"Shut up!" his father snapped.

"And I suppose you had a warrant allowing you to confiscate and *read* his e-mail?" Stockard said.

Star turned to Paresi, who produced papers from the folder he held.

"Here you go, Mr. Stockard." He handed them to the attorney. "You'll note that the warrant is signed by Judge Kelly, and it specifically states that any e-mail or writings on the hard disk are to be made available under the warrant."

Stockard's face grew nearly as red as his client's. He grabbed the papers and made a show of pulling his glasses from the slim brown case in his breast pocket. "This is outrageous," he muttered. "It's a violation of young Mr. Stevens's right to privacy!"

"In this case, Judge Kelly agreed that a murder investigation which turned up possible incriminating evidence was worth looking into," Star said

The attorney looked up at Star. His bottom lip was bloodless, due to his biting it.

"Charge them or let them go," he said.

"Nobody's charging anybody," Star said. "I'm just suggesting that cooperation is the key here, *Larry*."

"Give us a minute please," the attorney said.

"May I please be excused?" Butterworth was on his feet.

"The men's room is down the hall to the left," Star said.

"Thank you." He quickly exited the room. Star and Paresi followed.

In the anteroom, they joined Lewis.

"That Butterworth's a nervous customer," the captain said.

"Yeah," Star agreed. "I think Paresi scares him." Paresi smiled.

Star leaned against the wall, observing Lawrence Stockard huddling with the people at the table.

"He knows we're in here," she said.

"Damn straight." Paresi moved next to her. "But he's got nothing. He can't keep blowing smoke up their butts. He's going to have to give up something."

As if he heard, Lawrence Stockard's voice rose. "They're not arresting anyone. But due to their find, which was legal, they can ask any questions at all. So I'd suggest all of you co-operate and tell the truth."

Butterworth walked back into the room just as Stockard urged them to cooperate. He looked as if the attorney had stomped his mother.

Paresi laughed. "Which one d'ya think's gonna punk out first, Butterworth or the doc?"

"The *truth* is the only way everybody walks away from this station today. I urge you all to tell what you know," Stockard said.

Jay Stevens looked disgusted.

"I'll bet ol' Jay will be wearing out his tiny little fingers punching buttons on that cell phone like a son of a bitch, looking for new counsel on the way home," Paresi said.

CHAPTER THIRTY-THREE

Paresi reached into the bag on top of his desk and pulled out two ice-cold canned sodas. He popped the tops and handed the Pepsi to Star. He took a swig from his 7UP.

"What I wouldn't give to be a fly on the wall at the Stevens house right now."

"I know." Star opened the bag on her desk and pulled out two sets of paper-wrapped plastic chopsticks, straws, and a small bag filled with individual packets of soy sauce and hot mustard.

Paresi took out a white carton bearing the shape of a bright red pagoda stenciled on the outside. He opened it. The aroma of garlic chicken enveloped them both.

"Mmm." Paresi inhaled. "This smells great." He looked across the desk. "You got plates over there?"

Star opened her bottom desk drawer and pulled out two heavy-duty compartmentalized paper plates. She handed one to him.

"I almost feel sorry for Cody," she said.

Paresi looked up at her. "Don't." He opened another container.

Star handed him her plate. "I can smell that all the way over here. China Garden does the best fried rice in the city. Be generous."

Paresi tore the paper from his set of chopsticks and used them to dig the food out of the container and onto her plate. He opened another container. "Garlic string beans," he said. "Guess neither one of us is planning on doing any kissing tonight."

"Not unless you suddenly turn into Michael Jordan," she said. "Pile them on."

Paresi dug out the vegetables with his chopsticks and made a mound of green spicy beans on her plate.

He looked at her. "More?"

"That's enough," she said, reaching out. "Thanks."

"Man, this is good," Paresi said around a mouthful of chicken.

"The best," Star agreed.

They ate in silence for a while. Star looked at her watch.

"The shift's going to be changing soon."

"I know." Paresi wiped his mouth with a paper napkin. "But we should be hearing something any time now."

"Think Dr. Riley and his wife are going to be glad to see us tomorrow?"

"I think the doc is out of it," Paresi said.

"I agree," Star said. "He's *way* too broken up for this to have been just a coworker."

"That's my take," Paresi said. "My money says the doc was putting it to Camille."

The phone rang. She picked it up.

"Homicide, Lieutenant Duvall." She nodded at Paresi. "Hi, Sean. Yeah . . . mm-hmm. Thank you, we appreciate your doing this so late tonight. We owe you one." She hung up the phone.

"We've got our warrant. Now let's see what other goodies the future holds." She pulled a small waxed paper envelope from the bag. She took one of the fortune cookies and handed the other to Paresi.

Paresi cracked the shell of his fortune cookie and dumped the cookie shards on his empty plate. He unfolded the narrow pink paper fortune.

"What does it say?"

"The eye of the eagle star sees and knows. It sees even missing buttons on school blazers."

Star laughed. "It does not!"

Paresi smiled at her. "It should. If you hadn't spotted that missing button on Dave Riley's jacket, we might have lost the twins, and I know they're in this right up to their identical little eyeballs."

Star drank the last of her soda. "Noticing the little things is just something women do. If it's not quite right, we usually catch it."

"Good thing, because I didn't pay any attention."

"That's why we're so good together," she said. "You catch things I don't, and vice versa."

"Oh?" her partner said. "I thought it was because you're crazy for me."

"That too." She smiled and pointed at the fortune in his hand. "So what does it say, really?"

"Says you will be showered with good luck in the new day."

"Hmm," Star said.

"Read yours."

"Okay." She broke open the crisp brown cookie. "No need to look any further. True happiness is right in front of you."

Paresi spread his hands in a "here I am" gesture.

"So much for that." She smiled at him and tossed the broken cookie and fortune in the bag.

"I think you're going to have a real good day tomorrow," he said.

Star nodded. "I'm sure I will. It's going to start the minute we knock on Dr. Riley's door and confiscate his son's blazer."

Jay Stevens poured himself another Scotch on the rocks. His fifth of the night, and he was only now beginning to feel the buzz. What a bitch of a day this had been.

When they got home, his sorry excuse for a son locked himself in his room.

Maybe the little fuck'll hang himself, Jay thought, and sloshed another drink into his glass. He licked the spilled liquor off his fingers and picked up his case. He opened it, trying to look at the notes from the meeting he had left so abruptly that afternoon. His eyes wouldn't focus. He slammed the case shut, and added more Glenlivet to his glass.

"The only good thing about this day is that it's over." The antique clock on the mantel chimed the half hour. It was 10:30. Where the hell was Brenda, his loving wife? He'd started trying to reach her when he was in that hellhole police station, and she still hadn't turned up or answered his many pages.

From somewhere in the depths of the house, he could hear Donna Summer singing "Bad Girls."

"Bad girls," he muttered. "Bad fucking girls." He took a deep swallow of his drink. That stupid kid upstairs, picking up whores in that filthy park, running the risk of God knows what kind of disease. Why didn't Cody tell him he wanted to get laid? He knew where to go, he knew who to call.

Jay drained his glass. Marissa Pynchon ran a class-A house—he could have gotten his son a beautiful *clean* girl. Hell, he could have gotten Marissa herself for Cody. She still turned a trick every now and then, and God knows she gave great head. He felt himself stiffen thinking about it.

"Dammit!" He slammed the glass down on the table. The thick crystal bottom made a ringing noise but didn't break. "Why didn't he come to me?"

"Come to you for what, Jay?"

Brenda Stevens stood in the doorway of the living room. His wife of nearly twenty years, the mother of his two children, and his inspiration.

To Cody she'd passed her red hair and long legs. To Cheyenne, she'd given nothing. At least not that he could see as yet. If adolescence didn't change his daughter, she was going to be a very plain and unhappy young woman. Nothing like her mother.

Every time he looked at Brenda he was reminded of why he married her. A face like that of a chorus girl in some old Technicolor MGM musical and legs that were longer than most men's memories. He had immortalized her in various incarnations in all of the games he'd designed. She had been portrayed as everything from a warrior queen to a sexy female robot.

He'd first seen her when she was a student at UCLA. He was on vacation in Los Angeles, visiting his friend Alan Abbott.

Alan had left Massachusetts right after high school graduation, vowing never to return. After his first year at UCLA, he embarked on a campaign to get Jay to give up MIT and head out to the coast for sun, fun, and beautiful "babes."

After an all-night party in Alan's dorm, the two young men were headed out to the nearest 7-Eleven for Slurpees. Both had discovered that the frozen, garishly colored mush was legendary for its double whammy of satisfying the munchies and curing hangovers.

Alan was talking a mile a minute, trying to convince Jay to give up the slush and cold of New England winters and move to the land of eternal sunshine. Jay was adjusting his shades, trying to keep all that sun out of his eyes, and listening with one ear, when he saw her. She was striding across the lawn, her head high, red hair blowing back from a beautiful face in the warm breeze. Her long legs in white shorts were tan and bare. She wore thong sandals and a maroon colored UCLA sweatshirt that had been ripped at the right shoulder and cut off at the waist, giving him a generous view of tan, sleek flesh.

He knew in that instant that this woman was going to be his wife. He'd even said so, which caused Alan to just about laugh his guts out.

Ignoring his nearly hysterical friend, he walked straight up to Brenda and introduced himself. They were married eight months later. She left the university and the endless summer to live with him in a crummy little flat back in Boston. Seeing Brenda emerge dripping wet from the shower one morning inspired his first bestselling computer game, Mina and the Caves of Kronos.

Twenty years and two children hadn't changed her much. She'd had some work done—a little "maintenance" she called it. But he didn't think she needed a thing. It was just another way to spend his money and make him crazy. She played him. Even now, towering over him in the doorway, she was turning him on. Someday he was going to kill her.

"Answer me, Jay," she said. "What's happening with Cody?"

"Nothing." He got up. His pinstriped blue shirt was rumpled, and his red suspenders hung down over his hips like sad elephant ears. "Where have you been?" he asked his wife.

"You know it's my day at the spa," she said.

"Yeah." Jay poured himself another Scotch and looked at his watch. "The day officially ended about five hours ago." He looked at his wife. "I've been beeping you all day. It's almost eleven. Bren, where were you?"

She joined him at the bar. "I forgot my beeper." Her long hair framed her face, cascading over her shoulders in thick, fiery waves. He almost forgot to breathe. He hated her for making him feel like that.

"Your son was arrested today."

"What?"

In spite of the fact that his marriage was joyless and very nearly dead, Jay Stevens loved putting it to his wife, one way or another.

"Cody may be involved in a murder, Bren."

Brenda Stevens took her husband's drink from his hand and drained it. "Tell me what happened," she said.

Drunk and sloppy, Jay kissed her surprised mouth.

"In the morning." He groped her breast. "In the morning."

She grabbed his hand, stopping him, holding it in a tight grip.

"Now," she said, her eyes cold. "Tell me *now*."

Dave Riley opened the door to his brother's room.

"Danny."

"What?"

"You asleep?"

Dan Riley sat up in bed. "Yeah, that's why I'm answering you!"

"Don't be a shithead." His brother crept into the dark room and closed the door. "We've gotta talk, get our stories straight."

Dan turned on the light next to the bed. His brother flopped down on the quilt. It had been handmade by their maternal grandmother. Each of the boys had one. The quilts were also identical.

"The cops aren't gonna go away," Dave said.

"I know." His brother pulled back the covers and swung his legs over the side of the bed.

"Put something on," Dave said. "I don't wanna sit here looking at your dick."

"Why?" His brother smirked. " 'Cause it's bigger than yours?"

David pulled off his own pajama top and tossed it at his twin.

"We're identical, doofus, and that includes the dick!" The boys laughed. Dan tossed his brother's top back at him, and pulled the covers over his lap.

"That hooker said I was bigger," Dan said, grinning. "She said I tasted better too!"

They laughed again. David stopped first.

"They're on to us—I know it."

His brother, silent now, nodded his head.

"We've gotta tell the truth, Dan." Dave reached out for his brother's hand. "We can't let this stuff go down. We're gonna have to tell Mom and Dad, so we can get help."

Daniel Riley squeezed his brother's hand.

In his bed, with the covers over his head, Alex Monroe sobbed as quietly as he could. As big as this house was, his mother and stepfather had the bedroom right next to his, and the walls were paper thin.

Usually he stayed in his room at Bromleigh. He liked it there. When his mom first urged him to live on campus, he didn't want to, but now he was glad he'd done it. She'd just married Lee Garrett, and she was acting like some kind of love-starved cow. That's why he hadn't called her this afternoon, when he'd had to go to the police station.

He knew she would have made some excuse so she could be with her new husband. Or even worse, she would have come and brought Lee with her. They acted like Siamese twins, together all the time. And they did it constantly. That's why they wanted him out of the house. The thought that they probably did it in his bed sometimes made his stomach flip.

He'd moved into a room on campus nearly two months before, but he still came home for dinner, sometimes as often as three times a week. Every now and then he'd stay over.

Lee never wanted to drive him back to Bromleigh. That was his mom's job. Sometimes she'd be tired or something and she'd let him stay an extra night. Tonight had been different. He'd just turned up and said he wanted to stay in his room. They didn't look very happy about it, but they let him in. After all the grunting and groaning was over in their bedroom next door, he heard Lee tell his mom that he was going out of town on business over the weekend.

That was good. After Lee was gone, he was going to sit down with his mother and tell her all about this horrible day. He was going to tell her everything.

Marshall Butterworth stood in his shower, letting the hot steamy water rain down on him. He lathered his thick curly hair and shampooed it over and over and yet again.

He had to get hold of himself, get control. He turned off the shower and stepped out onto the thick white mat at the shower door.

He grabbed an oversized, plush white bath towel and wrapped it around himself. He went to the mirror. His image appeared distorted and grotesque behind the veil of steam. With his beefy hand, he wiped a small section of the glass clear.

Out in the bedroom, he heard her voice, telling him that the meter was running, and if he didn't hurry up, she was going to have to charge him extra.

Marshall Butterworth wiped the water from his face and dripping scalp. Without drying the rest of his body, he fastened the towel high around his chest, turned out the light, and stepped out into the cool hallway. In the dim light, he could see the whiteness of her naked body, lying on his bed. The black leather whip rested across her belly like a wound, cutting her in half.

When Star got home it was nearly midnight. She closed the front door behind her, and Jake, her fat gray-and-white striped tabby cat, came running. She picked him up.

"Hey, sugarboy." She hugged him to her breast, stroking him, listening to him purr. "I'm sorry I'm so late."

The cat rubbed his sharp little face against her cheek.

"You don't mind garlic breath, huh, Jakey?" She tickled him behind his ears. The cat's emerald eyes closed tightly, and he purred louder.

Star put him down. "Okay, I know all this affection isn't about me. C'mon, let's get you fed." She put her purse and keys on the hall table. "But first . . . messages." She pushed the button on the answering machine. Mitchell Grant's voice made her smile.

"My meeting was over at nine, and I was dragged, kicking and screaming, to the bar at the Hampton House Hotel," he said. "It is now nearly midnight and the switchboard informs me that the squad room is empty . . . should I be worried? Call me when you get in, doesn't matter what time."

She went to the kitchen and opened an individual

serving–sized can of chicken Iams. She spooned the cat food into Jake's dish and set a bowl of fresh water alongside it. The cat went immediately for the dish.

"So much for all that kitty adoration," she said, rubbing his head.

She went back out to the hall and lifted the mail from the woven bronze basket fastened beneath the letter drop cut low into the front door. She riffled through the envelopes and tossed them on the long hall table.

Heading upstairs, she unzipped her suit jacket as she went. In her bedroom, she turned on the light, picked up the receiver of the ivory 1930s-style telephone, and dialed Mitch. He answered on the first ring.

"Kicking and screaming, huh?" She sat on the bed, holding the receiver between her neck and shoulder, unfastening her plum-colored suede T-straps. She pulled them off.

"Like you wouldn't believe," he said. "Tell me, have you ever had to spend an evening with a bunch of meat cutters?"

"Meat cutters?" She grinned.

"Pathologist is too uptown for this time of night," he said.

"No." She stood up and unzipped her skirt. "I've only had to share my evenings with one."

"Well, that one missed you tonight."

"I missed you too."

"What are you doing?" he asked.

"Hmm?"

"It sounds like you're moving around," he said.

"I'm taking my clothes off."

"Oh . . ." Mitch laughed softly. "Want some help?"

"I've been able to undress myself for quite some time now, Doctor."

"I know you're a grown-up girl," he said. "But everybody needs help with those little snaps and buttons now and then."

Star peeled her skirt down from her hips and, again cradling the phone between her neck and shoulder, stepped out of it.

"What just went?"

"My skirt."

There was a silence.

"Mitchell?"

"I'm in the car."

She giggled. "Don't you dare, I've got to be up at the crack of dawn. Paresi and I are serving a warrant over at Dr. Riley's house."

"What for?"

She sat down. "Remember the Bromleigh button we found in the park, near Dolores?"

"Yes."

"One of the twins, Dave, has a button missing from his uniform jacket. I want to have it checked, to see if the one we found matches. We're going to pick the coat up in the morning, before the boys leave for school."

"I see," Mitch said. "That sounds promising."

"Hang on." She put the phone down.

"What was that?" he said, when she picked it up.

"My jacket and . . ." She felt herself grinning.

"And?"

"My bra. Lilac-colored, lace cups, with satin straps. It opens in the front."

"You're a cruel woman, Lieutenant Duvall," he said. "Lilac-colored, lacy cups, satin straps. I think I remember that one. Doesn't it have my teeth marks in it?"

They both laughed.

"I'll call you tomorrow, when I'm back in the house," she said.

"You mean I have to try to sleep with the image of that lacy, lilac-colored bra running around in my head?"

"Mm-hmm. I didn't mention the matching panties and plum-colored silk stockings that are going next."

"Stockings?" Mitch said.

"Stockings." She grinned.

"Not pantyhose?" he said softly.

"Nope." Star put her lips close to the receiver and whispered. "Stockings—thigh-high, lace-topped, plum-colored, *silky* stockings."

Mitch's low growl made her laugh.

"You *are* heartless," he said, his voice low and husky.

"Now you're making me feel bad."

"So why don't I come over and make you feel good?"

She didn't say anything. She couldn't.

"Star?" He said her name softly, as if his lips were touching her ear.

"Why don't I give you a rain check," she said, already kicking herself.

"For?"

"Anything you want."

"Sky's the limit?" he asked. She could tell he was smiling. Eyes closed tight, she nodded. "Yep."

Mitch drew in his breath, a soft, whispery, sexy sound that made her pause to rethink his coming over.

"Agreed," he said, finally.

She sat with her eyes closed, fingers pressed to her mouth, trying to keep herself from saying, To hell with tomorrow, get over here!

"Sky's the limit?" he purred. "Anything I want?"

"Do you know what you want?" The words tumbled out of her mouth.

"Oh yes," Mitch whispered. "I know *exactly* what I want."

"Are you going to tell me?"

"Tomorrow night, Lieutenant," he said. "No backing out."

"Sounds ominous . . . and intriguing."

He didn't say anything.

"Mitchell?"

"Rest up." He made a kissing sound. "Good night."

CHAPTER THIRTY-FOUR

Star looked up to see Loman Rayford enter the squad room. The detective stood six feet five and one half inches tall, and weighed in at nearly three hundred pounds. Though he walked with a limp, as a result of a college football injury, his bulk and his deep brown skin made her feel as if a giant redwood had uprooted itself and was headed her way.

"Big Man," she said. "A personal visit from BCI's head honcho, this must be good news."

Loman pulled up a chair next to her and settled his bulk into it.

"I brought you something to make you smile," he said.

Paresi pointed at the manila folders in Loman's huge hand. "The blazer?"

Loman nodded. "Yep, and some other things."

"We just picked it up this morning," Star said. "That was fast."

Loman opened the first folder. "You know I don't like making you wait for anything." He winked at her. "I've got a bonus for you too."

Paresi moved his chair next to Star's desk as she leaned in to see what the man was laying out.

"First, the button." Loman pointed to the photo of the Bromleigh button, enlarged to fill the whole frame. "This is the front. See the marks on it."

Star picked up the photo, bringing it closer. "Looks like it's been rubbed against something . . . scraped."

"That's right." Loman produced another photo from the file, and handed it to her. "Here's the back—notice the broken thread."

"The thread is yellow." Star looked at Loman. "I'm sure the tailor didn't use yellow thread on a blue blazer. It must have been sewn on by someone else."

"Exactly. Now take a look at junior's coat." Loman produced an extreme close-up of the area of the jacket that had the missing button.

"See that?"

Star leaned closer. "Blue thread." She sat back dejectedly in her chair. "Rats!"

"C'mon now, don't give up yet," Loman said, producing another photo. "This one shows the two other buttons on the blazer. What do you see?"

Star studied the photos. "I see that the button we found is different."

"Right," Loman said. "The button you found has *two* dates underneath the etching of the building." He pointed at the photo of David Riley's blazer. "These buttons have *one* date stamped on them—1895, the year the school opened."

"Damn," Star said. "That means it's not his button."

"Right, but that doesn't mean you're out of luck," Loman said. "Look again."

The two detectives pored over the photos.

"The buttons on this jacket have the same scrapings as on the button we found," Paresi said.

"Who said Italians are dumb?" Loman grinned.

"Hey!" Paresi shoved him playfully.

"That means that these scrapings on the button you found and the buttons on this jacket, being the same, both having come from being rubbed against something made of stone."

Loman produced a photo showing an extreme close-up of the button found near Dolores Causwell's body, and one showing a section of Dave Riley's jacket. "See here?" He pointed to the photo of the jacket. "See that streak of white?"

Star and Paresi nodded.

"That's stone and mortar dust on the jacket. It's also in the button crevices." He looked at Star. "I sent a team out to the old lab for scrapings, and guess what?"

"Match?" she said.

Loman nodded. "Match. It comes from the molding around the front door. Evidently they had to push and squeeze their way in sometimes."

Star looked at Paresi. "That puts David Riley at the lab."

"Yep," Paresi agreed. "But the button isn't his, so what next? A check of every blazer on campus?"

Star shook her head. "There's a reason that the buttons on Riley's coat don't have two dates." She looked at Paresi and Loman. "The ones with two dates must be special buttons, not ordinary uniform issue."

"I think you're right," Loman said. "It should be easy to check."

Star leaned back in her chair. "We're looking for somebody who sewed his button on with yellow thread. Somebody who didn't attach it securely, since it fell off in the park."

"Somebody who has been in the old lab," Paresi said, following her train of thought.

"Somebody who doesn't have a mother looking after him." She looked at Paresi. "Somebody who's on his own."

"Alex came in without a parent," Paresi said. "No mom or dad, and he's also porky enough to have popped a button!"

"That's a thought," Star said. "But you can bet that since Dave Riley was in that lab, his brother was somewhere close by. If Alex was there, he was following the crowd."

"And don't forget old Cody," Paresi said. "You know he's in on it. He's the King Vampire. What he says goes. My money says anything those twins and fat boy do is directly related to Cody's calling the shots."

"I agree," Star said. "But they're tight. They back each other up. You saw that yesterday."

"What I saw is that Alex is the weak link. We pull him in alone, and I guarantee, he's gonna crack," Paresi said.

"Before y'all pull out the rubber hoses, I've got more," Loman said.

"Sorry, Loman," Star said. "Just thinking out loud." She pointed to the folders. "Hope there's some *good* news in there."

"Let's see what I can do." Loman opened another folder and pulled a report from inside. "These are the lab results on the semen on Camille Westfall's clothes." He put the paper in the middle of the desk, and the two detectives again leaned close.

"According to this report, the semen came from a white male, approximately thirty-five to fifty years old. Type B Negative blood."

"That age group fits Dr. Riley," Star said.

Paresi looked at her. "And a lot of other guys," he said. "I'm betting Riley won't take kindly to your asking him if he bagged his clerk before he hacked her to pieces. We need to get a blood sample before we can rack him on this."

"You've got a point," Star said. "B Neg blood is kind of

rare, right? I mean, if we can type the doc at B Neg, he's a viable suspect . . . right?"

"Not necessarily," Loman said. "B Neg is not common—about twenty percent of Caucasians have it—but it's not really considered rare. If I were you, I'd wait for more pieces of the puzzle before taking on her boss."

He placed another photo on the desk. This one showed Camille's dirty, rumpled clothing. "We also lifted some hair from the woman's blouse and from the underside of her skirt. We got mud too, and the analysis shows that it's from the lab area."

"Anything else?" Star asked.

"Yep." Loman pulled out another report. "Grant's office gave us the hair found on her body. There were two kinds, head hair and pubic hair. Two different kinds of each type of hair."

"You mean there was more than one person?" Star said.

"Looks like it." Loman nodded. "Some strands showed a dark blond color."

"Dr. Riley is dark blond," Star said.

"Again, before you go to him, there were also gray strands. That means another suspect." Loman looked at Star.

"Riley's got some gray mixed in," Star said. "It could *all* be his hair. How do you know it's two different sets of hair?"

"Composition and color," Loman said. "Graying hair has two colors. The original and the gray, with the gray coming from the root. The first sample was gray head hair, with a thin shaft. The second sample of head hair was heavier, with a thicker shaft, but it too showed gray, with some sort of dye present."

"So maybe he dyes his hair," Star said, "and it's thinning in some areas and thicker in others."

"That's a thought," Loman said. "But it doesn't fly. They're two totally different types of head hair."

He pulled out a typewritten report. "Also, a couple of the head hair samples were found in her pubic hair combings, and they'd been ripped out at the root."

Star and Paresi looked at each other. He opened his mouth.

"Don't say it," Star said.

"I didn't say a word," Paresi said, winking at Loman, making him smile.

Star caught the interplay. "Both of you, behave!"

Paresi raised his hands. "No comment from over here."

Star shot him an "I know you" look and went back to the photo. "Since some of the hair was gray, are you saying the kids couldn't be involved? I mean she could have been killed later, after having sex with the gray-haired guy."

Loman nodded. "That's a stretch. What did she do, get laid and then take a walk in the park, down by the old lab?"

Star shrugged. "I don't know, but I *will* find out. I'm not eliminating those kids because of this hair evidence. They're solid, and it's possible that they got to her after she'd been with their father. Believe me, I know looks can be deceiving, but Dr. Riley doesn't strike me as a man who could make love to a woman and then viciously and brutally murder her.

"Besides, whoever did this was playing the game. They hacked her up, buried the pieces under the lab floor, dropped a note on Paresi's desk, and delivered the head and hands to me."

"Yeah, but don't rule out a copycat . . . somebody who knows the game, and is using it, and then coming to you because you're working it. It's no secret anymore that you and Paresi have this case."

"You're right. A lot of the details have leaked through the media, and Paresi and I got busted the other night working the park. We took down a pimp with an audience, so it's no secret what we're up to. Anybody could have been out there. But the note thing feels to me like something kids would do, you know, to try to muddy the waters and bust our chops at the same time."

Loman looked at her. "That note could have come from anywhere, even from someone who saw you in the park."

"But they brought it right into the station," Star said. "Paresi found it on his desk. If it was somebody who saw us in the park, it had to be somebody presentable, and at that hour, when we busted the pimp, I'm pretty sure there weren't any decent people around. I can't see some filthy wino or crackhead making it past the front desk and up the stairs. It had to be somebody who could blend in. Think about it, Loman. A kid in a school blazer could walk around here easily. There's always some field trip or youth group going through here."

Loman settled back in the chair. "I know, this place is busy—and *open*. Unless they're on fire, practically anybody could walk through the lobby and disappear anywhere in the building. But I still think somebody would notice a pack of Bromleigh kids roaming around. Maybe somebody else delivered the note for them."

"If one kid did it, nobody would pay much attention," Paresi said. "Maybe one came in here while the others put the ice chest in your parking space."

"Swell." Star slumped in her chair, then turned toward Loman. "Did you get the results on the note yet?"

Loman nodded. "The fingerprint results are in." He rooted through the folder. "And the results on the paper itself just came in. I haven't had a chance to really look at it yet."

He pulled out two sheets of paper. "Here's the fingerprint analysis. Neither the note nor the envelope showed fingerprints, other than Paresi's, so gloves were used from the beginning."

"That lets the bums off," Star said. "What about the paper?"

Loman looked at the second sheet.

"Maybe you should give up Homicide, Star, and come work with us."

"What?"

"According to this, the paper stock is a common one, but the watermark says Tiffany's."

Star sat up straight. "Tiffany's, like the store?"

Loman nodded. "Yep. They charge a bundle for their stationery and there's really nothing special about it, except the mark, and it can't even be seen by the naked eye."

"Would those kids have access to Tiffany stationery?" Paresi said.

"They would if it was in the house. . . ." Star looked at him. "Keep in mind, these are wealthy people."

"Here's something else that might help," Loman said.

Star looked at him. "What?"

"The note was typed on a typewriter, not a computer."

"Can you tell what kind?" Star said.

"An old IBM Selectric II, with self-correcting tape. One of the words was misspelled, lifted, and retyped."

"My money is still on those boys," Star said. "Were the hair samples checked for DNA?"

Loman frowned and shook his head. "Impossible."

"Why?" Star asked.

Because the roots are dried out. There's no source of DNA to check."

"I don't understand."

"Let me see if I can explain this," Loman said. "Hair is already dead. The only part that's alive is the root. DNA is stored in the roots."

"I know that," Star said. "What I don't understand is how all of the roots could be dead. How long does it take a ripped-out root to dry?"

"Anywhere from twelve to thirty-six hours, depending on whether or not it's exposed to air."

"And if it's not?" Star asked.

Loman shrugged. "Depends on conditions. Besides drying out, the root bulb decays and any DNA rots with it."

"No chance of getting even a trace?" Paresi asked.

"Not enough to make a difference," Loman said. "Since the body was found under the floor, it worked as a good and bad thing."

"How so?" Star asked.

"It's been getting warm early in the day, and the body was in an airless environment," Loman said. "Ordinarily, you'd think she would have just fallen apart."

"But she didn't," Star said.

"No." Loman leaned on the edge of her desk. "She lucked out. Even though the decomposition was advanced, during the day the heat produced a drying effect, and the nights have been cool. The boards provided a way to refrigerate or keep the cool air circulating around the parts. The soil was also relatively dry, even though there was insect infestation. It also contained an element that in all honesty probably would have eventually mummified the remains, had she not been found."

"Shouldn't all of that have *preserved* the hair roots?" Paresi said.

Loman pointed to the photo of the hair samples. "I know it sounds strange, but there were two different processes going on in the soil and on the corpse. The body parts, including the pelvic area, were found facedown. That means the skin, holding a lot of the hair samples, had first contact with the soil.

"The root bulb of the hair dried because of the minerals in the soil. It decayed because there was also moisture present, and the decomposition of the body began in the soil-covered areas. Insects got to those parts first, plus the fluids all drained and collected there." He pulled out another photo, showing enlarged hair strands.

"This is the dark blonde sample. See the root?"

Star nodded. "It's pretty fried, all right."

"Keep in mind what I said. Hair is already dead, and once it's yanked out, that's it. But it still tells the story. This—" He pulled out another photo. "—this is one of the other head hairs. See? It's gray at the root, but the change up the shaft isn't natural. This hair has been dyed."

"Can you tell what color?" Star asked.

Loman shrugged. "Something with a red, orange, or yellow base. There isn't enough hair to pull a strong color."

Star and Paresi looked at one another.

"Maybe the doctor is touching up his gray," Star said, "lightening a little, to bring back the blond."

"Riley doesn't strike me as a Grecian Formula kind of guy," Paresi said.

Star shrugged. "I don't know. Men can be just as vain as women. Camille was young, maybe he was trying to keep his appeal going."

"There was also gray pubic hair, different from the other, found in the examination," Loman said. "See?" He laid out another photo. "Here's the combings. This is Camille's pubic hair, but . . ." He put down another picture. "These two sets of pubic hair are totally different. One is gray and the other is mixed, dark blonde and gray, like the head hair."

"And you think it's two different sets of pubic hair," Star said.

"You agree?" Loman questioned.

"Nope," Star said. "I still think all of it belongs to the doc, because if he was all that concerned about age, he would have dyed his pubes as well as his head hair."

"Dye his pubic hair?" Paresi looked skeptical.

"Yeah," Star said. "People do it all the time."

"Themselves?" Paresi asked, amused.

"Sure, but there are beauticians who do it too," Star said.

"And sometimes I hate *my* job!" Paresi said.

"Mostly, I'd think it would be a private thing," Star continued. "You can do it yourself."

"And what happens if you spill it?" Paresi said, cracking himself up. "Talk about your burning love!"

The detectives laughed.

Collecting the papers and himself, Loman put all the materials back in the file. "Before we get too carried away here, Mitch said there was microscopic evidence that she'd had sex shortly before she died, but due to the degree of decomposition, he couldn't really pinpoint a time or tell if it was forced. My guess is she was willing, but somewhere it got out of hand." He looked at Star. "Have I helped?"

Star smiled at him. "Always. I owe you."

"I'll put it on your tab." Loman grinned.

"One more favor," she said.

"Anything."

She leaned back in her chair. "With this information, I think we've got enough to at least start tossing around the idea of hair and fluid samples, from the doc and possibly those kids. Can you turn the tests around quickly for me?"

"I'll do what I can," he said, standing, "but count on at least ten days, even if it's rushed."

Star nodded. "Thanks."

Loman winked at her. "I'll be in touch." He headed for the squad room double doors.

Star pointed to Paresi's phone. "You want to get Sean and see if we've got enough to at least start all the paperwork for the tests?"

"Okay. What are you going to do?"

"I'm going to see Dean Butterworth."

"Without me?"

"Definitely without you."

CHAPTER THIRTY-FIVE

Even though Star had called before she arrived, Butterworth appeared surprised to see her. She came alone, without her partner. She sat across from him with only the tea table separating them. He felt her warmth and allowed himself to think of them out for an evening, getting to know one another. He liked watching her.

"This is a lovely campus," she said, truthfully. Her nearly golden colored, amber eyes looked past him, through the leaded glass window behind his chair.

Butterworth thought the combination of her light eyes and dark skin was striking. He liked her hair too. It was short, closely cropped, and sculpted to the shape of her head. It set off her high cheekbones and provided a perfect frame for her face.

"Yes," he said, turning slightly in his chair. "It's like being in another time, a different place."

Star nodded. "It must be peaceful, spending one's days here."

Butterworth nodded. "Yes, it has been a sanctuary for me, at certain times in my life." He sipped his tea. "I first came here as a student."

"Really?" Star looked at him.

"Yes." Butterworth nodded, lost in her eyes. She was truly a handsome woman. Her face was much too striking for such a wimpy word as pretty. He imagined her in leather, wearing thigh-high spike-heeled boots, wielding the whip, making him her slave.

As if she heard his silent thoughts, Star looked directly at him. Her eyes forced him to look away. It excited him.

"This must seem like home to you," she said.

Butterworth nodded. "I have spent more years on this campus than I have at my family home in New York."

"Are you from Manhattan?"

"No." Butterworth put his cup down. "I grew up in Brooklyn," he said, searching her face for reaction. There was none.

"I'm a Brookport native," she said. "My dad was a police officer."

"Is that why you do what you do?"

Star smiled at him. "It started out that way," she said. "But I truly love my work."

"It seems a very demanding occupation for a woman," Butterworth said. "Especially working such an unpleasant assignment as homicide. I would imagine you've dealt with some very disturbed individuals."

Star didn't answer. She looked out the window again. "It's starting to warm up," she said, changing the subject.

He'd hit on something, but he dared not push it.

"Yes." He settled back in the chair. "The weather at this time of year is so unpredictable. One day you're freezing, and the next, you're searching for sunglasses and beach balls."

Star smiled.

Butterworth smiled back, and continued watching her. The way she held the antique bone china teacup, with the matching saucer perfectly balanced on her palm beneath it. . . . Someone had taken the time to teach her that. He wondered what else she'd learned . . . about pain and pleasure.

Star looked at the man sitting across from her, and then at his framed diplomas and accolades. They covered the cream colored wall to the left of his massive desk. She knew that even now, after so many years, he still thrilled to seeing his name engraved on the tasteful brass marker attached to the solid, heavily polished, ornate door of this office.

Without the frown, usually provoked by Paresi, Marshall Butterworth wasn't a bad-looking man. His eyes were intense, often a sign of myopia, but still they were dark, almost black and crackling with intelligence. His mouth was actually very pretty. His lips were full and beautifully shaped.

His nose, which was long, tended to be the only unbalancing aspect to his features. In profile it was beaklike, but like an eagle rather than a less majestic bird. The heaviness of his body added weight to his face. Even so, Star thought he was interesting.

His hands were huge, and as he reached for his tea, they dwarfed the fine china cup.

She's smiling, Butterworth thought. A tiny smile, almost hidden, but a smile nonetheless. She was enjoying his company. She wasn't wearing a ring. Maybe when this nightmare was over, he'd invite her to dinner. Perhaps his fantasy could become reality.

He sipped his perfectly brewed, imported, Fortnum & Mason's Royal Blend tea. All she could say was no.

"I'm certain all of this attention to Bromleigh is upsetting for you," she said.

Marshall nodded. His curly hair caught a ray of sunlight from the floor-to-ceiling windows. Star noted it was white at its winding roots.

"It's a nightmare, Lieutenant," he said.

"I'm sorry if we've been hard on you."

"Just doing your job, I suppose," Butterworth said wearily. "Although I suspect your partner enjoyed it very much."

Star smiled. He liked this smile. It was open, unguarded.

"Sergeant Paresi tends to get caught up in investigations," she said.

"Takes them personally, does he?"

She shook her head. "No. But he likes to make sure all the loose ends are tied and that we've done the best job we could in getting to the bottom of things."

Butterworth nodded. "I guess I can understand that. It's just that he rubs me the wrong way."

"Don't feel bad, he rubs a lot of people the wrong way," Star said.

"But you like him?"

Another smile, only different, more Mona Lisa this time,

secretive. Maybe he'd been wrong about her relationship with the Italian. Maybe they *were* lovers.

"I trust him with my life," she said earnestly. "Sergeant Paresi is a very good man. He's very dedicated," Star continued. "Believe me, all he wants is an end to the killings and justice for the victims."

"Something we all agree upon, Lieutenant. Would you like more tea?"

"No thank you."

"Then what else can I do for you?"

She set her cup and saucer on the table, and settled back in her chair. "I just wanted to come by and thank you for your cooperation in this investigation," she said. "I know having Camille Westfall's body and clothing found on Bromleigh property and then having to come down to the precinct and see your students in interrogation must have been difficult."

"It's been extremely upsetting." Butterworth furrowed his brow. "I still can't imagine my boys being involved in sex games . . . and seeing prostitutes."

"I know it's rough," Star said. "But I need to ask you something about the twins and Cody Stevens's family lives."

"I don't know much." He suddenly looked tired, and disappointed. "I've only observed their families at school social events, mixers, and the like."

"Can you tell me something about those?"

Butterworth shrugged. "I can't think of anything that would be of use to you."

"What about the boys and their interactions with their parents?"

"Nothing unusual," Butterworth said. "Although I do recall . . ."

"What?"

He sat forward, staring at her, his dark eyes almost hypnotic.

"We have lots of family evenings and mixers here. Mrs. Stevens usually attends alone," he said. "Her husband works such long hours."

Star nodded.

"The Rileys always come. They are very supportive of

the boys' education. However, we had a parents' evening a few months back, and I noticed that the Rileys came with another young woman. She was introduced to me as Camille Westfall."

"At a family event? That's strange," Star said.

"Yes," Butterworth agreed. "I'm not one for gossip, but it certainly appeared that Dr. Riley was very fond of the young woman."

"And Mrs. Riley was okay with her being there?"

"The three of them came together and they left together. Mrs. Riley seemed totally at ease with the situation. I did notice that the twins boycotted both their parents and Ms. Westfall that evening, though at their ages, that in itself is not unusual."

"No," Star said. "Teenagers never want to be around their parents."

"That's exactly how it seemed to me, and Mrs. Riley didn't appear to be bothered by it."

"How about the doctor?"

"He spent a good deal of time . . . how can I say it . . . uh, campaigning."

"Campaigning?"

"Yes." Butterworth nodded. "Dr. Riley is very well thought of in the community and he's very social. He always makes it a point to spend time with other parents at these get-togethers.

"And Mrs. Riley is left on her own?" Star said.

Butterworth nodded. "Usually. Sometimes she interacts with other parents, but mostly she'll be with Mrs. Stevens, which is understandable, since their sons are friends and as I said, Mrs. Stevens usually attends these events alone."

"Did Mrs. Stevens interact with Mrs. Riley that night?"

Butterworth folded his hands across his stomach. "Yes, I believe she did."

"Even though Ms. Westfall was there?" Star asked.

"Yes," Butterworth said emphatically. "I remember thinking they were such lovely women, and it was somewhat striking to see the three of them together."

"Did they stick together for the entire evening?"

Butterworth shook his head. "No. Mrs. Riley and Camille spent a great deal of the evening together, but Mrs. Stevens left about an hour after she arrived."

"But Ms. Westfall and Mrs. Riley stayed together," Star said.

"Oh yes, they were actually very close," Butterworth said.

"In what way?"

He leaned forward, nearly whispering, as if sharing an enormous secret with Star.

"After Mrs. Stevens had gone, and while Dr. Riley made the rounds, Mrs. Riley and Camille stayed together in the meeting hall. They seemed very happy in one another's company. They were almost like sisters, heads together, whispering and laughing. At one time, when I saw them, they were sharing the same glass of punch, and a small plate of finger sandwiches."

Star's mind went back to Mrs. Riley's description of her late friend, Irene Kavaraceus. Her "bestest girlfriend." Maybe Diane Riley was like Star herself. A woman who loved and respected her best friend.

Star let her mind race. However, if Vee died, she couldn't see herself forming that same kind of deep attachment with a new "best friend."

Maybe Diane just needed a female view. Living in a house full of men, she must have longed for the same kind of fun and spirit she'd had with Irene. Enter Camille, who, though younger, and though she was obviously fooling around with Dr. Riley, had still managed to make herself Diane's latest "bestest girlfriend." Star crossed her legs. "Interesting," she said.

"Very." Butterworth watched her face. She had left him for a few moments in her mind, and she'd be gone soon. He'd given her what she came for. Information.

"Dean Butterworth," Star said.

"Yes?"

"May I ask you something else?"

"Surely."

"I'm curious about the buttons on your school blazers. I've seen some with the emblem of the school stamped on them, and the years 1895 to 1995 under the impression of the school."

"Yes," Butterworth said. "Those are special issue. They were produced during our centennial, as a part of the celebration of Bromleigh's one-hundred-year history. At first we gave the buttons to teachers only, but later, during the year, we decided to award some of the buttons to our academically outstanding students. The regular buttons have the school emblem but only one date."

"Thank you," she said.

She had asked her questions. Gotten what she came for, he thought. Now, she was going to figure out some way to graciously exit.

Star indicated her cup. "You know, I think I would like some more tea. May I?"

The woman was *not* predictable.

Nearly four hours after she'd left the squad room, Star returned. Paresi sat at his desk, the contents of three folders arranged in front of him.

"Don't tell me you've been with Butterworth all this time."

She sat down. "Uh-huh."

"And?"

"And he's not a bad guy. He gave me a lot of information."

"Tell me later," Paresi said. "Mitch wants you to call him."

"Thanks." Star picked up the phone and dialed the doctor's private number. Mitch answered immediately.

"Hi, Paresi said you called."

"Yes. Tell him to pick up the phone," Mitch said.

Star signaled to Paresi to pick up his phone.

"Yeah, Mitch?"

"Hi, Dom," the doctor said. "I wanted you both on the line for this."

"Go ahead," Star said.

"On the Camille Westfall case . . ."

"Yeah?" the detectives said in unison.

"As you know, she was strangled, with the bruising inside the skin of the neck."

"Yes," Star said.

"And I told you before that this type of bruise usually happens when the killer doesn't have the grip strength necessary to really finish the job. Strangulation usually means a fighting victim," Mitch said. "You have to be strong to hang on."

"You told us the killer probably wore heavy workman's gloves," Star said. "That would have allowed him to grip tighter."

"Yes," Mitch said. "But I had to think about that, and when I did, I went back to the body."

"What did you find?"

"Lipstick."

"What?" the detectives said in unison.

"On the skin shreds of the neck, near where she was cut. I put her together and took one more look. There was a waxy, faded, russet-colored stain on her neck, below and nearly behind the ear, partially buried in and just below the hairline, very near the point of decapitation. I was able to excise enough skin to stick under a microscope," he said. "Lipstick."

Star exchanged looks with Paresi. "This is getting so bizarre."

"I know," Mitch said. "The hair samples we found on the body had dried bulbs, meaning they'd been pulled out at the root. The next question would be what makes one person yank another person's hair out?"

"Anger?" Star asked.

"Maybe," Mitch said. "But I opt for the other side of the coin, Lieutenant. Passion. Passion can make a person pull another person's hair out," he said. "Sometimes it's lust, and sometimes it's rage. But considering where the hair was found, I'm going with lust."

"Okay, that's enough for me." Paresi nestled the phone against his shoulder, closed the files on his desk, and stacked them to one side. "It's been a very long day," he said, "and I'm on overload." He held the phone again in his hand and looked across his desk at Star. "I'm taking Vee and the kids to Uncle Ange's restaurant tonight for dinner. You two wanna come?"

"Thanks, Dom, but Star and I have plans," Mitch said. "Another time?"

"For sure," Paresi said. "I'm out. Thanks, Doc." He looked

at Star. "You two have a good night." He hung up the phone, stood up, saluted Star, grabbed his coat, and headed for the door.

"Did Dominic leave?" Mitch said.

"Yep." Star watched her partner disappear. "He's had enough for one day, and I don't blame him. Now what are these plans you and I have for tonight?" she said.

"Last night you said this evening was mine." His voice became a soft whisper. "That I could have anything I wanted. Remember?"

Star swiveled in her chair, grinning like a five-year-old. "Yes."

"Be at my house in an hour."

"Dinner?" she said.

Mitch laughed. "Eventually."

CHAPTER THIRTY-SIX

"Homicide. Lieutenant Duvall."

"And just where were you and Dr. Long, Lean, and Fine last night?"

"Good morning, Verenita," Star said. "Did you enjoy your night out at the restaurant?"

"Actually, we had a great time," Vee said. "But no changing the subject. I thought you and Mitch would be going with us."

"We would have, but Paresi didn't say anything until the end of the day. By that time, we had other plans."

"Uh-huh, and you couldn't change them?"

"No," Star said, grinning. "But we're going to get together and do the restaurant thing with you guys next time. How are Angelo and Rosa?"

"They're doing fine. They're such sweet people, and

Dominic's uncle is so good-looking. He's like looking at Dominic in the future."

"Paresi should be so lucky," Star said.

"Hey!"

"Just kidding." She grinned. "I love Angelo and his wife."

"The kids had so much fun. Cole discovered he loves calamari, even after Angelo told him what it was, and Rosa took Lena into the kitchen and taught her how to fill cannoli. We all had a good time. I just missed you, that's all."

"I'm sorry we couldn't come. We'll do something soon, just you and me. How about that?"

"I could go for that. I mean I love having Dominic around, the kids are crazy about him, but sometimes I miss us."

"Me too," Star said, looking at the clock. "Speaking of Paresi, where is he?"

"He'll be in soon—he got a late start," Vee said.

"Uh-huh."

The two friends laughed.

"Don't say nothing to me," Vee said. "Cause I *will* tell you what you were up to last night."

"Okay, okay," Star said. "I'm quiet." She looked up. "Speak of the devil, guess who just dragged in, and looking pretty tired too!"

Vee laughed.

"Morning." Paresi hung up his coat.

"Hello," Star said. "Vee's on the phone."

Paresi tapped the lighted button on his telephone, and picked up the receiver. "Hey, baby."

"Hi."

"Did you have a good time last night?" Paresi said.

"Couldn't you tell?" Vee said, seductively.

"More than I want to know," Star said. "I'm off." She hung up and left them to talk. She went upstairs and got a double chocolate muffin. When she came back, Paresi was looking at the file on Camille Westfall. She tore the muffin in two and gave him half.

"Butterworth told me something weird yesterday," she said, sitting down.

"What?"

"He said that the Rileys showed up at a family night at Bromleigh with Camille Westfall in tow, and that she and Mrs. Riley were very, very chummy."

"Yeah?"

"Uh-huh. He said they even shared a glass of punch and a plate of food together."

"So? We're sharing this." He took a bite of the muffin. "And you and I have been known to drink from the same glass. I've seen you and Vee do it too."

"Yeah. But if I'm found murdered somewhere, you can bet Vee's lipstick won't be on my neck!"

"You think those two were . . ." He moved his hand in a see-sawing motion.

"What do you think?" she said, breaking off a piece of the muffin and putting it in her mouth.

"I think Riley was diddling his clerk."

"And you don't think she could have been maybe 'friendly' with Mrs. Riley too?"

Paresi shrugged.

"C'mon, Paresi, you watch Jerry Springer. This isn't exactly new. People are into freaky stuff."

"Maybe in trailer parks," Paresi said. "The doc and his wife don't strike me as swingers."

Star shook her head. "No . . . but you can't tell from looking at the outside. Butterworth said Mrs. Riley is friendly with Jay Stevens's wife too."

"Their kids are friends," Paresi said. "Makes sense."

Star took another bite of the muffin. "Yeah, but I'm thinking we should get hair samples from the entire Riley family, including the missus."

"You really think Diane Riley's involved in this?"

Star shrugged. "I don't know. But with what Butterworth said, and the lipstick, I don't think it's too far out to consider."

"Maybe the lipstick was Camille's," Paresi said.

Star arched one eyebrow. "And she was double-jointed so she kissed herself on the neck?"

Paresi laughed. "Okay, okay. Maybe the doc kissed her, got lipstick on his mouth, and when he kissed her neck, it came off on her."

"That's some theory," Star said.

Paresi finished his muffin in two bites, and dusted crumbs from his hands. "I'm just thinking out loud. It takes a certain kind of guy to be in the middle of a woman sandwich, and to my mind, Doc Riley ain't it."

"I agree," Star said. "But maybe he didn't know he was the filling." She looked at the report on top of the file. "Loman said there was dyed gray hair on the body."

"Yeah, but Diane Riley has brown hair. No gray," Paresi said.

"Ever hear of Clairol?" Star took another bite from the muffin. "Besides, her hair is a shade of brown that *nobody* has without help."

"Okay," Paresi agreed. "But he also said the dye had a red base. Brown ain't red."

Star finished the muffin, plucked a Kleenex from the box on her desk, and wiped her fingers. She tossed the tissue into her wastebasket and reached into her bottom desk drawer. She pulled out her rubber band ball.

"I've been burgled," Paresi said.

"Lock your desk." She opened her middle drawer and pulled out a handful of rubber bands, snapping one around the already immense ball.

"Loman said the dye had a red, orange, or yellow base, all warm colors. That would include the color of Diane Riley's hair."

"Okay, I'll give you that," Paresi said. "But the report also says there were two kinds of pubic hair. I think they made a mistake."

"How?"

"I was thinking about this."

"When, last night?" Star gave him a knowing grin.

"Yeah," he said, returning her smile. "*Late* last night."

She snapped another rubber band on the ball. "Let's hear it."

Paresi leaned forward. "The pubic hair found mixed in with hers was gray."

"Right. There were two kinds of hair in the pubic area," Star said. "Gray and dark blond mixed gray."

"It had to be the doc," Paresi said. "He was her only lover. Even though some of the pubic hair was all gray, I'd say it's all from Doc Riley. If he's going gray upstairs, he's more than likely already gray downstairs. It's Riley's hair."

"Which Riley?" Star said. "The doctor or the doctor's wife?"

"You're not gonna give on that three-way, are you?"

"Makes sense, don't you think?"

Paresi laughed. "I think you've been hanging around Mitch too long."

Star wound another rubber band around the ball. "I think we should go have a chat with Diane Riley. What do you say?"

"Let's do it," Paresi said.

Star put the ball in her drawer and closed it. As she reached for her coat, the young man came up to her desk.

"Lieutenant Duvall?"

She turned, surprised.

"I need to talk to you. Do you have time?"

Paresi's eyes across the desk held a little smirk, but he kept silent.

"I'll make time. Let me see if a room is free," Star said.

Alex Monroe's round, chubby cheeks flushed, but he looked relieved.

CHAPTER THIRTY-SEVEN

"Does he have to be in here?" Alex whispered to Star.

"Yeah, I do," Paresi answered, taking a seat near the window, facing Star.

"We work together, Alex," Star said. "You talk to me, you're talking to him anyway. He stays."

"I don't want him here," the boy said.

"Tough shit, junior," Paresi said.

Alex looked at Star. "He *scares* me," he whispered.

"Give me a break," Paresi muttered.

Star looked over the boy's head at him. "He's not going to hurt you, Alex."

"I know," the boy said. "He can't, because you're here, but he still scares me."

"Alex," Star said. "You came here for a reason. Sergeant Paresi and I are a team. If you've got something to say, say it. If not, you're not under arrest, you can leave."

Alex looked again at Paresi. He shrugged his shoulders. "Okay."

"What do you want to talk about?" Star said.

The boy looked sad, his eyes reddened. "About what happened."

"What happened?" Star asked.

Alex looked at her. "I'm not supposed to tell. They'd really hurt me if they knew."

"Wait, Alex," Star said. "If you're going to talk about the killings in the park, I'll have to read you your rights."

"Am I going to jail?" He looked at her, real panic in his eyes.

"I don't know," she said. "I don't know what you want to tell me."

He looked down at his hands. His knee bounced nervously up and down, beneath the table. "I gotta get this off my chest." He looked at her. "I'm so ashamed."

"I'll have to give you your rights," Star said.

Paresi stood up.

"I'll get the tape recorder," he said.

Star looked at the boy struggling not to cry. "Paresi," she said, "bring that box of Kleenex from my desk too."

"Right." He left the room, closing the door behind him.

Alex's fingers wound around and around one another. A deep sob escaped him. "I can't handle this stuff anymore," he said.

Star reached across the table and took his hand. Despite

what she knew was coming, she felt sorry for him. He was just a kid, not much older than Vee's youngest son.

"Do you want something, Alex, a soda, something to drink?"

He wiped his eyes with his free hand. "Yes, ma'am." He looked at her. "Got any Yoo-Hoo?" he asked.

"No, but I'll get you one." She got up and opened the door. "Stay put."

Alex nodded and wiped more tears from his face.

Paresi met her in the hall, Kleenex and tape recorder in hand. "He's gonna confess."

"Yeah, but to what?" she said. "Listen, you have to be in there, but don't spook him, okay?"

Paresi raised his right hand. "Promise."

"Yoo-Hoo," she said. "Where in the hell am I gonna get a Yoo-Hoo?"

"It's covered. I'll get somebody downstairs to run out to the Seven-Eleven on the corner."

"Thanks," she said. "I owe you."

"Take this." He handed her the Kleenex, the recorder, and a blank tape. "I'll be back in a second."

Star went back into the room. Alex had taken off his Bromleigh jacket and laid it across the table. Star noted that the third button was missing. There was a thin strand of yellow thread dangling from the navy blue fabric.

"Would you like me to hang up your jacket?" she said setting down the items she'd gotten from Paresi.

"No, it's all right." Alex stared at the table, unseeing.

"You shouldn't let it get wrinkled." She picked up the jacket. "It's nice."

Paresi came back into the room.

"What's nice?" he said, taking his seat.

Star looked at her partner. "This jacket." She turned the front of the coat toward Paresi. "I was just telling Alex that he shouldn't leave it lying around." She looked at her partner. "He's already lost a button."

The boy hadn't moved. His face still held the same mix of sadness, fear, and resignation. "I sewed it on, but it fell off again," he said, listlessly.

Star hung up the coat. "Too bad," she said. "These are very nice buttons." Again, she looked at Paresi. "I don't think I've ever seen any like this. They have a picture of the school and the dates of the hundredth anniversary."

"They were special," Alex said. "Another thing for me to get reamed about."

"How so?" Star took her seat, facing him.

"I got the buttons as an award for scholarship." He played with his fingers. "My mom was really proud. When she finds out I've lost one, she's gonna tear my head off."

"I thought you said you sewed it on again."

Alex looked up. "I did, but it fell off somewhere. I don't know where it is."

"It'll probably turn up," Star said. The boy looked at her. "Someone's gone out for your drink," she said.

"Thanks."

"Alex." She leaned close to him. "You're entitled to have your parents or an attorney here before you talk to us."

"I don't want anybody else in here," he said.

"I could call Juvenile, have them send an officer in to be with you."

"I won't talk if you do that," he said.

Star looked over the boy's head at Paresi. He shrugged.

"Okay," she said. "All right."

The door opened, and a young Hispanic civilian clerk with blue-black hair and thick eyebrows stuck her head around it. She looked at Paresi.

"Lieutenant Duvall?"

"Over here." Star turned and raised her hand.

The girl came inside the room. The badge on her white blouse read, E. MORALES, COMMUNICATIONS.

"Sorry," she said. "I'm new." She crossed the floor and put the paper bag on the table.

"I got a six-pack. They wouldn't sell it one bottle at a time." She pointed at the bag. "I made sure it's cold."

"Thanks," Star said.

The girl stood awkwardly, trying not to look at the officers or the overweight, unhappy-looking boy at the table.

"Something else?" Star asked.

The girl looked nervous. "Uh . . . I had to pay for it, ma'am. They didn't give me any money downstairs."

"You're supposed to get a receipt and give it to the desk sergeant, then he reimburses you," Star said.

The girl looked even more uncomfortable. "I didn't know that, and besides, the store was crowded and the clerk didn't give me a receipt."

"How much?" Star asked.

"Four dollars and fifty-two cents."

Paresi stood, reached into his back pocket, and pulled out his wallet. He handed the girl a ten-dollar bill

"I don't have any change," she said.

"Keep it."

"Thank you." The girl beamed.

"You're welcome." Paresi indicated the door.

She smilingly exited, nodding her way out.

"Thanks," Star said. "My purse is in my desk."

"No sweat." Paresi opened the bag. "I like Yoo-Hoo." He pulled three bottles out of the pack and handed one to Alex. He opened the other two, gave one to Star, and kept the third for himself. He set the bag on the table next to him.

"Chocolate soda." Star studied the cold bottle in her hand. "I've never had one of these." She took a sip. "This is good." She took another sip. "Why didn't I know about this stuff before?" She looked at Alex. "Thanks. You've turned me on to a new treat. I love this."

The boy's face broke into a grin. "Yeah, it's pretty good." He took a long swig of the drink. "Cody thinks it's kids' stuff, but I think it's real good."

"So do I," Star said. "Thank you, Alex."

Paresi sipped his soda watching Star, thinking about the ever-present six-pack of Yoo-Hoo in her refrigerator. He bet she even kept some at Mitch's right next to the champagne. She was good.

Alex took another drink from the bottle and set it on the table. His fingers laced around one another, and he looked sad again, anxious. "I guess I'm ready to talk now."

"Okay," Star said. She positioned the tape machine in front of him. "Paresi, do you have a pen?"

He handed her a ballpoint. She took the blank tape and wrote in the date and time. She added Alex's name, along with Paresi's and her own.

Alex chewed his nails as she popped in the tape and turned on the recorder. She announced the date, time, and the people present.

"Alex Monroe, you have the right to remain silent," she began.

A tear ran down Alex's chubby cheek and splashed on the table. He listened as Star went down the list of his rights.

"Do you understand these rights as given?"

He nodded.

"You have to speak, Alex," she said, indicating the machine.

The boy cleared his throat. "I understand."

"You can have your parents here, and I can have an officer from Juvenile come in."

"No," he said, leaning toward the tape machine. "I don't want a lawyer, I don't want a juvenile officer, and I don't want my mom here."

"Okay," Star said. "Talk to me."

"This is hard," he said.

"I know."

"I didn't want to get into trouble," Alex said, looking at her. "I just wanted to be one of the guys, you know?"

Star nodded.

"At first it wasn't so bad. I mean, I know they didn't consider me like them. In the game, they made me be Grendar, the malevolent gnome, because of . . ." He hung his head. "How I look, you know, how much I weigh and everything."

Star didn't say anything. She reached across the table and took the boy's hand. His fingers wrapped tightly around hers.

"I didn't like being Grendar." He looked at her. "But it still meant I was part of them, you know, I was with them."

"I understand," Star said. "Did you play the game often?"

Alex nodded and released her hand. He took another drink of the chocolate soda, draining the bottle.

"I coulda won a couple of times. But the twins, Dan and

Dave, they told me that Cody would be really mad if I won, so I let myself lose."

"Are Dan and Dave good friends to you?" Star said.

"Yeah." He turned to Paresi. "Can I have another soda?"

Paresi handed him a bottle. Alex opened it and took a long drink. "Am I gonna get in trouble if I tell you everything?"

"Honestly, Alex, I can't answer that," Star said. "I don't know what you're going to tell me."

The kid hung his head. "I want to talk about the old lady that burned up."

"You know about that?" Star said.

Another tear slid down the boy's face. "We did it."

"Who, Alex?" Star said softly. "Who is we?"

He looked at her, his eyes brimming. "The twins, Cody, and me." Tears rolled down his cheeks. "Cody started it," he sobbed. "He didn't mean to kill her, he just wanted to have some fun. We saw her sleeping there, on the bench, and he said let's just play with her, do something to wake her up."

He looked at Star. "Nobody meant to hurt her. We were drunk, and we just wanted to have some fun. Wake her up, make her yell at us and stuff." He sobbed again. "It all happened so fast, the fire, it just got away from us, you know?" He wiped his eyes and nose with his shirtsleeve.

Star slid the box of tissues over to him.

"Alex," she said, her voice soft, soothing.

"Yes, ma'am?" The boy pulled out two tissues and wiped his eyes. He gulped back the sobs into his throat.

"Are you saying that you, Cody, and the twins deliberately set that old woman on fire?"

"Cody did it," Alex said. "We were just there, but when she started screaming, we got scared. The twins shook up their beers and sprayed them all over her. I think they were really trying to put out the fire. But Cody, man, Cody was laughing. It made me sick when I realized what was happening." He wiped his eyes again. "We couldn't stop the blaze, so we just booked, ran out of there."

The boy pulled out more tissues and blew his nose.

"There's a basket near the cabinet," Star said.

Barely glancing at the metal wastebasket, Alex Monroe

hooked a shot over his head, and dropped the wad of soggy tissues into the center of the wastebasket. Paresi raised his eyebrows.

"Nice shot, Al."

The boy almost smiled.

"I like basketball," he said shyly.

"Tell me about the burning, Alex." Star gently led him back on track. "What led up to it?"

"We were at the park because we'd been partyin' over at the old lab."

"Whose idea was it for you to use the building?" Star said.

"Cody's." The boy looked down at his hands. "He'd been picking up girls in the park for a long time. He finally asked Dan and Dave to come along, and then they asked me."

"Prostitutes?" Paresi said.

"Yeah." Alex turned toward him. "He said it was surefire pussy." His round face reddened and he looked at Star. "Sorry."

"It's okay," Star said. "So Cody started the practice of picking up girls in the park?"

Alex nodded.

"How long had he been doing this?"

Alex shrugged. "I don't know. They only told me after they'd been doing it awhile. Dan and Dave wanted to stop. They thought the girls might have diseases, you know. But Cody made them keep doing it."

"What about you?" Paresi said. "Did you have sex with any of the girls from the park?"

Alex's face flushed. "No sir."

"You never did anything, with any of them?" Paresi said.

"I couldn't," the boy said softly. "I couldn't."

"What do you mean you couldn't?" Paresi said.

Alex turned in his seat, looking at him. "I couldn't," he said, his teeth gritting together, his eyes intense. "It wouldn't . . . I . . ."

"I get it," Paresi said. "I understand."

Alex turned back to Star. "They used to laugh at me, but I didn't care. I was still there, you know, still with them."

"What about the game?" Star said. "When did you start playing the game for real?"

Alex wiped his eyes with the heel of his hand. "Cody used to win all the time. Nobody could beat him, except me, and they told me not to. . . . Since he was the king, we had to do what he said."

"And he said, let's go pick up girls in the park and pork 'em in the old lab," Paresi said.

Alex nodded. "He said nobody ever went there, and we could have privacy and we could keep playing the game, doing it for real."

"Did Cody put the game piece in the old woman's mouth?" Star asked.

Alex looked ashamed. "He was just kidding. She was sleeping with her mouth open, we were stoned, it was a joke." He began to sob again.

Star took a deep breath, steadying herself. "Did Cody kill Dolores Causwell?" she said, her voice harsher than she intended.

"Dolores Causwell?" Alex looked confused.

"She was the prostitute who was found in the park. One of the game pieces . . ."

"Maylink," Paresi said. "The Seducer."

Star nodded. "Right, that piece was in her hand."

"I don't know," Alex said. "I stopped going to the old lab for a while. I know they picked up a woman and all of them took turns with her, but they didn't tell me everything."

"Did they tell you what she looked like?"

"Only that she was a big blonde."

Star sat staring at the boy.

"Why are you looking at me like that?"

"You said you weren't there when they took turns with her?"

"No, ma'am," Alex said, looking down.

"I've got your button, Alex."

"What?" He looked up as if he'd been slapped.

"The button you lost, your special achievement button . . . I've got it."

"Ma'am, I . . . I . . ." The boy began to stammer.

"It was found near Dolores Causwell's body."

His face reddened, he bit his lips.

"Tell me about the night Dolores died," Star said.

Alex began to shake.

"I . . . I . . ." He sobbed. "I wasn't there."

"The evidence says you were, Alex. And I'm going to be straight with you. You're sixteen now, and the Commonwealth recognizes seventeen as the age to be tried as an adult. But if you're lying to me, I will make sure that it won't make any difference. You will be charged as an adult in a capital murder case, and you will be locked away for the rest of your life."

Alex cried loudly.

Star kept talking. "The law says if you were there, you're just as guilty as if you'd killed her yourself. It's called being an accessory before the fact, and in this case, the fact is murder one, so, Alex . . ."

He looked at her, biting his lip, trying to hold the sobs back.

"If you know what happened, help yourself, and tell me now."

The boy put his head in his arms and wailed as if he were being torn apart. Star sat staring at him.

Paresi put his hand over his mouth. In spite of his feelings about rich, spoiled kids, something inside of him hurt for the boy.

The two cops sat, watching the boy sob. Finally he stopped, blew his nose on a handful of Kleenex, and looked at Star.

"Cody found her," he said.

"Dolores?" Star prodded him.

"Yes, ma'am. The big blonde." Alex wiped his nose again. "She was high, and Cody offered her some money to come with us. When she got into the old lab, Cody told her she was gonna be the seducer in our game, and she started saying she didn't want to do it."

"Go on," Star said.

"Cody told her he had some good stuff, something to make her fly higher than ever, something that would help her get into it. He told her he'd give her a major hit and pay double, if she'd do it." He hung his head. "So she let him shoot her up."

"What did he give her?" Star said.

Alex shrugged. "I don't know what it was, but she was out for a couple of minutes. We got her clothes off and Cody tried to fuck . . ." He looked at Star. "Cody tried to have intercourse with her, but she was so out of it, he couldn't."

"What happened then?" Star asked.

"We managed to get her awake, and she had oral sex with Cody and the twins. Then she passed out again."

"What happened after that?"

"Cody decided we should take some blood, you know, like she was the seducer, so we cut her."

"Where?"

"Cody said we had to cut her someplace it wouldn't show, so he spread her legs."

Star bit down on her bottom lip to keep from screaming in the boy's face. Dolores didn't deserve this.

"Dan said we should cut her up high, you know, near her . . . you know."

"Go on." Star's voice was controlled, cold.

"Cody made the cut. It was little, but he must've done something wrong, messed up, because she started bleeding all over the place. There was an old tube on the floor, so I grabbed that and Cody stuck it in her wound, to try to stop the blood, but she kept bleeding."

As the boy talked, Paresi watched Star. He looked in her eyes, and knew she was barely holding herself together. He moved his chair to the table, next to her.

"Then what did you do?" he said. Beneath the table, he took Star's hand.

"She was bleeding really bad. We had to catch the blood in something, since we couldn't stop it. Dan found a couple of old milk jugs, and Cody popped some kind of shot thing he had on the end of the rubber tube."

"Syringe," Paresi said. "A syringe."

Alex shrugged. "I guess, I don't know. Anyway, he put that on the open end of the tube, pushed the top thing down, and stuck it in a milk bottle. The blood was just gushing outta her, man, we didn't know what to do. When Cody pushed down on the top, that thing made it flow, stopped the spurting."

"It pumped her dry," Star whispered.

"Who put her in the park?" Paresi said. Beneath the table, Star gripped his hand. "Who moved her?" he asked.

"We all did," Alex answered, his voice small and soft. "We tried to get the bleeding to stop, but everything we did made it worse. Finally, it stopped . . . but by then we'd almost filled up two jugs."

He wiped his eyes. "We still thought she'd be okay, you know. We figured she'd just had too much dope, that she'd come to sooner or later, so we got her clothes back on and took her to the park. We left her against the wall, near the entrance, because we figured somebody would find her, you know, take her to the hospital."

"And it never occurred to any of you that a human being cannot live with that amount of blood loss?" Star asked.

The boy looked at her. "We thought she kept bleeding because she overdosed. We didn't do it to her."

Star turned to Paresi. Her eyes broke his heart.

"Do you know what Cody shot her up with?" he said.

Alex shrugged. "Something the twins stole from their dad's office. We didn't really know what it was."

"Coumadin," Star said. "You shot her full of Coumadin."

"What's that?" Alex looked at Paresi.

"Blood thinner, Alex," Paresi said. "Basically, you turned her blood to water. That's why you couldn't stop the bleeding."

The boy put his head in his arms and sobbed.

CHAPTER THIRTY-EIGHT

Captain Lewis hung up his phone. "The uniforms are on the way to pick up the Rileys, and Cody Stevens's father is bringing his son in. Where's Alex?"

"He's in Interrogation Two," Star said. "His mother just arrived. I don't want the others to know he's here. Especially Jay Stevens. He's a major pain in the ass. As it is, he's going to bring the building down when I charge his son. If he knows Alex is the witness, he'll destroy him."

"We'll handle Mr. Stevens," Lewis said. "You and Paresi just stay cool. Don't either of you punch his lights out. We're on shaky ground here."

"I think we're solid, Captain," Star said.

"No, Lieutenant, we're not," Lewis said. "These are kids, and you know how things work. Not only are they kids, they're *rich* kids, from rich homes. If we don't handle this just right, they're going to skate."

"In spite of all the get-tough-with-kids stuff the court's been rattling off lately, they'll probably skate anyway," Paresi said. "Money talks."

"I agree," Lewis said. "But since the eyewitness is one of them, and he's rolling over without any promises, maybe that will work in our favor."

"What about the trace evidence?" Star said.

"We don't really have any," Captain Lewis said. Molly Ludendorf was a charcoal briquette. Whatever might have been on her body was incinerated along with the rest of her."

"But Dolores . . ." Star said.

"Dolores Causwell is not the issue, Lieutenant," Lewis

243

said. "We're not bringing them in on anything but Molly right now."

Star's face clouded.

Lewis raised his hands. "I'm sorry. I know Dolores meant something to you, but right now, all we have is German Molly. That means Dolores and Camille Westfall are not a part of this picture, at least not yet."

"But Alex saw them kill Dolores. He participated! And more than likely, the semen found in Camille Westfall's body belongs to Doug Riley. If he was messing around on their mother, don't you think Cody could get the twins to kill her? Hell, Captain, even his wife is a suspect."

Lewis looked surprised. "When did all this happen?"

"It's just a feeling I have," Star said. "I think she's involved."

"Why am I just hearing about this?" Lewis said.

Star nodded toward Paresi. "We just found out about Mrs. Riley's relationship with Camille late yesterday."

"Have you talked with her?"

"No."

"Then it's out."

"But . . . Alex came in just as Paresi and I were about to move on it."

Lewis shook his head. "It's out, Lieutenant. German Molly first, and then we go on. If Dr. Riley was having an affair with Camille Westfall, the semen found in her body doesn't mean a thing, even if it is his. It doesn't say he hacked her to pieces, it just says they had sex."

Star looked frustrated. "Yes, Captain." She looked at her hands. "I still think the twins could have . . ."

"Star—" Lewis said.

"No. Hear me out." She leaned on his desk, her eyes locked with his. "Don't you think they knew about their father's affair? They share everything. More than likely, they told Cody, and *he* decided Camille should go. They do whatever he tells them. He calls the shots. I think on his word they lured her to that old lab, and all of them had a hand in killing her."

"You don't think Riley did it?" Lewis said.

"No sir. He's too distraught, and it's not an act. He's on the verge of a breakdown. He didn't kill Camille."

"You just got through saying you think Mrs. Riley is involved. Which is it?"

"I don't know." Star looked away. "I don't know . . . yet."

"As arrogant as I think these mooks are," Paresi said, "they *are* kids. But I gotta go with Star on this. I think they're involved in more than just Molly's death. I think she whet their appetite."

"You think the boys grew to like killing?" Lewis asked.

"They play games where people die, Captain," Star said. "Games that take a lot of cunning and ingenuity to win. I've played this particular one myself.

"You've got to be smart to win. And if you have nothing else, no other way to show people how smart and savvy you are, then that thrill of winning becomes everything," Star said. "It's not too far-fetched to think kids like that would want to transfer that experience in some way to life.

"Imagine the power," she said. "The power of being able to decide whether someone lives or dies, for real. To be able to read about what you've done and see it on TV. To be able to confuse and conflict an entire city and its police department.

"That's a hell of a thrill. The big win, the ultimate victory, maybe the only way to prove that you've got something, that you're not a zero. These kids live in a world that's defined by school, friends, and the games they play."

"What do you think?" Lewis asked Paresi.

"I agree with Star," he said. "These kids have crossed the line, and since Camille was found at the lab, they know about it, and they're involved. I mean they're not going to tell their fathers where they party, right?"

Lewis nodded.

"I think the twins talked it over with Cody, and he decided Camille had to go, so they lured her to the lab, and all of them had a hand in killing her," Star said.

"As part of the game," Paresi added.

Star nodded. "Exactly."

"But what about the lipstick?" Lewis said. "Didn't Grant say that lipstick was on the body?"

"Yeah, I don't know how it got there," Star said. "I can't figure it out right now."

"One thing at a time," Lewis said. "You make a good argument. But first, we find out just how deep these little bastards are in, and then we can look beyond them to their families."

Lewis took off his glasses, and rubbed his eyes.

"In the questioning, see if you can get Riley to admit to an affair," he said to Star. "If the man's on the verge of a nervous breakdown, he must be ready to start spewing. Let's see if we can aim him toward the truth."

"Okay," Star said.

"Did Grant give you anything else to bring to the party?" He asked. "Besides the lipstick?"

"He said the dissection of Camille's body was almost professional. The body was beheaded, bisected, and dissected neatly. The limbs had been severed at the joints, and the midsection was almost perfectly cut in half."

"That would take some medical know-how," Lewis said.

"Yeah, but I still say his sons could have done it," Star said. "They had to have hated Camille. She was breaking up their home. Besides, she was killed in accordance with the game. All Cody had to do was get them fired up and push them over the edge."

"Let's say I buy that," Lewis said. "But how would kids know how to cut up a body?"

"Anatomy class," Star said. "Mitchell said they stress anatomy for all the students at Bromleigh."

"But you said the cutting on this body was damned near professional," Lewis said. "Where would they learn that much about dissection?"

"Meat-Cutting 101," Paresi said.

Richardson stuck his head into Lewis's office. "Pardon me, Captain."

"What?"

The detective jerked a thumb over his shoulder. "There's a bunch of people here to see Star and Dom."

"The families." Star was on her feet.

"Kid gloves, Lieutenant," Lewis said.

"Got it," Star said, heading for the door.

"Paresi."

"Yeah, Cap'n?"

"Watch that BFM."

Paresi snorted derisively, "Gotcha, one big fucking mouth . . ." He clapped his hands together. "Shut."

CHAPTER THIRTY-NINE

Star walked into the room to find Jay Stevens scowling at her. His son sat to his right. To his left sat a woman dressed head to toe in cream-colored silk.

Star guessed she was Mrs. Stevens, and even though she'd never seen her before, the woman looked familiar.

She wore a turban-styled cream-colored hat that covered her hair and framed her exotic face. The hat was perfectly matched to her classically styled suit.

Her earrings were large chunks of ivory jade. She was an elegant woman, and a bored one. She looked as if she'd rather be pulling her nails out with rusty pliers than sitting in this room. She was not the kind of woman Star imagined would be married to a twerp like Jay Stevens. On his right sat the attorney, Lawrence Stockard, whom Stevens had evidently decided to keep.

The Rileys sat side by side. Diane Riley's hand rested lightly on her husband's pale wrist. Dr. Riley's hands were crossed on top of the table. He appeared drugged. They had shown up without an attorney.

"Thanks everyone for being here," Star said. She walked around the table and sat across from the assembled families.

"I'd like to begin by talking to the boys," she said.

"Cody doesn't say a word," Stevens's attorney said. "If you think you've got something, then charge him and get it over with."

Star looked at Paresi, who stood behind the families. He nodded slightly, and the expression on his face said, Get 'em!

"Nice to see you again, Mr. Stockard," Star said, her eyes on Cody.

The boy returned her look with a smug sneer.

Lawrence Stockard grandly produced a legal pad from his briefcase and began writing. Behind him, Paresi rubbed his fingertips together in the ancient sign indicating money. Star smiled.

"Cody, it's come to our attention that you've been picking up prostitutes in Saint Francis Park and taking them to the old Bromleigh chemistry lab for sex."

"What's wrong with that?" Jay Stevens's voice dripped ice. "He's a boy—he's growing up." His wife rolled her eyes.

"Quiet, Jay." Stockard raised his hand. "Prove it, Lieutenant, produce a witness."

Ignoring the lawyer, Star continued talking to Cody.

"Paying for sex is illegal in the Commonwealth," she said, her eyes never leaving Cody's arrogant face.

"Then why are you selling it?" the boy asked, his thin lips crawled open in a mean grin. "I saw you in the park, with him." He jerked a thumb at Paresi. "He was pimping you out. You got in a car too, I *saw* you!"

"Shut up, Cody!" The attorney's face flushed. "I said, produce a witness, Lieutenant."

Ignoring him, Star leaned toward Cody. "It's called undercover, Cody. It's part of what I do."

"I'll bet," the boy sneered.

They locked eyes. Star smiled. "Sergeant."

Paresi headed for the door.

Cody's smile faded. He looked nervous. "Where's he going?"

His father glared at Star. "They're bluffing, they've got nothing."

"Is there some reason we're here, Lieutenant?" Diane Riley leaned across the table, speaking in a conspiratorial whisper. "My husband isn't well, and if you don't need us, we'd like to leave."

"Please be patient, Mrs. Riley." Star turned to Diane. "I'll talk to the twins soon."

Diane leaned back and patted her husband's wrist. Doug Riley sat as if he'd been carved in the chair. Star looked at his chest to make sure he was still breathing.

Paresi came back into the room, and Jasmine Miller followed close behind him.

"This is Ms. Miller," he said, pointing at the woman.

In the harshly lit room, Jasmine presented an alarming sight, at least to these people. She stood close to Paresi, chewing gum that appeared with every bite at the corner of her heavily orange-lipsticked mouth.

She had given up her Tina Turner wig for a champagne-blonde '70s-style shag. Her bare belly, showing in the space between her gold lamé bra and gold hip-hugger hotpants, sported a shiny gold ring piercing her navel.

She had sprinkled her bare legs with golden glitter, and she wore ankle-length gold boots with five-inch heels.

"Hi, baby," she said to Cody, and turned her smile toward the twins. "How you guys doin'?"

"What's this?" Stockard jerked a thumb toward Jasmine.

"Aren't you asking *who*?" Star demanded. "*Who* is this?"

Jasmine squared her golden-dusted shoulders and aimed a gum-flashing smile at Star.

"I want to know what you think you're doing," Stockard said.

The twins hung their heads. Their mother looked at them and then at their father. Doug Riley hadn't even looked in Jasmine's direction.

"This is Ms. Jasmine Miller, an independent contractor who does a great deal of work in and near Saint Francis Park," Star said.

Jasmine beamed, gum momentarily tucked behind her smile.

"She knows your son, Mr. Stevens," Star continued, "and she's also familiar with the twins. She's seen them quite frequently, while addressing her line of work."

Dave and Dan colored, but kept their heads down.

The attorney shook his head, and Jay Stevens seemed on

the edge of an eruption that would rival Old Faithful. His wife looked bored *and* disgusted.

"You want to tell Mr. Stockard how you know these boys, Ms. Miller?"

The hooker grinned. "These boys always be comin' up to me in da park, axein' me ta party wif' 'em." She pointed at Cody. "He de one be always offerin' me money. I tol' him I don' mess wif' no chillren. He try ta show me his bizness, talkin' 'bout he a man!" Jasmine waved her hand in dismissal. "My dog bizness bigga den his!"

Paresi laughed. The other men in the room looked uncomfortable.

Jasmine continued. "I know som' other gurls say dey wen' wif 'em, dey tol' me 'bout goin wif dese boys to som' kinna secret place someweah in da park."

"That would be the abandoned Bromleigh chem lab," Star said to the parents.

"Chem?" Jasmine looked confused.

"Chemistry laboratory, Ms. Miller. It's on the far side of the park."

Jasmine's face lit up. "I knows dat place . . . dat whar y'all be takin' gurls?" She looked at Star. "It a awful place, it stink! De whole place smell lak bleach."

"Then you *have* been there, Ms. Miller?" Star said.

"Uh-huh. I ain't never be inside, but I be over close to dere one time, but not wif dem. One uh my frien's say som' folks be sellin' stuff over by dere."

"What kind of stuff?" Star said.

Jasmine shrugged. "Drugs . . . I just wen' wif my frien' ta keep her safe. I don' do none uh dat shit." She caught Paresi looking at her arms. The golden glitter didn't quite cover the track marks.

Jasmine folded her arms over her belly. "I ain' sayin' I neva' did no stuff, but I ain't into dat no mo'."

Paresi nodded at her. She hugged herself tighter.

"I'm tryin' ta gets my life right," she said. "I wen wif my frien' to proteck her. Dat place you talkin' 'bout smell really bad, even outside you can smell it. It be funky!"

"Thank you, Ms. Miller," Star said.

"Dat it, Star . . . uh, I mean Lieutenan'?"

Star nodded. "Yes. Thank you for coming in."

Jasmine grinned. "See y'all roun' de park, boys." She turned, heading for the door. Her hotpants rose high on her behind, exposing more than half of the twin globes of her butt.

Star repressed her laugh at the reaction of the males at the table. Even Mrs. Stevens and Diane Riley's eyes bugged out. Both round, jiggly spheres were covered with golden glitter.

Paresi left to walk Jasmine to the elevator. They passed through the squad room, with Jasmine waving at the detectives as if she were in a parade until she was outside the double doors.

"Thanks for your help, Jas," Paresi said.

"Dem boys in trouble?"

"Looks like it."

Jasmine shook her champagne-blonde, shag-wigged head.

"I know dey jes' kids," she said, "but dat redhead, he a sick puppy."

"What did he do?" Paresi asked.

Jasmine looked over her shoulder, as if expecting someone to be listening. She crooked a finger. Paresi leaned down, close to her.

"Damn, you fine!" she said to him. "Where you get dem pretty blue eyes?"

"I stole 'em." Paresi smiled. "What did he do?"

"Who?"

"The redhead."

"Oh!" She giggled. "Baby, when I gets dis close to you, I forget my *mama's* name."

Paresi leaned closer, whispering. "Tell me what he did."

Jasmine's smile was so wide, it looked like her face hurt. "Lawd ha' mercy!"

"Jas." Paresi spoke slowly. "What did he do?"

"He tol' me he wanna cut me."

"What did you say?"

"I tol' him to get his monkey ass on 'way from me, I don' do no kids, an' I don' do no sick shit."

Paresi burst out laughing. "Jas." He pulled her to him, hugging her tightly. "If I didn't have somebody in my life, I'd take you out."

"You jivin'." The whore grinned up at him.

"Yes I am," he said, hugging her again. "But don't let nobody sell you short. You're all right."

"So they paid for sex, so what?" Lawrence Stockard sat with Star and Paresi in Captain Lewis's office.

"They also set fire to Molly Ludendorf and murdered Dolores Causwell," Star said. "We've got an eyewitness."

"Another hooker?" the attorney said with disgust.

"No comment," Star said. "We've got their asses nailed. And your snotty little meal ticket, Cody Stevens . . . he's the ringmaster in this sick little circus."

Stockard jumped to his feet. "Captain Lewis, I suggest you inform your officers that they are on very thin ice."

"Sit down, Larry," Lewis said. "You're giving me a headache."

Star watched her boss, trying not to let the pleasure show in her face. She recognized the signs. Lewis was about to cut loose, and she loved watching him blow.

The attorney sat down, his game face leveled at the Captain.

"Get this straight, Counselor," Lewis said, his voice low and even. "Nobody comes into my squad and tries to undermine the work my officers do." He pointed at Star and Paresi. "These two have been busting their asses for weeks, trying to get to the bottom of these cases."

"Cases?" the attorney blustered. "What are you talking about, cases, there's nothing . . ."

"Shut up!" Lewis slammed his fist down on the desk. "Just shut the fuck up! My detectives don't make mistakes. They've tied the burning in the park and possibly two more killings to those fine, upstanding junior achievers in there, and they're not wrong.

"We've got motive *and* evidence. So I would suggest, Counselor, that you get your overpaid ass into that interrogation room and earn your money." He turned to Star. "You and Paresi get Sean Mallory down here."

"The DA?" Stockard sputtered. "They're *juveniles*!"

Lewis shot him a wicked grin. "They're all seventeen, Counselor, except for Alex Monroe, and his birthday's coming fast. Besides, with what they did, I wouldn't give a fuck if they were sucking on their mother's tits and shitting in diapers. It's murder one. Those little humps did adult crime and they're going to do adult time, *and* adult punishment."

His blue eyes blazed. "If that offends you, Counselor, then I'd be happy to go in there right now, line 'em up, and empty my weapon. That'll save you the embarrassment of losing in court, and the taxpayers can keep a few bucks. A twofer, whaddya say?"

Star thought Stockard was going to faint. She looked at Paresi. He covered his grin with his hand.

Lewis sat back in his chair. "My detectives will make the evidence available to your office. Now get the fuck outta here before I use your big-assed empty head for target practice."

CHAPTER FORTY

Paresi and Star stood outside the courtroom in the corridor of the courthouse with Sean Mallory.

"I expect the indictments to go down smooth, with no problem. This is a slam dunk," the DA said. "There's no way those kids are going to be able to get out of it. Even with Judge Fraser's hemorrhaging heart, there's no way he can be soft with this crew, especially after he hears Alex Monroe's testimony."

"Were you able to cut him a deal?" Paresi asked.

Sean nodded. "I've already got his bail arranged. But even though he's the star witness, I couldn't get him a clean walk. He's gonna do a couple of years, for complicity and accessory before the fact. There's an election on the horizon, and Fraser needs something to wave in front of the voters."

Sean ran a hand through his thick dark hair.

"I still feel for the Riley twins, though. They at least have some remorse. Stevens is playing it like some puke out of one of those 'killers are cool' movies. I think he feels going to prison is going to be some kind of adventure."

"And it will be, the minute he bends over," Paresi said.

"I hear you," Sean said. "Believe me, with his attitude, he's going to be hanging over a bunk about a nanosecond after lights out on the first night. As for Alex, I hope he does his time in a juvie lockup—you know, one of the camp-type places. Maybe he'll get it together in there."

"He's not a bad kid," Star said. "He just wanted to belong."

Sean nodded. "Right. Well, I think the twins might make bail, but Stevens . . ."

Sean's mouth turned down at the corners. "I don't think even Fraser is going to allow that little turd to walk. I know his dad's gonna throw a lot of money around, but I have a feeling old Cody might be resting in a whole new environment tonight."

"Speak of the devil," Star said.

They turned to see Cody Stevens and his father walking toward them.

"It couldn't happen to a nicer guy," Sean Mallory said.

Jay Stevens stared at the detectives and attorney as if they were insects marching across his chateaubriand. His son shot Star a look designed to drop her to her knees.

Paresi smiled at her. "How 'bout that look there, Buffy?"

Star shrugged her shoulders. "They don't call me the slayer for nothing!"

"What an asshole family," Mallory said, watching Cody and his father enter the courtroom. "A total waste of breath and skin."

Star looked at him. Profanity from Sean Mallory always shocked her.

He looked like central casting's idea of a young Irish Catholic priest. His eyes were deep set and crystal blue. They were the most startling feature of his craggy, heavily eye-browed face.

His dark hair defied cutting and always seemed to be expanding down the inside of his shirt collar. He had enough teeth to be a Kennedy, and most of them were on display in a wide smile.

"I wonder where the mother is," Star said.

"Divorce court." Paresi laughed.

"That would be a good move for Cody, actually," Sean said. "I know for a fact that Stockard is going to play the deprived-little-rich-kid samba in the courtroom," he said.

"He's going to plead that the father is distant and the mother is a self-absorbed bitch. So if they got a divorce, that would actually help the case. But the plain truth is that Cody, that little son of a sea cow, is a mean kid. He could have been born to the Holy Family, and he'd still be a murdering bastard!"

"Heads up," Paresi said. "The doc's coming."

They turned to see Dr. Riley, his wife, the twins, and an attorney they didn't recognize.

"Who's the suit?" Star said.

"Barry Aaronson," Mallory whispered. "Big money, big ego. He makes millions even when he's taking a piss, but he's going down on this one."

Star patted his shoulder. "You go get 'em, Sean."

The Riley family passed them without so much as a glance.

She turned to her partner. "Paresi, can you take care of this?"

"Sure. Where are you going?"

"I've got some business. I'll see you back at the station."

Eulala Boyd had been working in the city's license bureau since the days of 3 x 5 cards and wooden file cabinets. She showed no sign of ever retiring. She had always liked Star, considered her family. She was proud to see a black woman climb through the ranks of the police department, and so she was happy when Star popped up at her window.

"Hey, Eulala."

"Starletta!" The older woman's smooth-skinned chocolate face broke into a grin. "Girl, you bring yourself on in here and gimme a hug!" Eulala pressed the button that unlocked the big walnut door, and allowed Star access to her office.

"Baby, where you been? I ain't seen you in so long, James Brown done got old!" The woman enveloped her in a bear hug.

"I know I've been missing in action," Star said, as her breath was being squeezed out of her. She loosened Eulala's grip and stepped back. "But you look good, Miss Eulala. I promise, I won't take so long to come see you again."

"Well you just bring yo'self in here and sit down. Tell me what you been up to." Eulala indicated the coffeepot, an old-fashioned percolator. "Want some coffee? I just made some fresh a few minutes ago."

Star sat in the chair alongside Eulala's desk. "No thanks," she said. Eulala's coffee had been known to walk out of the pot and bench-press the cream. "I'm working on a case," Star said. "I need some help."

The woman pushed her electric blue, rhinestoned, cat's-eye '50s-style glasses up on her nose, causing the attached blue faux pearl chain to jiggle. "Tell me what you need, darlin'."

"I need to look at some records—marriage, birth, education, anything we can find."

Eulala waved her multiringed hand. She'd been married three times, widowed twice, and still wore all three wedding rings.

"Oh shoot, that ain't nothin'!" She pulled out a piece of paper. "Gimme the name, and any years you can."

"I don't know any years," Star said. "In fact, I'm not even sure the marriage happened in Brookport, or even in the Commonwealth, for that matter. I'm flying blind here."

Eulala pursed her Jungle Red–tinted lips. "Don't matter—I got a lotta friends in a lotta places. We'll find 'em."

"I've got the man's social security number, would that help?" Star asked.

Eulala Boyd's generous mouth opened in a smile. "Can't hurt. Now tell me the name."

"Riley," Star said. "The name is Riley."

Paresi hung up his coat and sat down opposite Star.

"How'd it go?" she said, barely looking up from the pile of paper on her desk.

"Great," he said. "Everybody went into custody, right from the courtroom."

She looked up, surprised. "The twins too?"

Paresi sat down. "Yep. I'm sure their superstar attorney will be able to get that changed, but they'll be in for a few days. Meanwhile, old Cody's going to rot till the next hearing at least."

"Wow," Star said. "Fraser must be campaigning hard to keep his seat."

"Yeah." Paresi nodded. "Looks like it." He smiled at her. "It's a pity you missed the look on Li'l Jay's face, though. He was so pissed, I thought he was gonna stroke out in the courtroom. I heard him demanding a plane to take him to New York."

"What's he doing?" Star said. "Booking on his family?"

Paresi shook his head. "They should be so lucky. The minute we hit the hallway, he yanked out his cell phone and set up an appointment with another big-gun attorney. Loud enough, of course, for us poor nobody jerks to overhear and be *intimidated* by his power."

"His son's behind bars," Star said. "Wouldn't you think that would be enough to make him realize just who's got the *real* power?"

"Amen." Paresi pointed to the pile. "What are you doing?"

She looked at him. "I went to see Eulala Boyd."

"The Bureau of Records?" Paresi asked. "Is she still there? She's got to be at least a hundred. I thought she'd retired long ago."

"She's still there," Star said. "And her reach is as long as ever." She pointed at the papers on her desk. "She's got friends in high places, all the way across the country."

Paresi recognized the look on her face. "You know something. . . ." He leaned toward her. "Tell Daddy."

Star grinned at him. "Did you know that Douglas Riley graduated from Stanford?"

"Impressive," Paresi said. "So . . . ?"

"Diane Riley studied nursing while they lived in California."

Paresi shrugged. "That makes sense—she married a doctor."

"Uh-huh," Star agreed. "But she never practiced." She waved a paper at him. "Still, she did get far enough along to choose a specific kind of nursing as her major."

"What?"

Star handed him the paper bearing Diane Riley's nursing school records.

They smiled at one another.

"Race you to the car," Paresi said.

"Uh-uh," Star said. "It's late. This will keep till tomorrow morning."

"Sure?" Paresi said.

"Yeah. Tomorrow morning's soon enough." She gathered the papers and put them into a manila folder. "The Rileys have had a bad enough day."

CHAPTER FORTY-ONE

The first thing Star noticed when Diane Riley opened her front door was that she was really angry.

"We need to talk to you, Mrs. Riley," Star said.

"Why?" Diane, cold sober, rested her head on the edge of the door, looking at the two detectives. Her eyes were bloodshot and tired. She'd been crying.

"We'd like to come inside," Star said.

"Do you have a warrant?" she bitterly replied.

Star looked at Paresi.

"No, ma'am," she said. "We recognize you're upset, but we still need to talk with you."

Diane backed away, widening the space, allowing them to enter.

"My living room is full of work from Doug's office," she said coldly. "Go down the hall to the family room. It's the one with the closed double doors. Take a seat, I'll be right with you."

"Where are you going, ma'am?" Star said.

Diane's dead eyes came to life. "To the bathroom, Lieutenant, is that allowed? May I go to the bathroom in my own house, or do you want to come with me?"

Star looked down. "No, ma'am. We'll wait in the family room."

She and Paresi went in the direction Diane had pointed, while she hastily walked to the rear of the house. Once she was out of sight, the officers heard her sobbing.

"This is when I really hate my job," Star said.

"Why? You didn't raise two killers." Paresi opened the doors. The sand colored walls, carpet, and pale furnishings made the room appear immense. Well-filled white pinewood bookcases lined one entire wall.

A huge television and speakers were housed in a built-in wood cabinet of the same hue. A VCR sat on the shelf beneath the TV.

Against another wall, under a large, brightly painted canvas featuring a field of red poppies, sat a CD player, a tape deck, and a turntable. The units were housed in a glass cabinet. Next to the cabinet, more built-in white pinewood shelves displayed a large collection of records and compact discs.

There were small, neatly mounted speakers in all four corners of the room, near the ceiling.

An unfinished chess game rested on an antique cherrywood game table, between two pale yellow Queen Anne chairs.

Paresi pointed to the board. "Who's winning?"

Star shrugged. "Damned if I know. That's Mitchell's game. I'm the queen of Yahtzee!"

Paresi laughed.

Star sat down on the ivory camelback sofa, across from the two yellow chairs, and Paresi walked to the French doors, which looked out onto the patio.

"I didn't notice this when we were here before," he said.

"We weren't in this room."

"Yeah, but I should've seen this."

"What?"

Paresi turned, and beckoned her to the leaded glass doors. Near the rear of the property, opposite a covered, in-ground swimming pool and a hot tub, stood a whitewashed, red-roofed cottage. Red-painted oblong wooden boxes, filled with budding spring flowers, were attached along the outer sills of two lace-curtained front windows.

"What do you think that is?"

"My studio," Diane Riley said.

The two detectives turned to see her standing in the doorway. She had washed her face and applied fresh makeup, including a very becoming russet shade of lipstick.

"Are you an artist?" Star asked.

"I sculpt, and I've worked in oils and watercolors on canvas." She pointed to a floral, iris-dominated painting behind one of the yellow chairs. "I did this when the boys were little." She turned to the poppy-filled canvas and pointed. "And that one about a year ago."

"They're lovely," Star said, truthfully. "Impressionism is one of my favorite styles."

Diane nodded. "Mine too. I love the softness, and the colors give this room a lift." She looked at Star, and the coldness with which she'd greeted them returned. "I'm sure you didn't come here to ask me about my art." She sat down in one of the yellow chairs, the iris painting behind her. "Why are you here?"

"How's your husband?" Star asked, moving back to the sofa, opposite the woman. Paresi remained at the doors.

"His sons have been locked up awaiting trial for murder. His employee has been hacked to pieces, and the practice he worked so hard to establish has been closed." She folded her arms. "How would *you* be, Lieutenant? Yesterday, after court, he signed himself into a care facility for a while."

"I'm sorry . . ." Star began.

"Can we see your studio?" Paresi interrupted.

"Why?" Diane Riley's eyes flashed.

"Just curious," Paresi said.

"Get a warrant," Diane shot back.

Paresi reached into his pocket and pulled out his cell phone.

"He'll do it," Star said.

Diane stood abruptly, her face red. "Oh, all right! What do I have to do to get you people out of my home? You've destroyed my life, my husband is practically insane, and my boys are in jail. What else can you do to me?"

"Calm down, Mrs. Riley," Star said. "We're just doing our job."

"Funny, that's just what the Nazis said!" She marched angrily across the room, and flung open the patio doors. "Follow me."

The two detectives trailed her silently to the cottage. She opened the door. There was an acrid smell in the air.

"Do you use heat in your work?" Star asked.

Diane Riley turned on the light. "I use lots of different things. When I work in metal, I solder. I also do ceramics—I have a kiln."

"Have you done any work lately?" Star asked. "I mean, I can smell the burning."

"Sometimes the smell of firing lingers. But it's been weeks since I've even been in this room, Lieutenant." Diane Riley's face was stiff and angry. "I haven't had the opportunity or inclination to work on anything for quite some time."

"Why do you have these books?" Paresi asked, pointing to several medical volumes, including *Gray's Anatomy*.

"I use them in my sculpting. They are invaluable for sculpting muscle and bone, getting things right for my pieces."

"Having been a nurse, with a surgery major, I would think that would have been easy for you," Star said.

Diane Riley spun around, her face wild.

"What are you trying to say? Yes, I studied nursing. Yes, I opted for surgical nursing, but I never practiced. I had the twins instead."

"Such lovely boys," Paresi muttered.

Diane's face grew angrier. *"Yes! Yes!"* she yelled. "They *are* lovely boys—they are my babies! How am I supposed to handle this?" She began to sob.

Star stood close to the woman and spoke softly. "Mrs. Riley, we've been given some . . ."

"Star?" Paresi interrupted her again. "I think you'd better come over here."

"Excuse me," Star said. Diane turned her back, wiping tears with the backs of her hands.

Star went to her partner. "What?"

"Look at this." He pointed to the canvas resting on the easel. It held an unfinished painting of a nude woman. She stood on a hill of skulls and bones. Long, thick Titian hair blew wildly back from her exotic face. Bat wings, full and open, sprang from her back, fanning out on either side of her naked body.

Star and Paresi looked at each other.

"Brenda Stevens," they said in unison.

"That's why she looked so familiar the first time I saw her," Star said. "She's the face of Maylink and Dorla in the game."

"That's not all." Paresi pointed to the paint-spattered table next to the canvas.

A polished wooden box rested near a jar filled with turpentine and paintbrushes. The lid was open, exposing a deep, blue-velvet-lined, compartmentalized interior. Attached to the inside of the lid was a gold plaque. It read, "To my darling bride. A gift for your future. With loving pride, Doug."

"Surgical instruments," Star said.

"Look closer."

Star leaned down. "Blood."

Diane Riley began to scream.

CHAPTER FORTY-TWO

The maid showed Star and Paresi into Brenda Stevens's study, off the living room. As they entered, she got up from her desk.

At the sight of them, her face hardened. "My maid said the police wanted to talk to me. She *didn't* say it was you two."

"Sorry, we gave her our names," Star said. "We'd like to ask you a few questions."

Brenda stepped out from behind the desk, her face cold and angry. She was again dressed in silk. Pale green, pants and shirt. Her flame-red hair was pulled back in a ponytail, tied with a green silk ribbon. She was barefoot. Star noted the pearl-colored polish on her fingernails and toenails.

Brenda folded her arms.

"I have only one word for the both of you. *Leave!*"

"Get the feeling we're not welcome?" Paresi said to Star.

"Very funny," Brenda Stevens said. "You people have destroyed my family. My son is behind bars. My husband is in New York, desperately trying to find yet another attorney to save our child's life, and you two want to come into my home and make jokes about it? Get out!"

"We just have a couple of questions," Star said. "If you didn't want to see us, why didn't you tell your maid not to let us in?"

"She's an idiot!" Brenda said. "She doesn't understand very much English, and the word police scares the bejesus out of her."

"Not you, though, huh?" Paresi said.

"Get out!" Brenda stalked out into the hallway, screaming for her maid.

"Paresi," Star whispered. "Look.'`

Paresi looked in the direction in which she pointed.

"Let's go," he said.

Brenda Stevens and her maid entered the room.

"Lupe, show these two people out," Brenda said. *"Now!"*

"Poleeces," the maid said in a frightened voice.

"I don't care, I want them *gone*!" Brenda screamed.

"No need to frighten the help," Star said. "We're leaving." She turned and nodded at the woman. "We're going," she said. Lupe looked blank. *"Adiós,"* Star said, "C'mon, Paresi."

Brenda Stevens watched them until they closed the front door.

"Did you see it?" she said to her partner as they walked toward their car.

"Yep," he said. "Let's get the warrant."

Dominic Paresi escorted Diane Riley toward Interrogation Room Two. He walked her past the small waiting room near the fax and copy machines.

Star had made certain the door to the waiting room was open. She stood nearby, watching.

Diane Riley's breath caught in her throat, and her hand flew to her mouth when she saw the person inside.

Brenda Stevens rushed to the open doorway.

"Bren," Diane said, as Paresi hurried her past.

"I've phoned my attorney," Brenda Stevens called out. "Don't say anything."

Paresi took Diane Riley inside the interrogation room and closed the door. Star stood in the open doorway, facing Brenda Stevens.

"Would you like some coffee or tea, Mrs. Stevens, before we begin?" she said politely.

"I'm not saying anything to you until my attorney arrives." Brenda Stevens folded her arms and glared at Star. "You can't hustle me, and you can't scare me. I don't have to say a word."

Star nodded. "That's true. I advised you of that very fact when I brought you in." She stepped back from the doorway and called Detective Richardson.

"Yeah, Star?" he said, approaching the room.

"Could you do me a favor, Chuck?"

"Sure."

"Would you baby-sit Mrs. Stevens here? I've got to check on something."

For a second, Brenda Stevens looked worried, but that look was soon replaced by one of icy indifference.

"Mrs. Stevens, Detective Richardson," Star said. "He'll keep you company while you wait for your attorney."

Brenda Stevens stalked to a chair and sat down, anger clouding her face.

Star went down the hall to Interrogation Room Two.

"Mrs. Riley," she said, entering.

Diane Riley sat clutching a handful of shredded Kleenex tissues in her fist. Her eyes were red and swollen.

"Why is Brenda here?"

Star ignored her and turned to Paresi. "Could you go out and check to see if what we're waiting for has arrived yet?"

"Right. I'll be back." He left, closing the door behind him.

Star sat opposite Diane Riley. "This shouldn't take too long. Did Sergeant Paresi offer you something to drink?"

"Answer my question, Lieutenant," Diane said, her voice edged with panic. "Why is Brenda here?"

"Brenda Stevens?" Star said innocently. "It's a police matter. It has nothing to do with you."

Diane jumped to her feet.

"The hell it doesn't! What are you people doing? What game are you trying to play?"

"We don't play games, Mrs. Riley," Star said calmly, and indicated Diane's vacated chair. "I suggest you sit down."

Diane stood for a second, then meekly took her seat.

"Where's my attorney?" she said.

Star shrugged. "I haven't a clue. You made the call, so we'll just wait."

Paresi walked into the room. "Everything's here, Star, it's out in the squad," he said.

"What . . . what's here?" Diane was again agitated. "What is this about? What's going on?"

Star got up. "Look after Mrs. Riley, would you?" she said to Paresi, and walked out, closing the door behind her.

*   *   *

Brenda Stevens sat with her legs crossed and her arms folded across her chest. When Star entered the room, the woman looked at her as if she wanted to rip her heart out.

"She's all yours, Lieutenant," Richardson said, leaving.

"Thanks, Chuck." Star sat down in front of Brenda Stevens. "Sorry I had to run out for a minute." She put a manila file folder on the table in front of her. "So many things to check on."

"I hope you know, you've gone too far," Brenda said.

"You might want to try your attorney, Mrs. Stevens." Star indicated the folder. "This has to go by the book."

"I've called him. He should be here any minute," Brenda said coldly.

"Good," Star said. "Would you like something to drink?"

Brenda glared at her.

"Oh boy," Star said. "There's just no pleasing anybody today." She folded her arms and leaned on the table. "Your friend Diane . . . Diane Riley, she's so upset, yet she won't let us get her even a cup of tea." She looked at Brenda. "Tea's very soothing, don't you think? Civilized and all that."

"What are you doing to her?" Brenda Stevens's voice rose. "She's been through hell. She can't take any more of this shit—she's fragile!"

"Unlike you?" Star said.

"What is *that* supposed to mean? Of course I'm upset, my son's been locked away for something he didn't do. . . ."

"You just handle things better, right?"

Brenda's face reddened. "If you people hurt Diane, believe me, I'll sue you all to hell."

"Why would we want to hurt your friend?" Star said. "In fact, she's in with my partner right now. I know you don't think too much of us, but believe me, he's the most gentle person. . . . He's especially good at calming and soothing women. It's something in his voice," Star said, leaning back. "Or maybe it's his eyes. . . . Did you notice his eyes? They're so blue, they're absolutely mesmerizing." She clicked her tongue. "He aims those eyes at women and they give up everything." She smiled at Brenda. "It's a gift."

*   *   *

Diane Riley looked as if she were about to turn herself inside out. She was so nervous that the ticking inside her body was visible on the outside.

"Is your partner with Brenda?" she said to Paresi.

"I don't know," Paresi said. "She had a lot of things to go over."

Diane shifted in her chair. "Where's my attorney?"

"He's been called," Paresi said, "he should be here any minute."

"Why is Brenda here?" Diane said. "Do you know? Your partner wouldn't tell me."

Paresi shrugged. "We went by to tell her what a great model she was, and she insisted on coming down to talk about her relationship with you."

Diane's eyes narrowed. "We're friends, that's all. Good friends."

"That's what she said." Paresi nodded. "Must be true—I mean, she posed nude for you and all, I'd say that makes you very good friends."

"That portrait was to be a gift to her husband."

"Really?" Paresi said. "Some present."

Diane stared at him. "Jay Stevens has made a fortune over the years, manufacturing computer games," she said. "His wife has been his muse—she's the model for all the female characters."

"Did you illustrate those too?" Paresi asked.

"No." Diane shivered as if a chill passed through her. "I agreed to do this painting for Brenda as a favor. She wanted to surprise Jay for their wedding anniversary, give him something different, something special."

"Yeah, she said something about surprising her husband when we brought her in," Paresi said.

Diane's eyes widened. "What are you talking about . . . what did she say?"

Barry Aaronson burst into the room. "I don't know what games you and your partner are playing, sergeant, but they've ended, right now!" He crossed to Diane. "Are you all right?"

"She's fine," Paresi said. "I haven't pistol-whipped anybody all day. Have a seat."

"Diane, they can't force you to say anything." Aaronson sat next to his client. "I'll get to the bottom of this, don't you worry about anything." He turned to Paresi. "This is unforgivable, bringing her in here, after all she's gone through."

"We're just about done." Star said, entering with Brenda Stevens and her attorney, Larry Stockard.

"Bren." Diane reached out. Brenda Stevens hurried to her friend, hugged her, and sat down next to her.

"I hope you've got a good reason for this, Lieutenant." Larry Stockard sat down next to Brenda Stevens. "This department has caused more than enough pain to these two women."

"Yeah," Star said. She put the file she was carrying on the table and opened it.

"Brenda Stevens, you are under arrest for the murder of Camille Westfall."

"No!" Diane cried out. "No!"

"What?" Brenda was on her feet. This is crazy!" She turned to her attorney. "Larry, do something."

"Lieutenant . . ."

Star took a sheet of paper out of the folder and held up her hand.

"My partner received a note, deposited directly on his desk, Mrs. Stevens. It stated that a gift had been left in the police garage for the two of us. That gift turned out to be the dismembered head, arms, and hands of the body of Camille Westfall. According to our tests, that note was typed on an IBM Selectric II typewriter. Tests on the IBM Selectric II typewriter removed from your home, by special order, prove beyond any doubt that it is the same machine used to type the note."

She put that sheet down and picked up another. "The stationery used was a brand manufactured and sold by Tif . . ."

A loud, agonized scream interrupted her.

Diane Riley was on her feet, shaking as if she were having a seizure. "No!" she screamed. *"No!"*

Her attorney moved to quiet her.

"Let me go!" she screeched at Aaronson. "I did it!" she sobbed. "It was me—Bren had nothing to do with it!"

Tears ran down Brenda Stevens's face. "Diane . . . stop, please."

"It was me!" Diane screamed. "I did it! I did it!"

"Diane . . ." Brenda reached out.

Diane Riley dropped unconscious to the floor.

CHAPTER FORTY-THREE

When Diane Riley regained consciousness, she found herself surrounded by concerned faces. The one she reached out to was Brenda Stevens.

The two women held each other as Diane wept.

"It's over, Bren," she said, again and again. "It's over."

Brenda Stevens helped her friend to her feet and into a chair.

"I did it," Diane said to Star. "I did it."

"No, it was me, Lieutenant," Brenda said, holding Diane. "It was me."

"You don't have to say anything," Larry Stockard said, putting an arm around Brenda. "You don't have to say a word."

"I want to talk," she said. "I can't stand to see her suffering." She hugged Diane again. "I love her so."

Diane sobbed and clung to Brenda.

"We planned everything together," Brenda said. "But it was me who did it. It was me. I'm the one who killed Camille."

Diane Riley wiped her face. She clung to Brenda's hand.

"We both did it," she said. "Brenda wasn't alone, I helped, that makes me guilty too."

"Diane." Barry Aaronson tried to move between the two

women, to separate them. "Diane . . . listen, you've said enough."

"Leave me alone, Barry." Diane's voice rose. "I want to talk. We want this to be over."

Brenda turned to Star. "We'd like to talk to you, Lieutenant, just you."

"Okay," Star said.

Diane kissed Brenda's hand. "I love you," she whispered. Brenda kissed her friend's tear-streaked face, and turned again to Star. She indicated the men in the room.

"Could you ask them to leave?"

"Guys . . ." Star said. "Out."

"No. We're not leaving, Lieutenant," Larry Stockard said. "These women need counsel."

Brenda Stevens wiped her eyes. "Larry, do you work for me or my husband?"

Larry Stockard's face reddened. "Even though I know Jay's in New York right now, trying to replace me, I'm working for you, Brenda."

"Then you're fired. I want to talk to the lieutenant alone."

Barry Aaronson and Larry Stockard looked at one another.

"Me too," Diane Riley said softly. "Please leave, Barry."

Barry Aaronson looked at Star. "We'll be outside," he said.

Paresi herded the attorneys out of the room. He looked back at Star.

"It's okay," she said.

Paresi nodded, closing the door behind him.

Star turned to the two women.

"Okay, it's just us now," she said.

Brenda put her arm around Diane.

"Please realize, Lieutenant, we didn't ever intend for all of this to happen."

"I'm sure," Star said, "but it has happened. So tell me how."

"My husband cheated on me," Brenda said. "He had one affair after another. I had to talk to someone, so I talked to Diane."

Diane nodded. "We were in the same boat. Doug was more discreet than Jay, but he was up to the same thing."

"How'd Camille get involved?" Star asked.

"We hired her," Diane said.

"Hired?"

"Yes," Diane continued. "Bren and I discovered, during our sharing, that we had feelings for each other."

"Feelings that went past friendship," Brenda said. "We became lovers."

Diane put her hand over Brenda's. "I love her more than I've ever loved anyone or anything."

"But we knew if we left our marriages to be with each other, there would be trouble," Brenda said.

"Doug would have cut me off without a cent." Diane wiped her eyes. "He would have destroyed me."

"What about your husband?" Star asked Brenda.

"He would have been humiliated, but I have money of my own, money he wouldn't have been able to touch." She caressed Diane's hand.

"How does Camille fit in to this picture?" Star asked.

"She was the niece of one of the women in my bridge club," Diane said. "That's how we met. She was a little coarse, but she was young, and she had a certain charm about her."

"More than that, she was hungry," Brenda Stevens said.

"Hungry?" Star echoed.

"Yes," Brenda said. "She wanted money, lots of money . . . and so we decided to work together."

"We hired her to seduce my husband," Diane said. "I introduced her to Doug, and just as I expected, he was taken with her. He put her to work in his office and she seduced him."

"Because you wanted her to," Star said.

"Yes." Diane cleared her throat. "The plan was to catch them in the act—that way, Doug would have to give me a divorce."

"And a handsome settlement," Star said.

"Exactly." Diane looked at Brenda. "We were going away together."

Star turned to Brenda. "So you have your own money, but you wanted hers?"

"No," Brenda said. "I wanted Diane to have what she deserves. She helped Doug build his life and his practice. Why should she be cheated out of all that? She deserved half of everything he had."

"What about your husband? You didn't want any money from him?"

"Lieutenant, I've always been a woman to look out for myself."

"I admire her strength," Diane said, gazing lovingly at Brenda.

"Like Diane, I helped Jay build his empire. But I also took care of myself. Ours isn't just a marriage, it's a legal partnership. I've got stocks and assets in my name."

"But if you left, couldn't he tie up your assets?"

"He wouldn't have," Brenda said. "For all of his fooling around, Jay really does love me. He would have come after me, if he knew where we were, but he wouldn't have taken the money away."

"He does love her," Diane said sadly. "He really does."

Brenda Stevens rested her head on Diane's shoulder. Her green silk ribbon had fallen off during Diane's attack, and her red hair tumbled forward, hanging loosely around her face. For the first time, Star noticed the beginnings of gray roots in the thick, abundant redness.

Diane lovingly ran her hand through Brenda's hair.

"Brenda makes me feel like I'm worth something," she said to Star. "She makes me feel pretty, and smart. She makes me feel like I can do anything."

Brenda kissed Diane Riley's hand. "I love you," she said, and sat up, looking at Star. "The night that Camille died, I got a call from Diane. She was very upset."

"Because of what she said . . ." Diane interrupted.

"Yes." Brenda squeezed her hand. "I went over to the house, and Diane and Camille were in the cottage. They were having a terrific row—you could hear them yelling from outside."

"I couldn't believe what she told me," Diane said.

"I went in, and Diane was beside herself," Brenda said. "Camille was totally out of control."

"She said the deal was off," Diane said.

"Why?" Star asked. "Why was she backing out?"

Diane gave Star a rueful smile. "She wasn't backing out entirely. She claimed she'd fallen in love with my husband.

She said he'd asked her to marry him, that she was going to say yes, and if I tried to stand in their way, she'd tell him about our deal. She said I'd end up with nothing."

"Diane was so upset, Lieutenant," Brenda said. "I couldn't stand to see her so miserable."

"What did you do?"

"I tried to calm her down."

"I'd been drinking," Diane said. "Heavily."

"So you were drunk too?" Star asked.

Diane nodded. "Yes."

"Things got crazy," Brenda said. "To add to everything, Diane had something in the kiln."

"I was firing a piece for Brenda when Cammie came over."

"It was mad, Lieutenant," Brenda continued. "They were screaming at each other. The room was hot, and you could smell that something was being fired. I looked at the kiln, and the lights were on, so I immediately went to turn it off. I really didn't know what I was doing. The kiln was hot, so I grabbed Diane's gloves and tried to turn the knobs, but nothing seemed to be happening. Finally I found the cord and yanked the plug from the wall."

"That's when Cammie hit me," Diane said. "I remember her hitting me, hard."

"Yes." Brenda nodded. "I turned just in time to see Camille haul off and hit her."

"She knocked me cold," Diane said.

"That's when I lost it." Brenda Stevens' eyes filled with tears. "I grabbed her, and just started choking her."

"You were still wearing the gloves," Star said.

Brenda nodded. "Yes. Everything happened so fast, I didn't have time to take them off. Before I knew it, she was dead."

"Then what happened?"

"I panicked. I had to get her out of there . . . I had to get her away from Diane's house."

"I came to, and Brenda was frantic," Diane said. "She kept saying over and over that she didn't mean to do it."

Star looked at Diane. "So, you had nothing to do with the actual killing?"

"No . . . Even though I was drunk, I knew what to do. I checked her pulse and her breathing. She was dead."

"We knew that we had to get her out," Brenda said. "And I thought of the murders . . . the game."

"Vampire's Lair," Star said.

"Yes." Brenda smiled ruefully. "Even though the media hadn't connected Jay's game with the murders yet, I was there when he created it. I knew those killings in the park were connected to Vampire's Lair. So I decided that we should take things further . . . make it look like whoever did the other killings did this one . . . playing the game."

"We never dreamed our children were involved," Diane said softly.

"What did you do next?" Star asked.

"I told Diane I needed her sober, so we got the liquor out of her, and then I told her how the body had to be disposed of."

"So you did the dissection," Star said to Diane.

"Yes." Diane nodded. "It was the only way out for us."

"Where did you do it?"

"In the cottage. We put down some plastic sheeting that I had in the garden shed," Diane said. "Cammie wasn't a very big girl. It was over fairly quickly."

"I went home and got my camper cooler," Brenda said. "We intended to put the entire body in it."

"Why'd you change your mind?"

"She wouldn't fit. That's when I thought that maybe if we sent something to the police, it would look even more connected to the other murders."

"So you sent the head, arms, and hands . . . and the game piece to me."

"Originally it wasn't meant for you," Brenda said. "Later, I decided to personalize it."

"So you put the figure in the bag and left it in her hand."

"Yes." Brenda nodded. "I have tons of those pieces around the house. I figured it would make things look more like it was all connected, a part of the game."

"Who left the note on my partner's desk?"

"I did," Brenda said. "I made sure I handled it and the envelope wearing gloves, like they do on television. Diane told me you two worked out of the Seventeenth Precinct, so I drove to the station and waited for the shift to change. With so many people going in and out, I figured no one would notice me. The downstairs directory said that Homicide was on the second floor, so I went upstairs.

"There was nobody in the room. I checked the nameplates on the desks until I found Duvall and Paresi, then I put the note on the sergeant's desk and left. It was easy to get into the police garage. It was open, and there was no guard. I'd intended to leave it by the elevator, but when I got inside, I saw marked spaces for captains and lieutenants, so I drove around until I found your space."

"That explains why the note had us go to the second floor," Star said.

"Yes. I couldn't very well go back and change it."

"Do you know where you slipped up?" Star said.

Brenda shook her head.

"The cooler. You wrapped it in a white bow. It looked like a Tiffany gift box."

"I thought that was a nice touch," Brenda said coldly.

Star smiled. "I guess you figured a working-class cop wouldn't recognize a Tiffany box, huh?"

"I'm not a snob, Lieutenant. That thought never entered my mind."

"Sure," Star said. "Well, for the record, Mrs. Stevens, I did recognize it. I also had the note that was left on my partner's desk analyzed, as you know, and lo and behold, Tiffany notepaper."

"I use Tiffany's stationery exclusively," Brenda said.

"And a typewriter," Star said.

"Yes. My old IBM," Brenda said. "I've never gotten used to computer screens. I like paper in front of me when I'm writing something."

"I noticed," Star said. "Our lab advised us that the note had been typed on an IBM Selectric II, with self-correcting tape. You made a mistake, lifted it, and typed it over."

"Very clever," Brenda said.

"I saw your collection of ceramic and crystal Tiffany boxes

this morning, along with the electric blue IBM typewriter in your study. It's the main reason I got the warrant."

"How astute, and correct. I typed the note after we'd taken Cammie to the old lab and buried what was left of her under the floor. Driving home, I saw you and your partner in the park.

"You had your guns drawn on a man who appeared to be abusing a woman. I assume they were a pimp and a prostitute. I watch a lot of TV cop shows. I especially find the real-life ones fascinating, so I couldn't help but look at the drama unfolding right in front of me. It was very exciting." Brenda's cold eyes locked on Star. "That was when I decided you deserved the gift."

They stared at one another. Star's face remained impassive. "Where were you?" she asked Diane.

"Asleep in the backseat," she answered. "After we got rid of the body, I just collapsed."

"Why the lab?" Star asked.

Brenda sighed. "When I was on the board at Bromleigh, one of the perpetual items for discussion was what to do with that abandoned building in the park. The city owned the land, but the building still belonged to Bromleigh. We never decided just how it should be used or disposed of." She smiled. "Bureaucrats, Lieutenant . . . the bane of progress."

Star didn't say anything.

"So . . . as it turned out," Brenda continued, "it was a lucky thing. It was there, dilapidated and filthy as ever. But it served its purpose, and actually, it was the perfect place, keeping in tune with the game and all."

"The castle and the trees of blood . . ." Star said. "The cherry trees."

"How did you know that?"

"I've played the game, Mrs. Stevens."

"Oh," Brenda said. "Did you win?"

Star looked at the two of them. "Big-time."

It was just after midnight when Star and Paresi finished the paperwork.

"Life's a bitch, ain't it?" Paresi said.

His partner sat staring at him. "And then you die," she said.

"Chopped up in pieces and left all over town. Whenever I think I've seen everything . . ." She shook her head. "I mean, can you even imagine this?"

"The more we do this job, the less convinced I am that we live in a civilized society," Paresi said, looking at his watch. "Quinn said the press is hanging around downstairs."

"At this hour?"

"Yep. The bookings leaked out somehow. It'll be on the early morning news."

"I'm sure the Larry and Barry team love that."

Paresi grinned. "Larry had them grease up the lenses so he'd look like Dylan McDermott!"

"Ain't that much Vaseline in the world," Star said.

They laughed.

"Yeah . . ." Paresi leaned back in his chair, stretching. "You know what I can't figure?"

"What?"

"The lipstick," he said.

"Oh . . . the lipstick on Camille's neck," Star said.

"Yeah . . . did you find out about that?"

Star looked at him for a minute. "If I tell you, you can't let it go to your head."

"What?" Paresi leaned toward her, a little smile working at the corner of his mouth.

"Promise?"

"Scout's honor."

"You were never a scout, Paresi," she said, laughing.

"Sons of Italy stickball champ, three years in a row—close enough. Tell me."

"You were right."

Paresi looked amused. "Yeah? 'Bout what?"

"The lipstick *was* hers."

"Get outta here!" He leaned back, laughing. "What? Did she have one of those spinning heads like that chick in *The Exorcist*?"

"No." Star giggled. "She saw the lipstick on Diane Riley, and liked it, so she bought some. That final night, before she went to blow out the deal she'd made with the missus, she made love to the doctor. She was wearing the lipstick, and when he kissed her, he got it on his mouth, and when he kissed her neck . . ."

"No shit!" Paresi said. "I'm putting in for a promotion. That's *some* detective work."

They laughed for a long time.

Finally, Paresi stood up, stretching and running his hands through his hair. "Is Mitch waiting for you?"

Star shrugged. "Probably. How about Vee for you?"

"I'm sure she's been asleep for hours," he said. "Her days are so long, with the job, the kids, and school."

"She's determined to get that degree," Star said. "I'm really proud of her."

"Me too." Paresi stretched again. "What say maybe you and me spend some time together? I don't really want to head home alone."

"Okay. Just let me call Mitchell and let him know where I am." She looked at her partner. "He worries."

"Call him from Uncle Ange's restaurant."

"Restaurant? Paresi, it's late."

"So? My uncle closes at eleven. He's probably still there. He likes to take his time, share some vino with the cleaning crew, do the receipts, all that. And if everybody's gone, I've got a key."

"If he's gone, who's gonna feed us?"

Paresi grinned. "Hey, I got talents you can't even imagine. You ever know an Italian who couldn't cook?" He reached for his coat. "Get your things, we'll have a nice antipasto, some linguine, a little wine. . . ."

Star got up and put her coat on.

"Let's go out the back," she said. "I am *so* not ready for my close-up."

"You'd knock 'em dead." Paresi put his arm around her shoulder, and walked her toward the door.

She slipped her arm around his waist. "It's after midnight, you know."

Paresi held the door open for her.

"That's when linguine tastes best."

Don't miss more cases solved by Starletta Duvall!

THE HOODOO MAN

by Judith Smith-Levin

๑ ๑ ๑

Desmond St. John, the legendary, supposedly immortal Haitian voodoo priest known as the Hoodoo Man, is found bound to his bed with six bullet holes forming a perfect cross on his body.

Homicide detective Lieutenant Starletta Duvall must find St. John's killer, but the case entangles her in a dangerous web of voodoo, magic, and terror, artfully spun by a spellbinding killer. Follow Starletta's progress on the case in *The Hoodoo Man* by Judith Smith-Levin.

Published by Ballantine Books
Available at a bookstore near you

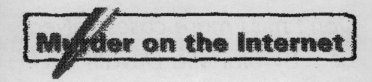
Murder on the Internet

Ballantine mysteries are on the Web!

Read about your favorite Ballantine authors and
upcoming books in our electronic newsletter
MURDER ON THE INTERNET, at
www.randomhouse.com/BB/MOTI

Including:
- 🕷 What's new in the stores
- 🕷 Previews of upcoming books for the next four months
- 🕷 In-depth interviews with mystery authors and
  publishing insiders
- 🕷 Calendars of signings and readings for Ballantine
  mystery authors
- 🕷 Profiles of mystery authors
- 🕷 Mystery quizzes and contest

To subscribe to MURDER ON THE INTERNET,
please send an e-mail to
join-mystery@list.randomhouse.com
with "subscribe" as the body of the message. (Don't
use the quotes.) You will receive the next issue as
soon as it's available.

Find out more about whodunit! For sample
chapters from current and upcoming Ballantine
mysteries, visit us at
www.randomhouse.com/BB/mystery